LINDA P. BA___ ___ novels, *The Irda* and *Tears of the Night Sky* (with Nancy Berberick) and several short stories in anthologies. Though she and her husband, Larry, live in Mobile, Alabama, they consider Ireland "home."

NANCY VARIAN BERBERICK has been writing fantasy for over a dozen years. Her DRAGONLANCE novels include *Stormblade*, *Tears of the Night Sky* and *Dalamar the Dark*. Nancy has also written numerous short stories in the fantasy genre. For fun, she translates Old English poetry, and now and then she threatens to have that long conversation with "Beowulf."

SCOTT BURACZEWSKI lives in Stevens Point, Wisconsin, with his girlfriend, a rabbit, and an emotionally disturbed television set that only works after it's been held.

JEFF CROOK is the author of the DRAGONLANCE novel *The Rose and the Skull*, as well as other short stories and game products. His new DRAGONLANCE novel, *The Thieves' Guild*, is due out in December 2000.

JOHN GRUBBER was unthawed only twenty-three years ago, and still finds our ways frightening and confusing. He recently graduated from a Masters Degree program in Religion and Culture at Wilfrid Laurier University, to compliment his previous Anthropology Degree. He contributed to *More Leaves from the Inn of the Last Home*, and "Blood Ties" is his first published story.

KEVIN JAMES KAGE lives in the state of denial. He is fond of singing, as it keeps the neighbors and dogs at a respectable distance. He's also been known to torture small musical instruments. He is an alumnus of the Clarion writer's workshop, and his works can be found in *Heroes and Fools* and *More Leaves from the Inn of the Last Home.*

Although well-known for his minotaur stories, RICHARD A. KNAAK has written several others featuring the Knights of Solamnia, including the *New York Times* best-seller *The Legend of Huma*. He is also the author of the ten-volume Dragonrealm series, plus many individual fantasy tales, both traditional and modern. His latest novels include *Reavers of the Blood Sea* for DRAGONLANCE and *Ruby Flames* for the Shattered Light series from Simon & Schuster. Among his current projects are a DRAGONLANCE novel taking place during the War of the Lance and another that will be the first in an epic fantasy trilogy of his own. He can be contacted through his web page at www.sff.net/people/knaak.

CHRIS PIERSON is a designer for a computer game company near Boston. His previous work includes stories in the DRAGONLANCE anthologies *The Dragons At War* and *Dragons of Chaos*, as well as the novels *Spirit of the Wind* and *Dezra's Quest*, both in the Bridges of Time series.

JEAN RABE is the author of several DRAGONLANCE novels, including *The Silver Stair, The Dawning of a New Age, The Day of the Tempest*, and *The Eve of the Maelstrom*. She works out of a small office in a small house, both of which are being made ever smaller by the number of books she insists on buying (and hiding everywhere so her husband won't complain).

KEVIN T. STEIN has written DRAGONLANCE stories for ten years. His screenplays "mindancer" and "Star's Revenge" have been optioned by the Hollywood production company Intrazone. His latest projects include work with Sony/Trimark, and authors Margaret Weis and Don Perrin.

PAUL B. THOMPSON is the author of nine novels, including *Sundipper, Thorn and Needle, Nemesis, Red Sands, Darkness & Light, Riverwind the Plainsman, Firstborn, The Qualinesti*, and *The Dargonesti*. (The last six were co-written with Tonya Carter Cook.) Thompson and Cook are working on a new trilogy in the DRAGONLANCE series collectively titled "The Barbarians." In addition to his novels, Paul has published a dozen works of short fiction and many non-fiction articles. He also co-edits an offbeat news website, ParaScope (http://www.parascope.com). Paul lives in Chapel Hill, North Carolina, with his wife Elizabeth.

MARGARET WEIS and DON PERRIN are a husband-and-wife writing team who live in a converted barn in Wisconsin. Weis and Perrin are co-owners of The Game Guild, a game store where they have entirely too much fun. Weis is currently working on the first Sovereign Stone novel with Tracy Hickman. Titled *Water from the Well of Darkness*, the book is being published by Avon Eos and will be out in Summer 2000. Perrin is working on the Sovereign Stone roleplaying game project and the second in the DRAGONLANCE draconian series of novels featuring Kang and the Dragonarmy Engineers. The book is titled *Draconian Measures* and is due out in November 2000.

Rebels & Tyrants

Tales of the Fifth Age

Edited by
Margaret Weis
and Tracy Hickman

REBELS AND TYRANTS
TALES OF THE FIFTH AGE

Cover art by Monte Moore
First Printing: April 2000
Library of Congress Catalog Card Number: 99-65626

9 8 7 6 5 4 3 2 1

ISBN: 0-7869-1676-1
620-T21676

U.S., CANADA,
ASIA, PACIFIC & LATIN AMERICA
Wizards of the Coast, Inc.
P.O. Box 707
Renton, WA 98057-0707
+1-800-324-6496

EUROPEAN HEADQUARTERS
Wizards of the Coast, Belgium
P.B. 2031
2600 Berchem
Belgium
+32-70-23-32-77

Visit our web site at **www.wizards.com**

TABLE OF CONTENTS

Introduction

In this anthology, readers will be treated to stories featuring some of the characters, major and minor, featured in the first book of the new War of Souls trilogy, *Dragons of a Fallen Sun*, by Margaret Weis and Tracy Hickman.

The mysterious elven rebel leader, the Lioness, is involved in the intriguing tale by Paul Thompson, "Freedom's Pride." Usha Majere, wife of Palin Majere, becomes involved in political intrigue, romance and magic in Nancy Berberick's "Lost Causes." Ulin Majere and Palin are both featured in the new story by Margaret Weis, "The Raid on the Academy of Sorcery."

We are pleased to welcome two new authors to our ranks. Scott M. Buraczewski opens our anthology with an interesting piece that is also the shortest story we have ever published, "Est Sularas Oth Mithas." John Grubber's young heroes must try to save their family from loathsome swamp monsters in "Blood Ties."

Don Perrin tells of a cursed clan of minotaur forced to relive the same horrific battle once every year for a thousand years in "Sargas's Night of Revenge."

Linda Baker has a new twist on the old saying, "thieves fall out" in "Sharing the Luck."

"War Chest" by Kevin T. Stein tells the tale of a knight who discovers that life's lessons are not best learned in the classroom.

"Flight of Fancy" by Jeff Crook is a gnome story. We just thought we'd warn you!

"The Deep, Deep, Dark, Dark Place" by Kevin Kage tells why adventurers should never try to out think gully dwarves.

Jean Rabe goes fishing in "Catch of the Day."

Chris Pierson brings us the tale of a dwarf's desperate search for her birthright in "Shard's Memory."

Solamnic Knights form a strange alliance with ogres in "Tactics" by Richard A. Knaak.

As always, it was a privilege and a pleasure to work with all the authors. We hope you enjoy their DRAGON-LANCE tales.

Est Sularas Oth Mithas
Scott Buraczewski

Est Sularas Oth Mithas. My honor is my life.

The ground races beneath the thundering hooves of my war horse, leaving a haze of dust in my wake. *Faster*, I urge him silently. *Faster*. Trees flash by us like barely glimpsed images in a fever dream.

Flash. I see my lady wife, laughing, stretching out her hand to me beneath the bright afternoon sky. She is beautiful, more so than I have ever seen her before. Her head is thrown back in the midst of her laugh. Her simple dress is green, the color of the salt sea on calm days.

The sun streaks in lazy arcs through the leaves of late fall, still hanging precariously in the trees. Although my horse and I are streaking along the path as fast as we can gallop, I notice these things, the small things that I had never before had the time or have thought to enjoy. We fly past a doe and are gone before the animal can even begin to run for the shelter of the deep woods.

Flash. She runs away from me, still laughing, bidding me to give chase. I am still clumsy in my unfamiliar armor, and slow. Far out of my reach, she spins in circles on the mountain-top, arms thrown wide. Out of breath for the moment, she stops circling to taunt me again, an impish grin on her face. I am still a dozen paces away when she turns her back and begins

---
3

to run, a careless laugh thrown over her shoulder to me like an afterthought. Oh, how I burn for her then.

The trail turns uphill, and we slow. I do not care if I run my horse to death anymore, for I must reach my destination. Yet it would not do for my horse to break a leg before his usefulness is fully served. I hear his panting breath, and I can smell his sweat. *A little farther*, I whisper to him. *Just a bit farther, and then you may rest.*

Flash. She disappears into a small grove of trees, but I can hear her moving about among the fallen leaves. A cloud passes beneath the sun, casting a shadow over us. Just as quickly, the cloud is gone. I do not even look up to mark its passage. I resume my search for my lady, my love.

I see it, now, looming above my horse, like a storm cloud on the horizon. It does not look like much, really, just a dark hole carved into a mountainside, but I am focused on it entirely. I feel the hate struggling inside me, and with a breath I give the hate free rein. With a vicious kick, I command the horse into one final gallop, and we cover the last thousand yards in what is seemingly the single beat of a heart.

Flash. I stumble through the underbrush in the tiny grove. A tree branch snaps up, striking me across the face. Anger builds in me at the burning line of pain across my cheek, and is forgotten just as quickly as I spot a flicker of sea green ahead, beyond the far edge of the thicket. I run towards it, heedless of whatever else stands in my way. I run to her.

I leap off of my horse and pause long enough to thank him for carrying me as he has, striking his flank with the flat of my hand, sending him to whatever the fates may have in store for him. He wheels and dashes back the way that we have come, galloping for joy at being masterless. I do not watch him go; I am already scrambling up the mountainside, my own breathing heavy in my ears. *Est Sularas Oth Mithas.* I repeat it to myself over and over, until it becomes a meaningless chant, whispered between ragged breaths.

Flash. I crash through the edge of the grove, and there she stands, arms spread wide in mimicry of the valley that lies far below us. Her face is solemn, but her eyes are still full of laughter. "Come, then," she whispers to me. I have to strain to catch her words. Only twenty paces separate us now, and I head toward her in wonderment, thinking that I will be crushed beneath the weight of my raging passion. Nineteen paces, fifteen, a dozen.

I have reached the top now, and I pull myself to my feet, panting from exertion. I am young and fit, but the heavy armor that I wear was not intended to be worn while climbing mountains. I rip my sword from its scabbard without missing a stride, and finally, I am standing at the beginning of the very end of my destination.

Flash. Ten paces, nine, the smile fades from her face, and she tilts her head slightly forward, still looking me in the eyes. She reaches up with her pretty hand and brushes a lock of her auburn hair from her face. Eight paces. Her head is tipping back now, and her lips part. I see them form the words "I love thee, Alric" but they are ripped away by the scream that erupts from behind and beneath her.

"I come!" I scream, stepping into the half dark of the cave. "I come now!" My right hand is clenched around the hilt of my sword, and my left is locked tightly into a fist, so tightly that blood drips onto the stone floor. From just beyond the spot where daylight holds sway, the spot where the darkness is nearly impenetrable, a voice like a nightmare answers me. In a mockery of my lady's words it says, "Come then. Fool."

Flash. A terrible shape suddenly blots out the sun, and my eyes begin to open wide. The green dragon hangs there, motionless, for what must be an eternity, although the smile has not yet begun to fade from my wife's lips. I feel my own lips begin to shout a warning. My heart gives a single beat.

The dragon lumbers out of the shadows as I bellow a war cry, breaking into a shambling run, my sword held high. The icy fingers of dragonfear wrap around me but my rage burns the fear to ash. Tears stream unchecked down my face. The dragon is surprised; I cover the space between us in a flash, so quickly that he has no time to use his foul breath against me. I am close enough to touch him, his head hovering over me. I slash at his neck but my sword bounces off of his scales harmlessly. He is startled at the boldness of my attack, but his surprise lasts only an instant. He opens his mouth, rows of fangs standing guard over his tongue, and his head plunges toward me like a bird knocked from the sky. I toss myself carelessly to the side, switching to an underhanded grip on my sword. I unclench my left hand and wrap it around the sweaty hilt just as his enormous head smashes into the cavern floor where I stood only a moment earlier.

Flash. The dragon wraps his talons around her, and she is nearly crushed in its powerful grip. I close my eyes in anguish.

I step forward again holding my sword facing point down. The dragon is ready for me this time, and does not underestimate me again. His jaws envelop me and I feel his fetid breath against my skin as I plunge my sword downwards with all the strength in my body and the agony that I carry in my soul. My strike goes home, and the blade slips beneath the scales that protect his evil heart, sinking to the hilt. His jaws close around me, crushing armor, flesh and bone. The pain is enormous, and I open my mouth to scream. As my vision fades, the dragon collapses in a boneless heap, still clutching me in its jaws. The darkness over takes me, and a voice follows me into the void. *I love thee, Alric.*

Est Sularas Oth Mithas.

Freedom's Pride
Paul B. Thompson

Wind scoured the sky, driving clouds across the set-ting sun and darkening the day before its time. The constant swirl of leaves and bowing branches obscured the sound of the oncoming scout, but Vytrad could see him well enough. He was riding hard, crouched for-ward over his horse's neck. The wind whipped at his mantle, and covered him helmet to stirrups in fine blown dust.

The scout reined up before his commander and saluted. "My lord!" he shouted above the wind.

"Report, corporal," said Vytrad.

"I reconnoitered three leagues ahead, my lord. I found ample signs of our quarry, but I never actually saw them. They're running for all they're worth, my lord. They can't keep up this pace much longer!"

Neither can we, Vytrad thought. He glanced back at his command: twenty knights and sixty-six men at arms, all mounted. When this mission started he'd had a hundred and twenty. Men and beasts both were sagging with fatigue, despite the fact they were all handpicked specimens. How could their soft, unskilled quarry stay so far ahead of them?

"The column will move up," Vytrad said to his sub-ordinates. "Flankers in the woods a hundred paces out.

Mark well the trees this time! I don't want any more ambushes, do you hear? We've already paid too high a price for these damned traitors!" He waved his map-bearer forward. The squire guided his horse alongside Vytrad's.

"Map!" Vytrad barked.

The youth found the most recent local chart and handed it to his commander. Vytrad unrolled the long scroll, tracing their path across the vellum with a single mailed finger.

"The Ahlanlas River lies six leagues ahead. What town is this, directly in our path?"

"Blancopa," said his senior sergeant, Benda. "Hardly a town, my lord. A few dozen timber and stone huts on a mud flat. Population, unknown; a few hundred at most. River trash, scum who live outside our law, or anyone else's."

"Defenses?"

"A log stockade on the three dry sides, defended by a town militia."

Light was rapidly failing. Vytrad swept the map into two loose loops and tossed it back to his bearer. "It seems clear the enemy is making for Blancopa," he said. "They'll be trapped there, their backs against the river."

"What if they have a boat waiting?" asked Llorn, Vytrad's chief subaltern.

"We'll commandeer a boat and follow them," Vytrad said confidently. "The prey we've chased so long and hard will not get away."

The warriors formed in column of twos to resume the pursuit. Vytrad closed the visor on his helmet and took his place at the head of his men.

* * * * *

It seemed like a polished-steel opportunity, the sort that makes a man's career. Vytrad Redlance, veteran member of the Order of the Knights of Takhisis, was summoned to wait upon Egil Liveskill, Lord of Black Hall. Lord Liveskill was the Order's chief of peace and order for southern Qualinesti, and as such, a very powerful and feared man. His stronghold, the newly built castle Black Hall, dominated the quiet town of Fara, at the edge of the great southern forest.

Being called to the Black Hall was a daunting prospect, but Vytrad savored the menacing atmosphere as he mounted the onyx stairs to Lord Liveskill's chambers. He'd long sought assignment to the Black Hall, where power dwelt in shadows and decisions of life and death were spoken of in whispers. Let others seek evanescent fame on the battlefield; Vytrad dreamed of serving the order in more subtle, effective ways.

He was silently received and ushered into Lord Liveskill's presence. The Lord of the Black Hall was but forty-six, his hair and beard still yellow. He was dressed entirely in black velvet, with a circlet of jet on his brow and the golden gorget of his office around his neck. Seated at a broad walnut table, Lord Liveskill set aside the document he was reading when Vytrad entered.

"You are Redlance?" he said, studying Vytrad with colorless eyes.

He bowed. "At you service, great lord."

Liveskill tossed a sheet of parchment to him. It slid easily across the polished tabletop. Vytrad picked it up.

"Do these names mean anything to you?"

He scrutinized them swiftly. Elven names all. "All prominent Qualinesti, my lord. I see cousins of the Speaker, members of the Verinthanlas and Ambrodel families, scions of House Gemstone, Cultivator, Forester . . . these are some of the most well-born folk in the province."

"Fully half those people have disappeared," Liveskill said.

Vytrad lowered the list. "Foul play, my lord?"

"The foulest. They've fled Fara to escape the authority of the Order, in some cases taking considerable treasure with them. I have been charged with the task of stopping this outflow of wealth and status."

Vytrad sensed what was coming. He said, "Any clues as to what has become of the missing elves, my lord?"

"None." Liveskill frowned, grasping his sharp chin with a thumb and forefinger. "They seem to have vanished completely. If any elves had turned up in other countries, our agents would have reported it, but none have. Their treasure hasn't turned up in circulation, either.

"We can't have the population draining away like sand in an hourglass. Where the rich and noble lead, lesser folk will follow, and if this exodus goes unchecked, the Order may find itself with an empty province on its hands."

Bad for prestige and the tax rolls, Vytrad mused. Aloud he said, "What shall I do, my lord?"

Liveskill rummaged through the loose papers on the table, at one point exposing a wickedly thin dagger. The greenish stain on the blade meant it was poisoned . . . the Lord of Black Hall found what he was looking for.

"An informant on the estate of a noble family named Verinthanlas has warned us his masters are fleeing soon. They've sold their household goods for gold and steel, and collected provisions for a trip. I have others watching the house. When they depart, I shall know. I want you, Vytrad Redlance, to lead a handpicked force of cavalry. You're to follow the elves, find out who they're meeting and where they're going. Then, and only then, I want you to bag them and bring them back to me."

Vytrad smothered a smile. An easy task, one well suited to his talents. "I will not fail, great lord," he vowed.

"See that you don't."

He was provided with men, superbly mounted and equipped. Most of the one hundred and twenty came from the elite light cavalry, and they could outride and outfight five times their number. They camped in the woods west of Fara for five days. On the sixth day, they received word the Qualinesti would be leaving that night. Sure enough, eighteen elves gathered on a grassy verge outside the town, veiled by the moonless night. They were met by a shadowy band of humans and Kagonesti, who loaded the refugees in wagons and made off, heading southwest. Vytrad began a distant, stealthy pursuit.

The first ambush was embarrassing. A scouting party rode right into a crossfire of arrows, loosed from the treetops. By the time Vytrad's main force arrived, the archers had melted away. The second debacle was horrifying. Seeking to trap the now openly fleeing elves, Vytrad divided his command in two, sending one column ahead to cut off their escape. The following column was supposed to drive the elves into the hands of the flying column, but instead the pursuers rode straight into a vicious trap. Nets and snares unhorsed many knights, and most were slain as they lay helpless on the ground.

Vytrad reorganized his command. It was plain the Qualinesti had put themselves in the hands of seasoned, dangerous mercenaries, and catching them was going to be a far tougher proposition than simply bagging a band of fleeing civilians. He sent a dispatch to that effect back to Lord Liveskill, requesting him to set up forces both in the passes leading to Thorbardin and the south shore of the Ahlanlas River. Vytrad was not going to fail in his first mission for the Lord of the Black Hall, even if it meant bringing home his command and his quarry more dead than alive.

*　*　*　*　*

Rain was falling by the time the rude wooden walls of Blancopa came into view. The stockade completely encircled the town, continuing right down into the river. There were two gates in the stockade, and both were standing wide open. Hooded lanterns hung on hooks by the gates.

Vytrad halted the column at the edge of the woods. Mist was rising on the river, and a few dim lamps bobbed in the darkness, stern lights on river craft.

Young Llorn rode up beside his commander. "How does it look, my lord?"

"Not good. The whole scene screams 'trap,' but I don't see we have any choice but to enter the town," Vytrad said. Rain was pooling in the small of his back, under his armor. The discomfort only added to his irritation.

"Could we summon them to surrender?"

"Unlikely. The Qualinesti might give up peacefully, but the mercenaries shepherding them won't. They've stung us too hard. They know what will happen to them if I get my hands on them."

Llorn tilted his head back, shielding his eyes with his hand. "At least the rain will put their bowmen out of action, my lord."

"Thank the Dark Queen for small favors."

Vytrad called his flankers out of the woods. He split his force into two bands, putting Llorn in command of the other.

"Take your men in through the west gate," Vytrad said. "Drive right to the water's edge. Keep together; don't let your men be drawn off in twos and threes among the houses. If you find the refugees, have the cornet sound on his horn."

"At your command, my lord."

Llorn cantered away, taking half the force with him. The rest remained quietly in line behind Vytrad. He stared through the downpour at the open east gate. When the sound of Llorn's group diminished, he raised his hand. Even the horses grew still. Wordlessly, he swept his hand down, simultaneously spurring his mount forward. The knights filled in behind Vytrad three abreast, swords glinting in the dark.

The gate was unguarded. Vytrad slowed, turning his horse in a circle, searching for signs of an ambush. Rain ran in streams off the rough thatch roofs, splattering in the muddy lane. A dog barked, somewhere close by. Vytrad steeled himself to ignore the eerie, empty streets. He waved his men on.

Blancopa was only four streets deep. Huts and hovels grew right up to the riverfront warehouses, which alone in the town were sturdy, straight, and made of stone. Hundreds of troops could hide in warehouses like those . . .

"My lord, what now?" asked Sergeant Benda.

"Look for a ship," Vytrad said. He stood in his stirrups to see the docks. "They must be crossing by boat!"

The knights rode slowly parallel to the docks. Most of the slips were empty, but ahead lay a low, lean galleot, oars run in. Striped awnings covered most of the upper deck. Vytrad saw this and slowed. Nobody put up awnings for cargo, only for passengers—

"There!" He stood in his stirrups and pointed at the galleot, three slips away. "That's it! Forward, for the Order!"

The words had hardly left his mouth before the doors of the nearest warehouse burst apart. A flood of ragged, unkempt people charged out, swarming over the knights, screaming at the top of their lungs. They were townsfolk, armed with whatever came to hand— hammers, axes, broken oars, anything. More foes appeared on the rooftops, hurling javelins and head-sized rocks down on Vytrad's men.

Vytrad turned his horse to face the mob, slashing hard at a nearly naked, long-haired man armed with a battle-axe. They traded blows until Vytrad caught the man's wrist on the tip of his blade. The axe fell to the ground. The villager tried to turn away, but Vytrad stabbed him in the back. He toppled to the mud.

"Cornet! Sound the call!" Vytrad shouted hoarsely.

The bugler raised the brass horn to his lips. His bleating notes were not answered by Llorn's cornet.

Just then, something heavy came hurtling out of the dark. It hit Vytrad hard on the shoulder and held there. Hampered by rain in his eyes, Vytrad couldn't see who or what had him. Then they both slid off his horse and fell heavily to the ground.

Cold metal scraped across Vytrad's throat. Had he not been wearing mail, he surely would have died then and there. He punched his attacker hard in the face with his gauntleted fist, and the assassin somersaulted away with remarkable agility. Vytrad sat up and saw his foe's wildly demonic face. A Kagonesti, in full face paint. The forest elf put his dagger in his teeth and sprang away, losing himself in the tangle of horses and men.

Gaining his feet, Vytrad saw what seemed like the whole population of Blancopa, turned out against them. The press was so strong the knights were being pushed onto the pier where the galleot was tied up. His horse was nowhere to be seen, so Vytrad picked up his sword from the mud and fought on. Most of his men were fighting on foot too, and they kept inching down the dock under pressure from several hundred belligerent villagers.

Vytrad bumped shoulders with Sergeant Benda.

"We're running out of fighting room, my lord!" the old veteran said.

"Can you swim?" Vytrad said. His question was meaningless; none of the knights could swim in their heavy armor. The only extra space available was the waiting galleot. Vytrad ordered his men to retreat up the gangplank, fighting all the way. When the last knight was on board, the walkway was thrown back on the dock.

"Any sign of Llorn?" asked Vytrad, panting.

Benda shook his head. "No sign, sir. If he met this kind of reception, it's no wonder."

With ropes and grappling hooks, the Blancopans tried to bridge the gap between the boat and shore to get at the knights. Vytrad's men were kept busy, fending them off. While the fight raged, Vytrad went below deck. To his amazement, the galleot had a full crew on board—forty oarsmen hunched over the benches, listening to the commotion overhead. Four better-dressed men Vytrad took to be the ship's officers. One, the tallest, stepped forward. He had to be in charge.

Vytrad accosted the man at swordpoint. "You! What's your name?"

The straw-haired fellow tugged a bandanna down low on his forehead. "Zoran, if it please your lordship." he said in a low voice.

"Are you the captain of this boat?"

"No, I'm only first mate."

Vytrad frowned. "What ship is this?"

"The *Water Strider*."

"Anyone else on board? Any mercenaries?"

Zoran exchanged telling glances with his mates. "No, your lordship."

Vytrad pressed the tip of his sword into the soft flesh under Zoran's chin. "The truth, or I'll have your head!"

"It's true, generous lord! The warriors took another ship!"

"What other ship?"

Zoran's face was rapidly becoming as red as a radish. He grunted, "*Swamp Adder*! Captain Luno's boat!"

Something heavy crashed to the deck above. Vytrad shifted his sword tip from Zoran's neck to his kidneys. "Up on deck, now!" he snapped. "The rest of the officers too!"

From the stern, it was plain the knights were slowly being overwhelmed by the villagers' mass attack. Vytrad sheathed his sword. "Get underway. This boat is now under my orders, is that clear?"

"My captain's ashore. I can't leave without him!" Zoran protested.

Furious, Vytrad grabbed the young mate by his leather vest and shoved him over the rail. Vytrad reached for his sword as the others tensed. The boatmen were held back by a look from an older officer with a paunch . No cries were heard, but a distinct splash marked Zoran's entrance into the river. Vytrad planted his hands on his hips and faced the remaining boatmen.

"Anyone else want to leave? No? Who next in command?" The paunchy fellow who gave his name as Hakan stammered that he was.

"Cast off at once," Vytrad said. "We must get away from these savages first. Is that clear?"

"Aye, your lordship!" Hakan bellowed orders, and the oarsmen ran out their oars on the starboard side, pushing the galleot away from the dock. A number of splashes occurred, following by cries for help from the water. Vytrad hoped they were townfolk and not his men.

Once clear of the slip, the other set of oars were deployed, and *Water Strider* backed smoothly way from shore. The knights on deck cheered their deliverance.

The rain had stopped, but the fog had grown denser. Torches appeared on shore, clustered around the western-most docks. Vytrad heard the close clangor of arms from that direction.

He pointed. "Make for those piers!" he commanded.

The galleot crept along, mindful of stumps and pilings poking out of the water. The sound of fighting grew louder. All at once the fog parted as *Water Strider* slid through. What was left of Llorn's band was likewise trapped at the extreme end of a dock. There weren't many of them left, and those that remained were under fierce attack.

Vytrad surveyed the situation and came to an instant decision. "Master Hakan, ram the dock! Ram it, I say!"

Hakan blanched. "That's madness! You'll wreck the ship and drown everyone on the pier!"

He seized the Hakan by the collar and shoved him against the rail. "Aim between the fourth and fifth pilings! Do it!" Vytrad cried. Out came his sword. "Do it, or die now yourself!"

Shaking, Hakan put the helm hard over and called for more speed. Water curled back from *Strider*'s sharp, downswept prow. Some of the mob fighting on the dock saw the boat bearing down on them and tried to withdraw, but the crowd was too thick to move fast. *Water Strider*'s bow smashed into the planking, crushing many Blancopans. The rest fell in the water or scrambled for shore. On the other end of the pier, the survivors of

Llorn's command saw their comrades on the galleot and climbed over the boat's apostis to join them. Bow battered but still watertight, *Water Strider* withdrew into the fog.

Bleeding badly from a scalp wound and cradling a broken arm, Llorn reported to his commander in the boat's stern. Saluting with his good hand, Llorn said, "My lord! Thank you for your timely rescue. A few more minutes and we would all have been fish-food."

"Why didn't your cornet answer ours?" Vytrad said sternly.

Llorn wiped the seeping blood from his eyes. "He was killed in the Blancopans' first rush. We were outnumbered ten to one, my lord, and had no room to maneuver."

Hakan, leaning on the tiller, politely offered the services of his vessel's sawbones to the knights' wounded. Vytrad agreed, and dismissed the staggering Llorn to the healer's attention.

"Your lordship?" Hakan began timidly.

"What?"

"Where am I to go? What course shall I set?"

Walled in by fog, *Water Strider* was paddling steadily up the river, more or less due east. Vytrad peered into the mist, trying to part it by sheer will power. The fog did not yield.

"This other boat, *Swamp Adder*; where was it bound?" asked Vytrad.

"I know not, your lordship. Luno took on passengers and rowed off into the mist. I couldn't see him . . ." The rotund riverman lowered his chin and frowned, deep in thought. "I think he had sea anchors on his bows when he left. Aye, I'm sure he did!"

"What does that mean?"

"Well, you see, your lordship, river craft don't need

much in the way of anchors. A slotted stone is all most of us use. But if you're planning to cross the Straits of Algoni, you need real anchors."

"So Luno took his passengers out to sea?" Hakan nodded. "Bring us about, then. We're going after them!"

"But lordship, *Water Strider* isn't equipped for open water! And the bows, the bows are almost stoved in—"

Vytrad brought his sword down on the rail, chipping out a wedge of seasoned oak. "Do as I say! If you balk once more, I'll put someone else in command, and you'll go over the side like your friend Zoran!"

"Aye, gracious lordship." Hakan looked pale, even in the fog. "To sea it is."

The galleot slowed, oars frothing. As one bank of rowers pulled forward, the other side rowed in reverse, spinning the light vessel on its own length. Vytrad ordered best speed, and *Water Strider,* helped by the current, hastened after the departing Qualinesti.

For an hour the galleot sped down the Ahlanlas on the track of its sister ship. Near midnight, stars began to appear through the clouds overhead. Wind, smelling of salt, played on their faces. Vytrad ordered the galleot to slow, then stop.

"All quiet," he said. "Listen."

Swells lifted the galleot's bow. At first all anyone could hear was the muffled sound of the surf. Slowly, as their ears grew accustomed to the background of wind and waves, the men on deck made out a faint, rhythmic thumping—the sound of oars working in their locks.

"Ahead slow," Vytrad murmured.

Water Strider crawled ahead, nosing through gouts of white fog. With hand signals, Vytrad indicated where he wanted Hakan to steer the ship. A pinpoint of light gleamed above the crest of a wave. Raising his left hand, Vytrad pointed to port.

A dull orange lantern glowed on the stern of craft dead ahead. It was a forty-oar galleot, just like *Water Strider*. The name on the stern had been effaced, but when Vytrad gave Hakan an inquiring look, the riverman nodded solemnly. It was *Swamp Adder*.

"All knights in fighting condition forward," Vytrad whispered. He sheathed his sword and started forward with his men.

They gained steadily on the slowly moving *Adder*. Both vessels were clear of the river fog, so *Water Strider* was plainly visible to anyone on *Swamp Adder*, had they bothered to look. Instead of leaping ahead, the other galleot slowed to a stop. A few soft splashes were heard, and muffled cries.

"At them, now!" Vytrad cried.

Strider charged, and at the last moment, the portside rowers withdrew their oars. The galleot slammed into the idle sweeps on *Swamp Adder's* starboard side, smashing them to kindling. The hulls scraped, and Vytrad raised the cry, "For the Order!" Some fifty able-bodied knights and men at arms echoed his cry and swarmed over the rails.

Vytrad landed on *Adder's* deck. A luridly painted Kagonesti cut at him with a saber. They traded thrusts and parries until Sergeant Benda jumped from the rail and landed on the elf. A torrent of armored warriors followed, sweeping the galleot's quarterdeck clear in an instant.

Hatches banged open and the rowers erupted, armed with knives, staves, and boathooks. They were a lurid gang—scarred, painted, missing limbs and eyes. For all their ferocity, they were no match for armored knights, and Vytrad's men cut through them like a needle through sailcloth. *Swamp Adder's* crew seemed determined to defend the forecastle, to the extent of raising a hasty barricade of casks and crates to impede the knights' charge. Men and elves with iron helmets and real swords appeared behind the makeshift barrier, and Vytrad knew they'd flushed out the mercenaries they'd been chasing.

The knights formed a wedge of steel and rushed the line of barrels. Despite fatigue and a heavy suit of armor, Vytrad leaped over a small cask, brandishing his broadsword in a wide arc. A human warrior stepped in and caught his blade on the boss of a small round buckler. The mercenary's weapon was a lighter, longer blade that flickered uncomfortably close to Vytrad. Rather than fence with the man (who was skillful), Vytrad picked up an oak bucket from the deck and used it catch his foe's sharp blade. Four inches of steel punched right through the tough wood, but the weight of the bucket bore the blade down. With a powerful two-handed swing, Vytrad tore the buckler from the man's grasp. His enemy leaped back, but Vytrad got him on his return swing, slashing him from shoulder to hip.

The flat of an axe caught Vytrad on the side of the face and send him reeling. He hit the port rail and slid to his knees. Yelling obscenities, a human with a gleaming shaved head attacked Vytrad with a axe in one hand and a cargo hook in another. The knight parried the axe with his sword hilt even as the hook snagged in his mail. Struggling to his feet, Vytrad pulled his foe off-balance and seized him by the throat. It was like trying to strangle a tree. After a few seconds' struggle, the mercenary dropped the hook and tried to use his free hand to gouge Vytrad's eyes. Vytrad snapped his head forward, butting the man in the forehead with his heavy steel visor. Stunned and bleeding, the mercenary tried to back away, collided with another knight, and Vytrad ran him through the throat.

Mercenaries and boatmen alike began dropping their weapons and jumping over the side. In moments the foredeck was empty of foes to fight. Vytrad ordered the wounded dragged aft, and any surviving mercenaries were to be detained for questioning.

"Sergeant Benda!" he called.

The tough old warrior appeared, panting but unwounded. "Yes, my lord?"

"Take six men and check below decks. I'll inspect the forecastle. I didn't see any Qualinesti , but its hard to tell who's who under all that facepaint. They must be on board somewhere."

Benda departed as ordered. With two men-at-arms, Vytrad climbed to the forecastle. To his surprise, *Swamp Adder*'s foredeck was covered in sailcloth. Something under the cloth was moving. At his nod, Vytrad's men whipped the covering aside.

People. The missing Qualinesti—most of them, at least. They were bound hand and foot and lying in tight rows, gagged. Upon seeing the knights, the hapless elves groaned against their gags and kicked their feet. Clanking revealed their ankles were wrapped with lengths of heavy chain.

"What in the Dark Queen's name is going on here?" Vytrad wondered aloud. His men pulled a mature Qualinesti male out of the squirming pile and cut off his gag.

"My lord!" the elf exclaimed. "I never thought I'd be glad to see the Knights of Takhisis! You have saved us!"

"What are you raving about?"

"Those bandits took our money to get us out of Qualinesti, but they intended to murder us all! They brought us out here with the intention of drowning us like kittens." The Qualinesti lowered his proud head. "Some of our friends were thrown overboard before you intervened."

Vytrad stood over him. "What's your name?" he said.

"Jerdato Verinthanlas, my lord."

Vytrad remembered the name from Lord Liveskill. The Verinthanlas clan was extremely wealthy and influential in Fara province.

The corporal at Vytrad's side said, "Shall we release the rest, my lord?"

There were fifteen elves lying on the deck, adults of both sexes, and barely twenty hale knights to guard them. Vytrad sized up the odds and said, "No. Leave them bound."

"My lord!" Verinthanlas protested. "What does this mean?"

"You're all under the displeasure of the Order for unlawful flight," Vytrad said solemnly. "That's why we were pursuing you in the first place. You will be returned to the Black Hall, where you will be tried for sedition."

Verinthanlas hung his head a moment, then raised it again and said, "So be it, my lord. We'll face your trial. It's better than the fate the mercenaries had in mind for us, at any rate."

Vytrad sheathed his sword. Don't be too sure of that, he thought.

* * * * *

A shout went up from the main deck. Vytrad turned to the rail. To his shock, there was *Water Strider*, already a cable length away and showing her heels. Hakan's boat was rowing for the mouth of the Ahlanlas as hard as it could.

"Damn the wretch! I'll gut him for this!" Vytrad roared.

Sergeant Benda emerged from the main hatch. He ran up the steps of the forecastle to report.

Paul B. Thompson

"The boat is ours, my lord. No one else here. The crew that isn't dead or wounded jumped overboard."

Vytrad thought fast. "Put the Qualinesti on the oars," he said. "The wounded prisoners, too."

Benda said, "Half the oars are destroyed, my lord."

"Then take half of what's left and transfer them to the starboard side!"

"At your command, my lord."

The elves and the least wounded prisoners were put on the rowers' benches under armed guard and ordered to row. With only twenty sweeps instead of forty, *Swamp Adder* could only struggle along. The tide was going out, and the currents around the river mouth were tricky, but the galleot wallowed through them under Vytrad's inexpert guidance. The fogbank loomed ahead.

Benda had a word in his commander's ear.

"My lord, there is something else to report. I didn't want to say it too loudly, you understand."

"What is it, man?"

"Treasure, sir. There are chests of steel and gold in the hold, bags of silks and jewels. I expect the mercenaries planned to murder the Qualinesti and divide the loot amongst themselves."

Vytrad agreed. Here was the answer Lord Liveskill had been seeking. Rich and noble Qualinesti fleeing the Order had not escaped, but met a crueler fate in the bottomless depths of the sea. That's why no word of them ever reached the Black Hall's extensive net of informers.

A lookout on the mast called out, "Unknown vessel astern, my lord!"

Vytrad gave the tiller to Benda and looked aft. Sure enough, the dark outline of another ship was cruising silently up behind them. It showed no lights, but skimmed along under shortened topsails only. An ocean going ship, likely a caravel out of Schallsea.

"Friends of the mercenaries?" asked Benda.

"Pray to our lady they're not," Vytrad muttered. "More speed! I want to lose them in the fog."

He ordered it, but the depleted, amateur rowers weren't up to it. *Swamp Adder* churned along, leaving a visible wake for the mystery ship to follow. And follow they did, even as Vytrad steered for the north shore. The dark caravel turned after them.

"All able-bodied soldiers on deck," Vytrad said. Weary and few in number, the knights responded.

All of a sudden fire blazed on the mystery ship's deck. A flame appeared, and a short time later, leaped into the air. It hurtled toward them and hit the water portside amidships. It burst there and continued to burn in the water.

"They've got a catapult!" said one of the knights.

"Yes, loaded with gnomefire." Vytrad's hands knotted into tight fists. Gnomefire was a terrible combustible, deadly to wooden structures like houses or ships. Water didn't extinguish it; the only way to put out gnomefire was to smother it with dirt.

A second flare glowed on the caravel's deck. This time there was an audible whump! and the blazing ball arced toward them. At the last second, Vytrad swung the tiller. The firepot hit dead in *Adder's* wake.

Fog thickened around them. Vytrad tried altering course to throw the pursuing ship off, but the caravel came on, guided by the broad wake left by their rowing. Soon they were in ballista range, and six foot long javelins whacked into *Adder's* planking.

"Ahoy, galleot!"

The voice was distant but strong. Vytrad ignored it. If he could keep ahead, the river was bound to get too shallow for the deep-hulled caravel. The question was, would that happen before they were riddled with missiles or set afire?

"Galleot, ahoy! Down your oars, or we'll sink you!"

The rowing did slacken. The Qualinesti had heard the cries, and they had no desire to die chained to the sweeps like galley slaves. They began shouting for help. Vytrad bellowed at them to continue rowing, but *Swamp Adder* lost momentum and began to drift backward with the current.

"All knights on deck! Yes, even the wounded—get up here! Every man is to have a sword in his hand!" stormed their commander. Bloody, bandaged, the injured knights, led by Llorn, joined their comrades on deck.

"My lord, it's not my place to say so, but we should parlay for terms," Benda said. Vytrad was shocked. The old sergeant wanted to surrender?

"It's an honorable end to a battle," he said. "They can pepper us with firepots until we're all just ashes on the water. What purpose will it serve for us to die like that?"

A volley of javelins hit the galleot, punctuating Benda's words. One iron-tipped missile drove straight through the old sergeant, pinning him to the galleot's single mast. Vytrad saw with a glance that nothing could be done for him. The rest of the javelins hit the deck and scattered the exhausted, bleeding knights.

Pulse pounding in his head, Vytrad hurriedly reviewed his options. He was hopelessly overmatched. Even if he wanted to resist, the caravel could stand off and sink them with no risk to themselves.

Vytrad climbed on the rail and cupped his hands to his mouth. "Ahoy, ship! Cease throwing! We'll parlay with you!"

The caravel turned broadside to the current and dropped anchors fore and aft. Pushed by the current, *Swamp Adder* came to rest against the larger ship's side. The caravel's deck was crowded with sailors bristling with weapons. Four large lanterns were placed on the rail. Vytrad was startled to see the caravel's crew were all elves—clean-faced Qualinesti elves.

The sailors parted ranks to admit another to the rail. The newcomer stood behind the shielded lanterns so that the light they cast was in Vytrad's eyes. All he could see was a suggestion of a face: pale skin, golden hair partly concealed by a dark bandanna. A slender hand rested on the caravel's rail.

"Who are you?" Vytrad demanded. "Why do you interfere with us? We are on a mission for the Order of the Knights of Takhisis!"

"I know who you are," said the shadowed one. The low, mellifluous voice was hard to place. "I also know what you carry on that boat."

"There is no one on this boat but subjects of the Order."

"I'll not bandy words with you. Release the Qualinesti and their property, and I will spare your lives."

Vytrad ran down the line of faces on the rail above him. None were smiling. "A gallant offer, since our lives are our own," he said sarcastically.

"Make no mistake, your lives are in my hands," the mysterious captain replied. "I've only to give the order, and you will all die. The only reason I grant you leave at all is because you saved my Qualinesti from those brigands. We meant to intercept the mercenaries before they left the river, but wind and currents were against us. For sparing their lives, I spare yours."

It was very quiet on both vessels. Vytrad thought about Lord Liveskill and his long cherished appointment to the Black Hall. If he failed in this first mission, he would never enter the ranks of Lord Liveskill's band.

Llorn laid a bandaged hand on Vytrad's shoulder. "My lord, you need say nothing. I will surrender the captives."

Face burning with shame, Vytrad slumped on a keg. Llorn ordered the Qualinesti nobles and their families off the rowers' benches. They climbed out, and though still burdened with chains, mounted the steep side of the caravel to freedom. The captured members of *Swamp Adder's* crew went with them. With Llorn's acquiescence, sailors from the caravel hauled out the treasure and stowed it on their ship.

"Will you tow us to shore?" Llorn asked the caravel's commander. "Our men are warriors, not oarsmen."

"Let them learn!" shouted a sailor. The caravel's crew laughed. Behind his lanterns, the shadowed master of the caravel smiled.

"I wouldn't want you to get to shore too soon," the caravel's commander said. "For all I know, you have reinforcements on land nearby, and we must make away. Farewell to you, and thanks again for saving my people."

Vytrad leaped to his feet. "Who are you? Show me your face, so I'll know you when I kill you!"

In answer, the captain had the lanterns removed, eliminating the shadows. Vytrad saw the face and didn't believe it. Zoran? The cowardly mate of *Water Strider*?

Zoran pulled the knotted scarf off his head, revealing a heavy hank of blonde hair.

"They call me the Lioness," the former Zoran said. "Mark my face well, knight. It may be the last thing you see in this life."

She tossed a white cloth to the galleot's deck. There was something heavy inside it. It thumped loudly on the planking and rolled to a stop in the scupper.

"Take that to your masters," she said proudly. "I regret not being able to plant it on Qualinesti land myself, but someday soon I shall. Farewell."

Sailors used poles to push the helpless *Adder* away. Turning with the current, the nameless caravel cracked on fresh canvas and sailed away in the mist. The last trace the knights had of the mystery ship was the faint echoing sound of laughter as the elves vanished.

Vytrad picked up the cloth-wrapped object. Inside was a stone catapult ball the size of his fist. The cloth proved to be a flag. Centered in the white field was the black and gold image of a rampant lion. The beast had no mane, and below the image were the words "Freedom's Pride."

"My lord? My lord?" Llorn had to call Vytrad four times before he answered. "My lord, who is the Lioness?"

"A bad dream," Vytrad muttered. "One that will be hard to waken from."

* * * * *

Kneeling, head bowed, Vytrad presented the flag to Lord Liveskill.

"This is what she gave you?" he asked, letting the banner fall to the onyx floor.

"It is, my lord."

"So, you met the Lioness. What did she look like?"

Vytrad raised his head. "I saw her clearly, my lord. She was not afraid to let me see her face." He described how she looked and what she said. "She's Qualinesti, without a doubt, and well-born. Of that I'm sure."

Lord Liveskill rose from his ebon chair and went to a high window. Clasping his hands behind his back, he surveyed the dark forest below.

"You failed, Vytrad. You're aware of that, aren't you?"

"Yes, my lord, but my mission was not a total loss."

"Oh?"

"I discovered where the Qualinesti were fleeing to, and how, and that route is closed now. I lost them and their treasure to the Lioness, but I saw her face and heard

Paul B. Thompson

her speak, which is more than anyone else in the Order has done."

Lord Liveskill turned his back to the window. Folding his arms, he said, "You find salutary lessons even in failure, Redlance. That's well. For that I'll give you another mission."

Vytrad jumped to his feet. "My lord is too magnanimous!"

"You don't know the mission yet." Vytrad snapped his heels together and stood ready for his orders. "Bring me the Lioness. For too long she has subverted our authority in this region. She must be found, and stopped. Bring her before me. I don't care how long it takes, or how many lives it costs.

"Find her, Vytrad. Begin immediately."

He saluted crisply. "I pledge my life to the task, great lord," he said, and he meant every word.

Sargas's Night of Revenge
Don Perrin

The banquet hall was bare and empty. The floor-boards that had been made of handhewn oak were rotted and split. The cracks between the boards allowed travel from the cellars and dungeons below easy for the rats who were now the keep's masters. Beneath the dust and the cobwebs and the rat droppings, fading blood-stains could still be seen on the rotting wood.

The walls had been made of stone, three feet thick, and they had withstood many glorious sieges, but they could not hold against the final enemy—time. The west wall had crumbled and fallen to rubble. The north wall was still attached to the main house, but was little more than a shattered hulk of its former might.

The roof had caved in some three hundred years earlier. The furniture had been stolen long before that. If Lord Trenak's rich tapestries had survived the centuries, they now hung in some other manorial banquet hall in Ansalon, the hall of some elf lord who would point to them and tell the tale of how his great-great-great someone or other had seized these as prizes of war during some valiant action against the minotaur in the year something. A year so far back that its count was meaningless. When in truth the great-great had stolen them as he had stolen the furniture out of a keep that had been abandoned.

Abandoned by the living, that is.

Once a year, once a year every year, once a year every year for a thousand years, the cracks in the boards were repaired by an invisible hand. The same invisible hand polished the wood to a high gloss and drove the rats—squealing in terror—back to the cellars. The tapestries returned to the walls. The weapons of the clan were once again proudly displayed on the walls. The massive oak banquet table took its place in the great hall. Food materialized on the table—roasted haunches of venison, rabbits cooked to a fine crispness, piled high on sizzling platters, all to be washed down with foaming ale. Torchlight flared again in the banquet hall and all was ready at last.

Sargas's Night of Revenge.

Vrass opened his eyes at exactly the moment when he usually closed them. Closed them in death. The young minotaur lay on his side on the floor of the banquet hall, one hand pressed against the gash in his belly, trying instinctively and desperately to hold his entrails inside him. Blood seeped from between his fingers, blood and his own life. The pain was agony. He was terrified of dying and, at the same time, he craved oblivion to end the torture. He would die, as those all around him were dying, die with the screams of his kinsmen in his ears.

And this night, he would return to life. Again.

Vrass watched the black blood that had gushed out of his body now flow back into his veins and arteries. The pool of blood disappeared. The terrible pain ebbed away. He drew in a deep breath. He spent a moment listening, feeling his heart beat with life, but the moment was never long enough. Never long enough for him to enjoy living.

He jumped to his feet. His dirk and his boot knife, both smeared with blood, lay on the floor beside him.

When he picked them up, the blood vanished. He thrust the dirk in his belt, slid the knife in his boot. The great tear in his best tunic sealed closed, sewn together by that same invisible hand. The bloody fabric was cleansed. He walked forward to the great banquet table to take his assigned place. All around him minotaur, males and females, their mates and eldest children, were heading for the table. Their own killing wounds had healed, their own blood was cleansed away, their own gore-covered weapons were returned to sheath or belt. All twenty-seven moved to the table and took their appointed places.

The minotaur formed the Trenak Clan, Warriors Noble, Protectors of the Northern Yeshall Passes, Commanders of the Northern Reach. They were one of the Great Houses of the Minotaur Kingdom of Kothas. All of the clan warriors were present, seven of them, sons and daughters to the clan chieftain, Lord Trenak. All of the warriors' mates were present, warriors proud in their own right. The eldest warrior son or daughter of each of these families was also present, grandchildren to Lord Trenak. Four of these grandchildren had mates who attended. Vrass was the eldest warrior son of Vormas, third son of Lord Trenak, and he had no mate yet.

Lord Trenak had convened this gathering. Sibling rivalry had escalated into near warfare and the lord was determined to have his clan at peace. The sons and daughters of Trenak had all come to the banquet in obedience to the head of the clan, but glowering looks went round faster than the ale and hands fingered the hilts of swords instead of the hilt of the carving knife.

Vrass sat across from Vromas, his father, and his mother. To Vrass's left sat the female warrior Lekcress, the mate of his uncle Emass, and to Vrass's right sat Hlell, warrior husband to his aunt Brossik. The members of Trenak clan sat in silence, sullen and defiant, waiting for the appointed hour.

An enormous minotaur took shape and form at the head of the banquet hall. Awful in his majesty, terrible in his wrath, the god of the minotaur, Sargas, glared down on his children from his great height.

"Clan Trenak! For nine hundred and sixty years, you have been cursed to relive the night of your foul treachery. On that night, your clan, Protectors of the North Yeshall Passes and Commanders of the Northern Reach, did slay each other in a blood-bath of betrayal and deceit such as our people had never before seen, or, thankfully, since."

Sargas drew in a seething breath. Over nine hundred years had passed, and his anger had not diminished.

"Not one member of the ruling warriors of this clan survived this night. Two days later, the Silvanesti elves entered the Northern Reach and seized them without a fight. Four days later, the Yeshall Passes were overrun. Countless minotaur warriors died because of your faithlessness. Your clan has been stricken from the record of clans and your name is cursed, never to be spoken again by any minotaur. You have shamed us all."

Again, Sargas paused. The minotaur hung their proud horned heads. Hands curled in on themselves, muscles twitched. Lord Trenak, head of the clan, shuddered visibly when it was announced that this clan had been stricken from the records. Of all the mortal blows he had received, that was the worst.

"You have been cursed by your deeds," Sargas concluded, "cursed to relive your fate again and again until time itself ends. Each year, on the anniversary of your treachery, you are doomed to reawaken, take your places in the game of death, and repeat your actions. Year after year, you will remember every death you cause. You will remember every death you die. Such is my command!"

A throne of carved black onyx appeared. Sargas took his seat. He raised his hands.

"The night begins!"

Vrass sat in silence, too overawed to speak. He had never before been invited to the Banquet of Warriors. This year, he had killed his man and now he was a blooded warrior, allowed to take his place at the table. Fearing he might make a mistake and bring dishonor on his family, he watched his elders closely. His mother and father sat across from him, but the table was enormous and piled with food and drink. He could barely see his parents. In the uproar of the hall, with brother shouting to father, mother shouting to daughter, and all of them bawling for more ale, he could not hear anything his parents were saying. Vrass decided he would emulate those closest to him, the warriors to his left and right.

His uncle by marriage, Hlell sat to Vrass's right and ignored the young minotaur completely. Vrass ventured to speak to his uncle, planning to ask him to pass the venison, for the young warrior was hungry and the smell of the roasted meat made his mouth water. Hlell did not even turn his horned head at Vrass's request, but continued to converse with a warrior neighbor. Vrass dared not reach across his uncle's plate to grab the food, a move that would have been disrespectful. The young minotaur would be forced to curb his hunger until the elder warrior saw fit to hand him something.

Trying to ignore the delicious smell, Vrass turned his attention to his left. There sat Lekcress, sister to Hlell and mate to Emass, Vrass's uncle. Lekcress was the most beautiful minotaur female Vrass had ever seen. Lekcress wore a tight leather jerkin that accentuated all the finest parts of her body. Her arms were tightly muscled from many battles, her neck short and stocky, and her chest was wide and rippled with powerful muscles. He wanted very much to speak to her, to make her turn her lovely eyes in his direction, but he had no idea what to say. If he said the wrong thing, he would disgrace himself and so he deemed it better to keep quiet.

As for the beautiful Lekcress, she paid Vrass no attention at all. He was a young warrior and not worthy of her notice. Her husband, however, was worthy, and her eyes were fixed on him. Emass sat on the other side of his wife and he was not paying attention to her. He was talking volubly to a shining-eyed minotaur female named Nekell, who sat next to him. The two leaned in toward each other. As far as they were concerned, no one else was in the banquet hall.

Lord Trenak rose to his feet, banged a mug on the table, counseling silence. He was an elderly minotaur with gray on his muzzle, but still able to take his place on the field of battle and lead his clan to war. He began to speak, to recount the past glories of the clan. No one was interested in past glories, however. They ignored the old man, talked among themselves. Emass and the Nekell continued to whisper together and once the young female laughed.

Vrass was extremely uncomfortable. He had heard his parents discussing Emass's scandalous behavior. All knew he was carrying on an affair with his lovely cousin. Did he think Lekcress was blind that she would not notice?

Lekcress noticed. As Vrass watched, he saw her hand drop to her belt, grasp the handle of her dirk and slowly began to slide it from its leather scabbard.

Vrass had no idea what to do. He saw murder in Lekcress's eyes, knew perfectly well what she intended. She was going to avenge herself on her unfaithful husband. Vrass could have dealt with that—even his parents would see that Lekcress had a clear right to avenge herself. No one of the Trenak would defend Emass in a fair fight. But this was not going to be a fair fight. Lekcress was not preparing to jump to her feet and denounce him in front of his family, demand that he give her satisfaction for openly disgracing her. She was sneaking the dirk from her belt, removing it slowly and stealthily. She was going to stab Emass in the back, a cowardly move that would bring dishonor to them all.

Confused, Vrass started to reach for his ale mug. His movement drew Lekcress's attention to him. She saw him staring at her with appalled eyes. Obviously, he guessed what she intended. She looked him up and she looked him down, and then, scornfully, she turned her back on him. She slid the dirk free of the scabbard and raised her arm.

Vrass was infuriated. This woman was going to murder his uncle in cold-blood, in his nephew's sight, and she obviously thought the young warrior was too frightened to try to stop her.

Vrass jumped to his feet, sending his chair sliding backward across the polished floor. He pulled his own dirk and launched himself at the female warrior.

An arm reached around Vrass from behind. A hand holding a dirk sliced Vrass's stomach open. Blood sprayed over the table, over Lekcress. Vrass stared down at the horrible wound. He saw parts of himself that should never be seen start to leak out. He stumbled, dropping his dirk. The hall erupted in chaos. He clasped his hand over his leaking guts and tried to reach for his boot knife. He managed to draw it, but he lacked the strength to hold onto it. The knife slipped from his bloody fingers. He slumped to the floor. His life seeped out from his fingers as chairs smashed and the minotaur of Trenak Clan roared in anger and screamed in death and the last sound he heard then was the sound of Sargas's voice, furious, outraged, cursing them for yet another year . . .

Vrass opened his eyes at exactly the moment when he usually closed them. Closed them in death. The young minotaur lay on his side on the floor of the banquet hall, one hand pressed against the gash in his belly, trying instinctively and desperately to hold his entrails inside him. Blood seeped from between his fingers, blood and his own life. The pain was agony. He was terrified of dying and, at the same time, craved oblivion to end the torture. He would die, as those all around him were dying, die with the screams of his kinsmen in his ears.

And this night, he would return to life. Again.

Vrass watched the black blood that had gushed out of his body now flow back into his veins and arteries. The pool of blood disappeared. The terrible pain ebbed away. He drew in a deep breath. He spent a moment listening, feeling his heart beat with life, but the moment was never long enough. Never long enough for him to enjoy living.

He jumped to his feet. His dirk and his boot knife, both smeared with blood, lay on the floor beside him. When he picked them up, the blood vanished. He thrust the dirk in his belt, slid the knife in his boot. The great tear in his best tunic sealed closed, sewn together by that same invisible hand. The bloody fabric was cleansed. He walked forward to the great banquet table to take his assigned place. All around him minotaur, males and females, their mates and eldest children, were heading for the table. Their own killing wounds had healed, their own blood was cleansed away, their own gore-covered weapons were returned to sheath or belt. All twenty-seven moved to the table and took their appointed places.

The minotaur formed the Trenak Clan, Warriors Noble, Protectors of the Northern Yeshall Passes, Commanders of the Northern Reach. They were one of the Great Houses of the Minotaur Kingdom of Kothas. All of the clan warriors were present, seven of them, sons and daughters to the clan chieftain, Lord Trenak. All of the warriors' mates were present, warriors proud in their own right. The eldest warrior son or daughter of each of these families was also present, grandchildren to Lord Trenak. Four of these grandchildren had mates who attended. Vrass was the eldest warrior son of Vormas, third son of Lord Trenak, and he had no mate yet.

Lord Trenak had convened this gathering. Sibling rivalry had escalated into near warfare and the lord was determined to have his clan at peace. The sons and daughters of Trenak had all come to the banquet in obedience to the head of the clan, but glowering looks went round faster than the ale and hands fingered the hilts of swords instead of the hilt of the carving knife.

Vrass sat across from Vromas, his father, and his mother. To Vrass's left sat the female warrior Lekcress, the mate of his uncle Emass, and to Vrass's right sat Hlell, warrior husband to his aunt Brossik. The members of Trenak clan sat in silence, sullen and defiant, waiting for the appointed hour.

The hour came and the hour went. Sargas did not appear.

The minotaur glanced at each other out of the corners of their eyes, not daring yet to lift their heads, each silently asking his neighbor what was going on. No one had the answer.

They sat for a few more moments, then heads began to raise. Brows furrowed. They looked around. All was as it should be. All was as it had been for year after year after year for a thousand years. The polished floor, the foaming ale, the sizzling meat. All except Sargas. The god of the minotaur was not here.

Vrass felt lost, bereft, uneasy. Sargas always appeared at the head table. He admonished them for their crimes against each other. He declared that the sins would be repeated, every year on the anniversary of the butchery, and that each minotaur at the table would learn his sin by millennia upon millennia of repetition. Vrass did not like being constrained to perform the same action year after year. He did not like being gutted, did not like dying a thousand deaths. But, now that he thought about it, that was better than this. This was strange and he didn't like it.

He noted other differences. The banquet was hot, stifling. He did not remember such heat before, it was as if the world outside were being consumed in flame. In front of Vrass sat his tankard of cool foaming ale. Thirsty, suffering in the heat, Vrass grabbed up his tankard and prepared to take a long draught.

Lord Trenak rose to his feet. He banged the ale mug on the table and started to launch into his usual speech. "The glories of Clan Trenak stretch back to the time when the gods themselves first walked upon Krynn—" He stopped. The minotaur were, as usual, muttering and whispering.

"You are ungrateful, spoiled children!" Lord Trenak suddenly shouted. "I watched every one of you die with pleasure! You got what you deserved. And so did I," he added, slumping in his chair. "So did I."

He sat, his head bowed. The minotaur fell silent. Some looked ashamed. All were uneasy.

The female warrior Lekcress should have been watching with jealous fury her husband flirt with the young minotaur Nekell. Instead, she kicked Vrass savagely under the table.

"Put that mug down! You have never touched the mug before! You are not supposed to be doing that."

Vrass kicked her back. A thousand years before, he would have never dared touch her, but he had built up inside him a thousand years of anger at her for having been the cause of his death.

"Leave me alone, Aunt Lekcress! It's damned hot, and Sargas is late. I haven't had ale in a thousand years and by the gods I mean to enjoy this one before I die again."

"And speaking of dying, Uncle"—Vrass turned to Hlell—"it's a right bastard thing to stab me in the belly from behind! What did you have to go and do that for anyway?"

Hlell snorted. "Hah, Nephew! You are free to plunge your dirk in my sister's chest, but you consider it a damned trick when I gut you, is that it? Why were you going to stab her anyway?"

"I was defending my uncle's honor!" Vrass returned. "She was going to kill Uncle Emass. I saw her and she knew I saw her. She pulled her dagger right under my nose, figuring I was too much a coward to try to stop her. If I hadn't gone for her, she would have stabbed him in the back."

"What?" Uncle Emass roared, leaving his conversation with Nekell to glare around at Lekcress. "Is that true, Wife?"

"Of course it is," she said in frozen tones. "For a thousand years I've had to endure watching you flirt with that heifer—"

"And to think I died avenging you!" Emass said, scowling.

"Did you?" Lekcress asked, startled and softened. "I never knew that." She put her hand to her breast, looked across at Vrass's mother. "I am always dead by her hand before I know—"

"Heifer!" Nekell was on her feet. "Who are you calling a heifer?"

Lekcress pointedly ignored her rival. She reached out her hand to Emass. "So you do still love me?"

Emass shook his horned head. "I am a terrible flirt, Wife. But that is all it is. I swear to you—"

Disgusted with the lot of them, Vrass leaned across his Uncle Hlell, grabbed hold of the meat platter and dragged it toward him. He ripped a leg from the roasted venison. His behavior was rude, but he'd been starving for a thousand years. Being the first dead, he was never able to eat or drink at any of the dinners and if his belly was going to be ripped open tonight, he intended for it to be full.

Just as he brought the juicy meat to his mouth, his uncle Hlell caught hold of his hand and slammed it down on the table.

"Lekcress is right. We are doomed to repeat our history. We must reenact our darkest hour. You didn't have any food or drink that night, and that's the way it should be."

Vrass thrust Hlell's hand aside and started to bite into the meat. Angrily, Hlell drew his knife.

"We'll see who's a heifer, you stupid cow!" the female minotaur Nekell shouted and hurled her ale, mug and all, at Lekcress.

The aim was bad. The mug struck Vrass on the snout, jarred the meat from his hand and covered him with foaming ale.

Lekcress laughed.

Vrass jumped to his feet in rage. His chair went skidding backward. He made a dive for Lekcress. She kicked him in the gut, sent him staggering. He fell onto Hlell's dirk.

The long blade slid into Vrass's back and came out

his belly. He stared down at it in shock. Horrified, Hlell snatched the knife from Vrass's body. Blood gushed from the mortal wound.

"Vrass, I'm sorry!" Hlell cried, catching hold of the dying young minotaur. He lifted a stricken face to Lord Trenak. "My lord! I swear! I didn't mean to do that!"

Vrass slumped to the table, scattering plates. The hall was in an uproar.

"By the gods, Hlell!" Vrass heard his father yell. "This time I will have a chance to avenge my son's death before I die!"

His father brandished a battle-axe from the far wall. The blade come crashing down onto Hlell's head, splitting open the minotaur's skull, spattering Vrass with blood and brains and shards of bone.

Vrass was dying. He was dying, but not the way he was supposed to die. Nothing was happening the way it was supposed to happen.

His father's body crashed onto the table, felled from behind by someone who fell at the hands of Vrass's mother, before she too was killed . . .

Death seized Vrass as it seized all the others. But this time Vrass died with a smile on his lips.

* * * * *

Once a year, once a year every year, once a year every year for a thousand years, the cracks in the boards were repaired by an invisible hand. The same invisible hand polished the wood to a high gloss and drove the rats—squealing in terror—back to the cellars. The tapestries returned to the walls. The weapons of the clan were once again proudly displayed on the walls. The massive oak banquet table took its place in the great hall. Food materialized on the table—roasted haunches of venison, rabbits cooked to a fine crispness, piled high on sizzling platters, all to be washed down with foaming ale. Torch-light flared again in the banquet hall and all was ready at last.

Vrass watched the black blood that had gushed out of his body now flow back into his veins and arteries. The pool of blood disappeared. The terrible pain ebbed away. He drew in a deep breath. He spent a moment listening, feeling his heart beat with life, but the moment was never long enough. Never long enough for him to enjoy living.

At least, not until now.

Vrass took his place at the table. All around him, the other minotaur were doing the same.

Vrass looked to his father and bowed before he sat down. "Thank you, Father, for avenging my death last year."

"You are my son," his father said gruffly, though he was well pleased. "I have the family honor to uphold."

Chairs scraped. The minotaur took their seats. All looked toward the place where Sargas usually appeared. He was not there.

Lord Trenak sat in his chair, nursing his ale. He glowered round at all of them, said nothing.

Beside Vrass, Lekcress and Emass sat close together, hands touching beneath the table. The young female Nekell was speaking quite loudly and pointedly to a young male at her side.

Vrass gulped his ale quickly, before someone killed him again. Reaching across his uncle, Vrass grabbed hold of the roast venison. He ripped off a leg and then, acting on impulse, he tore off the best portion of the meat and placed it on the plate in front of Lekcress.

She looked at him with a startled expression.

"You never get to eat before you die, either," Vrass said.

"Thank you, Warrior," she said, regarding him with new respect.

Hlell glowered at Vrass and Lekcress. "Sargas forbids us to do other than to reenact the events of our night of treachery."

"Sargas is not here," Vrass said with his mouth full. "I'll do what I damn well please."

Hlell drew his knife. "You will show respect to the god of our people!"

Vrass rose, dirk in hand, to meet Hlell's challenge. A violent shove from behind sent the young minotaur stumbling into his chair. Lekcress stood protectively in front of Vrass, facing her brother.

"We none of us have shown respect for the god of our people. That's why we're here year after bloody year. Either put down your knife, Little Brother, or use it on me."

Hlell eyed his sister, perhaps to see if she meant what she said. He apparently decided she was bluffing, for he made a sudden sideways lunge at Vrass. Leckress blocked him with her body. Seizing hold of her brother's wrist, she gave it an expert twist. Bones cracked. Hlell gasped in pain and dropped the knife.

"I've wanted to do that ever since you were born," Leckress said with a sneer.

"You have dishonored our family, Sister!" Hlell cried, nursing his wrist.

"Yes, dishonor!" First cousins, second cousins, aunts and uncles leapt to their feet. Swords flashed in the torchlight. Axes raised.

Vrass jumped onto the table, scattering the plates.

"Trenak Clan, hold your weapons!" he yelled. "Sargas is *not here!* Don't you understand what this means? We do not have to reenact the night of our worst treachery!" He turned to face the elder minotaur.

"Lord Trenak, we are your family. Do not renounce us. True, we turned on one another, and did this family such a disservice that we are cursed throughout time. Yet for two years now, Sargas has not come to continue the curse. It seems that we are still doomed to repeat the night, but no longer the actions of the night. Have we learned nothing in a thousand years?"

Lord Trenak rose to his feet. He stood silent for a few moments, looking searchingly at each of the minotaur present. He looked last and longest at his grandson Vrass, who had now resumed his place at the table.

The elder minotaur lifted his head, glared around at them.

"I am your liege Lord, and I am your Father or your Father or Mother's Father. You will obey me when I order you to take your weapons and place them on the table in front of you."

No one moved. Lord Trenak drew his own sword and tossed it on the table. Slowly, the warriors began to comply. Swords, short spears, battle-axes and several hand-crossbows clattered onto the table, smashing the dishes and upending the mugs of ale.

"All of the weapons!" the Lord commanded, his voice stern. He took four blades from out of his leather vest and tossed these onto the table.

The minotaur exchanged glances and then began pulling knives from their boots, dirks from belts or bosoms. These too were added to the pile.

"No one will move until I give the command," said Lord Trenak. "No one."

The assembled warriors sat quietly, obeying their lord's order. They sat through the long hours of the night, staring at the weapons on the table, weapons that had meant their deaths for the past thousand years. At length, as dawn was drawing near, Lord Trenak broke the long silence.

"Vrass, son of Vormas, is the youngest amongst and yet he is the wisest. Can we not, after all these years, see our folly?"

A low murmur came from the assembled minotaur. They nodded their horned heads and a few began to thump loudly on the table.

"Can we not correct our folly?"

The murmur rose to a shout, the thumping to a crescendo.

Lord Trenak raised his voice. "It seems that Sargas has given us the chance to redeem ourselves. Shall we take it?"

The minotaur yelled in unison, "Yes, Lord!"

The first rays of the sun filtered through the windows. The warriors sat and waited, not knowing what would happen. None of them had ever lived to see the dawning.

The sunlight glinted on the weapons and slowly the minotaur faded away.

* * * * *

Vrass opened his eyes to find himself seated at the table. The food was piled high, right where it always was.

Hlell sat beside Vrass. He glared at Vrass, daring him to repeat his action of last year. Vrass returned the glare, undaunted, and started to reach for the meat. Suddenly, recalling his words of last year, Vrass arrested his movement. Keeping his hand in plain sight, he reached instead for the pitcher of ale.

"Uncle Hlell," said Vrass respectfully, "will you grant me the very great honor of allowing me to fill your mug, the mug of a gallant warrior?"

His gaze fixed on Hlell, Vrass could not see Leckress, but he felt her behind him, approving, supporting. Vrass could not see Lord Trenak, but he could hear the elder minotaur's low murmur of approval, a murmur that was echoed around the table.

Hlell hesitated. He had been taken by surprise, caught completely unaware. If the young warrior had suddenly plunged a knife into him, Hlell would have been less astonished. At length, grudgingly, Hlell grabbed his mug and held it for Vrass to fill.

"I drink to your health, Vrass, grandson of Lord Trenak," Hlell said gruffly and drained his mug.

Lord Trenak raised his voice. "Weapons will be stacked in the corner of the room."

All the members of the minotaur clan, Hlell included, marched to the southwest corner of the room. They tossed their knives and dirks, axes and swords, crossbows and spears onto the floor, then they returned to their seats. Vrass surrendered his own dirk and boot knife, pleased to see that this time they were not covered with blood.

Once all had resumed their seats, Lord Trenak looked to Vrass.

"Will you do us the honors, my grandson?"

"Every year we have drawn blood on this night," Vrass said. "Last year, we changed that. This year, it is my pleasure to welcome Clan Trenak to the annual celebration dinner." Vrass raised his tankard. "Let us come together in peace!"

He turned to Lekcress. "Peace, Aunt?"

Lekcress smiled and lifted her mug to touch his.

"Peace, Nephew."

Vrass turned to Hlell. "Peace, Uncle?"

Hlell lifted his mug and clashed it against Vrass's.

"Peace, Nephew!"

A loud cheer roared from the minotaur.

The merriment lasted throughout that night, far longer than did the ale. The minotaur emptied the last drop an hour before sun-up. As the darkness began to diminish, Lord Trenak rose to address the clan.

"I am proud of you. We have restored our honor. Yet, in one thing, I am displeased." Lord Trenak looked sternly around.

The minotaur hushed, glanced at each other, wondering what new offense they had committed.

Lord Trenak glanced sadly at the empty keg. "Next year, and all following years, we must pace ourselves with the ale so that we don't run dry before the end of the feast." He winked. "We wouldn't want a fight to break out over the ale, would we?"

Laughter dissolved into dust, as the banquet hall dissolved to ruins.

The next year, the laughter started right where it had left off the year before.

Sharing the Luck
Linda P. Baker

Kraco killed the dwarf.

He didn't mean to do it so quickly, but behind the bushy reddish beard, the little man glared at him, menaced him with his gleaming brown eyes. And so Kraco just slipped the blade in between the dwarf's ribs, quickly, efficiently, and pushed.

There was the surprising resistance of a body stronger and tougher than he'd expected, the bruising grip of the dwarf's fingers as he tried to push away, the smooth, slushy slide of the dagger going in. Then the dwarf gasped and slid to the ground, all the menace slipping away with his last breath.

Kraco looked up at his partner and managed to look a little shamefaced "Sorry."

Risha just grinned and went back to guarding the dwarf's traveling companion, an old man wearing the robes of the Academy of Sorcery. Moonlight glinted off his dagger in lovely jagged patterns as Risha wove it back and forth in the air, warning the old man to stay where he was.

Kraco easily withdrew his dagger from the soft, squishy flesh. It had been a good, clean kill, right between the ribs, no chilling, eerie scrape of blade on bone, which he hated. Blood welled up as the dagger came free, soaking the dwarf's dirty brown tunic and leeching into the earth in a widening pool. Kraco wiped his blade clean on the hem of the dwarf's tunic, then leaned in to rifle the pockets.

He found only a cloth pouch that rattled pitifully with two silver coins and few coppers and a length of braided leather that would make a good lace for a shirt, but then, he hadn't expected to find much. Risha had picked these two out of a crowd back in Hangman's Harbor, assuring him that they were good marks. The mountain dwarf because he was a bit too plain, too conspicuously inconspicuous. The old man because Risha had been listening to too many travelers' tales about the magical artifacts spit up when the Blood Sea burned away during the Summer of Chaos. Supposedly, a man could walk along the shores of Karthay and gather them up like picking dandelions in a summer meadow. Supposedly, the wizards from the Academy had been sent out to do just that, prospect for artifacts. Risha was convinced that the old one, who looked as if he barely had the price of supper, had treasures from the lost city of Istar rolled up in his blanket.

Kraco cursed again as he climbed to his feet and brushed wet grass off his knees. He dropped the meager findings into his partner's palm. "This is all he had." After weeks of cold and sleeping in stables and eating others' leavings, he'd been looking forward to better pickings, to a long stay in a warm room and plenty of flowing ale.

Risha rolled the coins around before taking one of the silvers and half the coppers and dropping them into his pocket. The other half, Kraco's pitiful share, he handed back. But he didn't seem terribly upset at the small take. He looked around the area that the dwarf and old man had chosen for their campsite, at the two bedrolls consisting of scraggly blankets, one under a tree, the other a few feet away.

Risha waggled the dagger. "So where are your real valuables, old one?"

For a moment, the old man's eyes reflected the dim light. For a moment, they glowed silver, with all the fire of an enchanted dagger, and Kraco's heart leapt in his chest. For a moment, he thought they'd seriously miscalculated and this was a formidable enemy. All those tales of great and terrible magical spells that his grandmother had used to threaten him when he was a child popped into his head.

Then the old man straightened, and all that was staring at them were a pair of amazingly clear gray eyes in a wizened face. He moved slowly, keeping his hands in plain sight as if he'd had experience with thieves. "I have nothing that you would want, young man. Only a few coppers and my traveling gear, which has seen better days." He lifted his robe a few inches to show boots even more shabby than the ones Kraco and Risha were wearing. His sleeve billowed out with the movement, sliding up his arm to gather at his elbow, revealing a glint of silver and the flash of jewels on a bony wrist.

Before Kraco could say anything, Risha stepped forward. "What's that?" he demanded too loudly. "Give us that, around your wrist."

The wizard held out his arm and the sleeve fell away again. Kraco peered at the bracelet encircling the old man's wrist. He blinked, leaned closer, and blinked again. The wrist was bony, pale and blue-veined, skin papery thin. And what had at first flashed bright and shiny in the moonlight was actually dull and gray. Instead of a finely polished silver bangle, etched with intricate designs and encrusted with jewels, the bracelet was actually a dull metal circle, scratched with wear. Upon closer inspection, the fine jewels looked like glass.

Kraco made a rude sound. He started to turn away, disgusted, but was pulled up short at the expression on Risha's face. His partner was looking at the bracelet as if he was about to fall on the old man and cut off his hand. His eyes were so hot they actually glittered. Desire steaming out into the darkness.

"Give it to me!" Risha demanded, knife tip dancing as dangerously as his eyes.

The old man put a hand up. Kraco braced, expecting resistance. Risha shifted with him, unison movements borne of long years fighting side by side. But all the old man did was twist the thin band around so that the narrow opening in the back of it lined up with the shallow part of his wrist.

Risha shivered with his eagerness to have the thing.

The old man wriggled his wrist free and extended the bangle out to Risha. "I give it to you freely," he said. "And you must take it freely."

Risha stuffed his dagger into the waist of his trousers. "I take it freely."

Kraco watched them both, mouth open. Such fuss over a piece of junk. Time wasted when they should be on the road, looking for more likely prospects. Unless . . . he grabbed the bracelet as the old man extended it towards Risha. It was still warm from his skin. So warm in contrast to the cold, moisture-laden air that it made his fingers tingle. It was rough and beaten on the outside, worn satin smooth on the inside.

No, it was just a cheap piece of junk made of pot metal and decorated with glass. He passed it to Risha. Slowly. Turning it just once more before he allowed the tug of Risha's fingers to take it. "It'll turn your skin green."

Risha, who had been glaring at him while he examined

the bangle, grinned and slipped the thing onto his wrist. "It'll bring us luck. I feel it."

"Hmph." Kraco frowned, still eyeing the thing. Risha was a great believer in luck, always crossing his fingers at things and tossing salt over his shoulder and picking up stones to carry around in his pocket until they were polished shiny. Kraco believed in making his own luck, which didn't seem to be happening tonight. "Maybe it'll bring us a rich mark to make up for these two. We've wasted our time here."

Risha shook head his head, peering up at him through a shank of hair as curly as Kraco's but pale as bleached bone, hanging down over his brass colored eyes. His partner thought it looked rakish, but Kraco thought it looked messy compared to his own neatly brushed back, brown curls. Like most times when Risha looked at him as if disappointed in him, Kraco felt like grabbing his dagger and the hank of hair and shearing it off .

As always, before he could act on his irritation, Risha grinned his lopsided grin, taking the sting out of his expression. He pointed at the other blanket lying half-hidden beneath a stand of scrubby bushes. "Krac, you should have more faith" he said softly, with just the slightest jeering reproach. "Would an old man carry two bedrolls?"

Kraco whipped around. Barely visible, near the corner of the dwarf's blanket, was another blanket, still tightly rolled and bound with strong leather strips. He snatched up the roll, cut the ties and quickly unrolled the blanket.

Then the first trinket fell out of the folds. He gasped and dropped to his knees, scrabbled for it with his free hand. It was a tiny silver dagger, sized for the hand of a kender, but fit to hang on the belt of a king. The scabbard was decorated with gold wire, and the hilt capped by a blood red, cabachon stone as big as his thumb. Clutching the dagger clumsily, he gave the blanket another turn, and loose jewels fell free, twinkling green and red and deep blue and fiery in the moonlight.

Kraco looked up at Risha. The worth of such stones was enough to keep them warm and fed for two winters. Cool and dry for two summers. Maybe more, if they were frugal and wise.

Risha, rubbing his wrist and the cheap bangle, threw his head back and laughed aloud.

Kraco carefully tucked the sharp-edged stones into his pocket, the dagger back into the blanket. Then he untied the ruined strips of leather and tied the lengths together, making them once again into two strips long enough to circle the roll of blanket. He bound up the bundle and tested it, ensuring that nothing precious could slip free. When he was done, he looked up to find Risha watching him, smiling. And in the warmth of his friend's smile and the cold bite of the breeze, he could feel the turning of their fortunes.

"Finish him and let's go." Kraco jerked his chin at the old man as he climbed to his feet, tucking the rolled blanket securely under one arm. He peered up at the sky. It had cleared for a while, after the rain, but now clouds roiled overhead, threatening to blot out the moon. "Let's hurry. It's going to rain again."

Risha looked back at the old man, then back at Kraco, back at the old man again. He shrugged. "He's an old man, no threat to us. It's not worth the effort."

The skin across the back of Kraco's neck prickled, but not from the cold. In all the years since they'd met in a farce of amateurish bungling, both stumbling around in the dark, trying to rob the same merchant, they'd never left a witness alive. Since that night, when they'd first tried to kill each other, then recognized each other as kindred spirits and decided to work together, they'd never disagreed on their method of operation. Choose a mark, take anything of value, leave no witnesses, split the spoils.

Risha looked at Kraco, as if his every thought was written upon his forehead. "Come on," he said, motioning back towards the road. "He brought us luck. He was the one convinced the dwarf to come this way. I heard them back in town." He quirked his head to one side and lifted one shoulder. "T'would be back luck and bad manners to kill such a benefactor."

Kraco believed making his own luck, but he had received the benefit of Risha's on more than one occasion. And one old man, incapable of catching up to them if they moved quickly, wasn't important enough to be the source of his first serious disagreement with his partner. "All right," he growled, menacing them both, partner and prey, with a scowl. "But if this one causes us trouble down the road. . . ." Kraco glared at the old man.

Risha shrugged again, conveying that dealing the old man a painful death would have been as easy a task as leaving him alive. He strode away without looking back.

"Don't follow us," Kraco warned. Then he trotted away up the slope to the road. He glanced back once, and the old man was standing where they'd left him, dazedly watching them go. The body of the dwarf was a shadowed lump at the edge of the clearing.

Kraco ran to catch up to his partner. They stayed on the road for several minutes, then Risha veered off into the forest. The night and the trees swallowed him up.

Clutching the bedroll to his chest, Kraco had to duck beneath several branches, then work his way through a thicket to keep pace with his companion. "Slow down! Where are we going?"

"Back to town." Risha grinned back at him, his teeth gleaming white and ghostly in the near darkness. "If the old man reports us to anyone, they'll expect that we went on. Nobody would expect us to double back. They won't even look there."

"If we'd killed him, we wouldn't have to worry about it," Kraco huffed and ducked to avoid a branch that Risha let snap back towards his face.

"All right, then." Risha paused to get his bearings, peering up through the thick foliage as if he could see the stars. "How about The Drunken Piper? Nobody would expect us to go there."

"That's because nobody in their right mind would go to the Piper." The Drunken Piper was a rundown, squalid inn so far off the main road that few travelers even knew it was there. During the worst of the winter, the majority of the customers were like them: thieves, card sharks, cutthroats. The few good marks who happened in usually left quickly.

They pushed on. A big raindrop splatted onto the tip of Kraco's nose. Another splashed the back of his neck as he ducked to avoid a branch. He patted his pocket, fingers lingering on the sharp edges of the stones, clutched the bedroll tighter and reminded himself that this was the last night they'd spend looking for shelter for a very long time.

The inn was packed with travelers when they finally stepped out of the trees into the muddy yard that surrounded it. Cold, tired and wet to the skin, Kraco sighed as he pushed open the doors and allowed Risha to precede him. What luck! On another night, he would have been overjoyed to see the inn bustling with possibilities. Now he only saw competition for the few upstairs rooms.

Apparently the wind and rain, which had set upon them before they had gone a mile, had driven many travelers inside. Twenty plus of them, all taking shelter from the storm, drinking and eating and talking so that the common room sounded like a combination of bustling kitchen and magpie gathering. It smelled like a herd of wet dragons had moved in, smoky and leathery and crowded.

Yet in the light of the dancing torches, the Piper looked almost as good as one of those nice inns that bordered the market square in Hangman's Harbor, instead of a dive along the bay road outside the city. The shining wood floors showed through the tracked-in mud, and the bar top, beneath droplets of spilled ale, was oiled and gleaming. Between booted feet and spots of tarnish, the brass railing shone .

Kraco put one foot up on the rail and heard the metallic ring as Risha did the same. He lifted the wet bedroll up, lay it along the edge of the bar and leaned his chest on it. Water squished out and dripped down his ribs.

None of the crowd of faces along the bar or at the tables, not even the slatternly barmaid who was serving the group before the fire, looked familiar. A couple of women returned Kraco's perusal, and he preened a little, reaching up to wipe the rain off his face. Woman always responded to the exotic evidence of his mixed heritage, his black hair courtesy of a plainsman grandfather, the slanted green eyes from some Dargonesti ancestor. There was even a touch of minotaur in his background, or at least that's what his grandmother hissed at him when he pinched her egg money or stayed out too late drinking. He didn't know if it was true, but he had broad enough shoulders to fancy it possible.

The little blonde sitting just a couple of chairs away blushed and fluttered her eyelashes, first at him, then at Risha. But her father noticed and yanked her chair around so fast he almost toppled her over. Risha snickered, elbowed Kraco in the ribs, and turned his attention to the burly innkeeper halfway down the bar, polishing the mahogany wood.

"Hey, Maryl, did you save a room for us?" Risha leaned forward on his elbows, hanging half over the edge of the bar, trying to see what Maryl had stashed underneath.

The innkeeper turned, frowned. "You!" he spat. He wiped his way down to them. "For you, double and money up front."

"Pleased to see you, too, old friend." Risha grinned as Kraco scowled. Risha slapped his half of the coins that had come from the dwarf's pocket onto the bar.

Maryl didn't even look at them close. He just sneered. "That'll get you ale and stew. And maybe you can stay out back in the storehouse."

"We don't exactly have coin. But we're good for it, and we'll pay you double." Kraco gaped at his partner. Double!

"Are you mad!" he hissed. "What do you mean, 'double'!"

"Whaddya mean, 'good for it'?" Maryl growled.

"We've got something better than coin." Risha leaned towards him and winked. He motioned towards Kraco's pocket.

Maryl made a sound, a cross between a snort of disbelief and outright laughter, and turned away, still rubbing circles on the gleaming bar. Another snort and the circles grew bigger.

Kraco didn't really want to pull out the gems until he'd had a chance to look them over for himself, but Risha motioned again, so Kraco reached in his pocket, shifting the bedroll carefully. Maryl came back a little too quickly, his big brown eyes on the bedroll, until Kraco brought up three gems and lay them on the counter.

Linda P. Baker

He leaned in eagerly to peer at them. They sparkled like fire. An emerald no bigger than a small fingernail but cut round instead of the usual square. An oblong stone as red as blood that might be a ruby or a garnet, so flawless that even if it was a common bloodstone, it was worth more all the things they'd stolen in the last year combined. But the third stone . . . Kraco could almost feel the other two pairs of eyes move with his, widen like his, dilate like his. The third stone was tiny but beautifully cut into a faceted triangular shape, like the emerald, an unsual cut. The color was striking. It was mauve, clear as a diamond and as shiny as a puddle of water slicked with oil.

"Taaffeite" Maryl breathed.

"A what?" Risha asked, his own voice low.

"Taaffeite. By the long departed gods . . . It must be. I've never seen one, only heard them described. They come from the mountains, and there's only ever been a handful found. They're rarer than dragon's teeth." The innkeeper reached out a single finger, touched the stone reverently, turned it so that a different face showed.

Before he could do any more, Kraco scooped up the gems, and stuffed them back into his pocket. He glanced at the roomful of strangers to make sure their attention was elsewhere. "So . . . a room for the night, and maybe longer."

Maryl made another sound, but the tone was completely different than before. This time there was only respect. And greed. He reached out, almost a plea for Kraco to pull out the stones again.

"The room," Kraco prompted.

"Sure," Maryl said without even blinking, his big eyes narrowed to slits as they once again shifted to the bedroll.

"And a bottle of wine. The warm stuff."

"And some stew," Risha added.

"Sure."

"We're good for it," Kraco assured him again, unnecessarily. Just to prove it, he pulled out the silver and three coppers from his pocket and added them to what Risha had already laid upon the bar. One of the coppers still had blood on it. He started to wipe it clean, then didn't, just left it on the bar as it was, glowing redder than its coppery-red companions. "Here's a down payment."

Maryl eyed the coins, his gaze flicking from them to the rolled blanket. But the message of the bloody coin was not lost on the innkeeper. Without protesting, he went and got a bottle of the wine from the hearth and brought it back.

Kraco took the bottle from him and turned towards the stairs. "Is the room with the big fireplace empty?"

Maryl nodded. "Yeah. Go ahead. I'll send her up with something to eat." He jerked his thumb towards the barmaid.

"And something dry to wear," Kraco added. He'd seen Maryl's back room once. And in amongst the barrels of ale and shelves with row upon row of whiskey in dark glass bottles was a hoard of goods. Maryl had shrugged with a show of innocence and said, "Sometimes, people can't pay what they owe."

The room with the big fireplace was Maryl's best. It was the warmest, despite its high ceiling, the largest, with the softest bed. The fire was already lit when they entered, blazing hot and high. The bed, though not the cleanest Kraco had ever slept in, was already turned down and heaped with extra blankets and pillows. Kraco kicked the door shut with his foot, then bolted it.

He looked at his partner, rubbing at the gray bracelet that bound his wrist. Then Risha looked at him and laughed like a delighted child. By unspoken agreement, they knelt on the floor in front of the fireplace and tore at the leather strips binding the blanket. They unrolled it, so that the treasures tumbled free. Besides the dagger were three small bundles in fine swatches of silk.

Wrapped within the silk bundles was a miniature gold crown encrusted with tiny seed pearls and a tiny figurine of a dragon with flashing sapphires for eyes, probably made of silver because of the tarnish around the edges of the engraved scales. There was also an enameled egg with a miniscule gold clasp that opened to reveal, nestled inside, a perfect replica of a fine coach. It was surely platinum, because unlike the dragon, it's exquisite surfaces had no tarnish.

Risha lined up the three precious items on the edge of the hearth. They flickered in the firelight. They both stared at them while Risha once again ran his finger around and around the inside of the bracelet he'd taken from the old wizard.

"Why do you keep doing that?" Kraco asked irritably.

A knock at the door forestalled any reply , and Risha rose to answer it. Kraco flipped the edge of the blanket across their treasures and pretended to be sitting by the fire, unstrapping his boots, as the barmaid struggled in under the weight of a pile of clothing and platters of stew, bread, cheese. She managed to set the plates and clothing onto the bed without spilling or dropping either.

After he'd once more locked the door behind her, Risha stripped off his wet things, wrapped himself in one of the fine cloaks Maryl had provided, brought the plates of food and empty tankards over and put them on the floor beside Kraco.

While he poured wine, Risha asked, "What do you suppose all this is? What was a lone dwarf and old mage doing traveling with hidden riches fit for a king?"

Kraco took a big swig of the wine. It was warm and sweet and spicy. "Probably taking them to some rich client. What better way to disguise themselves than to look poor and unimportant? Or, who knows, maybe they stole them themselves."

They finished taking off their wet clothes and dragged chairs over next to the crackling fire. The food they ate was better than anything they'd had since the bitter winter began. None of it was the slop Maryl served in the common room, but the rich stew and the sharp cheese and crusty bread he kept in the back for himself. As they ate they contemplated the small fortune they had laid out in the firelight.

Unfortunately, there was only one of the strangely pink/purple colored stones Maryl had called taaffeite. But there was another emerald, and a few diamonds, a couple of yellow gold quartzites, and an even bigger red stone like the small flawless one. They would have to take everything to Hangman's Harbor, maybe even a bigger city, to get the prices they were worth.

Kraco took another big drink of wine, tore off a big bite of bread. "How do you want to divide it up?" He hoped the words sounded pretty casual.

Risha turned the bracelet on his wrist as he surveyed the goods. Then he took a sip of wine and reached for a piece of cheese. "Oh, it doesn't matter. You decide."

The words were thrown out so with such indifference that Kraco thought it was a joke. Risha had a wicked sense of humor that cropped up at the most unusual times, especially when he was trying to be clever or nonchalant or sneaky. He waited for the punch line, for Risha to say something else. To choose the taaffeite first, for himself, leaving Kraco with a pitiful second choice. But Risha's only interest seemed to be in deciding which piece of cheese to eat next.

Dutifully Kraco separated the gems into two piles, one for himself, one for Risha. He kept the one sapphire for himself, giving Risha the oddly cut emerald. Risha was busy with a corner of the heavy cloak, folding it to make a small point and polishing his bracelet. The poor stones in it sparked dully in the light. Compared to the quality of the dwarven jewels, they were paste and colored glass. There was a time . . . in fact, only a short time ago, that Kraco would have been very glad to steal a few poor quality stones and a tarnished bracelet. Tonight, he could not understand his partner's fascination with it.

"You don't mind if I have the taaffeite?" He added the mauve gem to his pile, gave Risha the two red stones to offset it.

"No." Risha continued polishing.

"What about these?" He indicated the miniatures.

Risha contemplated the array. "Well . . . I like the little dagger. But it doesn't really matter. Whatever you think is fair."

Kraco stared at him. Except for the little silver dragon, the dagger was probably the least valuable. Unless, of course, in the middle of the night, it was slipped between the shoulder blades of a partner. Then its value would be . . .

Risha saw his partner's hesitation. "It's all right. If you want the dagger, take it. Just give me whatever you think is fair." He went back to polishing the bracelet.

"You're being exceedingly strange!" Kraco snapped. He jumped up and stomped over to the pile of their wet, cast-off clothing. He dug through it until he found his leather shoulder pouch. He dropped it on the hearth with a wet smack and began rewrapping the miniatures back into their silken protection. "You act as if you don't even care about these things. Like it doesn't even matter that we've enough money to live well for a very long time."

Risha smiled placidly at him,. "Not at all, Kraco. I'm very glad we've done so well. I just trust you to divide everything fairly. We're partners, right? We share everything, right? That's all. I mean, it's not like we're going to be spending it right away. Everything has to be sold first. Right?"

Kraco glared at him, though everything he said was true. They did always split their spoils, the same way they split the work. They shared whatever they had, coin, women, food, water, killing, thievery. But Risha had always done the dividing, he never trusted him to take care of it before.

It made the hair on the back of his neck stand up. It made him remember that all Risha wanted, supposedly, was the dagger. It made him get up and find Risha's dagger and his own, where they'd laid them on the table, and move them to the washstand on the far side of the bed. Risha, busy polishing, pretended not to notice.

Kraco went back and completed the division of their spoils. If all Risha cared about was that fool bracelet, fine, He took the largest red stone from Risha's pile and put it in his pile. He wrapped the two piles of gems in scraps of silk and put them away. He put all the trinkets, save the little silver dragon, into his pouch. The most miserly piece of everything they'd taken went to Risha.

Risha still pretended not to notice.

Annoyed, Kraco even stuffed the little dagger into his own pouch.

Risha looked up at him, smiled beatifically, and said, "I'm tired. Are you ready for bed?"

The skin between Kraco's shoulder blades puckered, as if it could already feel the prick of a blade sliding in. He shivered although he was sitting close to the fire. His partner was definitely up to something.

He glanced the bracelet that encircled Risha's wrist

from beneath his eyelashes. Risha's industrious polishing had lent it a little shine and, with the other treasures tucked away, it looked a bit less disreputable. "What do you supposed we'll be able to get for that? We could claim it's magical."

Risha pulled the edge of his cloak down over his wrist. His eyes flashed for just a moment, defensive and sharp, then he smiled. "You don't mind if I go to bed now, do you?"

Kraco shook his head and pretended to forage amongst the leftover cheeses as Risha washed his face and hands, then slipped beneath the thick covers of the bed. He took the side of the bed nearest the fire, away from the table where their daggers lay. And he left his treasure trove lying forgotten on the floor, at Kraco's feet.

Risha yawned widely, showing white, even teeth and pink tongue. "Kraco, you can take charge of all of it if you want."

"What?"

"The jewels. The miniatures. You can carry them. I don't mind." Then he yawned again, turned over and went to sleep.

Kraco sat by the fire for a long time. He would have liked to finish off the warm wine, but he didn't dare. His mind was fogged enough already by Risha's inexplicable behavior. He didn't need wine clouding his judgment further while he guarded their backs from other guests in the inn . . . and his own from his partner.

Finally, after checking that the shutters were barred and the door was locked, he joined Risha. With the hilt of his dagger clutched in his palm, he allowed himself to doze, knowing that if his partner moved he would feel it.

* * * * *

The sun was already up over the trees when Kraco woke. A bright spear of light flickered over his face. He stirred, then jerked up, remembering. But he was safe despite his negligence. The dagger was still in his hand, the treasure in his pouch.

But his partner was no longer asleep at his side. He ran his fingers through his hair, trying to smooth the kinked up curls. Rubbed his tongue across his teeth, trying to eradicate the leftover taste of onions from the stew and herbs from the wine.

The door of the room was closed, but no longer bolted. The heap of wet clothing was still where they had left it, but the pile of new clothing that Maryl had sent up had been sorted through. Half was missing. One pair of boots was gone.

The fire had burned down to winking embers, and the air was cold on his skin. He snatched up items of clothing from the jumbled pile and yanked them on. Slipped his pouch over his neck and shoulder. Slipped both his and Risha's daggers into his waistband, draped his new, thickly woven cloak over his shoulders, and set out to find his partner. To find out what trickery he was up to.

Though it was less populated, the common room looked much the same as it had the night before. Maryl behind the bar, polishing away, a family of husband, wife and three quarreling brats pawing over their morning meal, the same merchants near the fire. Their table was littered with the remnants of porridge and milk instead of ale, but it appeared they'd never even gone to bed. Just stayed up the whole night gambling amongst themselves and telling tall tales.

At the table in the back corner, half hidden in shadows, was a handful of old acquaintances. Ark and Nova and the always sneering half elf whose name Kraco could never remember, a couple of others whose names he'd never bothered to learn. They were all frowning, eyeing his new, clean clothing with a mixture of greed and jealousy and speculation.

Kraco nodded to them and started outside. Before he could reach the door, Risha shoved it open and barreled through. His pale hair was dark with water, dripping as if he'd just dunked his head in the water trough, and he was carrying an empty bowl and mug.

"Kraco! Good morning!" He plunked his empty dishes down on the bar and motioned to Maryl. "Get Kraco a bowl of your delicious porridge for his breakfast. With honey. And a mug of milk." He slung an arm around Kraco's shoulders and beamed. "Isn't it a beautiful day?"

Kraco wanted to punch him. Whether it was for the radiant smile or because he'd gone off by himself, unarmed, or for leaving his partner asleep in an unlocked room with an unguarded treasure trove, or for assuming he'd eat anything as disgusting as porridge with honey, Kraco wasn't sure. "What in the name of the dungeons in Neraka is wrong with you?" he snarled in Risha's face. "Have you lost your senses?"

Risha's arm dropped from around his shoulders. He moved back a half step, his brow creasing in a frown. "What's wrong, Kraco?" Kraco didn't even know where to begin in the face of such well acted innocence. He settled for the one thing even a befuddled Risha could understand. "You left the room without your dagger." He snatched the heavy thing out of his belt and slapped it into his partner's palm.

Risha looked at the wide black scabbard with its silver studs and threading as if he'd never seen it before. But his expression lifted from worried to relieved. "Oh. I'm sorry. Of course, how careless." Risha tucked it carefully into its spot in the small of his back, rearranging his new cloak so that it dropped free of the dagger and swirled in folds down his back. "Thank you."

So . . . for all his seeming surprise at seeing the dagger, he remembered exactly where it went, and that both reassured Kraco and chilled him at the same time. This new game of his partner's was beyond his fathoming. But it wouldn't stay so for long. He would slip, and Kraco would be there, watching, waiting.

Bright smile back in place, Risha raked his hand through his unruly hair and wandered away towards the group of noisy, laughing merchants. Across the room, Ark sat up taller and bristled. Kraco watched them as they watched Risha.

The merchants weren't rich. He could tell by their hill country accents and the cut of their clothes. And despite their leather bottles and heavy ivory dice and beautifully painted cards, they were using pebbles for coin in their game. No merchant on the road played dice with pebbles if he had coin to flaunt.

Risha circled the merchants, eyeing their pebbles, reaching out to touch a pair of dice, to rub the smooth cube between his forefinger and thumb. He leaned over the shoulder of one of the merchants and said something to him. The man looked up at him, held out his hand for the dice, surprised and suspicious.

From across the room, Ark glared with much the same expression. He rose, slowly pushing his chair back.

The innkeeper slid a mug of milk and a bowl of steaming porridge across the bar. Maryl, too, had noticed the movement in the back corner and was watching Risha. "What's your partner up to? I don't want any trouble."

Linda P. Baker

He didn't answer Maryl's question because he wasn't sure himself. Before Maryl could ask again, Risha was back at his side, grinning, and Ark was settling back into his chair, scowling.

"What are you doing?" Kraco hissed. He snatched up the mug of sweet milk and downed half of it without taking a breath.

Risha just smiled at him. It was his feral grin, the one that showed more teeth than one man should have in his mouth. "Just having a bit of fun. Ark has been eyeing those merchants like a dog waiting on a bone. I just warned that one that if he joins in a game of chance with anyone here, he should take care that the cards he uses are his own."

Kraco choked on his spoon and spit porridge across the expanse of Maryl's gleaming bar.

Risha laughed and pounded him on the back. "Well, it's only fair," he said in a tone of oozing sincerity. "They've all come all this way from a small town near Neraka. They banded together to make the trip to Hangman's Harbor to buy supplies for the coming year. The money they're carrying with them is everything that their village owns."

Kraco choked on another spoonful of porridge. Now that was the Risha he knew, all teeth and cheerful meanness. And at last, he understood what Risha was up to, although he didn't know why. The wealth of an entire village . . . that might be a lot indeed. "Risha," he said with affection. "Are you planning another job?"

"Job?" Risha raised an eyebrow. "There's no job. I just told you, I was only trying to warn these gentlemen that they might be cheated."

Kraco stopped himself with his spoon midway to his mouth. It was plain he was going to strangle before he finished his meal. Laughing at Risha's obvious joke, he simply scooped up his bowl and mug and took it to a table near the other end of the bar. Settling in where he could watch his partner, and his partner's new marks and the table of competing cutthroats, he put his feet up and finished his meal , watching everything unfold as the morning sun crept across the plank floor of the inn.

An older woman, trailed by a servant, came down the stairs, paused at the bar to order food, then seated herself midway between Kraco and the merchants. The gold threads in her shirt and the gold highlights in her hair sparkled in the morning sun. The servant deposited a satchel, decorated with brass fittings, at her feet.

Risha, visiting now with the barmaid, ignored the woman. Ark didn't. He sat up straighter, fairly brimming with greed, the gaggle of merchants forgotten in lieu of an easier, richer victim.

When the woman and her servant finished their meal, Ark rose. He hastened across the room towards her as she leaned to grasp the handle of the satchel. But Risha was a step ahead of him, neatly swiping the leather from the woman's small fingers and Ark's large ones. "Here, lady, let me help you with that."

She smiled at both men. Ark bristled. And Kraco noisily pushed back his chair.

The woman wavered, clearly not wanting to give offense. And Ark wavered, glancing first at Risha and then at Kraco, clearly not wanting the bigger man to come to the aid of his partner. Risha ignored all of them. He put a proprietary hand on the woman's elbow and led her away, telling Ark, "I'll do it." Telling her, "It's all right, lady. That one will only cut your purse strings and be gone with your coin before you board your carriage."

Ark's hiss of astonishment followed them out the door.

Kraco slumped back down in his chair and tried not to guffaw. It was too priceless, Risha's guileless insult, the expression on the ruffian's face.

Ark wheeled on him, booted heel scratching the floor. "I'm going to gut your partner," he snarled.

Kraco couldn't stop the laughter then. It was just too funny, seeing the fury in Ark's face. Seeing the shiny spittle fleck his chin. He knew Risha would make it right with Ark later, probably giving him half the money he took from the woman.

"You tell him," Ark spit out the words. "I'll kill him."

"I'll tell him," Kraco assured him as he stormed past, turning his chair casually on one leg, to make sure Ark didn't double back.

When, a short time later, Risha returned, steps light and carefree, Kraco was grinning from ear to ear. Ark had raged out the back door, cursing loudly and promising dire consequences. Risha dropped into a chair and returned his smile. "What a lovely lady," he said.

"What did you get?" Kraco whispered. Images of a fat purse, strings cut, danced in his mind. "You know we're going to have to share with Ark, else he'll cut both our throats."

"Get?" Risha looked at him as if he was losing his mind. "Well, she offered me a coin for helping her to her carriage, but of course, I refused."

Kraco looked at him in wonder.

"By the way, do you have that little dagger on you?" Risha asked. "I wanted to show it to Maryl."

All Kraco could do was shake his head. The fool didn't really expect him to pull out his shoulder pouch in front of everyone and sort through it, did he? He didn't expect to show the greedy innkeeper still more of their hoard? Was Risha losing all sense? Was he trying to get them killed? Or was he just trying to get Kraco killed?

* * * * *

Kraco woke the next morning, much the same way. With a snort and a jerk and surprise at having slept at all. With the late morning sun punching through the shutters and crisscrossing his eyelids. In a bed empty of his partner. With the door closed, but not locked.

He'd spent the day before, the entire evening, playing along with Risha's weird game. Helping families load their children into wagons. Carrying wood for Maryl. Playing cards with a table of idiot merchants for pebbles. Pebbles! He'd never played for pebbles in his life, not even when he was a child intent on cheating the other village children out of their lunch buckets. But he'd gritted his teeth and played along, because he knew Risha must have a plan.

Whether it would benefit or kill him, he wasn't sure. Either way, it was safer to stay close to him, watching.

Now, for the second morning in a row, he went in search of his missing partner.

The common room was even more empty than the day before. There was a group of four strangers at the fireplace. Nova and her elf companion glowered from the same back corner. Behind the bar, a woman making a desultory attempt at mimicking Maryl's wiping technique. Maryl was nowhere in sight. Neither was Risha. Neither was the group of village merchants.

Kraco snatched up a hunk of the bread and cheese that was sitting on the end of the bar and stuffed it in his pocket. "My partner," he said, addressing the woman tersely. "Blonde, curly hair, funny colored eyes, wearing a black cloak. Have you seen him around this morning?"

She jerked her thumb westward. "Towards the inland road."

"Ark won't have to kill him," Kraco muttered as he stomped the length of the room and out the door. "I'll do that myself." He set off after Risha, hoping that his partner had stayed on the road. Risha knew the woods better than Kraco and could move through them faster. Kraco wasn't much of a tracker anyway. But he didn't really have to track Risha. All he had to do was find the merchants, and he knew where they were heading. Hangman's Harbor. He knew that Risha would follow.

It was night when Kraco finally scame upon a camp-fire barely flickering, well off the road, shielded within a thicket. He was lucky to have spotted it. He'd had a long, hard day. He'd been in such a rush he'd left the inn without a waterskin or supplies, or his old, comfortable clothes. By midday, his new, unbroken boots were killing him, and his new clothes scraped his skin until it felt he'd been flogged. With only dry bread and cheese for suste-nance, he was in a keen rage when he noticed the flicker-ing amongst the trees. It hardly seemed enough of a camp for the group of merchants, whose muddy wagon tracks he'd been following all day.

As he edged down the slope and in amongst the small trees, he saw that he'd been on the right track, but not the one he'd thought he was following.

Sitting on a familiar faded, barely striped blanket was the old wizard. And beside him, legs folded, hands rest-ing in his lap, head turned in a way that indicated he was giving a person all his attention, was Risha. The old man was staring at the fire, but he was speaking quietly, in a voice so low that Kraco could only hear the drone of it. The harmonious, clandestine silver of it. As if the old one were imparting the secrets of the ages. And his partner was soaking them up.

Their heads both jerked up as Kraco stepped out of concealment.

"Kraco," Risha smiled a welcome as if he'd only just left his side moments ago. As if he hadn't run away and double-crossed him.

The anger that coursed through Kraco was irresistible. He snatched up one of the burning logs and rushed towards Risha, intent on smashing his fragile skull with it. At last, he understood what Risha was up to. Or he thought he understood. The bracelet. The damnable bracelet that looked so innocuous and cheap, yet was worth enough to make his partner betray him. At last he understood that it had been the bracelet all along. That Risha's strange behavior had been designed to cover up some new partnership with the mage and betrayal of Kraco.

Risha stood up, faced him calmly. Strangely calm he was.

Kraco slid to a halt. Stood, looming over the smaller man, his breath huffing out in visible clouds of steam. Smoke billowing from the end of the log in his hand, flames skipping up the length of it, licking at his fingers, adding blisters to his fingers to match those on his feet.

He tossed the log away. "At last," Kraco said with fuming breath. "I discover what you're up to." He shoved the tips of his fingers into Risha's breastbone for emphasis. "What plan you've set in motion to cheat me."

"I'm not trying to cheat you," Risha said reasonably. He took the shove to his chest by rocking back, then settling back into place. All he said, still using that calm, conciliatory voice, was, "This is Leryc . . ." He glanced back at the old man. "I needed to talk to him. That's all. I would have returned."

Kraco stared into the eyes of the old man, into the power of him. He heard Risha's words, but he didn't believe them. But he knew how to discover their truth.

"Then give me the bracelet. If you don't want to cheat me, give me the bracelet. It's my turn to wear it."

All the blood drained from Risha's face. His fingers dropped away from Kraco's arm. He took a step back. "No. I— I—" He shook his head. "You don't understand. It's not worth anything. Not the way you think."

Kraco reached up under his cloak and yanked at the pouch of jewels that he'd carried for two days, hidden in safety against his body. The strong leather strap resisted, digging into his shoulder, bruising the flesh, tearing his shirt before it gave. "Here. You take this. Give me the bracelet."

Risha stepped away again, covering the bracelet with a solid grip. He glanced back at Leryc for support.

Leryc said to Risha, "You must give it freely. He cannot take it from you by force, else it has no value."

Risha faced him again, squaring his slender shoulders. "Then I refuse. Kraco, take the jewels. The trinkets. You can have it all. I only want the bracelet."

The rage that had been boiling up inside him, so hot he could feel it burning his skin from the inside, suffused Kraco. He yanked at the ties of his cloak, tossing it aside, fingers curling into tight fists.

Risha pleaded with him. "Kraco, please understand. It has no value in gold and silver, only in here." He thumped his heart. "If I could share it with you, I would. If I could give it to you, and not lose what I've gained, I would."

Kraco heard only his partner, refusing to share what was rightly his, at least by half. He grabbed Risha, tearing the protective hand away from bracelet. He thrust his fingers around it, feeling the warmth of the metal band. The strength of it, refusing to yield as he tried to wrest it from his partner's arm.

Risha struggled with him. "I won't give it to you!"

Risha was all wiry strength and resistance, but Kraco was bigger. Stronger. His strength was one of his contributions to their partnership, and now, he used it against his partner. Holding him easily with one hand while he slipped his dagger free of his waistband.

Leryc finally made a move to come to Risha's aid, but Kraco brushed him off as if he was a pesky bug. Tossing the thin, weak body away from him. "You're next, old man," he growled and swiped at Leryc with the blade as he fell back. "And I'm going to kill you this time," he promised. Whatever happened, whatever came of this, he vowed to keep that promise. He would kill the wizard, slowly, carefully, he would slit his gut open and leave his innards spread upon the ground to rot and be picked apart by weasels.

Risha twisted free with one hand and wheeled, trying to turn away. Kraco clung to him, to his wrist, grinding the bracelet into the flesh, the flesh into the bones. He knew if Risha got free, he'd be gone in an instant. He was no match for his fleet-footed partner in any race. He yanked hard, using Risha's own momentum to swing him back around and into his arms. He used Risha's weight to bear him down. Risha was soft and warm, the ground cold and hard.

Kraco fell on his partner, pinning him to the dirt, still holding this wrist. The scent of crushed grass and wet earth filled his nostrils. "Just give me the bracelet. As you like to say—a sign of faith. Give it to me, and we'll forget this. We'll go back to Hangman's Harbor and sell the jewels and everything will be as it was."

Risha shook his head, grimacing in pain. "I cannot," he gasped.

Kraco eased back on Risha's arm and pressed his dagger to his partner's ribs. The tip pressed through the tunic, baring flesh and bringing a shining drop of blood to the surface. The flesh gave. Thin rivulets of blood soaked into the earth. Kraco could feel the bracelet beneath his fingers, so warm, so hard. Sharp edged gems cutting into his fingers.

"Kraco, don't . . ." But then Risha's voice faded away, drowned by the slide of flesh on metal.

After a while, a long drawn out time in which the only sound was his own strained breathing, Kraco eased the pressure on the dagger. Risha was still. Pale. Staring sightlessly up at the stars.

Kraco pushed himself up to a sitting position. He wished his cloak was within reach. The air in the thicket, was cold, a damp chill. The fire kept back the shadows but did nothing to dispel the night air. He glanced over at Leryc.

The old man had dragged himself back to his blanket, his left arm twisted oddly beneath him. There was no threat there. And no longer any threat from his partner.

He touched Risha's face tenderly, feeling the silky curls, the smooth skin of his temple and the stubble along his jaw line. He closed his friend's eyes with gentle fingertips, eased the dagger from his cooling flesh. Then he slipped the bracelet from his friend's yielding wrist. "He gives it freely now, doesn't he?"

Leryc had pulled himself to a sitting position all the way onto his thin and threadbare blanket. "Yes," the old man croaked. "For the dead, there is no choice of giving or not giving."

There was blood on Kraco's fingers and it smeared onto the bracelet as he turned it over and over. When he had slipped it from Risha's arm, the circlet flashed bright and clean the way it had at first glimpse. But now when he turned it in his fingers, it once again seemed only ordinary, tarnished metal.

He twisted his wrist sideways and wedged it on. His arm was bigger than Risha's, and it was a tight fit, but Risha's blood slicked the way. Yet it scraped the flesh and the metal felt cold. But just for an instant, then it warmed to his skin and formed to his wrist as though it had been made to order for him.

He would have liked to sit for a while, just enjoying the feel of it, the tingling on his skin, the warmth radiating up his arm. But he had promised himself that he would kill the old man. There was still work to be done.

Leryc barely glanced up as Kraco's shadow fell over him.

As he stared down at the old one, Kraco slipped his finger between the bracelet and his arm, slid it around. It relieved the slow, sensuous itch of the metal against his skin. At the same time, when he pulled his finger away and the bracelet again caressed his wrist, the renewed contact seemed stronger. "I already feel it. It . . . burns me with the sweetest fire. What will happen now? Riches? Power?"

Leryc rocked back and forth, holding his injured arm tight against his body. "There are no riches. No power. At least, not the way you think of them," Leryc said. "The bracelet does not impart gold or power or any way to gain it. It will only make you . . . whole."

"Make me whole?" Kraco threaded his finger inside the bracelet again. "You speak in riddles, old man. I'm already whole. How could I be any more whole?"

The homey scent of woodsmoke washed over him. Kraco strode over, picked up the still smoldering log he'd jerked out of the fire and threw it back on top of the blaze. What was there about a fire, outdoors at night, that smelled so good and warm? The fire blazed up, massaging his chest and his legs.

He squatted down, stuck the dagger into the ground

and held out his hands, warming his fingers. The fire heated the metal of the bracelet so quickly he had to pull away. He glanced at the old man, still sitting in the same place, too far away from the fire to feel its warmth. "You'd do better to move closer," he said, almost kindly.

Leryc struggled to his feet, still favoring his left arm.

Kraco picked up his dagger and headed towards the old mage. He caught up his cloak and spread it across the thin shoulders. "Here." He guided Leryc around to the other side of the fire where there was a rotted out tree trunk, helped ease him down onto it. "Let me look at that arm. It's not broken, is it?"

Leryc shook his head, gazing at the bloody dagger, but allowed Kraco to push the voluminous sleeve up high, to probe the thin appendage.

Just as Kraco'd thought, there was a dark purple bruise forming across the papery, dry skin . But the bone, though poorly cushioned by the old man's stringy muscles, felt whole. "It's not broken, just bruised," Kraco told Leryc, pulling the sleeve back into place and looping his cloak more tightly around the old man's bony shoulders. "It'll hurt for a couple of days, but then it'll be fine."

Leryc nodded, clutched the cloak and watched him, flat, gray gaze flicking back and forth between Kraco's face and the dagger still clutched in his hand.

That reminded Kraco that he was going to kill the old man. Slowly, painfully. But Leryc seemed so pitiful, so frail. There was always time to kill him later, if such a thing was needed. Maybe he would just let him go.

For luck.

The War Chest
Kevin T. Stein

Sir Dammerman held the binding thread in his thumb and forefinger. He missed the hole in the heavy needle twice, dropped everything to the workbench, lit another candle. He smiled. He picked up the needle and thread. Without squinting, he got the thread through the hole on the first try.

Dammerman's fingers were discolored by ink. The pot, nearly empty, sat nearby. He had spread a linen cloth over the pristine tabletop to prevent staining. Ten quills he bought earlier rested in a jar of water mixed with spirits and gum-maple to make the quills last longer, prevented their chiseled tips from shredding. The water was murky, blue-black.

The knight placed the needle in a binding tool. The tool was a gift from the Order when he had retired from the field to teach. He put the tool aside, checked the sheaf of collected papers. He forced a long nail through the bottom hole, another through the top, aligning the individual sheets. The other binding holes were just as clean.

Dammerman riffed the outside edge of the papers. He had written thousands of words on the the actions of the Knights of Takhisis, their attempts to finally open passage from Neraka to Haligoth. The horizontal ruling he had drawn on the pages with light charcoal lines kept his script perfectly aligned and spaced.

Dammerman sighed, still smiling, stood and arched his back, then bent from side to side. He ran a finger across his long blonde mustache. When he clenched his hands the knuckles cracked. The loudest were three fingers of his left hand, once broken and never properly healed. He straightened.

Dammerman glanced at his old sword, well oiled and mended. The scabbard was a few years old, the standard issue of the Solamnic Order of the Sword. Checking the remains of his first candle, burning more than two hours, Dammerman realized he had left his young charges too long to their studies. He checked his belt for its hanging sheath-loops, found they had migrated behind him. He tried pulling them back around. They caught in his linen shirt. Rather than force them, tear the shirt, he left his sword behind, picked up the comfortably worn binding tool.

"All right, boys!" he said, voice carrying through the silence of the library.

The heavy books that filled the shelves of the two-story building muffled some of the sound, but the marble ceiling and walls carried the rest. From below he heard the rustling of papers and books, murmuring. He left his private alcove, which was located away from the general study areas. He leant over the rail to peer down onto the main floor's conference table, well lit by the skylight. The sun was heading toward mid-afternoon.

Ten faces peered up, three with full knightly mustaches, two with the beginnings, and the others too young.

"Now?" asked Jared, oldest of the group, self-appointed spokesman.

"Let me see your notebooks first."

The boys groaned and gathered their things. Dammerman laughed, gestured with the binding tool. "Just open them for me to see."

The ten boys opened their notebooks. They were filled with lessons on the Oath and the Measure, especially as they pertained to the Order of the Sword. Dammerman leaned further over the edge. All ten notebooks were covered with diagrams from *Answers to Steel*, a treatise on the use of the hand-and-a-half sword. Dammerman recognized what was considered the most important figure in the work, a knight holding his weapon above his head, with subsequent strokes across the belly of the opponent, an ogre. Most of the boys had drawn the ogre like the artist, or had tried. One boy held up his notebook for the others to see.

The younger boys laughed, the ones with moustaches maintained respectful silence, their lips pressed tight against smiling.

"Let me see your book, Master Raye," Dammerman said.

Raye smirked, then held out his notes at arm's length. Instead of rendering an accurate drawing, the boy had scrawled a stick figure complete with teeth, the word "Ow!" coming from its mouth.

The younger boys giggled into their hands. Raye and Dammerman's eyes met.

Dammerman frowned and pulled back, searching the faces of the other boys. "Anybody have questions?" he asked. Raye lowered his book.

Rithjonson raised his hand. He was the youngest of the ten. Dammerman nodded to him.

"How many ogres were defeated when you wrote this book, sir?" Rithjonson asked.

Jared elbowed his classmate. The other students rolled their eyes.

Dammerman waved his open hand for silence. "Now, why do you all think that a foolish question?"

The giggling subsided.

"Why shouldn't he wonder? All teachings of battle need proof, otherwise they're just conjecture and guess-work. Boys, these writings will not only save your life, but more importantly, allow you to achieve honor and glory for the Knighthood!"

"Honor and glory?" Raye asked. A crooked smile cut his face.

"Yes, Master Raye?" Dammerman replied. "You have a question?"

Raye purposefully closed his notebook. "I'm sorry, Sir Dammerman. Did you say honor and glory?"

Haverc said, "What's wrong with that, Raye, you twit?"

Haverc was a head taller than Raye. Raye was not intimidated.

"Nothing," Raye answered, running a finger along the edge of his book. "Just seems strange."

"Strange?" repeated Haverc.

"Strange, you bloody parrot. For a respected knight to abandon the field, and then tell of honor and glory. What good is that?"

"What do you mean?" Rithjonson asked with interest.

"Aren't the best lessons to be learned from the tales we hear of heroism?" Raye demanded. "Isn't that what the Order teaches?"

Vigille drew a finger across his blonde mustache. "You mean, 'Better to die in battle?' Isn't that what your father has said?"

"Isn't that what all the teachers say." Raye sneered. "And yet, here they are, unable to follow their own lessons. It's enough to make you vomit."

All the boys spoke at once, some to each other, some

to Dammerman. All tried to get more answers from Raye, but the boy sat back, folded his arms across his chest, maintained his crooked smile.

Dammerman stared down at the boys, tapped the binding tool against the railing. He made out Rithjonson's high voice.

"What is your question, Master Rithjonson?"

"So what's the answer, then?" Rithjonson asked. "How many ogres?"

Dammerman waved his hands for silence. "An exact number?"

"Yes, please."

Dammerman thought. "A hundred and thirty-seven."

Rithjonson's jaw dropped. "A hundred and thirty-seven?"

"Give or take," Dammerman said.

Vigille raised his hand. "How many by you, sir?"

"Does that really matter, Vigille?"

"Dodging the question, of course," Raye whispered.

Vigille heard Raye, but waved away the comment. "Just curious, sir."

"Vigille, that text, and the others like it, have been compiled over many years of long study, hard work, and lost lives," Dammerman said. He left the balcony railing, made his way down the marble stairs to the first floor. "Let's wrap it up, boys. I've got something to show you."

All the students slammed their notebooks shut and began to talk excitedly, even the older Jared. Dammerman ushered the boys away from the table toward the library door.

"Go on outside, go on, this is no day for you all to be inside."

As Vigille moved toward the door, Dammerman pulled him back.

"If you must know," the knight whispered, "I can account for half of those defeated ogres."

"How many is that, sir?"

"Use your math, my boy!" Dammerman admonished.

Vigille thought a moment. "That leaves a half, sir."

"Just so."

"Sir?"

Dammerman made a motion with the binding tool, holding it in both hands, as if drawing a sword across Vigille's middle. "Imagine one knight attacking from here."

Dammerman switched sides. "Imagine another knight attacking here."

"Half each, sir?" Vigille was delighted.

"Half each."

"Good story, sir."

Dammerman drew a finger across his mustache. "Honor and glory, Master Vigille."

The knight made to pat his student on the shoulder, stopped. Dammerman turned, faced Raye, who had been standing, unnoticed, behind him. As he stood aside to let the boy pass out into the sun, Dammerman stared at the young man's back a few moments. He made the motion with his hands again, as if holding a sword. The binding tool was old and worn comfortable in his hand. He turned and tossed it on the study table.

*　*　*　*　*

The air was filled with the scent of the tended trees in the Solamnic fort. Northern Ergoth's weather remained clear and bright. The few clouds moved lazily east toward the ocean. The boys rushed out into the afternoon, slung their strapped books and papers over their shoulders. The younger boys, led by Rithjonson, spread out and started a game of catch with a ball left in the grass. The older boys gathered together to talk. They emulated the lessons they copied in their notes, bringing their hands down and across as if holding swords. They complimented and critiqued each other like veterans. Dammerman kept away from Raye. Raye, hanging back, hands in pockets, glared at the nearby storehouse. His father sat at the storehouse entrance.

Dammerman saw ink under his nails and frowned. He rubbed his fingers together, but the ink did not come off. He looked at his students. Their hair was trimmed, their clothes clean. They walked with straight backs. He ran his dirty hands over his hair, smoothing loose strands.

The older boys walked up to the knight. Karle ran hands through his red hair in unconsious imitation of Dammerman. Karle's voice was low, though he was only fourteen. He held his hands as if holding a sword and brought them down across Vigille's middle. "Is this correct?"

Dammerman gestured for the boys to walk, then waved for the younger boys to follow. Rithjonson grabbed the ball from the air and put it back on the ground where he had found it. The students followed obediently. Raye turned his glare toward the ground and strode after.

Dammerman maneuvered the boys between himself and Raye.

"To answer your question, Master Karle, it's not a matter of your stroke being 'correct,' but rather, if it will succeed."

"If the stroke is correct, won't it always succeed?" Karle asked.

Dammerman said, "Master Raye?"

Raye did not answer. Dammerman waited, then said the boy's name again.

"What?" Raye shot back. His gaze did not leave the ground.

"Would you care to answer Master Karle's question?"

"No."

"Please reconsider, Master Raye," Dammerman responded. "You are the best swordsman of the class."

Raye shrugged. "Must be my father's doing."

"Of that, I have no doubt!" Dammerman laughed. "He taught me everything I know."

"Of that I have no doubt."

Dammerman leaned forward. "What did you say?"

"Just pondering the lessons of honor and glory, sir," Raye replied, pointed toward the storehouse. "If you others want to learn all the lessons taught by my father, why don't you go ask him?"

Raye's face was blank and set under Dammerman's gaze. Finally, the knight nodded toward the storehouse. "All right, let's find the answer to Master Karle's question."

Sitting on a chair outside the door of the storehouse was a man whittling a cane from a length of ashwood. A well-worn cane lay beneath his chair. His long hair and mustache were white like the wood. He was not old. When he looked up from his work, the boys lowered their heads diffidently.

He said, "Good afternoon to you all."

"Good afternoon, sir," the boys replied together.

"Good afternoon, Master Raye," the knight said.

The young man's face did not change expression. He bowed stiffly from the waist. The knight's face was fixed like his son's.

"We have a question for you, Sir Raye," Dammerman said.

The other knight stared at his son, said, "You have a question?"

Dammerman motioned for Karle to respond. The boy stepped forward. "If a stroke is correct, will it always succeed?"

Sir Raye pressed his lips in a thin line, then frowned. "Why don't we find out."

The old knight stood, using his unfinished cane to force himself from the chair. Several of the boys stepped forward to help. He waved them away, took the worn cane from under his chair. Dammerman took the unfinished cane and stepped back. The two men faced each other, brought the canes up like swords.

"This," Sir Raye said, bringing the cane across Dammerman's middle, "is the correct stroke." The white-haired knight nodded to the other man. "At regular speed." Sir Raye brought his cane up and around. Dammerman stepped back a half-pace, returned with an attack to Sir Raye's head, stopped before the cane hit. Sir Raye had missed. "Correct is not always successful, boys. Nicely done, Sir Dammerman."

Dammerman bowed and the boys politely applauded, whispered compliments to each other. Dammerman bowed again as he returned the unfinished cane to the other knight, then ran a finger across his mustache.

"How do you like the teacher's life, Sir Raye?" Dammerman asked.

Raye let out a long breath as he lowered himself to his chair. The knight smiled and took up his knife to resume his work. "Our order should all die in glorious battle. Don't you agree?"

"Glorious battles are hard to come by," Dammerman said.

"That's why we should go out and find them."

Dammerman laughed. "To that, I definitely agree." He turned to the boys, whose attention was wandering. "Can any of you tell me why our Order concerns itself with courage and acts of heroism?"

Some of the students raised their hands.

Sir Raye said, "You have excellent students, Sir Dammerman."

"Thank you, sir," Dammerman replied. He pointed to Haverc.

The young man stepped forward, brushing aside his curling black hair. "The Order of the Sword is an inspiration not only to the other Orders, but to those outside the knighthood."

"And how is that, Master Haverc?"

"In my opinion, sir, those outside the knighthood often find in their lives times when they must stand forth and be courageous. This courage can often be found in the strength and examples of others."

"And the Order of the Sword provides these examples?"

"Just so, sir."

Dammerman nodded. "Just so, just so. Very good, Master Haverc. I accept your statement."

Haverc bowed and stepped back.

"Stooge."

"What was that?" Dammerman asked.

The younger Raye stepped forward. "I called him a stooge."

Vigille and Karle grabbed and held Haverc's arms, to keep him from fighting.

Raye ignored them. "He just repeated what he read in a book. Books written by you and others like my father."

"You disagree with what he said," Dammerman stated. "That's no reason to—"

Raye interjected. "We don't learn from books. We don't learn from these 'lessons.' When we're out in the world, then we learn."

The older Raye said, "You take these lessons and—"

"—find out how they work or don't in the field, and you know damn well nothing works like it's supposed to." The boy laughed, pointed at Dammerman. "I learned that in a book written by you!"

The teachers stood in silence. The younger Raye stared, fists clenched, then turned on his heel and left the group.

Dammerman said, "I promised these boys a look at the spoils from our last action against the ogres. Permission to enter the storehouse."

"Permission granted," Sir Raye replied, waving his cane at the entrance.

Dammerman leaned closer. "And I also promised a bottle of wine to my teacher. Permission to deliver it tonight after sundown?"

Raye shook his head and frowned deeply. "Not tonight, Dammerman. Tonight, I have things to remember. What do you think of the enemy who threatens us?"

"The enemy?" Dammerman considered. "The knights of Takhisis are capable."

"And they are led by the Glass Hand."

Dammerman nodded. "The Glass Hand."

"Who is the Glass Hand," Rithjonson asked.

The two teachers regarded each other. Raye said, "The Glass Hand is the name given to the commander of the armies invading Haligoth."

"Why the 'glass hand'?"

"That is not important, my boy," Raye answered. To Dammerman, he said, "Take your boys in, what you seek is on the second floor."

"Are you sure you won't reconsider my offer for tonight?"

With the knife, Raye shaved a long, curled sheet of ashwood from the new cane. He said, "Teach your boys of glory, Sir Dammerman. Teach them well. Learn better than I." He shaved another strip from the cane. "I think my son is right. Better to die in battle, Dammerman. I was wrong to teach you otherwise."

* * * * *

Like many of the buildings in the fort, the store-house was a two-story woodframe building of stone and white plaster. There were no windows. The interior was lit by lamps whose oil was regularly refilled. The students walked into the building single file. The cool air was heavy with dust, and the plaster held in the scent of sweat and the iron taint of blood. Rithjonson sneezed, held his nose, sneezed again. Jared pulled a kerchief from a pocket, handed it to the younger boy. Rithjonson nodded his thanks and wiped his nose.

Wooden frames and wire fencing formed alcoves holding the rewards of the Order's battles. Parchment labels with names, dates, and geographical information were tacked to each doorframe. In the lamplight, the gems, steel, and other spoils glittered. The boys held back their wonder.

An unlit stove, black-iron potbelly, stood at the end of the corridor formed by the alcoves. Stairs leading up flanked the stove. Dammerman pointed, ushered the younger boys toward the end of the hall. "What you want to see is upstairs."

The boys shuffled forward, awed. They had no words, though a few gasped when they saw something of particular interest, a sword or shield. Dammerman saw even Jared was amazed.

Dammerman whispered, "Wait till you see what is upstairs."

The group walked up the stairs, lit with more lamps. Dammerman led the way, pulled a lamp from its holder. He partially closed the lamp's bullseye, shielded the rest of the light with his body, gave the boys minimal illumination. They gathered at the top of the stairs in the small room formed by more wood frames. Dammerman stood behind them

"Before we enter, each of you must swear not to reveal the contents of this room, until the Order deems it time."

Each boy held up his right hand and in unison said, "I swear."

Dammerman turned the lamp toward the front of the room and opened the bullseye.

The yellow arc from the light first caught the gold, then was reflected into the gems piled knee-high. The gems colored the light, made rainbows, made lines of ruby red or sapphire blue. Arms and armor carefully placed on holding stands caught the refracted rays, lit as if on display. Filled with treasure, the upstairs storeroom was the length and width of the entire building.

The boys were awed, silent.

Finally, Sir Dammerman said, "In time, you will learn these things mean nothing. Only the Oath, the Measure, and the glory of war have value. For all the reasons cited by Master Haverc." He stepped past the frozen forms of his students, opened wide the door leading to the room. "For now, you may see, you may browse, these rewards of glory, buried before the Chaos War."

A moment passed before Rithjonson jumped forward, walked through the door. He was followed by Jared, then Haverc, then the rest. Dammerman lit other lanterns near the entrance and watched his students head in different directions. Dammerman hung the lantern from a peg on the doorframe. He leaned against the creaking woodframe, listened to the sound of his boys in the storeroom. They whispered.

The whispering from his students grew silent. The lanterns dimmed. A soft glow came from the back of the storeroom, where no light should be.

From where he stood, Dammerman thought the light was far away, almost a league. He walked forward, slowly, curious, pressing against the gloom. He grew tired, feet and legs aching as if he had been force marched. He walked through a desert, where the sands clutched at him, dragging him back, dragging him down if he were not strong.

He moved around dunes of treasure, brooding mounds without detail. The glow was not far. It was hidden around a hillock. Dammerman pressed forward, sweating, laboring against the distance. He put his hand out for support, his fingers touched something, dirt or gold. He rounded the last dune.

Dammerman fell. His breathing was shallow and fast, he felt surrounded, felt enclosed by darkness thicker than castle walls. He pushed himself to his knees, brought his head up. Dirt or gold, he saw himself in a cave, though if there was a roof, it was just more darkness. A box sat in the center of the cave, surrounded by a lazy halo. The box was the size of a traveling pack, big enough to carry maps or daggers. The sides and bottom of the box were encased in complicated, symmetrical joists, all made of either wood or metal, Dammerman could not tell. He touched the box.

The joists unfolded, clattering loudly. The box rose to knee height, waist height, chest height. More joists unfolded, forming thin legs, a thin body. Thin arms ending in wiry hands pushed away from the body. A neck appeared and a head snapped up. The stickman smiled.

"I've been waiting so long for you, Sir Dammerman," the stickman said. He held the box forward, fingers clutching the sides. "I have a proposition."

Dammerman did not raise himself to his feet. He stared at the stickman and the box. The stickman's eyes were the color of metal, his skin had a hard sheen. His short hair stuck out from his head as if carved from iron.

"I'm sure you're wondering what this is about," the stickman said. "It's very simple, really. I have been sent to offer you a deal."

"Sent by whom?" Dammerman said. His tongue was thick and dry.

The stickman shrugged. "That is not so much important as the deal itself."

The boxlid sprung open. The stickman rotated his hands so Dammerman could see the contents. Dammerman saw two things, one mundane, the other, impossible. First was an hourglass, an ordinary construct of wood, glass, and sand. He also saw the Abyss. The dark red of the Abyss, held in the box.

The stickman said, "It is not the whole of the Abyss, just a small place where men like you might go."

"I don't know what you mean."

The stickman shook the box. The suspended hourglass did not move. "In this place there is strife eternal. Fighting for the sake of fighting. Suffering without end."

Dammerman tried to wet his lips. "You sound pleased with that."

"Why should I not be pleased?" the stickman asked. "It is my portion of the Abyss. I am sent to stock it with great warriors. Knights, specifically. Good, bad, or otherwise, it makes no difference to me. There are as many servants of Takhisis as there are Paladine."

"You serve neither Takhisis nor Paladine?"

The stickman smiled. "And they are gone. Gone from the world and stars. A shame, a pity. A necessary sacrifice, all the gods, in my rather humble opinion. I would not be here, otherwise." The stickman bowed his head. "Thanks to Father Chaos for my life."

"I want nothing to do with this." Dammerman slowly stood. He turned to leave.

"You have not heard my proposal!" the stickman shouted.

"What could you possibly have to interest me?"

The stickman's mouth twisted. "That's a good question. Let me start with a quote. 'Better to die in battle.' Familiar?"

Dammerman did not respond.

The stickman nodded. "Yes, familiar. Did you know Sir Raye needs no cane? It's true. He just believes he does."

"That is not true," Dammerman turned away.

The stickman slowly shook his head, smiled. "He just thinks he does. As you think . . ."

"As I think what?" Dammerman demanded.

The stickman raised his eyes, smile fixed. "Let's just say your cane, your crutch, as it were, are words, when you know, and I know, and more importantly, the boy knows that you should have no crutch, no cane. Only deeds."

"I have retired from battle to teach—"

"I believe the more accurate word is 'abandoned.' Don't you know why young Master Raye is so angry with his father? Or with you for that matter?"

"No," Dammerman admitted. "I don't know."

"Need it be spelled out for you in stately words, in words of the Order? Very well. The boy, Sir Dammerman, is everything you could hope for. Bright, honest—seemingly to a fault, skilled. He wants to believe, but what is there to believe? His own father has abandoned the very lessons he once taught. And you . . . well. . . ."

"Well, what?"

The stickman shrugged. "Well, you've become a bookbinder."

"What is your proposal?"

"What I have to offer is better even than death in battle."

"What could that be?"

The stickman stepped forward. His thin legs moved like a bird's, his body bobbed, his arms were steady. Near Dammerman's ear, the stickman said, "Glory, without death."

Dammerman turned back. "How can that be—"

"Possible, you ask?" The stickman tilted the box forward again. "Take this hourglass, and our deal is made firm!" The knight could not keep his eyes from the box, from the hourglass and dark red glow of the Abyss. "Glory without death I have promised, and with the glass, I can provide!"

Sir Raye's words were loud in Dammerman's thoughts. He ground his teeth.

The stickman persisted. "I know, I know, you would rather find death at an enemy's hand than by withering slowly in a fort. Leaning on a cane you don't need."

"I have never known a greater wish than to leave behind a legacy of courage and honor," Dammerman said, more to himself.

"The foundations of the Order," the stickman agreed. "You have done so many great deeds already."

"But there are always greater deeds."

"Greater and greater! And I will give you the means to leave that legacy, your name forever in word, in song. In deed and battle cry!"

"How?" Dammerman demanded. "How can this be done?"

The stickman laughed. "Nothing could be more simple! Once you have found that 'perfect moment,' that time when you believe you have achieved the culmination of your legacy, turn the hourglass over, and you shall live in that perfect moment forever!"

"Forever?"

"Forever. Glory, without death."

Dammerman hesitated. "What if I am killed before I turn the hourglass over?"

"Ah," the stickman said. "As to that, if you do not use the hourglass before your time is ended, you shall fight here, in my portion of the Abyss, for all time." He hold the box higher. The red glow within shone in the stickman's eyes.

The stickman continued. "I see you have doubts. Very well, I will offer you a better opportunity. I will ensure, that by the end of the year, you shall war against a foe worthy of your steel. No more of these ogres and draconians, but a true foe. One you would be proud to defeat, and just as proud if you lost."

Dammerman widend his eyes. "You cannot mean—"

"Of course!" The stickman shuffled, nearly danced. "Enticing, is it not?"

The knight shook his head. "The Glass Hand. Abraxis."

"Abraxis! Abraxis the Cursed, Abraxis the Great, Abraxis of the Glass Hand, and the host of other names by which he is known. Abraxis, the Warrior in Jet."

"The Warrior in Jet," Dammerman whispered to himself. A legend among the Solamnics, a name never mentioned outside the chambers of council. It was said Abraxis was born from the blood of Chaos. Rumors were his black armor was a thing washed up on the shores of the Blood Sea, and the Warrior was trapped within. He commanded the new armies of the knights of Takhisis toward Haligoth. He never failed.

Dammerman turned on the stickman. "You assure me I will face the Warrior!"

"Take the hourglass, and your fate is sealed."

The knight could read nothing in the flat metal eyes of the stickman. Dammerman reached out, put his hand in the box with the Abyss. He removed the hour-glass.

The box snapped shut. "I will visit you from time to time. Just to see how you're doing. Offer advice," the stickman said.

"How soon till I face the Warrior in Jet?"

"Soon enough, soon enough. But for now, your students await. Better to die, Dammerman."

"Were you saying something, sir?"

Dammerman turned and the dunes were gone, the darkness fled. He stood empty-handed. Rithjonson held a lantern, lighting the knight's face. "Is there something wrong, sir? You don't look well."

"No, I'm fine, fine, my boy," Dammerman answered. He wiped sweat from his forehead, ran a finger across his mustache. "I'm fine. Let's go back, now. I have to prepare. I have to stop the knights of Takhisis. I'm going back to the field!"

* * * * *

Dammerman and his knights marched over the grass, each yelling the name of their fathers. Dammerman carried no shield, holding his hand-and-a-half sword one handed, to his right. He pointed toward the train of wagons with his left.

"Dammerman!" he shouted, honoring his father, for whom he had been named, just as Raye had been named for his father. "For the Oath and the Measure, forward!"

The Solamnic's foot soldiers pressed forward, recruits from the mountains of Throt. They were a black wave hundreds of paces to the right and left of the charging knights, whose red-bronze armor shone bloody in the sun. The first rain of arrows launched from the surrounding hills fell among the foot soldiers, none reaching the knights. The soldiers held shields, and at their distance to the archers, they were safe.

Dammerman saw pavices move down from the hill-tops. The tall shields were held by stands, providing the enemy archers with cover from returning fire. Skirmishers with short swords and bucklers planted cavalry stakes, waited patiently for the onrush of Solamnic soldiers. A white hand against black background was painted on every pavice and every buckler.

The hand of Abraxis. Dammerman grinned.

The archers were the concern of the footmen. The skirmishers were outnumbered by the soldiers from Throt. Dammerman continued to force march his men through a shallow valley formed by the hills. The centerline of the valley was at the far edge of archer range, and he doubted the bowmen would waste their arrows on the knights when there were hundreds of targets rushing at them.

Five squadrons of Solamnic light cavalry maneuvered for position. They were first behind the foot-knights, then to the sides, then past. They charged toward the first line of fully battle dressed enemy knights, a screen for the soldiers behind them. The cavalry held light ashwood lances in single-handed grips. The lances were tipped with old hardened silver. The cavalrymen gave their battlecries, they spun their weapons in circles to the side, making a bulrush roar.

The knights of Takhisis did not break their lines. The screening force waited unmoving. Dammerman was impressed by their discipline, but he knew that discipline and courage were different things. He hoped the enemy would break when they were finally struck, doubted his hopes would be honored. The troops of Abraxis were among the elite of Takhisis. The only thing they feared more than their missing Dark Queen was the wrath of their commander.

Behind the screen of knights were three more brigades of enemy footmen, not knights, all in blackened armor emblazoned with the white hand of Abraxis. They fought the rearguard brigade the Solamnics had left to protect the baggage and supply train. The Solamnics had closed ranks around the train, and used toppled wagons as balustrades and cover from missiles.

Without healing magic, the brigade wouldn't last long against the assault. Dammerman ran over a rise in the field, looked beyond the enemy screen. The black-clad soldiers concentrated their attack on the left side of the balustrade. All the other wagons were set aflame. Smoke rose straight up in the breezeless day. Dammerman decided he would lead the men against the soldiers furthest from the wagons once past the screening enemy. The forces of Takhisis would have to move or be trapped by two opposing forces.

The Solamnic cavalry suddenly broke left, the horses rearing up, some backward. Cavalrymen were thrown from their mounts, and Dammerman expected the enemy to rush forward. The screening knights held their ground. Dammerman did not stop his charge, nor did the captains of the other charging footknights. The horses without riders rushed after their companions, leaving their riders on the ground. Some of the horses tried to walk, but stumbled and fell.

One horse rose, put a hoof to the ground, lifted the hoof quickly.

Caltrops. Dammerman was sure the other captains had come to the same conclusion. Caltrops were not much danger to a knight with armored boots.

He shouted, "Watch your step!" and laughed.

The fallen cavalrymen jumped to their feet, expecting

attack. Fifteen had fallen, three from each squadron, and five were unable to rise on their own. Those capable helped the injured to their feet. The intact squadrons lost their impetus and rallied a hundred paces from the screening knights. The Solamnic foot soldiers shouted a defiant cry and flooded toward the skirmishers and pavices.

The archers ignored the foot soldiers and directed their shafts toward the cavalry. The first volley decimated a squadron. As the remaining squadron commanders turned their mounts, the second volley fell among them. More men and mounts were killed, but the rest scattered.

The cavalry's advantage was gone. Dammerman lost his smile and again shouted his father's name. Fifty paces from the enemy, the screening knights stabbed their swords into the ground, pulled long darts from quivers. Like the caltrops, missiles were used to break a charge. Dammerman supposed young knights might lose their courage. Veterans did not. He saw the Warrior in Jet had underestimated the Solamnic rearguard.

The enemy knights as a unit threw their black darts. Dammerman raised his sword to shoulder height, stepping over caltrops spread on the grass. He heard screams, men wounded by the darts. He was at the front of his unit, and four darts struck his red-bronze armor and glanced off with the sound of hammers against metal. The first knight Dammerman faced pulled his sword from the dirt as Dammerman cut him down with a single stroke, neck to shoulder. Dammerman turned to the right, backhanded the next enemy.

The enemy knight snapped his hand back as Dammerman's sword dented a vambrace. Dammerman rushed his shoulder into the man who shieldblocked and was knocked off balance, weaponless. Dammerman stabbed the point of his weapon under the knight's helmet and put the weight of his body behind the thrust.

Pulling the blade out, he shouted, "By the Oath and the Measure!"

Two enemy knights attacked at once. The first swung down in a long arc. Dammerman stepped to the left, deflecting two-handed the cut off his angled sword. The second knight stabbed toward Dammerman's stomach. Dammerman lifted his blade, caught the second thrust with the edge of his own blade, turned it aside. He counterstroked the first knight as the man recovered from his swing. Dammerman cut edgewise into the man's side through the chainmail, laid the man open.

Dammerman turned left, sword down at his right, swung up toward the other knight's arm. The knight blocked the attack with his shield. Dammerman's swing scored a gash across the painted white hand. The knight drew his weapon back for a second stab, toward Dammerman's throat. Dammerman stepped back, crashed his sword against the man's helmet. The helmet's cheekguard sheared from the skullcap. The man fell without a scream.

Dammerman's arms ached with strength. His red-bronze armor was patterned with other men's blood. He turned to face the next knight, but they were fleeing to regroup opposite the reforming ranks of Solamnic cavalry.

Dammerman shouted, "Carry the day! To the wagons!"

The remaining footknights repeated Dammerman's cry.

"Carry the day! Carry the day!" To the cry they added, "Dammerman! Dammerman!"

The knights of Solamnia formed a single unit, Dammerman at its fore, sword in both hands. With a single wordless cry, the knights rushed forward, smashing sword against shield. The footmen at the rear of those attacking the baggage train turned, weapons lax in their hands, but only for a moment. Their discipline returned, and they formed a defensive line of spears.

Dammerman curled the newly formed Solamnic unit around the spearwall to let the rearguard of his knights engage the spearmen as the rest of the knights attacked the unprepared footmen. The wall of spears did not move quickly enough to defend the whole of the footmen. Knights discarded their spear-pierced shields and charged in, swords held in both hands.

The enemy footmen were not as well trained as the knights of Takhisis, though Dammerman noted their training was excellent. He killed ten. His men continued to shout his name, the soldiers behind the balustrades took up the cry, deafening the enemy until they were maddened with fear. But they fought to the last man, and none were taken prisoner.

Dammerman saw fear of the Warrior in Jet was great.

The archers and skirmishers were driven off rather than slain. The enemy knights regrouping in the field retreated. Dammerman jumped atop a wagon and watched them leave, watched the white hands painted on their shields fading into the distance. The setting sun turned the sky orange. Dammerman shielded his eyes. Atop a hill was a single man in shining black armor. Across the great distance, Dammerman saw the white left gauntlet of the Warrior in Jet.

"Dammerman! Dammerman!" the knights of Solamnia shouted.

He was lifted from his perch, carried on the shoulders of his men. Dammerman was paraded through the circle of baggage wagons, the fires still trailing lines of smoke straight into the sky. He heard some shout,

"Carry the day!" He grinned widely and ran a hand across his mustache.

Dammerman was finally let down. He ensured the wounded were gathered together for treatment. He finally sheathed his sword, the battle over, unbuckled the bottom of his breastplate and let a cool breeze dry off his sweat.

"Dammerman?"

Dammerman turned toward the voice.

The stickman held out the box and the lid snapped open. "How about it, Sir Dammerman? Quite a victory, eh?"

"Yes, an excellent victory!" Dammerman replied. "A perfect day."

"A perfect moment, now, I'd guess. When have times been better?" The stickman nodded toward the crowd of knights around the train. "They've taken up your cry and your name! I, myself, would be very excited." The stickman held the box up higher.

Dammerman looked inside the box, saw the hourglass, the red glow of the Abyss. His arms still ached with strength. He felt he could fight until dark. The smile on his face faded.

He said, "Not this time, I think."

"Are you sure? I mean, you have proven the Warrior in Jet can be defeated. In fact, you're the first!"

Dammerman was humble. "Yes, I suppose I have. But you've said I will face the Warrior himself."

The stickman's shoulders curved, the box lowered. "Yes, I suppose I have. And Father Chaos made me promise I would keep my word. But let me add this. If you accept now, I'll tell you a secret about the Warrior. A great secret!"

"Not this time. I have to face the Warrior in Jet. There will be a more perfect day."

"I really think you should reconsider. No?" The stick-man shrugged his thin shoulders. "Very well. If today you will not take the hourglass"—the lid snapped shut—"it will have to be another day. But a good victory all the same!"

"Yes, thank you, thank you," Dammerman said. He could not take his eyes from the closed box.

The stickman said, "Congratulations again, then. I'll be leaving." Without a glance back, the stickman stalked into the crowd on his thin legs.

Dammerman sighed loudly, leaned against a wagon. He wiped sweat from his face.

"And I'll take my secret about the Warrior with me!" the stickman called out.

* * * * *

Stepping past the day old bodies of goblins, hob-goblins, and humans, two hundred footmen charged the castle gate. They named their battering ram Grendel. It was seventy-five feet long, shod with iron and mounted with a snarling steel wolfhead at its tip, a fortune in metal. Grendel's length was studded with handles. Seventy-five footmen on each side held a handle in one hand, a shield in the other. The remaining soldiers carried an oilskin canopy over their comrades' heads to repel hot oil or boiling water.

Dammermen's knights walked close behind Grendel, followed by more soldiers. Archers walked with men carrying tower shields, each shield emblazoned with three crossed swords, crested by a shining crown. Every fifty paces, the shieldmen stopped and the archers fired a black hail of arrows against the castle's defenders. The defenders flew the flag of the Warrior in Jet.

A hundred paces from the gate, Grendel pushed forward at a fast march. The men holding the ram chanted the engine's name with their steps. Dammerman picked up the pace, turned back and pointed his sword toward the commander of the archers. The commander waved his sword in return, shouted for his men to run past the knights. The lightly armored bowmen quickly passed the knights, stopped and readied their bows fifty paces from the castle.

The first siege missile arced up from the castle proper. It was poorly aimed, landing far behind the line of bowmen. Dammerman knew this was only ranging fire and hoped the Solamnic forces would quickly be under the minimum range of the catapults. He wondered why the forces of the Warrior waited so long to employ the engine, which they had captured when they took the castle from the Solamnics the day before.

When Grendel reached the line of the archers, the ram's footmen bellowed a wordless shout and rushed toward the castle gate. The men holding the canopy followed, their off hands holding shields close to their sides. Arrows fired down from the castle's high walkway pierced the oilskin and struck the soldiers' shields. A few men fell, not enough to prevent the canopy fulfilling its purpose.

Dammerman heard the distant cry of soldiers from the other sides of the castle. He was eager to push forward, but there was nowhere to push until Grendel had smashed open the gate. The foot soldiers supporting the knights quickly followed in Grendel's path, yelling, carrying siege ladders. The Solamnic archers fired blindly at the castle's walkway, the enemy archers hidden behind crenellations, or firing from arrowslits.

Grendel bit into the thick oak doors of the castle, bending iron reinforcements. The men drew back ten paces, charged forward again, shouting. Boiling water fell on the canopy, cooled, fell to the sides without causing much harm. Rocks were dropped from the walls above the gates. Some punched through the oilskin, some fell and came to rest suspended. Grendel tore a larger hole in the gates, but they did not fall. They were built by Solamnic engineers.

Dammerman held his sword above his head, parallel to the ground, and his men stopped. The footmen behind moved forward and past. The siege ladders went up. Grendel chewed the hole wider. Wood splintered and rivets popped. Dammerman felt something was wrong. The defense of the castle was relying on nothing but high walls, heavy gates, and the occasional missile. Dammerman searched for the Warrior's uncommitted resources.

To the left, the ground near the castle wall buckled and fell away. "Sappers!" Dammerman shouted. "Look out!"

The lightly armored men were silent as they streamed out of the hole. Another tunnel opened and more enemy soldiers crawled out. Fifty men drew their swords and charged forward.

Before Dammerman could give his order, one of his men shouted, "Carry the day!" The retinue took up the cry.

Dammerman shouted his father's name and ran at the emerging enemy. His knights changed their cry and shouted his name.

Dammerman's unit matched the soldiers of the Warrior one for one. He fought hard to quickly repel the soldiers, to prevent his men being outnumbered. The first man to face him lost a shield, then his life in two strokes. The second was killed in three. Dammerman wanted to press on, but his hand-and-a-half sword was too long for close fighting. He forced himself to hold back his advance.

The enemy was slowly pressed back toward the wall. A few scattered and regrouped away from the tunnels. They were chased and engaged by trailing Solamnic footmen. Dammerman changed technique, stabbing with the tip of his long blade. The man facing him stepped to the side and stabbed in return. Dammerman also stepped sideways, moved in and struck his armored elbow into the man's unprotected face. The man fell and fouled the advance of a footman coming up from behind.

Jumping back, Dammerman picked up a shield with his right hand, held his sword next to his left cheek. He struck down at the advancing footman who blocked with his broadsword. Dammerman's hand-and-a-half sword notched the other blade and knocked it from the man's hand. The footman lunged forward, arms out. Dammerman dropped him with a kick.

The ground fell out from under Dammerman's feet. He fell to one knee and brought up the shield. A mace glanced off the shield. Dammerman sprang forward, threw himself at his attacker. He felt an arm break and the weight of a body fall backward. The sappers must have worked through the night to create the tunnels. The tunnel was lit by lanterns and reinforced with wood beams. He saw daylight at the far end, ten feet away.

"By the Oath and the Measure!" he shouted. The press of dark, featureless soldiers moving at him suddenly stopped.

"Dammerman!" he shouted.

The soldiers turned and ran.

Dammerman fought through five footmen before reaching the light. Arrows from outside rained in. He kept himself close to the wall for protection. His knights fell in behind him, attacking the nearest enemy. Dammerman ran through the gatehouse entrance.

The capstan used to open the gate required at least

four men to operate. The Solamnic engineers who had built the castle used counterbalances as a substitute for a heavy locking bar, the balances housed in shafts on either side of the gates. Dammerman tore open the inner gatehouse door and dashed up the stairs.

The stairs were slick with moisture and mold, forcing Dammerman to check his footing. He burst out of the stairwell and threw himself at the first archer, cutting through the heavy bow and the man's leather armor with a single stroke. Dammerman pushed forward to the next bowman, and the next. A broadhead arrow struck the wall near his arm. Dammerman turned on his heel, brought himself behind the next bowman, stabbed the man behind him, then the man to his front. He shouted his father's name again, and the bowman who fired the arrow dropped his bow and ran across the wall.

Dammerman jumped to the open shaft housing the lefthand counterbalance, hacking at the rope. The coils spliced open, and Dammerman hacked again. The rope shredded and the counterbalance crashed to the bottom of the shaft. Dammerman ran back to the other housing shaft, raising his sword to strike.

Across the compound, through the tangle of men in red-bronze and men in black, Dammerman saw the Warrior in Jet standing among his captains. The Warrior's helmet was turned up toward the high wall. The Warrior raised his left hand, gauntlet crystal-white, and saluted Dammerman. Dammerman cut the thick rope with a single stroke.

Grendel charged forward and the gates swung freely open. Dammerman waved his sword above his head. Hundreds of Solamnic soldiers rushed into the castle proper. Inspired, they shouted his name and his cry. There were remarkably few enemy soldiers. Dammerman returned the Solamnic call, then laughed.

"It seems you have done it again," the stickman said at his side.

To the sky, Dammerman shouted, "Yes!"

The box in the stickman's hands snapped open. "Take the glass!"

"No!"

"But you must! A greater victory you will never know! Your name in the mouth of every soldier, every knight! A more perfect moment—"

"No!"

The knights and soldiers of Solamnia ended the battle, taking prisoner the remaining enemy forces. The compound grew silent. The Warrior and his captains had vanished.

Dammerman swept his sword down. "I have not yet faced the Warrior in Jet."

The stickman held the box up. "Take the glass now, and I will tell you my secret about the Warrior."

As Dammerman watched, every soldier, every knight turned their faces toward him. They raised their weapons to their eyes in solemn salute. Then from every mouth, his name was whispered, chanted, shouted.

"Change your mind now?" the stickman demanded.

Dammerman resisted the urge to take the glass. "The final, greatest glory will be to defeat the Warrior himself. It is not enough to defeat his armies. He, himself, must be conquered. Then will my life be given its greatest worth. There will yet be a more perfect day."

"I really think you should reconsider. No?" The stickman shrugged his thin shoulders. "Very well. If today you will not take the hourglass"—the lid snapped shut—"I'll be leaving. And I'll take my secret about the Warrior with me!"

The soldiers grew quiet. Dammerman raised his

sword to his eyes and saluted. He shouted, "By the Oath and the Measure!" His words echoed against the castle walls.

* * * * *

Sir Raye's modest house was made of the same plaster and wood supports as the rest of the compound's buildings. The furnishings were classic Solamnic, most inherited long before the Chaos War. The dinner table's top was made of a number of blond wood slats, joined seemlessly to the legs, which ended in stylized column bases. The chairs were low-backed.

Sir Dammerman and Sir Raye sat straight as all of Dammerman's students stood silently near, ready to take orders or bring in dishes. The house was nearly silent as the two older knights drank the red wine Dammerman had promised earlier in the year.

Sir Raye held the wine glass under his nose and breathed, closing his eyes. Dammerman saw the man's hand shook.

"This must be from your private stock," Raye said.

"Yes, sir," Dammerman replied. He couldn't take his eyes from the shaking hand.

"Let me think," Sir Raye muttered. He breathed again. "This wine is from the region of Teyr, near Mount Brego."

"That is an amazingly accurate guess, sir."

Raye opened his eyes. "Oh, not really, Dammerman. You brought me this same vintage two years ago."

Dammerman raised his glass in a salute. "Then here's to your health and memory, sir."

"Health and memory," the older knight returned. "One the storehouse of the other. Or do I mean prison."

"Sir?"

Raye put the glass on the table, wiped his lips with a linen napkin. Raye took up his new cane and painfully pushed himself to his feet. On Dammerman's glance, none of the boys moved to help. When he stood erect, Sir Raye looked from one boy to the next, then back to Dammerman.

"You see what you have inspired?"

"I don't understand, sir?"

"One time, they would have leapt to help me," Raye replied, indicating the students with his cane. "Now, with less than a word from you, they stand like statues. If you told them to dance a jig, they would do it without question. If you told them to fight, they would rush in empty handed if need be. A shame my son was not willing to join us tonight . . ."

"Sir Raye, please don't—"

"Dammerman, Dammerman, don't misinterpret what I say. You have given your boys the greatest gift a teacher can bestow. You have shown them the truth of your lessons. They have given you faith, and you have given them glory." The knight turned to the attentive students. "Is that not so, Master Haverc?"

"Yes, sir!" Haverc snapped.

"Just so." Raye smiled. He slowly walked around the room to a free-standing cabinet matching the table and chairs. Dammerman heard the man's heavy breathing. The cane struck the floor and the man's right foot shuffled to catch up in three-count walk.

When Sir Raye reached the cabinet, he said, "I was going to ask your students to leave, because I wanted this to be a private moment between the two of us, student and teacher, friend to friend. However, I think I can still teach them a last lesson, even if I did not die in battle as I should have."

Sir Raye opened the cabinet, took out a wood crate.

With effort, he held it out toward Dammerman, who took it, put it across his knees.

"Open it," Sir Raye said.

Dammerman forced his thumbs under the lid, pried upward. The lid popped open, hinges creaking. The box was lined with blue silk emblazoned with the Ergothian Order's three swords and shining crown. Dammerman moved the silk aside.

The older knight said, "I had thought it lost."

Dammerman removed a hand-and-a-half sword. The blade's length was unmarred, and the metal was dark, not iron, obviously strong, not steel. The crossguard and grip were one piece of the same metal, and it seemed to Dammerman the weapon was forged as a whole. There were no gems, no carvings. It was weightless in his hand.

He asked, "What is its name?"

"Name? My memory is sharp, Dammerman, but your wits are sharper still for you to know it must have a name. It is called Bar." Sir Raye laughed.

"I do not know it."

"You do not know it because it has been generations lost. Found among the spoils of the ogres. In fact, it belonged to my grandfather, many times removed."

Dammerman jumped to his feet, dumping the crate. He held Bar out in both hands, head bowed. "I cannot—"

"You can and will!" Sir Raye said with a sweep of his cane. "Of the things the Order can provide its knights, the weapons of the past are one."

"But, Sir Raye—"

"Sit down, Sir Dammerman!" The older knight's voice softened. "Sit down, Sir Dammerman."

Dammerman complied.

Sir Raye walked slowly to his seat at the table. "Bar cannot be harmed, it cannot be broken. It can never lose its edge."

Dammerman tried to see his reflection in the blade, but its metal was too dark.

Sir Raye continued. "You have shown the Order, all the Orders, that the Warrior in Jet can be defeated. I don't understand how or why but some strange force is bringing you and the Warrior together. Abraxis, whom I would be proud to defeat, and just as proud if I lost. If only to face him."

Dammerman decided he must reveal the bargain with the stickman to his teacher. He made to speak, but Sir Raye cut him off with a sweep of a hand. "I don't want an explanation, Sir Dammerman. You are the finest of our knights, the exemplar of the Order, and I believe you now have all you need for your final encounter."

Dammerman breathed deep. Emotion threatened to overwhelm him.

Sir Raye put his hand on Dammerman's shoulder. "Would that I had been as great as you."

"You once said the student must be greater than the teacher, or there would be no one to build the future."

"Then these boys are your future, Sir Dammerman. Go forth, and show them how to build." Sir Raye gestured toward the door. "Go and think on this."

Dammerman raised the sword to his eyes, saluted to his teacher, to the boys who would build the future. He left the house, walking in the half-light of the moon. He heard a snicker and turned.

"Was it a nice dinner, Sir Dammerman?"

"You might have attended, Master Raye."

The younger Raye stepped out of the shadows. He wore a tabard with the Order's heraldry.

Seeing Dammerman's surprise, Raye shrugged. "You don't understand."

"Perhaps I do," the knight answered.

"Don't think I haven't been listening to the tales of

battle, nor reading reports, nor . . . gathering information in my own way. Being the son of a respected teacher can have its advantages."

Dammerman waited for the boy to continue. Raye smiled his crooked smile. "I believe that despite my age, I have a keen sense for the ironic."

"What do you mean?"

"Here I am, wearing the tabard of the Order, the tabard of an honor guard," Raye replied, gesturing. "I, who was the golden worm in the golden apple of your class."

Dammerman said, "I think you may have seen your father in me."

"Or wanted to," Raye said. "Or wanted to find him."

"Astute. More than astute. Still," Dammerman replied. "I have it on authority that you are the best of your age, and a great hope."

"Who told you that?" Raye asked, startled.

Dammerman smiled. "Not important. It was authority enough." He thought a moment, then said quietly, "I believe, I trust, I hope that your new-found faith will protect you from bargains . . . certain bargains . . . in the future."

"Bargains?" Raye was puzzled.

"Never mind. No apologies are necessary, Master Raye."

Raye's crooked smile widened. "I was not offering any. I regret none of what I said. But I can say, I will say, in your hands lies my faith in the Order. That is, by your hand, I have found the faith."

Dammerman shuffled his feet, said nothing. Clouds passed before the moon. Dammerman patted the boy's shoulder, said, "Goodnight, Master Raye." He left for his quarters.

* * * * *

On the fields of Haligoth, the army of the Solamnic knights was lined up in battle order. Regiments from Solamnia and supplementary units from Fenalysten lined the western edge of King's Plain. The plain was green with the season's new grass, the ground firm, rolling no more than a few feet. The tallest plant was the occasional dandelion.

The soil was compacted where the cavalry waited, a long track leading back leagues toward the fields near Fangoth. Light cavalry, shock cavalry, lancers with pennants, four squadrons of specialty horse archers waited patiently. The infantry flew the banners of the Order, three crossed swords beneath a shining crown. Longbow flanked the heavy infantry, skirmishers make up a line in front of them all. Footmen with spears stood ready. All were silent. Even the irregular units, mercenaries, and foot soldiers waited without sound.

Across the field stood an equal force flying the banner of the Warrior in Jet, white hand against black. They were the personal units of Abraxis, culled from the armies of the Dark Queen over the years, before and after the Chaos War. There were no irregulars, no mercenaries. Every soldier was human, disciplined and trained to the service of the Warrior. They also stood silent.

Dammerman's captains formed a small retinue in the center of the Solamnic line. Maps were spread over portable tables, weighed down to the parchment rolls with daggers. King's Plain was too flat and wide for a hidden flank attack. The forces of Takhisis were ready to fight a stand-up fight, as were the forces of Solamnia. Dammerman considered ordering his forces forward but reconsidered as he gazed across the field to the other side. The Warrior in Jet and his captains stood directly opposite Dammerman's.

An honor guard, a retinue of ten young men wearing tabards with the Order's heraldry, stood near the command table. Haverc held a trumpet at parade rest. The other nine held torches in red-bronze sconces. They carried swords, wore leather beneath their tabards. They were ready in spirit to follow the path of the Order, the Oath and the Measure. The younger Raye was at their lead.

"I'm going across," Dammerman said. He strapped Bar in its sheath to his belt. He checked Bar's scabbard, walked toward the middle ground.

The Warrior in Jet left his retinue at the same time as Dammerman. They met between the armies, two hundred paces to either line. The Warrior was a head taller than Dammerman, broader in the shoulders. His black armor had the same mournful shine as obsidian glass, the same depth as black marble. The armor's edges were raised in a fashion generations old. There was no scrollwork and no chasing. Dammerman saw black chainmail between the breastplate and leggings, chain under the helmet. The helmet covered the Warrior's features. There was no sound of breathing. The eyeslits were dark. The left gauntlet was the translucent white of new snow.

Behind him, Dammerman heard footsteps. He did not turn, knew it to be one of his honor guard, one of his students. Master Raye.

Dammerman drew Bar, the metal sung. The Warrior reached over his shoulders, slowly drew twin steel short swords.

"Are you the Abraxis of legend?" Dammerman asked.
"I may be."
"Are you Abraxis of the Glass Hand?"
"I may be."
"Are you the Warrior in Jet?"

"All these and more, I may be. Are you the Dammerman of legend?"

"I know of no legend," Dammerman replied.

"You are a legend, a name, and a song among my own troops. It will be an honor to defeat you."

Dammerman saluted, sword to eyes. "It will be an honor to have you try."

The Warrior saluted in return, crossing swords over his chest. From behind, Dammerman heard blades brought up, spears raised, every footman, every man on horse saluting the two. Dammerman heard the same from the lines of the enemy.

"They, all, salute you," the Warrior said.

"Carry the day!" a voice cried from the Solamnic lines. The voice was joined by another, then by hundreds. Every man, officer and soldier, cried Dammerman's words. Dammerman swept his sword down, stepped back from the Warrior's reach.

The Warrior held his left sword low, the other high, near his head. Dammerman held Bar two-handed, left hand over his left eye, right hand near the cross-guard. His stance was tall, relaxed. The two moved in a slow circle to the left, Dammerman kept his feet apart, at the same distance. The Warrior was fluid, swords swaying with his steps. His left shoulder pointed toward Dammerman.

Dammerman leaned forward, brought his left hand down, back up. The Warrior brought his right hand up, left blade moving under his arm. Dammerman swung Bar, pushing his left hand forward, other hand down in an arc. The Warrior fell back a step, and Dammerman recovered. Holding Bar above his head, Dammerman pressed the attack, moved in a half step, thrust his left hand forward and released the right. Bar shattered the Warrior's right blade as the Warrior blocked and stepped to the side. The Warrior ran his sword through Dammerman's chest.

Dammerman fell to his knees, red-bronze armor shorn front to back. The Warrior sheathed his weapon and did not turn to face the dying man.

Dammerman moved Bar's tip toward its sheath, missed, used his finger and thumb as a guide. He tried to hold his flesh together with a hand. He was suddenly lying on his back and looking at the sky. He heard laughter. Dammerman saw sunlight gleam on an object close to his face.

The hourglass was running out of sand.

The stickman leaned down near Dammerman. "You should have listened when you had the chance! 'There will be a more perfect moment,' you said. 'I must face the Warrior in Jet,' you said. Do you now want to know my secret of the Warrior?"

With his ebbing strength, Dammerman propped himself up on one arm. He saw the troops of Takhisis, still in battle order.

The stickman said, "Very well, if you insist, I'll tell you. The secret is, you cannot defeat him! You could never have defeated him. And now you're mine!" The stickman's laugh was dark and hollow. "I asked you, I practically pleaded with you to take the glass, and now you're mine!"

Dammerman turned his head. His own troops were still in battle order. "You're here to punish knights like me," he asked, gasping with the pain. "Aren't you? Knights who lost their way on the road to glory."

"Astute!" the stickman said, mimicking Dammerman's words to Master Raye. "More than astute. Just the same, you'll fight in my Abyss for all time. You'll never know rest, you'll never know joy, you'll never have a moment's comfort. You will suffer beyond suffering, as have all the other fools before you. And the best part? Someday, I will offer the glass to Raye!"

Dammerman coughed up blood. He looked toward the Warrior. Around the haze, around the pain, Dammerman felt as he had been promised. He was proud to have faced the Warrior, even in defeat. The sands of the hourglass were nearly gone.

The red light of the Abyss bathed Dammerman's face, hurt his eyes. The stickman said, "And just between you and me, my good knight, nobody ever chooses the perfect moment. Nobody ever uses the glass."

The stickman's laughter filled Dammerman's ears. His heart throbbed. He knew the roar in his ears was the last herald of his ebbing life. He breathed deeply, chest heaving around the blood. The last few sands of the hourglass trickled down.

"Dammerman!"

From the enemy, Dammerman heard his name.

"Dammerman!"

From his friends, Dammerman heard his name.

"Dammerman. Carry the day."

From the Warrior's mouth, Dammerman heard his name.

"Dammerman!" the stickman cried. "You are mine!"

"Father!" Raye cried. He held aloft the torch. "Father, these torches represent your guidance. We do not walk in your shadow, but carry your light."

The stickman laughed aloud.

Dammerman smiled. He looked to Raye. "As you sought yourself in me, I have found a self in you. Any suffering is worth your faith restored. Your faith will protect you against certain bargains."

With a shaking hand, Dammerman ran a finger across his mustache.

The stickman stopped laughing.

A Flight of Fancy
Jeff Crook

Klaus uth Elester peered wistfully through a port-hole at the wind-rippled waters of the Sirrion Sea, sparkling hundreds of feet below. In the deep cerulean of the sea, whales appeared as small, dark, streamlined shadows, like tiny overturned toy boats. The great seagoing vessels sailing from Palanthas looked like little bits of paper floating on blue oil, and their crews scurrying about on their decks like so many fleas. The gulls, flying high above the sea but still far, far below him, were like motes of dust swirling in beams of sunlight. But of all the crashing waves, crying gulls and shouting ships' crews, Klaus heard not a sound. Not even the wind reached his ears, only the deafening infernal buzzing of his flying machine, and the whine of the gears and wheels that drove it.

And he could no more pause and enjoy the view than he could pause in the endless cycle of oiling and lubricating those gears and wheels, lest they seize and send him plummeting to the sea. Nor could he rest from cranking the winch, which wound torque into the springs, which turned the gears, which flapped the wings, which flew the machine that Klaus built (actually rebuilt, from the wreckage). He had to steer the craft's rudder with his feet, because he had no more hands to spare. The rapid beat of its wings shook the ship. The space around him was barely large enough to hold his six foot tall frame, and this after he'd relocated or removed from the original design numerous devices, gears, and pulleys for which he could find no use. Meanwhile, the heat generated by the wheels and gears made him feel less like a bird on the wing than a bird in an oven, while the oil spraying from the gears kept him as well-basted as a Yule goose. For a brief moment, a design for an automatic basting oven began to form in his mind, but it was quickly driven out by the need to check his course against the direction-finding device he'd invented. He had no desire to end up on the other side of Krynn (at least not today).

Between oiling and cranking and steering and adjusting, he somehow managed to light a candle and open a map on his lap. By his best estimate, the Isle of Sancrist ought to already be in sight, but a glance out the porthole only showed an endless expanse of water. He cursed the inaccuracy of seafarer's maps, vowing that once this was over, he'd make aerial maps of the length and breadth of Krynn. What he really needed was a time-keeping device, but no waterclock invented by man or gnome worked aboard this flying machine. The vibration of the machine caused the water droplets to fall at much too rapid a pace, speeding up time. Although no waterclock was on board, it did seem that time moved at its normal pace. He hadn't quite worked out the theory behind this, but it certainly intrigued him. Perhaps without devices to measure time, time wouldn't exist at all! A frightening thought indeed.

He turned in his seat to reach for another flask of oil, only to find he'd already used his last one. An errant droplet of grease, flying off some rapidly spinning gear, snuffed out his candle with a puff of oily smoke. Now, only the weak light from the smoke-stained overhead porthole provided any illumination at all, but it didn't matter. Without oil, he only had a half hour or so of flight time remaining before the gears seized up, and his bronze and iron, bee-shaped flying machine fell like a stone from the sky. With a dirty rag, he frantically cleaned the glass of the floor porthole to look for a landing site —an island, or even a small bar of sand or coral somewhere in the waters below. With the machine's hovering capability, he only needed a few feet of dry, cleared space. To his surprise and great relief, the coastline of Sancrist passed below him at that very moment. Gnawing his beard, he cranked a few more rounds into the drive springs and swore that if ever he safely reached the ground, he'd first install self-lubricating gears (after inventing them, of course), then he'd add forward portholes so he could see where in blue blazes he was heading in this infernal flying machine! While still scrubbing at the floor porthole and peering searchingly at the ground, he aimed the ship's nose downward and began his descent.

He swore profusely when a cloud shadowed his craft and pitched him into even greater darkness. But the darkness was a red one, a deep crimson as of blood, and he realized why: the gears had begun to glow with heat. Sweat, he realized, was streaming down his nose. As the craft neared the ground, he couldn't find any object or landmark to guide him, and he lost his bearings. The craft began to swerve and bank.

He cranked round the angle of the wings to try to slow his descent, but as he did so, the gears grew redder and hotter. Soon, he knew, the heat would be intolerable; it scorched his hands and his face and, he now noticed, the soles of his feet. Suddenly he realized the soles of his boots were on fire. Frantically, he tried to stomp his feet, which only sent the craft spinning totally out of control. As it rolled over, the gears began to seize with a series of pops and clangs. For a brief moment, he saw the huge bulk of Mount Nevermind rise in the overhead porthole, only to be replaced by sky, then ground, then the mountain again. A sudden thought occurred to him then, a remembrance of something he'd heard but forgotten, something that had been nagging at him ever since he first climbed into the flying machine to fulfill a vow—that there was a newly-arrived red dragon lurking about Sancrist Isle. His name, the sailors said, was Pyrothraxus, and he was a terror to both man and beast. He'd taken Mount Nevermind, the home of the gnomes, and Klaus's destination this day.

Not that it mattered. Soon, only the roaring of the wind could be heard. A hundred ideas flashed through Klaus's mind in those last brief moments, ideas for inventions to account for a sudden and catastrophic loss of altitude. He envisioned an umbrella-like device, with strong yet light collapsible ribs, attached to the machine by ropes. It could be stowed atop the machine, between its wings, and opened in times of emergency. As a redundant feature, a large pillow case could be folded into a military backpack and worn on the back. Should the umbrella fail, the machine's pilot could escape the machine while still in the air, and then float gently down to earth by holding the pillow case open above his head. Or better yet. . .

But he had no more time for thinking up ideas. Just before impact, there was an odd explosion just below (or above—everything was spinning rapidly) the machine. For a thousandth of a heartbeat, he pondered its significance. Then he pondered no more.

* * * * *

Jeff Crook

"Thesubjectwasfounddiscumbentinaprofoundstate-ofrigormortis," a curious voice said just behind Klaus's head. His eyes flashed open.

"Doctoritsalive," said another small, rapid, whiny voice, almost like the buzzing of a mosquito. Klaus blinked in the brilliant white light shining in his face, wondering if this were the afterlife. It didn't seem to be quite what the priests had promised.

"Don'tberidiculousasimplenervousreactionhappens-allthetime," the first voice pronounced importantly. "AsIwassayingthesubjectwasfoundinprofoundstate-ofrigor. . ."

"Am I dead?" Klaus asked.

"Ofcourseyouaresopleasedonotaskquestionsorthe-philosophyguildwillhavetobecalled," whispered the second voice.

"What? I don't understand," Klaus complained.

"NeitherdoIyouaresupposedtobedead," said the first, a bit cross now.

"You are talking too fast. What is that light in my face? I can't see," Klaus cried.

"Howcanhenotseeyetknowthereisalightinhisface?" whispered a third voice.

"You . . . are . . . dead . . . that . . . light . . . is . . . the . . . afterlife . . . so . . . move . . . into . . . it . . . and . . . stop . . . causing . . . philosophical . . . puzzles."

"Why are you talking so slowly?" Klaus now asked.

"Idonotbelievethissubjectisdead. Ceasetheautopsy," ordered yet another voice, this one from somewhere high overhead.

"Maywenotexaminehimtodiscoverwhyheisnot-dead?" the first voice asked.

"Suchanexaminationwouldsurelykillhim."

"Where I am? What language are you speaking?" Klaus cried.

126

"You are home now, Glepstickgloggerwollicking-winking. You've taken a blow to the head, but you'll soon be able to speak and hear at a normal pace," said the second voice.

With a clang, the light in his face winked off, leaving him nearly as blind in the sudden darkness. Large green and purple blobs floated before his eyes. Blinking, Klaus asked, "Home? Back in Solamnia? How did I get here?"

"No, you are home, in Mount Nevermind. Don't you remember?"

"I'm from Solamnia," Klaus said, as someone began to loosen the straps binding his arms to his sides. "From the village of Trebeign. My name is Klaus uth Elester." Quickly, the straps were retightened, as the strange-voiced creatures began to whisper excitedly.

"Obviouslydelusionalasaresultoftheblowtothe-headaswellastheunusualtransformationofhisbody. Fur-therstudyiswarranted."

"Somethinghasstetchedhimalloutofshapeheisatleast-twiceastallashewaswhenheleft. Perhapsitstretchedhis-brainaswell."

"Iwouldliketoperformadissectiontodiscover-howdeeplythetransmutation . . ."

"Transformationtransformationhowmanytimesmust-Irepeatmyself? Atransformationofthebody . . ."

"Istillbelieveatransmutationhasoccurredhere."

"Perhapsweshouldcallinsomeonefromthelinguistics-guild." A bell rang somewhere.

"Where am I?" Klaus cried in frustration.

"You are in the examination room of the Mishaps Investigation Guild," the second voice answered.

Slowly, the green and purple blobs around him lost their weird colors and shapes, and began to look more and more like people—short, nutty-brown-skinned, white-haired people with broad smiling faces and nervous, deerlike movements. They all wore strange white overcoats which had innumerable pockets covering every available space, even their backs where it was obviously impossible for them to reach. Some of the shorter ones tripped over the hems of their coats as they scurried about, putting away various machines and instruments which looked uncomfortably like tools of torture.

"Oh, I see. You are all gnomes," Klaus exclaimed.

"As are you," said the second voice. Klaus turned his head and found a rather pretty-eyed young gnome watching him from behind some sort of cloth mask covering her face. "Granted, your body has gone through some sort of grotesque transformation, probably a side effect of the machine which carried you away three months ago, and then brought you back today. It stretched you all of out shape. The Time-Sciences Guild theorizes some sort of time distortion effect. But I'd know you anywhere, Glepstickglogger." She began to rerelease the straps binding his arms.

"That name sounds familiar," Klaus said, when his hands were free. He rubbed the back of his head, where a walnut-sized, painfully tender knot throbbed on his aching skull.

"Of course it does. It's you. The Medical Guild will soon produce an antidote which will return you to your natural state," she pledged.

"But this is my natural state, this is my natural state!" he shouted. The room grew quiet, as all eyes turned to him. Klaus hadn't realized just how many gnomes were around him until they stopped moving. Dozens of small, brown faces gazed wonderingly at him.

"Listen, I am not a gnome," Klaus pronounced. "I am a human. My name is Klaus. I am from the Solamnic village of Trebeign. I too am an inventor and designer, of mechanical toys. I came here in a flying machine—"

A snort of laughter interrupted him. "Preposterous! Everyone knows that intentional flight is a physical impossibility," said a voice from the balcony. "And humans never invented anything of merit." An important-looking gnome rose from his chair and wagged a finger at Klaus. He wore a long leather robe decorated with numerous mathematical and engineering symbols.

"But it did fly," Klaus argued anachronistically. "Although I can't take all of the credit. Glepstickglogger, now I remember, made valuable contributions." He noticed that more and more gnomes were crowding into the chamber. Most of them wore some sort of uniform, from the leather aprons and hammer-and-tong symbols of the Metalworkers Guild, to the black jackboots, breeches, and jackets of the Weapons Guild, distinguished by their finger-over-the-lips-enjoining-silence emblem. Soon, a veritable sea of little brown faces gazed up at him

"The machine's unfortunate tendency to fly was an accident, nothing more," the important gnome pronounced. "I should know, for I myself designed it originally."

"Really? How wonderful! I have so many questions, I—" Klaus began excitedly, but the important gnome waved his hand impatiently.

"Later, later," he said. "First, you must tell us what happened to Glepstickglogger, for it is obvious to some of us that you are not he. Your authentic Solamnic accent proves that."

"Hecouldhaveacquiredtheaccentduringhisabsence," the young female gnome argued.

"Nonsense, Zeeberwhindhodimplingwillow. This creature is a man, nothing more," the important gnome said. "Have him brought to my study at once." He turned and strode importantly through a doorway, followed closely by a train of jabbering attendants.

The female gnome stared at Klaus over her mask for a moment longer, as though sizing him up with her twinkling brown eyes. She loosened the strings which held the mask in place and let it drop to hang about her neck. "I suppose you aren't Gleps, after all," she sighed. "Well, come along. I hope you have news of dear Gleps."

"Who was that gnome?" Klaus asked as he swung his legs over the side of the table and prepared to drop to the floor. To his surprise, the examination table proved to be only a few inches off the ground.

"He is the master of the Agricultural Sciences Guild," Zeeber answered. "He is very important indeed, a great inventor of labor saving devices. He invented the can opener."

"What's a can?" Klaus asked as he rose to his feet, groaning in pain from his bruises and injuries. As though cued to action by his movement, or perhaps by his agonized cries, the gnomes in the room burst suddenly into motion. Most scurried away to other jobs or duties, a few moved closer to examine him with professional curiosity.

"Well, as we all know, the more flavorful the food, the quicker it decomposes," she answered as she led him from the examination room. "Our engineers believe that if fruits and vegetables can be cooked down until most of their flavor has been removed, then a small cylindrical metal container, called a 'can' for short, could be used to store such food indefinitely. It's called hermetic sealing, after Hermeticiticus, who first proposed the notion in 353 PC. Professor Hagginsbottombortembutting has already invented a device to open the containers, once they have been designed. He is quite the genius, you know."

They turned a corner and entered a circular space many times taller than it was wide. As Klaus looked up, he saw that balcony after balcony ringed the shaft-like central chamber, one atop the other, until the highest levels were lost in the sunlight shining down from above. All around the floor of this, the lowest level, stood numerous large catapults and siege engines of various designs. It seemed a strange location for an artillery emplacement, being deep within the mountain. However, as he watched, a gnome approached one of the ballista and climbed into its basket. A bell rang, then another seemed to answer it from somewhere above. The catapult's attendants scurried about a siege engine for a few moments, then (much to Klaus's alarm) one of them pulled its firing mechanism, thus launching the hapless gnome up the center of the shaft, many hundreds of feet into the air. Just as the poor fellow reached the apex of his flight, a net shot out from one of the balcony levels, catching him and pulling him to safety. Klaus breathed a sigh of relief.

"This way," his guide directed, pointing to a rather antique-looking catapult machine.

"What is this?" Klaus asked as he warily scrutinized the contraption. A group of gnomes gathered nearby, eyeing him expectantly.

"Transportation system. Much safer than walking," Zeeber noted. "Just climb aboard, then tell the operator which *skimbosh* you wish to reach."

"Skimbosh?" Klaus asked.

"Level. We want to go to *skimbosh* nineteen," she explained. At his dubious expression, she continued, "It's quite safe. Every year, the number of terminal mishaps decreases as more safety features are added."

"Terminal mishaps? Don't you have any stairs?" Klaus exclaimed. "I've had my fill of flying for now."

"Oh, I hadn't thought of that. Most unfortunate, your recent flying experience," she said. "Stairs, yes, we have many, but they are rarely used these days. Most dangerous, very few redundant safety features. Are you sure you want to use them?"

"Quite," he said tremblingly as yet another gnome was flung out of sight. They turned back the way they had come and followed the passage until it led to a low rusty door. With considerable effort and noise, she managed to open it, but not before a large group of gnomes had gathered to watch and offer suggestions. Finally, she pried it open wide enough for Klaus to squeeze through. They popped into a dusty, narrow staircase filled with cobwebs.

With much coughing, choking, and sneezing (and a few lengthy discussions about various self-cleaning ventilation system designs) they made their at last way up to skimbosh nineteen. Here, approximately midway up the central shaft of volcanic Mount Nevermind, the Agricultural Sciences Guild had recently established their new headquarters. Gnomes wearing the grand plow design on their sleeves scurried about, busily anticipating the next quantum leap in the agricultural sciences, to be provided by the much-whispered-about Professor Hagginsbottom. Like all the other main levels, the agricultural skimbosh spread out like a great spider's web from the central shaft of the volcano. However, unlike most of the other levels, skimbosh nineteen had its own exits from the mountain. Doors let out to the fields and terraces where the guild members were able to test their theories and inventions on the main food supply of the gnomish city.

As Klaus and his guide made their winding way along the maze-like passages of skimbosh nineteen, they met more than one gnome coming in from the fields, some covered with dirt and looking dejected, others proudly and gruntingly bearing some monstrous vegetable recently produced by gnome-engineered methods. Klaus saw tomatoes the size of pumpkins, peas as big as tomatoes, and pumpkins no larger than peas. Eventually, they arrived at a heavy, bronze-bound door with an important looking row of brass plates down its center. A closer examination revealed these were not a list of offices or occupants, but the single, encyclopedic appellation of Professor Hagginsbottombortembutting (this being but a brief translation of his full name).

Zeeber opened the door and led Klaus into a large elaborately-decorated office. It was filled not only with books and desks and worktables, but also museum-quality specimens of innumerable labor-saving devices stretching back over dozens of generations of gnomish inventors. Behind the largest and most cluttered of these desks sat the important Professor H. He rose as Klaus and his guide entered the room, and crossed to them, his stubby-fingered hand extended before him, a huge toothy smile on his face.

"Let me welcome you officially," he boomed as he vigorously shook Klaus by the hand. "I am so glad you were not killed during the accident."

"So am I," Klaus answered.

"It is a good thing I included those emergency features, the explosive self-inflating shock-absorbing bladders—you didn't happen to notice, did you?" he asked, motioning for Klaus to find a seat. Most of the large comfortable chairs were filled to overflowing with tools and instruments, plans and schematics. Klaus managed to squeeze into the corner of one by pushing aside what looked to be an automatic seeding device.

"Would that have been the strange tar-sealed compartments lining underside?" Klaus asked.

"Exactly," the gnome smiled appreciatively. "So tell me, how did you come to be here?"

Before Klaus could begin his story, there came a knock at the door. It opened a crack, and a small, thin, rather red-faced gnome peered inside. "Lord Pyrothraxus demands that the Solamnic spy be brought before him at once," he squeaked plaintively.

"Yes, yes," the professor waved abstractedly. "I am interviewing the prisoner at the moment."

"Prisoner!" Klaus exclaimed when the door closed.

"DGR spies," the professor snarled to himself. "They must have had someone in the examination room. I am sorry," he apologized. "Our dragon is quite sensitive about outsiders. We go along with it, up to a point. Have to, no choice really."

"Your dragon?" Klaus asked incredulously

"Yes, well, officially of course, Pyrothraxus took Mount Nevermind and we are all his thralls and slaves. That's the image the DGR, the Draco-Gnomic Relations society (which is but a division of the Diplomats Guild), tries to purvey. And so of course, the presence of any human, much less a Solamnic, is in their eyes as well as His Majesty's, a spy. So I named you my prisoner. That should keep you safe. For a little while at least."

"I see," Klaus said worriedly.

"I can't even begin to explain the complexities of the situation, as you might well imagine. It isn't every day that one has a dragon move into one's home and try to take over operations. It's most inconvenient, but what is one to do?" the professor complained.

"Is that why you built a flying machine, to try to find a way to escape?" Klaus asked.

"Why would we want to escape? This is our home," the professor said with a sweeping gesture of his hand. "No, I did not build a flying machine. I built a device to increase food production. I built a spring-powered bee-juice extractor."

"A what?"

"A spring-powered bee juice extractor. For years, we've been wrestling with the best way to extract bee juice from the bee. Dangerous things, bees; they don't readily or peacefully relinquish their juice. After many years of design and experimentation, I came up with the spring-powered bee juice extractor. Come, I'll show you."

They rose and Professor H. led them through a door into a wide low-ceilinged chamber. Two-dozen machines of ever-increasing complexity lined the farthest wall, in the center of which was another larger door, obviously an exit to the outside as evidenced by the sunlight shining through the cracks.

Professor H. pointed to a large, square white box with a hinged lid and small horizontal slots at the bottom. "This is the first prototype," the genius of a gnome said. "It produced large quantities of bee-juice, but at great personal danger to the beekeeper."

"We have these at home," Klaus commented. "We call them hives."

"Hives? Isn't that a nervous condition?" Zeeber, who had followed along, asked.

"Forgive her. She is in the Medical Guild," the professor laughed. He continued on to the next prototype, one much like the first, but with a nest of glass tubes and beakers underneath it The next one had a large copper cauldron beneath it.

"We tried various external collection systems, but the original problem of danger to the collector persisted. So we determined that if the juice could be extracted directly from the bee, a needless step in the collection process could be circumvented, and the danger to the collector eliminated. To that task we directed our efforts with these models," he said as they continued along the wall, passing larger and more complex devices with each step.

"This model," the professor said, indicating an empty space, "is the one you flew here. The previous model reached such internal temperatures that its operator was invariably burned to a state very much like bacon. So I added a set of winglike vanes on top, hoping these would cool the hull. However, they were the cause of its unforeseen tendency to leave the ground. Which brings us at last to your story, for somehow you gained possession of my machine. Is poor Glepstickglogger okay?"

"It crashed in my back yard, three months ago last Tuesday," Klaus said.

"Ah, of course. To the very day when my assistant, Mr. Gleps, climbed aboard the extractor for her initial trial run, started her up, and vanished into the blue," the professor said.

Zeeber sniffled.

"Mr. Gleps was also Miss Zeeber's promised betrothed. You can understand her interest in this matter," the professor explained. "So how did you find Mr. Gleps?"

"Much the same way you found me, I should imagine," Klaus said. "Only much worse. Numerous broken bones, contusions, bruises. He is recovering upon my daybed. I expect he will be fine with a tincture of time."

"Very good indeed. We are glad to hear it, aren't we, Miss Zeeber?"

"Indeed we are," she answered with a relieved sigh.

"But come now, tell us how you managed to effect repairs to the craft?" the professor asked.

"Well, it's a funny coincidence, but I am a bit of an inventor myself," Klaus explained. "Upon discovering the crash site, I immediately recognized the nature of the machine, and determined to fly it myself. After seeing to the bandaging and dressing of Mr. Gleps' injuries, I set about repairing the damage, removing in the process those elements for which I could find no purpose or which seemed ridiculously redundant."

"Hmph!" the professor snorted.

"Over the last month or so, I've been taking her on short test flights, trying out her systems and exploring her flight envelope. I think I put her back together pretty much as you built her, minus the redundancies, except for one thing. I found a great quantity of glass at the crash site, for which I failed discover its designated purpose—a mystery element, you might say. In addition, there was a large number of bees flying about the crash, and until this very moment, their presence remained a bafflement to me."

"Did you discover any bee juice?" Professor H. asked excitedly. "Any honey at all?"

"I'm afraid not," Klaus said.

"Drat! Confound it. Well, no matter. I think I've solved all the problems with the previous model. The newest version of the spring-powered bee juice extractor should work perfectly." He turned and snatched the cloth covering from the last machine in the line.

This version, unveiled, was indeed the largest and most complex of them all, and it also looked the most like a giant bee. It stood fully twelve feet high, and had a double-set of wing-like ventilation vanes resting along its back. Forward-facing portholes allowed for a full field of view through the bulbous black eyes. Its six multi-jointed stabilizers looked remarkably like legs, while its rear drain spout frighteningly resembled a stinger.

"The second set of vanes is meant to provide negative

lift, offsetting the positive thrust of the cooling vanes and thusly holding the machine safely upon the ground," the professor said.

"However," he continued, whispering, "this morning I reversed the pitch of the offsetting vanes, anticipating your possible need for a mode of escape. Do climb inside, both of you. Give it a try." He glanced back at the door. Some sort of commotion was going on behind it. Suddenly, someone hammered noisily at the door, then rattled the lock.

"Quickly," the professor urged.

"Professor! I am a representative of Draco-Gnomic Relations. His Majesty demands the Solamnic prisoner be brought to him at once," shouted an officious voice behind the door. Meanwhile, an apprehensive Klaus opened the bottom hatch.

"Zeeber, you must go along with him. Unlike the previous versions of the spring-powered bee juice extractor, this one requires two operators," the gnome professor said.

"ButIdon'tknowhowtooperatethemachineryproperlyyouarecertainlymorequalified," she said excitedly.

"Imuststaybehindtoexplaintheescapeoftheprisonerwhileyoushouldbeatthesideofyourpromisedbetrothed," he explained hurriedly.

With a quick wave of her hand and a huge smile, Zeeber scrambled up and inside the machine.

"Professor, I must insist that you open this door at once," shouted the voice from behind his office door.

"What?" Professor H. said elusively.

Klaus followed Zeeber into the craft.

"Good flying to you both. And hurry!" the professor urged.

"Professor, one final thing," Klaus said. The office door rattled in its frame as something large and heavy was thrust against it. "Smoke. You might try smoke. It calms the bees," he said.

"Smoke?" Professor H. asked, somewhat puzzled.

"That's what Solamnic beekeepers use."

"You don't say," the professor mumbled, as he thoughtfully scratched his head.

"Thank you, professor," Klaus said as he closed the bottom hatch with a clang.

At that moment, the door burst open and a dozen gnomes poured into the room. Seeing the professor alone, they hesitated. The spring-powered bee juice extractor began to whir and buzz, and then it suddenly lurched into motion, emptying the room of intruders as quickly as it had been filled.

"Stop them! They are stealing my machine!" the professor said, holding back his laughter. A few gnomes peered timidly around the door.

The machine unfolded its wings, turned round on its spindly legs, and crawled from the chamber. No one gave chase.

* * * * *

"Crank that spring until it is tight," Klaus ordered from his upper seat inside the machine. A second, lower seat had been added for the co-operator, down where a bank of switches and levers controlled the automatic oiling devices (a tremendous improvement!) and where the two main cranks which wound the drive springs were located. Klaus could concentrate his efforts on flying the machine, while Zeeber oiled and cranked and wound things. Front and rear portholes provided an almost 360 degree field of view, the only obstacle being the large tear-shaped glass container hanging directly before the pilot's seat. The container was black with bees, probably thousands of them, and had a number of glass tubes and copper hoses running off it and into the tangle of machinery behind the seats.

Klaus walked the machine outside, onto a level terrace several thousand feet above the base of Mount Nevermind. He launched the drive system and, gazing up through the overhead porthole, saw the wings fan slowly a few times, before they melted into a gray haze of fluttering speed. That is when the machine lurched into the air, bobbed a few times, then shot away, pinning him back in his chair. The ground dropped away beneath them. Even over the deafening noise of the machinery and buzzing wings, Klaus heard Zeeber's screaming (whether with delight or fear he could not immediately discern).

As the machine reached top speed and the mountains of northern Sancrist sped away beneath them, Klaus began to get the feel of the controls, trying the new flying machine in several banking and turning maneuvers. She handled like a gem, although each gyration sent Zeeber into new fits of terror. Finally, Klaus leveled her off and relaxed. Under his directions, Zeeber calmed enough to begin the self-oiling procedures.

In the new version of the spring-powered bee juice extractor, the numerous improvements and the addition of a second operator allowed Klaus more time to observe his surroundings and enjoy the view. It truly was wonderful, zooming amongst the clouds. The horizon spread out blue and (to his surprise) slightly rounded. Only the sun above flew higher than he. After staring in wonder through the bottom porthole at the world so tiny below, then at the deep, almost night-like azure of the sky in the upper porthole, he glanced back through the tiny rear porthole at Mount Nevermind receding in the distance. As he watched, a dark red speck lifted from the summit. Slowly, it grew in size.

"It'sworkingit'sworkingit'sworking!" Zeeber exclaimed.

"Keep those drive springs cranked up tight," Klaus said worriedly, still looking over his shoulder. The dark red speck had become a ruby sparkling in the sun.

"It's working!" Zeeber said.

"What's working?"

"The bee juice extractor. The tubes are full of honey," she said.

Inside the large, tear-shaped glass container dangling before him, the bees were still angrily buzzing about, but the tubes had filled up with a thick, slow-moving amber fluid. Klaus started at the honey in wonder and amazement, but only for a moment. He turned back to the porthole and saw that the ruby had become a small scarlet creature, no bigger than a bee. Every moment, it seemed to draw a little closer, a little faster, becoming a ruby breasted hummingbird, a bright red cardinal, and then a vermilion hawk. At the same time, the ground seemed to be drawing nearer, as though they were dropping from the sky.

"Why are we slowing down and losing altitude?" he cried. "Keeps those springs cranked!"

"They are cranked!" Zeeber shouted. "What's wrong?"

"Pyrothraxus!"

Below them, the shores of Sancrist slipped away. Now, they were crossing above the deep blue of the Sirrion Sea. Behind them, Pyrothraxus grew ever closer, gaining on them as their craft unaccountably slowed, as though it were obeying the will of the pursuing dragon. In mere moments, it seemed, he was almost upon them. The great leathern wings and powerful, rudder-like tail, the crested spine and sinuous neck, the fanged mouth hanging open in anticipation, the claws clutching eagerly at the air, the eyes burning with hatred, all held Klaus spellbound. Terror clutched his heart, terror mingled with awe.

Now, the dragon was but a few dozen yards behind them and closing. Its great body seemed to stretch across all the sky. The sunlight reflecting off its vermilion scales filled the interior of the craft with an eerie red glow. Yet, the beast seemed at that moment to hesitate, as though puzzled by the nature and appearance of its quarry. Then, Klaus noticed a thin trail of amber fluid spraying out behind them, and he realized it was honey overflowing from the stinger-tube. Probably, it looked rather like venom. The dragon dipped a little lower, as though trying to get a closer look at the curious craft.

A desperate thought occurred to Klaus. "Zeeber, see if you can find the release valve for the bee juice storage tanks!" he shouted.

She turned in her seat. "You mean these copper kettles?" she asked, pointing.

"Probably. The weight is slowing us down. We have to dump the honey," he said.

"Dump the honey!" she cried.

"We can always make more. Do it, quickly!" he shouted. She clambered over the back of her seat and vanished into the machinery.

Klaus glanced back. A flash of lightning starkly illuminated the dragon's hate-filled eyes. It had risen in the sky, probably to gain altitude before making its final diving attack.

Meanwhile, they had flown into a sea squall. Huge black clouds rolled before them, dumping gray sheets of rain which obscured the sea. Occasionally, a bolt of lightning leaped from thunderhead to thunderhead, or flashed downward, vanishing into the blowing rain.

"Hurry!" Klaus shouted frantically. Pyrothraxus lowered his head and plummeted toward then, his jaws gaping, fire spewing forth. Klaus felt his stomach sink into his shoes. A thick stream of amber fluid billowed behind them as Zeeber finally managed to open the dump valves.

Then, there was a brilliant flash. It seemed to surround them entirely, stunning their minds and their eyes to blindness. Some concussive force seemed to strike the craft from behind, shattering the portholes and blasting them into their seats. Wind and rain screamed through the empty holes, hissing on the gears. From somewhere way in back of his head Klaus watched the dragon became a tiny red speck again. Then everything went black.

* * * * *

"That's how it must have happened. . . ." Zeeber finished as she daubed an herbal salve on her pink, swollen, bee-sting bloated nose. "The resulting sudden release of large quantities of honey into the sulfurous dragonfire, combined with the lightning strike, created a remarkable explosive quality. A rather remarkable development, wouldn't you say?"

"Hmmm. Sulfur and honey. I wonder . . ." the young man said, his eyes thoughtful.

"The next thing I knew, we were crashing into your barn," the gnome said.

The young man tossed another log on the fire, then stood and stared thoughtfully at a strange device resting on the mantle. It had a circular face with numbers running around its circumference, and two small needle-like pointers affixed to a central pin. Below the face, a pendulum swung with an annoyingly regular ticking noise.

"I'm something of an inventor myself," the young man averred. "Perhaps I could attempt to repair your machine."

"No!" a voice roared from the other room. A mummy-like creature wrapped head-to-toe in loose bandages lurched stiff-legged into the room. "No! Let it rot and rust! We'll walk back to Solace. If the gods had wanted us to fly, they'd have given us wings," he bitterly declared.

Zeeber eyed the streamers of bandages fluttering from Klaus, wildly waving arms. "Hmmmm. Wings," she purred as she reached into a pocket and withdrew a bit of charcoal. She began to sketch on the rough top of the wooden table.

"Wings?" their host asked.

Klaus grew still and examined the wing-like shape of his bandage-wrapped arms. "Hmmm," he pondered.

The Deep, Deep, Dark, Dark Place

Kevin James Kage

Two years passed, and once again men came to the deep, deep, dark, dark place.

Glug heard them long before he saw them. Their boisterous laughter raced through the tunnels faster than the slippery things that Glug often caught to eat. They had low, heavy voices that thundered through the caves. Sometimes, they sang. Glug liked that. No one had sung in the deep, deep, dark, dark place for a very long time. He wanted to join in, but he didn't know the words, and he didn't want them to hear him anyway.

He took Lurd to listen to the voices, and they sat for a long time in the darkness. Lurd frowned as they listened.

"What they say?" Glug asked her, for she was smarter than he was, and she knew some of the words men used.

"Me not sure. They not speak like other men."

"Why they come? For Treasure?"

"They not come to eat slippery things."

"Oh. Think they find Treasure?"

"Not know," she said.

For two days, Glug kept waiting to see the men. Lurd let him do it, even though he was supposed to find food for them. He crept through the darkness, looking for the men whose voices rang in the caverns all around him.

They had started off very distant, and after a time they grew nearer and nearer.

One night he dreamed he found them: men in shiny armor with swords and nice boots. When he woke up, there were no men to be seen, but they sounded very close. Glug became excited and he went to tell Lurd, but Lurd was busy picking mushrooms, too busy to listen. Glug anticipated seeing the men at any moment.

Still, when he finally saw them they caught him by surprise. One day, Glug was crawling up through a tunnel, and there they stood. They didn't see him in the shadows, so he sat very still and watched.

They had big bright boxes that sat on poles and made light that hurt Glug's eyes. There were many men: maybe more than two. They talked in gruff voices that sounded like rocks grinding together. Glug didn't know what they said, but it sounded like important man-talk.

They were shorter than the other men he remembered. These men weren't much taller than himself, and they had big, thick beards. They were men though. In the deep, deep, dark, dark place, there were only slippery things, and sometimes men, and Glug, and . . .

"Hey!" he said softly to Lurd, who had just appeared in the hole, "You remember what that other thing in deep, deep, dark, dark, place is?"

Lurd crawled up beside him and screwed up her face while she thought.

"Me?" she said.

"No, me meant the other, other thing, not you or Glug or slippery things or men . . . other thing."

"Treasure?"

"Yes, Treasure!" Glug said.

The men laughed loudly, and Glug and Lurd slid behind a rock. The men had sticks with shiny curvy ends, and they were hitting the rock with them, and pulling bits of stone away, making the natural tunnels wider.

"They have rock breaking sticks," said Glug. "They are trying find Treasure!"

"They fail unless we help."

"Me think they will succeed."

"How many men try before?"

Glug thought about it for a long time.

"Two men."

"Two?" Lurd said, frowning, "Must be more than two! Lot of men come!"

"It two! Me remember!" Lurd was smart, but Glug had a better memory.

"So it two," Lurd said. "But those men not smart. Not like Glug and Lurd. Men need help to find treasure!"

"You right! We help new men find Treasure! But how?"

Lurd thought again. She was good at thinking. Glug liked her because she was so smart.

"We make trail," she said.

Glug grimaced, "Last time Glug do that, men saw Glug. Hit Glug. Bad plan."

Lurd frowned for the moment. In the light of the men's boxes, Glug could see her one green eye and one brown eye fixed in concentration. Her hairy upper lip twitched a little. Glug thought she looked very pretty.

"They not see us," Lurd said. "We use magic vanishing stick."

* * * * *

Raddoc Stonedelver drove his pick into the rock, and a shower of limestone cascaded to the cavern floor.

"So if we organize—unionize—we can demand higher wages, safer working conditions, and more benefits," he said. "It's the wave of the future. No one will be employed without an organization that safeguards their interests."

"I don't know," said Thurgood Strongarm. "It sounds like something gnomes would think of. Why do I need one of these . . . unions . . . anyway?"

"Everyone needs the union. It protects us from unlawful work practices."

"Ain't no law to it! We dig. We get paid. Where's law come into that?"

"That's what I'm saying! Unionize and we'll get better work, higher wages."

"And if we don't?"

"We refuse to work."

Thurgood snorted. "Sitting around refusing to work? Sounds about as much fun as digging, and digging pays more. Say, what time is it?"

"How should I know?"

"I say it's lunch time."

Thurgood sat down on a stone and brought out the wrought iron box he kept his rations in. He pulled out a piece of stale bread and chewed on it noisily.

"If we unionize, you'll get a longer lunch break."

Thurgood gave him a look. Raddoc shut up.

They ate and went back to work.

"Doesn't matter anyway. When we find this treasure, I'm going to retire," Raddoc said at last.

"The boss won't let you retire till you're dead," Thurgood bellowed, "And then he'll use your bones for tunnel bracing."

He heaved a support beam into place with a loud grunt. Normally the job took two dwarves, but Thurgood Strongarm lived up to his name.

"When we find this treasure, I'll be so rich, not even the boss can stop me!" Raddoc said, "I'll tile my home in gold and silver, and I'll drink spirits out of the Diamond Bowl of Dougan Redhammer!"

Thurgood snorted. "No such person, and no such thing."

"Was so! My great-great-uncle's second cousin knew a fellow whose grandfather owned an inn where Dougan Redhammer once stayed. And he had a diamond bowl too!"

"First gnomish ideas, and now kender stories!"

Raddoc grumbled, "There is so a diamond bowl, and it's down here with the rest of the treasure. The man said so."

Thurgood guffawed. "You mean the man in town? The man who sold the boss the treasure map? The man who said he also had maps of the Dwarf Mines at Naroc, the sunken city of Istar, and the Lost Temple of Reorx? The man who said he knew how to get to an island where all the treasure that ever sunk into the sea is kept? The man who said he could show us the Hammer of Kharas for a steel piece each? Don't tell me you fell for that!"

"So why are you here?"

Thurgood shrugged, "The boss pays me. He says dig. So I dig. It's more steel than I made splitting logs in Haven."

Raddoc didn't say anything after that. He set his pick back to work. Thurgood went back to setting beams.

"How long have we been down here, anyway?" Raddoc asked finally, mopping sweat from his brow.

"I'd say we've been down here a week, nine days maybe," Thurgood said. He hefted another beam.

Raddoc said, "I'd say you're about right, judging by the oil we've used. Wish we'd brought an hour candle though."

Thurgood set the beam into place. "Time means nothing down here. Let's just hope the boss decides to quit before we dig ourselves clear to the other side of the world!"

Raddoc nodded, hefted his pick and drove it into the wall again. It stuck deep, and when he pulled it out, he felt the wall start to give. The rocks slid.

Then Thurgood had him by the arms and was pulling him away from the cave-in. The rocks crashed down over where he had just been standing. The noise thundered through the tunnels. Thurgood's beams groaned, but held. A great cloud of dust washed over them both, leaving them gasping for air. Then it was over.

"Reorx's teeth and toenails!" Raddoc said, once he had stopped coughing and heaving. He stood with arms akimbo and regarded the rubble with a sad shake of his head. "There goes a day's work!"

"There'll be other days," said Thurgood. He slapped his friend on the back.

The Warden came running down the tunnel, his legs pumping furiously.

"What are you two doing?" he said. "You're making enough noise to wake my deaf grandmother!"

"Sorry, Boss!" Raddoc said. "The cave collapsed. I lost my pick to it."

The Warden frowned. His steely eyes scanned the rubble.

"Lost another lamp too," Thurgood said, picking up the damaged casing.

The Warden nodded. "We don't have any more extras, you'll have to make do with the ones you've got."

"What about my pick, Boss?"

"Use your hands if you're going to be so careless," the Warden said. Then he said, "I'll have Slate bring you down a new one. Mark me, Raddoc. You lose this one, and you *will* be using your hands!"

"Yes, Boss!"

"And don't let me catch you spouting any more of that union nonsense either. Bad enough I've got to supply work helmets to you sorry fools."

"Yes, Boss!"

"Hey! What's that?" Thurgood said.

He pointed into the darkness.

"You see it?"

"What?"

"Is it the gold?"

"No. Looks like a gully dwarf."

It was, in fact, two gully dwarves. They stepped forward into the light, beaming bright smiles full of broken teeth. They held a thin, rotting branch between them and they walked around the dwarves without even acknowledging their presence.

"They not see us?" said one of them.

"Not see us. We carry magic vanishing stick. Men not see us! We smart!"

"Men not see us!"

"Not see us!"

They danced and skipped about the stunned dwarves, singing something unintelligible and dropping little stones on the ground.

"That enough. We go now."

"Okay. Bye men! Good luck finding Treasure!"

With that, they strolled off into the darkness.

The dwarves stood stiff as boards.

"Well, take me out of the fire and hammer me!" Thurgood said, "That's about the strangest thing I've ever seen."

"Spooked by gully dwarves, Thurgood?" the Warden said, but his voice wavered too. "These caves are full of vermin. There's silverfish the size of cats down here! Making a mess of our rations. A few gully dwarves is nothing."

"I'm not spooked," Thurgood said stiffly, "I just didn't know they were down here."

"Boss! Look!"

Raddoc held up one of the stones the gully dwarves

had dropped. It sparkled a deep blue in the light.

"A sapphire!" said the Warden.

"Look at the size of it!" Thurgood said.

"And there's more!"

They knelt down and picked up the stones that the gully dwarves had dropped: an emerald, a ruby, a bright yellow topaz, and a fire opal. All of them were finished with the care and precision of the finest dwarven gem cutters. The smallest of them was the size of the Warden's thumbnail.

"I don't believe it!" said Thurgood. "There really is a treasure!"

"Why didn't you grab those gully dwarves!" the Warden said. "They know where the treasure is!"

"Sorry Boss, it's not in my contract." Raddoc stifled a grin.

"I just lift beams, Boss. How was I to know?"

The Warden grumbled. "Well, we know now. Much good that it does us!"

"Should we grab them if we see them again, Boss?"

"Not unless they start stealing or being a nuisance. They seem harmless enough, and I don't have the supplies to feed them, nor the manpower to watch them either. Maybe we'll get lucky and they'll do what they said—lead us straight to the treasure!" He had a good laugh at that. "Meantime keep an eye peeled for any more gems! And, get back to work!"

* * * * *

"They see us?" Glug asked.

"Not think so," said Lurd. "Magic stick very strong."

He clutched one end of Lurd's magic stick tightly, and she held the other end.

"Me liked using magic stick." Glug said.

"We still have lots work," said Lurd. "Leave men shiny stones. They follow."

"Me know," Glug said, "But men close! Very close! If they keep going, they find treasure soon!"

* * * * *

"Men stupid!" said Glug sourly.

"Me know," said Lurd. She fished a shiny green stone out of her ragged skirt and tossed it among the men.

One of the men turned around, picked up the green stone, and tucked it into his belt pouch. Without so much as a nod, he turned back to the wall and started working again.

Glug picked up a clear glittery stone and hurled it at one of the men. It hit the man's shiny helmet—*clang!*— but the man only stooped down, picked it up, and went back to work.

"Men still go wrong way!" Glug snorted! "Stupid men!"

"I got idea!" Lurd said. "Give Lurd shiny stone!"

Glug handed Lurd a shiny red stone and Lurd held it above her head. In her other hand, she clutched the magic stick.

"Lurd? How come me still see you when you hold magic stick?"

"Lurd want Glug to see."

"Oh."

"Now watch!"

She crept forward, until she stood in the middle of the group of men. Then, she held the red stone high up in the air.

"Me magic red shiny stone! Me very powerful! Me got news for digging men! You go wrong way, not find Treasure!"

The men turned and looked at the stone. Glug thought at first they might be looking at Lurd, but then he remembered Lurd was invisible.

"Uh," said one of the men, "Yes—uh—magic red shiny stone. Thank you! Which way do we go?"

"You go back to where big stone teeth point down, then you follow more stones. Only go where stones lead! Caves very dangerous! You might fall and not find Treasure!"

"Thank you, magic red shiny stone!" said the man, "We'll go back there and look for stones. You heard the gully—uh—stone, boys. Let's go!"

"Good! Magic red shiny stone go now!" Lurd said, and she stepped away and walked back to Glug.

"You so smart, Lurd!" said Glug.

"Come quick!" said Lurd, "We go drop more stones."

* * * * *

It took the men two more days to dig through the rock and widen the narrow passes. Glug and Lurd led them easily, dropping stones every few yards. Once more, the men turned in the wrong direction, so Lurd and Glug led them in a circle until they found their way back to the path. It took quite a lot of work making sure the stupid men went the right way. They took turns. Sometimes, Glug borrowed Lurd's stick and he crept right up next to the men, and pretended to be the magic red stone. It was a lot more work than he expected. Sometimes he wished the men would just go away. But only sometimes. Sooner or later these men would find Treasure, and that was going to be better than all the quiet days he knew before the men came.

Glug was half-dozing and Lurd was snoring at his side when one of the men started shouting loudly. Glug sat up. Making sure he was still touching the magic stick, he peered out from behind his alcove.

154

A great cavern yawned where the man had been breaking rocks. Light filtered in from the boxes on poles, and among the shadows there came the gleam and sparkle of jewels and gold. Treasure.

Men poured down the tunnel while the first man continued to shout. They pooled at the cavern-mouth until Glug could no longer see the treasure beyond them. Glug had never seen so many men in his life.

"Look, Lurd! Look!" he whispered happily, shaking his companion.

She stirred and looked at him with bleary, uncomprehending eyes. Glug grinned and pointed.

"Look at men!" he said, "Many men! Much more than two! Maybe three! They find Treasure!"

Lurd peered over the rock and watched the men for a long time. She remained very quiet.

"Quiet!" she said sharply. "Come with me!"

She took him by the hand and led him out of the alcove. Silently, they crawled toward the cavern. At the opening, Lurd slid Glug into a niche into the wall, then slid in beside him.

The men stood very close at hand.

"Hold onto stick!" Lurd said, "No let go!"

Glug didn't, though he stood mesmerized by the glittering treasure. It filled the room in rounded piles each taller than the last. Each pile sparkled in showers of silver and gold. Some held brightly-colored gems as well. On top of the pile in the center, sat a great clear bowl that sparkled more than anything else in the room. Glug wondered if it was a stew bowl.

One of the men shouted something that Glug didn't understand. The other men cheered, and they all ran headlong toward the glimmering piles of wealth.

Then it happened.

There came a hiss like the sun falling into the sea,

and out of the cracks of the floor oozed a thing like running tar. Its flesh glistened wetly in the torchlight, and its body lay covered in loose scales fashioned from stone. Hundreds of luminous eyes like moonstones dotted its skin, and great silvery teeth lined its wicked grinning maw. It reared above them all, towering in the high cavern like a wave waiting to crash.

The men stopped dead and stared.

They ran.

With a lightning flash, the thing had one, and then another, rending them with its teeth and crushing them with the weight of its stone scales. It grasped them with tentacles and dangled them above its mouth. It hurled them screaming into the cavern walls. Men collided with piles of treasure. Men fell broken to the floor. The thing scooped up their bodies, peeled off their armor, and swallowed them whole. The floor became a mess of helmets, pickaxes, mail shirts and hammers.

The creature reared its head and made a deep, hideous noise like a laugh. It shook the caverns. Then it sank—into cracks, into shadows, Glug could not say— back down to the deep, dark places where all the things without names dwell.

When all was silent Lurd pried free of the niche, and Glug followed. Nothing moved in the cavern.

Finally, Glug said, "Look at great stuff! Me got rock breaking stick!"

He hefted a pickax and scooped up a helmet to put on his head.

Lurd called out. "Good Treasure! Good Monster! Thank you!"

A final rumble came from the deep.

Glug smiled, "Treasure good pet."

They gathered the men's things and went home to eat stew.

Catch of the Day
Jean Rabe

"This is an art, and I am an artist."

"One with no paint in his pot!" This was punctuated by a loud, derisive snort and a sharp slap on the thigh. "Have you ever fished before, Redge?"

"Shhh! You'll scare 'em away." Redge swung his skinny legs over the bank and scooted forward just enough so his toes could stretch down to wriggle in the pleasantly cool water of the Gold River.

A pale gray mist hung over most of the river, early-morning finery that the rising sun was attempting to chase away. It obscured the opposite bank, cloaking the thick roots of the shaggybarks that stretched deep into the cool water and hiding a pair of nested bluebirds which were singing. It also concealed the occasional fish that somewhere cleared the surface and returned with a soft splash.

Redge's small fingers gripped a polished cane pole and with a motion so deft he surprised himself, he jerked the rod back, then forward, the line that was tied to the tip arcing gracefully toward the center of the narrow river. The lure landed in the mist with an almost imperceptible plop.

"How you supposed to catch any, Redge, if you can't see . . .?"

"I can see you, Molay," Redge returned. He stared at his yellow-skinned companion, who'd settled behind him, and he reached a clawed hand back to tug playfully on his friend's stubby horn.

Molay grinned, revealing a row of needle-fine pointed teeth the shade of dying birch leaves. Molay was a kobold, a diminutive goblinoid creature with a face that was vaguely human, though it looked more like a cross between an overlarge lizard and a rat, with a smattering of bristly brown whiskers sprouting from his leathery bottom jaw. His skin was a mix of hide and scales, dotted with warts the color of mud, and his eyes were tiny and bright red, practically glowing like hot coals despite the thick brow that attempted to shadow them. The kobold's snout looked oddly stunted, as if he'd compacted it by running into an unyielding object, the nose shiny black and dripping something green. And his horns . . . they were perhaps his best feature, smooth and shiny with the dampness from the mist.

Redge looked nearly Molay's twin, save his skin, which was a shade darker—the hue of rotting yellow apples. On close inspection, a peppering of gray could be seen among the bristles that sprouted from the bottom of his jaw. And his brown ratlike tail was a few inches longer than Molay's—though that couldn't be noticed when it was curled tight, like it was now.

Redge nodded respectfully toward the river. "The gods invented fishing, you know."

Molay gave him a quizzical look.

"Havahook, god of the seas and rivers and of all the fishes. I'd worship him, I'm certain, if he was still here."

"That's Habbakuk, Redge."

Redge wriggled his nose and huffed, a sound like dry leaves rustling together. He pulled back on the cane pole until the tip touched the grass behind him, then he flipped it to the right and forward several feet, plopping the lure in a different, closer spot, where he could watch it sink this time. The water was dark, perhaps because it was deep or because the sun hadn't yet touched it or because it was shadowed by the massive oak that clung to the bank and stretched its great limbs over the water.

An impressive spiderweb, damp with the mist, spread from the lowest branch to a rotting log lodged in the bank. Molay stretched toward the log and snatched up a fat grub, sucking the wriggling thing into his mouth with a smacking sound and quickly swallowing it.

"I'm hungry again, Redge." Molay's stomach snarled as if to punctuate the sentiment.

Redge tipped his head back, indicating a large shad-blow bush a few yards behind the pair. A swarm of blue bottle flies buzzed around it, some landing on a worn boot that peeked out from beneath the bottommost branch. "Plenty more gully dwarf over there, Molay."

The young kobold spat a gob of something viscous into the river. "Big one was too tough, Redge. Yuck. Can't get the taste outta my mouth."

"The little one was good, though, wasn't he?"

Molay nodded. "Wasn't much meat on him, though. I'm hungry, Redge." The young kobold picked at a wart on his cheek and scratched his stomach. "Maybe we shouldn't've been so quick to kill them gully dwarfs. Maybe we should have watched them do some magic, first. Maybe we should've let them catch the fish for us."

Redge made a face. "Don't need no stupid gully dwarfs to catch us some fish to eat. Weren't you listening to them?"

Molay didn't answer, he was watching the spot where the line cut into the river, licking his lips in wistful anticipation.

"Well, *I* was listenin' good, Molay. Them gully dwarfs said this fishing pole and lure was magical. They went on for quite some time about it, chatting to each other all the while we was sneakin' up on 'em. We don't need no gully dwarfs. We got the magic right here!"

Molay's stomach rumbled again.

"The big one said the lure was passed down from his gran'father, and that the little one was gonna get it passed down to him one day after he was dead. Course he is dead and that ain't happening now, Havahook be praised." Redge jiggled the end of the line. "Now it'll get passed down to you—after it catches me lots of fish."

Molay skeptically raised an eyebrow.

"Do you doubt it?"

"Redge, maybe before we killed and ate them we should've asked them gully dwarfs how to use that magical lure."

"Shuddup," Redge scowled. "How hard can it be? It's just a matter of time before I get me a big fish."

When the older kobold pulled the pole back again, Molay's clawed hand shot out, grabbing the line and lifting it up. "I want to get me a good look at this magical lure, Redge."

Molay cupped the thing in his leathery palm. The lure was roughly the size of an ogre's thumb, segmented in the middle, the sections held together with a gleaming silver link. One half was painted blood red, the color slick and glossy. Two blue beads with black centers were affixed to it, mimicking eyes. The other half was painted sun-bright yellow and had a thin green squiggle on what passed for its stomach. It had a tail, a collection of downy feathers from a bluejay, surrounding a longer gray feather that had likely come from a hawk. And there was something inside the thing that made it heavy enough to sink and that rattled when Molay shook his hand.

"What's that, Redge?" Molay pointed to the green squiggle.

"It's writing. Secret writing. Magic writing."

"Maybe it's the name of one of them gully dwarfs." On either end of the squiggle gleaming silver hooks hung, each with four wicked-looking barbs that sparkled.

Redge shook his head. "It's not a name. It's a rune or whatnot. Magical writing. The writing . . . well . . . it tells the thing what it's supposed to do. Like in this case: catch fish."

"Why haven't we caught any fish yet, Redge?"

Redge whipped the tip of the pole back again, jerking the lure out of Molay's hand. "Magic takes time, is all. You gotta have patience. Everybody knows that about magic."

"I'm really hungry." Molay reached for a canvas satchel that sat behind Redge, throwing open the flap and peering inside. There was a collection of lures all nicely separated by thin wooden slats. Some looked like plump beetles, but were painted unnatural colors—pinks and pale blues, bright greens and white with purple spots. There were a few that resembled dragon-flies and horseflies, and strips of leather that looked a bit like nightcrawlers. Others looked like no insect the young kobold had ever seen. One that caught his eye was vaguely frog-shaped, green and spotted black. It didn't have any legs, but it had a tail of tiny yellow feathers. The young kobold flipped it over to make sure there was no magical writing on the bottom. Then he worried the two hooks free and popped the lure in his mouth. He crunched it quickly, swallowed, and chewed thoughtfully. Then with a grimace he closed the satchel again and nudged it away.

His stomach rumbled louder, and he glanced back at the bush, considered for a moment trying another piece of the big gully dwarf. Redge hadn't touched the nose. Maybe the nose wouldn't be so tough. Maybe. . . . Molay's beady eyes narrowed as he saw the bush move. "There were only two of them gully dwarfs, right Redge?"

Redge nodded, though the gesture was lost on the younger kobold, who was transfixed by the big bush. "Yup, two. We killed 'em quick. Gutted both of 'em, first thing. Ate 'em quick, too."

Molay stood, shifting back and forth in his new boots, then took a tentative step toward the bush. "Dead. Dead. Dead. Both of 'em!" His mouth fell open when a head appeared behind and well above the leaves, an arm following it to bat at the blue bottle flies.

"Redge—"

The older kobold dismissed the interruption with a wave of his clawed hand, brought the pole back and flicked the line again, this time trying to place the lure in the shadowed water under the spiderweb.

"Redge . . .."

"Shhh. You'll scare the fishes."

"Something's about to scare *us*."

Redge finally turned, just as two other heads joined the first. They snarled in unison and stepped out from behind the bush.

"Bugbears!" Redge exclaimed, slowly pulling the line back to the shore and carefully laying down the pole.

The three creatures were roughly seven feet tall—more than twice the height of the kobolds. Coarse brick-red hair sprouted haphazardly from mottled yellow-brown hide. They were nearly humanoid, looking like a cross between an overlarge goblin and an ogre, and smelling worse than either. Redge found himself staring at the center one's nose, which resembled the snout of a bear.

Bear-snout's lips curled up, showing a row of jagged yellow teeth, and he growled.

"Redge. . . ." Molay's word came out as a thin squeak.

"Help yourself to some gully dwarf to eat," Redge began, gesturing exaggeratedly to the big bush and pointing a slender finger at the fly-dotted boots. "We only ate the little one. There's plenty left."

Bear-snout growled again, a sound that was echoed by his two companions. Then he thumped his chest, which was broad and heaving.

"Wh-wh-what do you think they want, Redge?"

"What do you *think* they want?" the older kobold softly retorted. Lowering his voice further, he added, "Us. If you was a bugbear would you eat stringy gully dwarf when there's a couple of juicy. . . ."

"Magic." This from the tallest of the bugbears, the one who looked the most formidable of the trio because his right ear was jagged from a fight and because of the numerous thick scars that crisscrossed his chest.

Scar-chest was striding forward now and leaving his fellows at the bush. He was the only one wearing clothes, an old, faded red tunic that was ripped down the front to accommodate his large frame. "Magic lure you waz talkin' about. Me want that."

The other two growled and made a series of barking sounds, hinting that they only spoke bugbear or that they were letting Scar-chest do the talking for them. Scar-chest glowered at the kobolds, then grinned, a trail of spittle running from his bottom lip and stretching to the ground.

Redge ground his heel into the earth, puffed out his chest, and met his stare. "What magic lure?" he bluffed.

"The one on the end o' that stick."

Molay's fingers were nervously fluttering. "Let's give it to them, Redge. Maybe they'll leave us alone."

Redge swallowed hard when the tall one took a step closer. The blue bottle flies left the gully dwarf corpse and swarmed around the approaching bugbear. Scarchest didn't bother to swat them away. A series of barks and Bear-snout moved forward, too. The third bugbear, which had one eye, was poking in the bush and prodding the gully dwarf corpse.

"Well . . . I suppose you can have this old stick," Redge offered. He glanced at Molay, who was shivering. *Run!* Redge mouthed. Then he spun on his heels and headed toward the river, leaping off the bank and belly-flopping with a splash. Small arms and legs pumped rapidly, as he awkwardly swam as fast as he could toward the other side.

At the same time, Molay darted inland at an angle, but in his panic he tripped over his own feet and went flying. His small hands clawed at the ground, then he felt himself being lifted. An instant later he was face to face with Bear-snout. The young kobold gagged and practically passed out from the stench of the bugbear's fetid breath.

"Redge! Help me, Redge!"

One hand clamped on the scruff of the screaming kobold's neck, Bear-snout reached the other around to the top of Molay's head and gave a twist and a yank. Then Bear-snout sat and began to feast on his prize as his fellows trundled toward the bank.

*   *   *   *   *

Nearly all of the mist had burned off, revealing the river as a gently curving blue ribbon that reached to the east and west as far as the bugbears could see.

So smooth on this still Yurthgreen day, it mirrored the clouds and merrily sparkled gold here and there.

Perhaps it was the river's ability to catch pieces of the sun and hold them, wildly shimmering for long heartbeats, that had birthed its name. About eighty miles south of Palanthas, the Gold River cut through the Vingaard Mountains that virtually ringed the famed city and meandered into the Plains of Solamnia, almost paralleling the course of the Knight's High Road.

Bear-snout glanced at the mountains, the peaks white with the last remnants of what had been a brutal winter. The sunlight glared off the snow and he squinted. Somewhere out of sight, bluebirds were singing, and he allowed several minutes to slip by as he listened to them. There was a hint of lilac in the air, and he inhaled deep.

A curt growl broke the mood.

"No. Me first. I try fishing. It was my idea." Scarchest gripped the pole and held it up so his one eyed companion could ogle the lure. "Magic!" After he too scrutinized it a moment, he added softly, "Looks like a bug, don't it?" He shook the lure, hearing it rattle. Then he perched on the bank and dangled his long legs over the side, the water coming up to his knees. He gripped the pole awkwardly, as it was uncomfortably small for his long fingers.

There was a series of growls from One-eye, and from Bear-snout who was stuffing his maw with chunks of Molay.

"Me knows all about magic. Me learned from watching them kobolds."

One-eye snarled and glanced back and forth between the pole and his Bear-snouted companion, who hurried to finish the last of the little kobold. Then One-eye settled himself next to Scar-chest and pretended to study the river.

The older kobold was climbing up the opposite bank and scrambling toward the cover of the trees. He looked across the river ruefully and then rushed off, almost comical in his awkwardness.

Scar-chest was happily attempting to plop the lure into the river. Instead, he managed to wrap the line around his forearm, and he yelped when the hooks of the lure bit deep into his flesh. His two companions made a cackling sound, as he tore the lure free and struggled to unwrap himself.

Bear-snout cackled louder and brushed by him. He stepped into the river to wash the kobold blood from his claws and face.

"Get out of the water! You scare fish!" the tall one ordered. He'd managed to untwist the line from his arm only to get his fingers tangled in it. He howled in frustration and contorted his head and shoulders down to the line, trying to bite at it to free his hand.

Bear-snout ignored him and waded out deeper, until the river swirled about his hips. He paused while the water stilled around him, then he bent slightly, edging his big hands beneath the surface. He held his breath and waited.

Scar-chest struggled harder, the line cutting into his flesh and drawing blood.

Finally, One-eye turned to help.

"Hold it there," One-eye instructed. "Now pull." Scar-chest howled, but a moment more and he was free. He wiped his big hands on his tunic, took a couple of deep breaths, and reached for the pole again. But before he could get the line in the water, Bear-snout was trudging back to shore, a big trout held out in front of him.

"We fish like men!" cried Scar-chest. Rising, and still holding the pole in one hand, Scar-chest batted the fish away. It fell onto the bank, wriggling. The two other bugbears argued in their guttural growling language and dove on the flopping trout, shredding it with their claws. Guts and scaly-skin flew as they hurriedly devoured it, the last bone swallowed just as the tall bug-bear had managed to settle himself again and get the magical lure into the water.

Scar-chest let the lure just dangle below the surface, not moving the pole, scarcely breathing, waiting for the magic to take effect. He stared at the water, so clear he could see several feet down. It wasn't deep close to the bank, where he preferred to fish, and he could easily make out the pebble-covered bottom, which looked a bit like the hide of the beaded lizards he was fond of eating. He spotted several crawfish ambling over the pebbles, and he fought the urge to bend over and snatch one.

Behind him, One-eye and Bear-snout grew bored and turned their attention to the gully dwarf corpse. They tugged the stiff body out from underneath the bush, not bothering to swat away the flies. Bear-snout turned up his muzzle and made it clear he wasn't interested in eating the thing—not yet anyway. One-eye gave it a try by sampling the bulbous nose. He spit out the flesh with a growl and began searching the body's clothes for trin-kets and sweets. When they discovered nothing but dead nightcrawlers, hooks, a spool of line, and a couple of pieces of red and white-painted corks, they shoved the body back under the bush and returned to the river, intent on wading in and grabbing another fish.

"No!" Scar-chest barked. "We fish like men!"

"You fish like idiots!" This from behind the trio of bugbears.

The three bugbears turned.

"Id-eee-uhts," a second voice parroted. A form fol-lowed the voice out of the woods, two voices and one body far bigger than any of the bugbears. "Want to try magic," the second voice continued. "I like magic."

"An ettin," Scar-chest snorted. He sat the pole on the bank and shuffled toward the visitor, his two fellows following close behind.

The ettin had two heads extending from a thick neck that sat in the middle of his massive shoulders. Otherwise he had the form of a giant man, pale-skinned and muscular, with a hairy chest and hairy legs. Even the tops of his bare feet were covered with hair. One head had a hawk-shaped nose perched above a long black mustache. The other head, looking similar save for its pug-nose, had a bushy black beard that hung down one side of its chest, thinning to a twisting hank just above the top of a deer-skin loincloth. The giant's left hand reached up to stroke the beard, an almost thoughtful gesture. The other hand was concealed behind its back.

"Ettin ain't gettin' the fishin' stick," the tall bugbear growled. With that he charged, snarling and snapping as he closed the distance. He didn't need to issue a verbal invitation to his fellows, they were fast and close on his hairy heels.

One-eye growled the loudest, claws raking the air. Bear-snout hooted and dropped his head, meaning to ram the ettin's belly. Both were several steps behind their tall scarred companion, however.

"Squash bug," the bearded ettin head said. "Like squash."

In a graceful movement that seemed incongruous with appearance, the ettin drew its right hand from behind its back, revealing that it held a huge log. Sweeping the arm forward, the end of the log connected with the tall bugbear's head and forced it back with a sickening pop. The bugbear fell heavily, and the ettin stepped forward to meet the two remaining creatures.

One-eye paused to regard his dead friend for only an instant, then he darted in and raked the giant's belly, dropping beneath a second swing of the log. Jumping back as Bear-snout barreled forward, One-eye whirled to the ettin's side. It appeared that the two bugbears were used to fighting in tandem. And for a moment their practiced routine of dash in and strike, jump back and shift around, worked.

The ettin found himself bleeding from a dozen deep gashes, his loincloth stained red and blood running down his legs. The head with the beard cried as One-eye darted in again, this time raking his broad back with sharp bugbear claws.

"Ow!"

"Quiet!" the head with the mustache shouted. "Turn!" The giant two-headed creature spun, whirling the log and catching Bear-snout on the side of the head. Momentarily stunned, the bugbear wobbled and couldn't get out of the way when the second head took over. "Kick!" The giant's right leg shot up, the knee striking the bugbear's jaw and cracking it.

At the same time, One-eye came at the ettin from behind once more, gouging the the giant's back.

"Ow, bug hurt!"

"Step, kick!" the head with the mustache bellowed again. In response, the giant's right leg shot up, the heel landing against Bear-snout's stomach and stunning him. The bugbear crumpled and the giant trundled forward, jamming his foot down on the bugbear's back, the force snapping his spine.

"Squash bug. Like squash. Ow!"

One-eye jumped up to claw at the Ettin's shoulders.

"Drop club!" The giant's right hand released the log. "Turn!" The massive body pivoted, facing One-eye. "Grab!"

Both hands shot out, snaring the remaining bugbear and pulling it close against the ettin's stomach. The giant squeezed the bugbear until it suffocated. Releasing the body, the giant stepped over it and headed down to the river.

* * * * *

The sun was setting, painting the Gold River a fiery bronze that managed to captivate both of the ettin's heads. The water looked like molten metal shimmering wildly in the slight breeze. It was shot through with fingers of black, the lengthening shadows of the shaggy-bark trees stretching outward from the opposite bank.

The birds had stopped chirping several minutes ago, settling down for the approaching evening. From somewhere along the bank frogs started to croak, their throaty tones long and deep and musical.

The sun dropped lower, its rays brushing the massive spiderweb that spread between the shaggybark and the rotting log. As the orange spread from the edges to the center, huddling spiders began to stir. One crawled almost tentatively to the edge, where it hung suspended, reflected in the water's surface. The spider paused there, then suddenly started inward again. Too late! A fat trout rose, all but its tail clearing the water. Curved jaws snapping, rainbow colors glimmering wetly in the setting sun, the fish skillfully plucked the spider from the web, swallowed it, and disappeared beneath the surface.

"Wow." The head with the beard stated.

"Bend." The ettin picked up the fishing pole with its right hand and held it up so that both pairs of eyes could admire the polished smoothness of the cane. It was so small, and yet the giant's hand held it gently. The left hand fluttered down the line and reached the lure, cupped it almost reverently and turned it over.

"What's that writing?" This from the bearded head.

"A signature," the other noted, eyes fixed on the green squiggle. "No doubt, of the sorcerer who crafted it. Closer. Closer. Yes. A famous sorcerer. One of Krynn's greatest, brother. I've heard of him. It was fortunate for us that we came across a thing so fine. Sit."

The ettin slumped down on the bank, both heads groaning slightly as the cuts from the bugbears were jarred a little by the movement.

"Ow."

"We should tend to our injuries, brother. But first . . ."

The right hand drew the pole back, until the tip touched the ground over his shoulder, then with a quick motion, he cast forward, the line flying out and the lure landing and plopping below the surface. He passed it to the left hand, which began moving the pole back and forth, making the tip bend prettily as the segmented lure wiggled with the motion.

"I am convinced, brother, that there is no finer way to pass a spring day than to fish. The air is so sweet next to this wonderful river. The water so cool."

"Cool," the bearded head parroted.

The left hand brought the pole back, passing it to the right for another cast. This time when the lure arced away and toward the spot shaded by the oak, the water dripping from the line caught the sun and formed a miniature rainbow. The pole was passed back to the left.

"I think the gods must have invented fishing, brother. Indeed, I—"

Both heads turned to stare at the left hand. A plump brown spider had found its way from the web and was skittering up the ettin's long, muscled arm.

"Ow. Bit us."

"Indeed." The left hand quivered and shook, the fingers releasing the pole. "Dear brother, I think it's . . ."

". . . poison," the bearded head finished.

The ettin pitched forward into the river with a loud splash.

The water was darker under the overhanging limbs of the great oak. Darker and deeper. As the two-headed giant sank beneath the surface, the cane pole began to move away from the bank. Slowly at first, as if the abandoned rod were floating with the current, it drifted away from the great tree and its web. Then it seemed to stop and turn around and pick up speed as it moved in the other direction.

Lost Causes
Nancy Varian Berberick

Well, I never saw a homelier girl than that rawboned
creature sitting on the edge of the deeply cushioned sofa
in Usha Majere's reception room. Her big hands she
folded carefully on her lap, you could imagine she'd
arranged each finger, one by one, to hide the knobby
knuckles. Her hair hung poker-straight and it was the
color of mud puddles. She had a long horsey face; unfortunately, with teeth to match. I don't say these things to
be cruel, but the drabness of the girl was actually startling, surprising because everything, everyone, around
her was so lovely.

She is an artist, Lady Usha, a woman whose portraits
are much sought-after. The least of them is valued for its
execution, the fairest and the rarest—well, those you tell
stories about. She surrounds herself with paintings and
sculptures and weavings from all around Krynn. Artists
are like that, hungry for beauty, for color and shape and
texture. Lady Usha, whose husband is the premier mage
of Krynn, does not suffer for lack of what she loves.
These collections, however, were but backdrop for the
jewel that is the lady herself. If songs ever lied about the
charms of Usha Majere, they lied only in that they did
not praise her beauty highly enough. Ah, it was a lovely
place, the lady's chamber, and were her artifacts and the

lady herself not enough resplendence for one parlor, two elves kept watch just inside the doorway, one facing outward to the corridor, one inward. They had the same beauty it seems all their kind receive as a birthright, elegantly canted ears, shining golden hair, lithe limbs and long eyes as clear as starlight. Among all this splendor sat the drab girl.

"There you are," said Lady Usha, holding out her hand to me. "Come in, Madoc. Here are people I want you to meet."

Tarya was the elfwoman's name, Raethe her companion's. Raethe didn't so much as nod to me when introductions were made. Tarya looked at me with winter eyes. "Madoc ap Westhos," she said. "Yes, I know your father."

Thus, the winter eyes. For if she knew my kin who live out in Sancrist, no doubt she'd heard one or another of them go on at length about the dismal matter of Madoc, our father's lastborn son who turned aside a knighthood for magehood, then failed to use his sorcerous skills to benefit the knights. Well, that's what they'd tell you, those brothers and sisters of mine. I'll tell you this: He was an old man, my father, and like so many of his generation, dedicated to lost causes and lost gods. He remembered the time before the Chaos War, before the vanishing of gods and the coming of the dragons who portioned out most of Krynn among themselves. He believed that Solamnia, the old borders shrunken by a dragon's will, could be restored to its former glory, that Qualinesti and Nordmaar and the lands round Thorbardin be restored to freedom, ay, that all of Krynn could become a world of Free Realms again. He wanted his children to embrace this lost cause with the same fervor he did. Both my brothers joined the knighthood, and my two sisters each married a knight, eager to rear sons to feed the fight. Living in the past, dying in the present, it was a fool's game. Me, I wasn't of a mind to throw away a decent talent in sorcery so poets could stir the hearts of the foolish with one more doleful tale of a life flung into the breach.

A knight's errant son, not on the borders; a knight's son, not in the underground. A knight's disgrace, said elven Tarya's cold blue eyes. To Lady Usha, she said, "Is there no other you could have chosen than—" Her pretty lip curled in disgust."—this one ?"

The lady smiled, as though nothing unpleasant had passed between her guests. "Madoc is the very man I require, Tarya. Imperfect, as it seems you've noticed, but he has some notable skill as a diviner and a pyromancer. Yes, I think he's probably the man for the job."

Diviner, I am, but not so bold as to attempt to divine the thoughts of Lady Usha Majere, and so I was left wondering whether I'd been handed a complement or something less as she guided me to the center of the room to stand before the homely girl. "Here is Aline Caroel. She is soon going to be married, away down in Haven. Aline," she said, her voice softened into motherly tones. "My dear, this is Madoc ap Westhos, the mage of whom I spoke."

Aline glanced up long enough to acknowledge the introduction, then lowered her lashes again. Long enough, and too long. Madoc Diviner they call me, and for good reason. I know how to tiptoe into your mind when it pleases me and leave not the least hint that I'd been there. In Aline Caroel's mind, for that one moment her eyes were unveiled, I saw sudden panic, then swiftly imposed calm.

"I am pleased to meet you, sir mage," she murmured. Ah, the poor thing, her voice was as rough and nasal as a boy with the ague. "And I thank you for your assistance."

I raised a brow, not to her but to Lady Usha, who did not hasten to reply. She seated me in a comfortable chair near the window that looks down upon the campus of her husband's academy.

"Now," said the lady. "Aline spoke a little beforehand, but she expresses my hope: I have a little job for you, Madoc, and if you take it I'll see your bar tabs paid in Solace." She hesitated, tapping her finger against her white teeth, then smiled. "Yes, the bar tabs, and if all goes well, you'll have more besides."

The bar tabs, long as my arm, would have been enough, the promise of more besides made me answer her yes before thinking much more about it. Having my agreement, she inclined her head, a simple nod. I didn't see her move in any other way, yet the two elves grimly guarding her doorway bowed to her, more deeply than one would imagine elves bowing to anyone not of their kindred, and left the chamber. Lady Usha's skirts whispered as she went to sit on the sofa beside Aline. She held something small and silver, a coffer about the length of her hand, perfectly square, with a little silver latch snapped into place. I felt a little tug, looking at it, a nudge deep down in my mind. The coffer itself was not magical, but the stirring in my mind told me that what it held was.

"This coffer," said the lady, "contains a gift. And yes," said she who had been around mages for many years and knew what one looks like when he has his ears up. "The gift has qualities. That's why I've called you here, Madoc." She held up the coffer to watch . . . the sunlight slide on the silver. "This contains a thing that must not fall into the wrong hands, and who better to carry magic than a mage? It is for Aline to present to her husband on their wedding night." A little flutter, the white hands of Aline Caroel rearranged themselves into a tighter clasp.

Lady Usha covered those two hands with her own. To me, just as though no one had moved, she said, "Until the moment it is presented, this gift must be guarded. Will you carry it safely for me, Madoc?"

Still thinking of the bar tabs and the more that might be, I said, "My lady, when do we leave?"

"Soon." She glanced at Aline who lifted her lashes again to look at me.

"In the morning tomorrow, sir mage," Aline Caroel said. "We will take a south-running way."

I frowned. "There are no roads running south out of Solace to Haven. The road runs north around Darken Wood."

Aline nodded. "And the rivers run south around Darken Wood."

"You'd travel along the Qualinesti border?" I smiled, as you do at a child. "Right along the edge of a dragon's realm? Are you so eager for your groom?"

Her knobby knuckles whitened a little. "We are going south, sir mage, because the Sentinel Gap is blocked by a rock slide. I doubt there'll be a way round the north of Darken Wood till spring."

No way north, and only fools would travel through Darken Wood. She didn't say that, and she didn't have to. More folk went in there these days than came out.

Aline rose, smoothing the skirt of her blue gown. "My lady," she murmured, "Will you excuse me now? I want to rest."

Lady Usha excused her graciously, handing her over to the elves. When we two were alone, I said, "My lady, I'm wondering why this human girl is so closely warded by elves."

"Because I have asked the elves to guard her, they come to guard her." She sat a moment silent, then: "Madoc, you're too young to remember the time before the Chaos War, but I do remember. I remember when the Knights ruled Solamnia, when the elves of Qualinesti did not live under a dragon's heel and the dwarves of Thorbardin held their gates open to friends. Many of us in the Free Realms still remember when all of Krynn was free, and many of us work for the day when it will be again."

Lost causes, I thought, but I didn't say so.

"What will save us?" she said, musing. "Who can tell? The Knights in your homeland? Some think so. My husband puts his faith in the mages here in Abanasinia." She lifted the small silver coffer, tracing the space of needle-thin darkness where the lid met the case, firmly latched. "I put my faith in heroes less grand. They are like the stars in the sky, Madoc, these small heroes. One alone sheds little light. All together make the night lovely. Aline Caroel is one of those stars upon which one's hope may hang. She is the granddaughter of Galt Caroel. Do you know the name?"

I didn't, and she told me Aline's grandfather was a wealthy man, a rich merchant who had made his fortune before the Chaos War. He'd managed to keep that fortune even in the disastrous years after the war when the dragons came to carve up the most of Krynn among them. His only son had wed young and fathered a daughter, but the son and his wife died in a boating accident, leaving Aline to be raised up by a grandfather who had dedicated his riches to subsidizing the network of spies that slipped in and out of the various Dragon Realms, and to the underground efforts to bring refugees out of the Dragon Realms to freedom.

Galt Caroel was now, said Lady Usha, poor as a mouse at winter's end, his fortune spent, his schemes soon to go unfunded, starved for lack of money. But a way had been found, discovered in a marriage pact

between the House of Caroel and that of his longtime
rival on the battlefields of enterprise, the House of
Wrackham. Aline would marry Lir Wrackham, join the
two competing houses and, for that concession, funds
would again flow to support the spies and the secret
dark-moon flights of refugees from the Dragon Realms.
Their deal struck, the old coin-counter and the girl's
grandfather waited in Haven for her now.

"I wish," Usha said upon a lovely sigh, "that I could
go with Aline, but I dare not. My presence would call
attention to the journey and the wedding." She spoke of
spies, secret men and women slipping in and out
of Abanasinia from the dragon lands, men and women
in thrall to any one of the deadly dragons who guarded
their stolen realms so jealously.

"Too much attention would be dangerous, Madoc,
for there are those who are happy enough these days to
think Galt Caroel's work is at an end. But if Aline can
go safely to Haven, well, his work won't end, will it?"

"That's a hard bargain to make, my lady. Especially for
a girl—" I stopped, and then shrugged. "Well, she's not
going to win the old man's heart with her beauty, is she?"

"No," said the lady, "she is under no illusions about
that." She balanced the silver coffer on her pretty hand,
looking at me long from sea-colored eyes. "And I am
giving her the help she asks for. But there are other
things than beauty of face or form, Madoc."

I cocked a crooked grin. "Among them, perhaps, a
vial filled with a love potion, or a small charm to turn
an old man's heart? Is that the kind of magic concealed
in your little silver coffer? Well," I said, giving her back
her earlier words, "I will endeavor to be the perfect
man for this task. I'll see your gift safely to Haven." I
swept her a bow, the kind one of my knightly kin might
make. "For you, my lady, and your lost causes."

Usha turned that bright blue gaze on me again and, in a sweep of silk skirts and lavender scent, she rose and she kissed my cheek.

"Come back after the wedding." She tapped my shoulder with one elegant finger. "With your bar bills paid, you can treat me to supper in Solace while you tell me what Madoc Diviner has divined from his trip."

* * * * *

I didn't pack much for the trip to Haven, naught but a book on pyromancy I'd been studying and a change of clothes for the marriage feast. These I shoved into a small canvas scrip and took with me to Crystalmir Lake the next morning, there to meet Aline and her traveling party. Eight elves accompanied her, six of them boatmen to tend the small skiff, two of them Tarya and Raethe armed with bristling quivers and strung bows. No provision for privacy or comfort had been made on the boat for any but Aline, who had a small tent of blue and gold striped canvas for a bride's bower.

We left the lake when the sun banished the morning mists, and entered Solace Stream beneath the bridge connecting the road round Solace to the one running north around Darken Wood. The stream was so narrow in the morning hours of our journey that the tall oaks stood like walls of wood and bronze leaves, the willows lining the banks hung like curtains drifting in the slightest breeze. Asters nodded in patches of sunlight, their thin leaves dark, their flowers blue as a faded sky. My scrip near to hand, I drowsed in the warming sun.

In half-sleep, I heard the cry of kingfishers, the rough voices of the boatmen—"Steer left of that log. Watch out for that rising stone. Ai! Look out for the shoal!"—and I heard Tarya speaking in low elven tones to Raethe. They spoke of the bandits in Darken Wood and, sometimes, in tones even quieter, of Qualinesti, the lost homeland. Lost causes, I thought, drifting on the edge of sleep. Defeats unacknowledged, useless striving . . .

A hand touched my arm lightly. I looked up into the long, homely face of Aline Caroel. She cleared her throat self-consciously, once and then again, before she announced that I'd slept past noon then asked whether I was hungry. When I told her I was, she reached behind and took bread from a little sack, and cold meat and a leather wine flask.

"Will these do for a nooning?"

They would, and I spun out one of those airy courtesies we of the knightly houses learn in our cradles. Ah well, why not? How much of that had the homely girl heard in her time? I told her all would taste better if she shared the meal with me. Behind her the elf Raethe murmured to golden Tarya. That one lifted her head and gave me good view of her hard cold eyes.

"Oh, don't worry about Tarya," said Aline, settling near me. Near, but not close. She kept the homely girl's distance, the distance she'd no doubt learned to judge early. Pretty girls settle close, they lean near to tease and flirt, but homely girls, horse-faced girls whose teeth are too large, whose hands are knob-knuckled, those girls learn early their place. She cleared her throat self-consciously. "She takes her work very seriously, and she's afraid every moment that I'll jump over the side of the skiff and swim away."

That much I knew, but something I didn't. "Should she be?"

"No. Promises have been made, and one of them is mine." Aline lowered her eyes again. "I am," she whispered, "pleased to be going to my marriage."

Liar, I thought, who carried a charm she had begged

from Lady Usha. I thought so, but saw no reason to say so.

Aline passed me the flask while she broke off portions of bread and sliced two fat cuts from the chunk of peppered venison. We ate in silence, observed by Tarya as though by a keen-eyed old duenna fearing for the integrity of her charge. The current ran slow, it only needed two boatmen with poles fore and aft to guide us now. Oarsmen passed flasks around and tossed each other little sacks of food. Only Raethe and Tarya seemed uninterested in eating. Bows strung, quivers at the hip, the elves watched the shadows and the overhanging willows.

The banks slid by, the oarsmen returned to their work as the current freshened. We passed Gateway and turned a little east. Soon the Solace Stream widened and joined the Whiterush River, and the wood fell away, replaced on both sides by flat moorlands, treeless expanses where autumn's sun shone hotter and brighter. Aline looked past me, westward to the line of low hills and Darken Wood. Beyond those hills lay the Dryad Forests, the oak wood where live the trees and the dryad sprits who inhabit them.

"Have you ever heard a dryad sing?" she asked, eyes on the shadowed wood.

"No. I've never been in Darken Wood. And dryads don't come out."

She sighed. "Oak tree and dryad, one cannot live without the other, so says legend. They're as entwined as soul and body." A flush crept across her cheeks. Not a lovely rosy blush, not for Aline. Her cheek went mottled, red and blotchy. "I wonder," she said, "if that's what it's like to be in love?"

I told her I didn't know if love is like dryads and oaks and she laughed. "You? Not know? I've heard some things about you, sir mage." She shrugged her cloak from her shoulders and let it spill onto the deck. "Tarya says all the barmaids in Solace know you."

"All? Not true. A few of them do, but that's not love."

She didn't have her eyes on me, she watched past me, looking at the river running. "What is it then?"

"Happy exercise."

The mottled color of her cheeks deepened and in that moment she seemed not merely homely but ugly, all jaw and startling over bite.

"Aline!" called one of the elves, Raethe with his strung bow in hand. Aline looked around on a quick breath, startled. "Come forward and sit in the middle of the skiff. It's safer there."

She gathered up the remains of the meal and went to obey. In moments, two of the boatmen came to her and began to roll down the four sides of her little canvas chamber. Soft, a step behind me. Tarya stood, her shadow fell dark on the deck. Her lips pulled a mirthless grin as she squatted beside me.

"Mage," she said, her voice pitched for only us to hear. "I'll tell you something: The girl is meant for better things."

"Better than an old man in Haven? I don't—"

Tarya leaned suddenly close, her blue eyes steely. "Better things than a dalliance, mage." She drew my eye to her dagger, her fingers tapping on the bone handle. "Better things than you, Madoc ap Westhos."

I laughed, heads turned. Tarya never moved. "Me? For pity's sake, woman, do you think I'd steal a bride from her bower?"

"No," she said. She slipped the dagger from the sheath in a slow, thoughtful way. Sunlight glinted on the edge. "I don't think you'd have the courage for that."

"Why? Because I don't clank around in armor or run with the underground, spiriting people out from under a dragon's nose? No, thanks. I'm fine as I am, and I don't care a bent copper, my girl, for what you think."

Her sun gilded face became like a bronze mask, her eyes slits as her lips curled in a sneer. Me, I just laughed.

"Leave it alone, Tarya. I have no interest in the girl. Who do you imagine would have? Perhaps an old man in Haven, and if that's the case, she's luckier than she'd likely ever thought she'd be."

I don't know what made me turn my head, the hiss of breath taken was little different that the hiss of water sliding by the boat. I turned, though, and saw Aline standing beside an oarsman, caught in the moment between pained surprise and sudden shame. When she felt my glance on her she turned, hurrying into her tent.

"Oh, elegantly said," Tarya sneered. "And so very sensitively put."

One and another, each of the boatmen looked at me, some full in the face, others with that sliding kind of glance best used for disdain. It was very strong, that elven scorn, and there's no one better at ignoring the mental chatter or the constant spate of emotion running out from his companions than a diviner, but no matter how I tried to insulate myself from it or ignore it, I felt their disgust.

No one had a word for me all the rest of the warm autumn afternoon, nor even a glance, and when the sun set, I settled to sleep. I did not dream and no intuition shivered in my mind to trouble me. Madoc Diviner slept like stones.

*   *   *   *   *

"Bandits!"

I woke hard, a man flung out of sleep and dashed

into the waking world. Inside my skull whirled a kaleidoscope of emotion, fear and rage and great thrusting gouts of greed. Voices lifted, some in anger, some in pain. The first words I could make out were Tarya's, shouting to someone to wait till he could see.

On my feet, I clung to the side of the skiff. Above me the sky spread from bank to bank, and those banks were closer now than they had been. Stars and bursts of orange light filled the sky. Fire-arrows arced high, those simplest of eye-baffling tricks, shafts wrapped in oil-soaked rags and set afire. Each fiery bolt drew the eyes of our archers, leaving them blinded, for deadly moments unable to see what foe harried them. Beneath us, the skiff rocked, then heaved. My heart lurched, even as the little craft did. Someone was in the river trying to overturn the skiff.

Cold, steel-tipped arrows wasped from the northern shore, the Darken Wood side. One struck the side of the skiff, inches from my hand. *Thok! Thok!* Two more followed, humming in the wood. I grabbed up the scrip and scrambled my feet. Someone hit me hard from behind, flinging me to my knees.

"Idiot mage!" Tarya shouted. "You're supposed to be a pyromancer—give us light!"

Idiot mage? Ay, idiot elf to ask for more of what was killing her. I kept my head low and pulled myself into myself, shutting out fear and the cries of the bandits and the arrow-struck. I reached down, past my physical body, past the deck, past the water and the stony riverbed. I reached right into the heart of Krynn itself, that well from which sorcerers are born knowing how to drink. Overhead, fire-arrows arched and I thrust my hand into the sky, all my will running in sinew and bone. One by one the flaming arrows went dark and the night held only it's rightful torches again, the stars. Cheers arose from the skiff, and curses from the river's bank.

I lifted my head, and Tarya shoved it down just as a steel-tipped arrow whizzed by. "Keep low," she whispered, forbearing to name me idiot. She slipped that long-bladed knife from her belt, the steel glinting in the starlight as she pointed to the little canvas chamber. "Listen," she hissed, thrusting the dagger into my hand. "If all this goes to ruin, and I find out you didn't give your last breath to save her, the ghost of me will drag through every corner of the world till I find you and kill you."

I never doubted it. Armed, head low and hauling my scrip after me, I scrambled across deck. Someone screamed, arrows flew rasping. The skiff rocked again, heaving. I fell over, rolled, and crawled up as an elf toppled silently into the water. I looked, I couldn't help it. An arrow had her neatly in the neck, the bloody steel head pointing to the sky as her corpse turned over. Tarya's dead eyes stared up at me, her golden hair spread out around her on the water.

I crawled to the tent, Tarya's knife banging on the deck, my scrip dragging behind me. Someone screamed in sudden pain. Heart slamming against my ribs, I plunged inside. Aline's hand clutched mine. Terror screamed in her mind, howling into mine. I shut it out as best I could, clamping down my own defenses until only small whimpers of her fear leaked through.

The skiff rocked, outside elven war-cries, elven death-screams, became curses in rough voices laughing. They had no more fire-arrows, those bandits, but they had numbers. They would overwhelm the boatmen in good time. Aline trembled, her breath shuddering in her throat. She tried to speak, I hushed her with a hand across her mouth. The deck rumbled under running feet, someone screamed high, the cry suddenly cut off. Aline struggled against my hand, I held harder.

"Hush. Not a sound." My hand still on her mouth, I went past her, obliging her to come with me. Two swift strokes of Tarya's knife and the back of the little tent gaped wide. "Out," I whispered. "Head straight out— and right over the side."

The thunder of booted feet roared outside. "Check the tent! Someone's—Hey! They got a woman in there!"

I grabbed Aline back. I caught the waistband of her skirt and slashed it, dragging the blue wool from her. She stood in her blouse and her pantalets, lace-edged and reaching only to the knee. Her green eyes filled with indignant protest as I shoved her toward the opening.

"You have to swim! Go. *Go!*"

My scrip over my shoulder, the dagger in my belt, I was right behind her, forcing her onward, through the slashed canvas, out onto the burning deck. She stumbled, I caught her and in the same motion flung her over the side. Behind us someone howled. Arrows plunged into the water, from the skiff now and from the shore. The night filled up with cursing, then with wild, hooting laughter. Swimming, I turned and saw bandits on the deck, some lop-eared goblins, a few humans among them. The bandits had the skiff.

Loud in the night, a voice like fury shouted, "There goes two of 'em! An extra measure for the one who drags the woman back!"

I turned to find Aline and hit a jutting rock. The impact blasted air from my lungs. I gasped as the current caught me, spinning me away. Without breath, I couldn't fight the river's grip and when my empty lungs filled again, they filled with water.

*   *   *   *   *

Aline said, "You're alive . . ." as though it were some kind of wonder. She pounded on my back like she wanted to break all my ribs, and she said, "You're alive . . ."

Well, I was. Alive, puking up half the Whiterush River, and certain I'd be spewing blood if she didn't stop banging on me. I tried to turn over, coughing, retching, and she did the work for me, getting her hands under my chest and rolling me onto my back.

Her face shone pale in the light of the lately risen moon. Shadows made her too-wide mouth look like a wound. Awkwardly, her hands fumbled at the neck of my shirt, not sure whether to pull it tight against the cold or open to help me breathe. I stilled those hands with my own, then pushed her away.

"I can breathe," I said, shoving up onto my elbows. With effort, I managed to sit. I looked around me, expecting to see the burning skiff. The river flowed blackly by, little ribbons of starlight weaving on the surface. The skiff was nowhere in sight. "What happened? Where are the bandits? Oh," I said, groaning. "The elves?"

"They're all dead." Her lips trembled, my gut did the same. I was afraid she'd start to cry. Perhaps she saw that fear, for she took a breath, steadied herself, and said, "The bandits are upriver—we came a dark distance in the water, sir mage."

Sir mage. She'd never called me otherwise and it seemed that, lying there, just then, I realized this for the first time.

"Madoc," I said. "My name is Madoc. How far have we come?"

"We went round two bends in the river, and we fetched up on the Darken Wood side." She pressed her lips together, on the edge of weeping. To forestall that, I lifted my hand.

"What?" she asked.

"Light," I said.

Lying there, I felt the earth beneath my back, hard stone, dirt and sticks and leaves. In me I felt more, the strength of Krynn welling. You don't have to do it, that little dance of fancy gesture that mages used to have to make. You don't even have to speak, all you have to do is let the strength of the world be guided by your will. Still, I gestured. I thought it would take her mind from her gathering tears. One flourish of my hand and fire leapt into being, another and flames went to dance tamely upon a boulder as happily as though they feasted on kindling and logs. Aline's face, blotchy and mud-stained, didn't relax.

"Have you salvaged anything?" I asked, sitting up and looking around me at the darkness and the wood.

She dumped my scrip into my lap. "Only this."

The book on pyromancy lay a soggy mess in the bottom, my white linen shirt, brown cotton trews and a red and gold sash meant to make me presentable at the wedding feast were but wads of muddy cloth. I pulled Lady Usha's coffer out of the scrip. The cover was dented and the latch broken, the river's rocks had dealt no more kindly with the box than with my aching body.

Aline came closer, spying the silver. "Is that the, well, the gift? The thing I'm supposed to give to . . . to him?" Her voice trembled on the words.

"Yes." I tossed the scrip to her. "Or the case of it. The gift itself—"

Tarya's dagger lay near. I took up the sodden book, with the dagger prying clumps of paper free from leather covers. Within one of those clumps I found something small and hard. I held up a little rectangle of platinum studded with ruby chips, a locket strung upon a golden chain. So, I thought, it's not a potion but a charm, and just as well. Who knew what mischief a love philter dumped into the river would do?

Aline leaned closer, her breath warm on my cheek. "It's lovely! Like forged starlight." When I slid her a sideways glance, surprised by the turn of her phrase, she blushed. "It must have fallen between the pages of the book when the coffer opened."

Hesitantly, she reached for the locket, but I held back. Slipping the chain over my head, I said, "Getting this to Haven was—is—my task. I'll keep it till we get there."

She looked at me a long moment, a long moment silent. Then, folding her hands in her lap, shivering in the night cold, she said, "Then, we will get there?"

I snorted. "Staying here isn't an option, is it?"

Little comforted, she nodded nonetheless. If not encouragement, at least it was agreement. An owl called, far away in Darken Wood another answered. I looked around me at the forest and the night. I hadn't the first idea where we were, just a "dark distance" from where the skiff had been attacked. I closed my eyes, trying to imagine a map, trying to imagine where we sat on that map. The best I could reckon was that we were a day's drift from Haven by boat, probably two or three days walking. The only thing I really knew was that we must head west.

"We'll get there." I tried for heartiness, managed only hopefulness. "You'll be safe in the arms of your groom before you know it."

Aline's face became like stone. "And luckier than I'd likely imagined I'd ever be."

I winced, I tried to say something, to take back the hard words she'd not been meant to hear. None of my fumbling helped. She rose briskly, gathering my soaked and muddy feast gear.

"Take off your boots," she said, pulling off her own little shoes. And when I frowned, not understanding, She gestured to the wet clothing and wet boots I wore. "I'm not going to Haven half-naked, mage. Are you prepared to walk there in wet boots?"

I was not. Neither was I, it seemed, fit to keep watch over the fire. "Just do something to keep it going—you can do that, right?—and leave the watching to me."

I could do that, I did do that, and then went gratefully to sleep. It wasn't an easy sleep, though, and often disturbed. Each time I woke, I saw her sitting near the fire, sometimes tending the drying of our shoes, sometimes simply watching flames dance on stone. Not till the darkest hour did she let me take watch, and even then she didn't sleep. She curled up on the ground before the fire, arms wrapped around herself, head tucked low, but she didn't sleep. She lay there, face hidden and hearing, no matter how hard she tried to forget, the carelessly cruel words of an idiot mage who'd bleated the opinion that she'd consider herself lucky to be going to the bed of an old man, a stranger who'd as much as bought her, rather than to live a spinster's life.

And that's not guessing. I'm a diviner, I know what she thought.

* * * * *

In older days, so say all the stories, Krynn had undergone times of great re-shaping as mortals failed to please gods and must bear the brunt of their tempers. The shores of the Whiterush, however, stayed much the same through all the upheavals of gods, repository for stone and boulders dragged up from Icewall when glaciers advanced and retreated south across the world. Along the banks of the river, beyond the stone, the soil was rich, dark and deep. Berry bushes grew and that year autumn had been gracious, not so cold at night and full of warm days. The bushes along the Whiterush River yet hung low with their burden even as the oaks in the forest readied their acorns.

We weren't the best of companions, the bride astray and I. She went ahead of me, walking west and had very little to say. What shy attempts to converse she'd made the day before might well have been made by someone else. To end my useless attempts at conversation, at last she said, "Look, you don't have to talk. Save your breath for walking and soon you'll be in Haven, your duty discharged and, I'm sure, a pretty girl to keep you company at the feast." And so, you see that we didn't go companionably down the Whiterush, but at least we didn't go hungry.

The land rose, the river dropped, and we kept ourselves always on the stony banks, below and out of sight of Darken Wood. Thus sheltered, I didn't worry about bandits spotting our fire but I did wonder whether it was wise to have a fire so close to a dragon's realm. Aline, breaking another of her long silences, said it wasn't like the dragon herself was going to spot it and come winging to murder us or steal us away.

"She's not interested in such small gain as the two of us." She pointed across the river, to Qualinesti. The trees, once the boundary marker of the dominion of a proud race, now made the walls of the green dragon's country. "They are all different, the dragons of Krynn, and the name of this one, this Beryllinthranox, could be another word for "greed." She has all of a rich nation to torment and plunder, elves who were once the lords of the forest now work to fill her coffers. The guards who watch her borders are Qualinesti, corrupted by the power she lends them, and they aren't interested in keeping us out. They keep their own people in."

"You know a lot about it," I said, gutting the trout that would be our supper.

Aline shrugged. "I've known a lot about it all my life. Helping to aid refugees to escape from that place—from all the dragon lands—has been my grandfather's work since before I was born." She looked across the river to the dark wall of the elven forest. "Now it's mine."

"But why must it be yours? They're elves, and they never cared a damn about what went on outside their forest in the days before the dragons came. Why should anyone care about them now? Why should you?"

She looked at me sideways, a small, sardonic glance. "I thought you knew. To get a husband."

"Aline—"

Her expression softened. "I'm sorry. You've apologized for that, and I shouldn't bring it up again. But I don't fear a spinster's life as much as you imagined I should. My life is my life, mage, wed or not. You assume it's one of waiting desperately for a man to come and claim me. It isn't. Or . . . it wasn't. My life has been one of books and study and bards—yes, bards, they come to my grandfather's house often, I grew up among them, and one of them made a poem of mine a song for his lute . . ." She bit her lower lip, her long horsey face went mottled with blushing.

I spied, slipping in and out of her mind like a shadow sliding on the ground. She'd thought she was in love with that song-maker. For a time she'd spun dreams for herself, fantasies in which the bard figured, but soon she'd let them die. Who, after all, would imagine that a fair and handsome bard would be truly interested in a homely girl? Not Aline.

Unaware of me, Aline sighed. "But I am to be wed, and perhaps it would be easier if I had a pretty face." She lowered her lashes, hiding.

"And yet," I said, stuffing the gutted fish with onion grass, "married to a husband who welcomes you happily or simply married, what is it you hope to do? Empty the Dragon Realms one by one until one day the beasts all look up and find their slaves gone?"

Ah, hers was not a pretty face, not at all, but I saw it in that moment a thing I hadn't recognized in the days we'd been together. Aline's were strangely searching eyes.

"Mage," she said, honestly curious, "what kind of life do you lead, a man who studies with Master Palin, who knows the Lady Usha, and yet doesn't know what we hope to do?"

"Not such a bad life," I muttered, suddenly defensive. "And if I'd known what you hope, I wouldn't have asked."

"Why, you could divine the answer, couldn't you?" Eyes wide in mock innocence, she corrected herself. "No, that wouldn't do. This kind of answer you have to *feel* your way to, sir mage. You can't spy it out or guess it. But you're not much for that kind of thing, are you? Girls and taverns, your magic and a running bar bill, those are the things of your life, aren't they? And if you knew what we hope to do, what we so desperately try to accomplish, would you care? I don't think you would." She leaned close, with one finger lightly touched the platinum locket where it hung round my neck. It was a gentle gesture, and I was not the object of that tenderness. "And yet, Lady Usha sent you with me, with this."

"A mage to carry the magic," I said, surprised to hear bitterness in my own voice. "You heard what she said, imperfect, and the very man for the task." I looked at

Aline, at the food cooking. "I don't suppose I'm doing so bad at the job, after all."

In the face of my sarcasm, Aline withdrew.

When at last the fish were baked, the meal eaten and the remains of it buried so foxes wouldn't come prowling round our camp, she walked away from me. It was only a few yards to the waterside, and she stood there looking into dragon-bound Qualinesti.

After a time, her voice trembling, Aline said, to me or to the forest, "If I didn't have to do this, I wouldn't do it."

* * * * *

An owl's long winding call drifted on the night. Sleeping, Aline shuddered as the forlorn cry slipped into her dreams. Soft, the river ran past the stony banks, the first frost of autumn glittered on the rocks. I sat close to my magic-made fire, shivering and hoping that my reckoning of the distance to Haven was a good one. I'd grown weary of sleeping on stone and eating only sometimes, weary of guiding this bride to her wedding.

Delicate hoofs made little clicking sounds at the water's edge, small splashes. A stag trumpeted and when I shifted a little I saw it, head back, wide rack of horns spread like a thick web against the starred sky. He stood in perfect stillness, listening, breathing. Watching, I recognized the quiet, the change come upon the night. In the moment I did, the stag burst into motion, plunging up out of the river, dashing downstream.

Aline jerked awake.

"Hush!" I whispered, a breath, hardly a word. I slipped my hand over her mouth. Eyes wide, she struggled. Then she stilled, seeing what I saw.

Two dark figures appeared at the far bank, one taller than the other. The taller was armed, starlight shone on the steely tips thrusting out from a full quiver. The other was a woman, and she went hunched over, carrying something. In utter silence the man lifted a canoe out from the concealment of bushes and put it into the water. Steadying the craft, he held out his arms and took the woman's burden, an infant wrapped in dark cloth. The woman alighted next, took back her child, and in utter silence her companion turned the canoe into the current, crossing the river on a moonless night. Their faces shone white in the starlight, their eyes were dark as holes. These two, perhaps lovers, perhaps husband and wife who in the days before the dragon might never have dreamed they'd leave their beloved homeland, went out from the banks of the Whiterush River, forever away from Qualinesti.

The child cried, an infant's piercing wail suddenly muffled against its mother's breast. My heart jerked, the cry sounded so loud in the night. Aline rose, before I could stop her she crept to the edge of the water. Quickly I caught her back.

"Be still! One of them is armed—"

"They have a child with them," she breathed. "Mage, we must go help."

"No." I gripped her arm. "No. Stay here, Aline. If he catches sight of you that child's father won't stop to reckon if you're friend or foe. He'll defend his family."

She held, but not willingly, and we watched the elven craft draw closer to the Darken Wood side of the river. Skilled with the oar, the elf used a little eddy to carry his craft safely round a jutting of stone to thread the narrow passage between rock and shore.

"He'll make it," Aline whispered, her breath warm against my neck.

He would, I thought so. I took her hand to draw her farther back into shadow.

High, a cry of pain tore the night's stillness. The canoe wobbled, suddenly out of balance as the oarsman toppled over the side. Another cry soared, a woman's scream as she lurched up, then fell into the river. Wailing, her child fell with her. It made only a little splash when it hit the water. By the light of stars I saw an arrow quivering in the mother's shoulder as she fell.

"No!" Aline cried. She struggled, twisting in my grip. Sharp, her elbow caught me between the ribs. In that moment of startled pain, she broke my hold and ran splashing into the Whiterush. Gasping in the cold water, she struck out for the mother and child. And me—well, what was I to do? Cursing, I followed, plunging into the icy water.

Cold sapped the strength from my muscles, each stroke seemed more difficult than the last. The more I swam, the more the river seemed to run harder, faster, carrying the elfwoman out of my reach. Bobbing in the current, she tried to turn onto her back, to keep herself that way. She had but one good arm, with that she must hold her child out of the water. An arrow flew, then another. On the far river bank, rough laughter as someone hooted derision at the archer who'd missed his target. River-caught, the elfwoman spun and went down again, child and all. A cheer rose up on the Qualinesti side of the Whiterush River.

She's gone, I thought, drowned.

The elf broke the surface again, again holding her infant high.

"There!" someone shouted, "There are more with her! Shoot!"

An arrow buzzed past my ear, another splashed into the water in front of me. The river pulled at me, trying to drag me down, even as I looked around me for Aline. She'd not fought to cross the current as I'd been doing, she let it carry her, swimming with it. She was but a few strokes from the luckless mother and her child.

Her face a white oval, the elfwoman saw me, on her lips a wailing prayer to a vanished god. "E'li!" she cried, "E'li—!"

I swam harder, kicking against the river, and the elfwoman fetched up against a jutting boulder, slammed so hard I heard the breath blasted from her lungs. Blood ran in the frothy water whirling round the stone. Held high, the infant wailed. The water spun the woman around, her eyes great and dark fastened again on me.

"In E'li's name—!" She gasped, she coughed, held against the boulder by the force of the current. Blood ran out from her mouth. "Take my child—!"

I reached, still too far from her, yet I reached. A hand burst up from the water, one thrusting white arm followed. Aline flashed out of the river between the elf and me, reaching for the baby.

Bleeding, the mother tried to hand off her child. Sobbing, Aline reached. The river, jealous of it's take, held the elf with hard hands, pulling her down, the baby with her. Blood-stained frothy water closed over their heads, Aline cried out, a long wordless sound of grief. She dived down, searching, and she came up again, gasping. I caught her and held her, my body pressing her against the boulder.

Voices came muffled from the far bank, the sound of searching. Then, "Gone?" one called? "Dead," another said, laughing.

Aline wept, her whole body wracked with shuddering.

Far down the river, whirled away on the current, a small white shape went bobbing. There, the drowned infant. Nowhere to be seen, the murdered mother. And, in time, no more arrows flew, no more voices could be heard. In time, we left the shelter of the boulder and plowed the water back to shore.

* * * * *

She sat, bereft. As though the elves were her own kin, the child torn from her own breast Aline Caroel sat before my mage-fire, white and weeping. I didn't know how to comfort her, no word of mine made any difference to her sorrow. "They are lost," she sobbed. Tears running, her eyes swollen and red, she looked up at me and moaned, "I couldn't save them. They—" She stopped, shuddering. Eyes wide, some sudden fearful thought gripping she reached for me, her fingers brushing my neck. "The locket—it's lost—!"

"No," I said, reaching into my wet shirt, "no it's here. It's all right, I have it." I slipped the chain over my head, let the little locket sit in my hand. "See."

In the dark she came closer, still sobbing, shivering so hard I thought she'd shake her bones apart.

"Look, here it is," I said, snicking open the locket. I held it out, the two halves wide. I drew breath to say something more, to assure her perhaps that if three elves were lost to the river and their fate, surely others would be saved. I let the breath go, a mute ghost.

In my hand lay a portrait of Aline Caroel. Ay, Aline, long horsey face with a nose to match, her hair the color of mud puddles, her teeth too big. Lady Usha hadn't sought to gild matters, she simply presented the girl as she was, but it seemed she paid the most attention to her eyes. They were, I only noticed then, green as springtime, bright and lively as sunlight dancing on water. They caught me, those eyes so delicately pictured by the brushes of Lady Usha Majere. A thrill ran through me, bone and blood. So lively the eyes that I was drawn to look long, and looking I saw reflected back to me a spirit filled with generosity and deep strength, with such beauty as had nothing to do with fairness of face or loveliness of form. This beauty, more precious than jewels, had come with the soul and it would ever reside with the soul, no matter the vessel.

"In the name of all gods," I whispered, me, a man born in the time after gods.

This portrait had been meant to turn an old man's heart toward his young bride, the gift meant to ease Aline's way. I didn't care. I didn't care, for in one flashing instant I saw in the eyes of the living girl what I had seen in portrait, an expression to make me feel I could tear down towers for her and lay waste to cities only to be seen, truly seen by her, my heart to be known by her in the same way I had been given to know hers.

This, this was the girl I had so carelessly hurt, the girl I'd implied was unlovable simply because she was not pretty, fortunate to find any husband at all.

Aline said, "Mage," and hesitantly, her hand shaking, she touched my cheek with her finger. I knew then I was weeping. I felt my tears because she did, I felt my sorrow because she saw it. I knew with fierce suddenness the terror of a love so deep it could break me, a love I could not imagine living without.

"What is it?" she said, eyes wide, lips trembling. For the first time in all the days we'd known each other, she spoke my name. "Madoc, what's wrong?"

I showed her the portrait, the precious charm made of brush strokes and paint and the secret magics of Usha Majere. Aline looked at the portrait, then again at me. She said nothing, but her lips moved, shaping protest, shaping regret, and shaping words of fear.

"Aline," I said, groaning.

Her breast rose on a taken breath. I don't know what that old man in Haven would have done, the portrait in hand, the living girl in his bed. I knew, even as I reached to touch her cheek, what I was going to do.

I had no sense in me that night. I had no conscience. I had only the great need of this woman, her heart and the sweet loveliness that touched my soul as none had ever touched. I drew Aline closer, she resisted, but not much. There was in her eyes still that lorn emptiness, that grief for the mother and the baby drowned, for the father who had not, after all, guided his little family to safely. She felt empty, I knew it looking at her. I knew it as I slipped gently into the heart and mind of her, Madoc Diviner like a silent shadow. That emptiness I embraced, eager to fill it up with what I knew about her, her true loveliness, her courage and her tender heart. I tipped back her head and kissed her, looking into those deep wells, her green eyes shining. She struggled, but only a little, the hand that pushed at me soon moved to draw me closer.

We loved long that night, she a maiden not so shy, I the man determined to bind her to me, to have her and keep her, the elves and Lir Wrackham—Lady Usha herself—be damned. Something turned in me, though, that will to bind became a will to be myself held, and I, who had said to her not so long before, that my bed sport with women had been happy exercise, knew the poverty of those nights, the shallowness of those days. As I can set fire dancing on naked stone, so did that girl kindle a fire in my heart, with each touch igniting, with each kiss feeding.

Yet in the morning, with the sun shining down on the river to make gray curtains of the rising mist, in the morning I woke alone, my arms empty, only the faint scent of her skin clinging to my own flesh. Aline was a long reach away, on the opposite side of a crackling fire. Fed on kindling and wood, this was Aline's own fire, and with it between us, she said, "It's time to leave, you must take me to Haven, mage."

Mage, not Madoc.

I looked at her like a witless man, my blood running cold in me. "To Haven?" I said, as though I'd never heard of the city. "No, I—Aline, no. I can't do that now. You can't—" I sat up, struggling to understand. "I love you," I said, as though that alone would turn her, would make her understand. "I love you and I can't take you to Lir Wrackham." The name fell like stones from my lips.

I reached for the locket, the little love charm, as though it would make my case for me. It was gone from my neck, and when I looked up, startled, I saw it now round her own neck, the little platinum rectangle studded with ruby chips.

In the morning sunlight, her long face shone pale. "You love me, Madoc." She lingered on my name, that name she'd seldom spoke, and it sounded like a sigh. "So you think. But you know about magic, you know about charms." She held up the locket. Like forged starlight, that's how she'd described the platinum. "I am the same woman I was when first you saw me in Lady Usha's chamber, no different. And so," she said, "surely it is the magic talking through you, the charm making you think you love me."

I know about magic, I know about charms. I knew how cunning a sorcery the lady in Solace had performed. No enchantment of hers had changed my mind, it had not rendered Aline suddenly beautiful, her loveliness a mask of magic to confuse my senses. No, nothing like that. Lady Usha's charm had opened my eyes.

"Aline, listen," I said, fumbling, tripping on words and thoughts and sudden hopes. "Listen, you said—I heard it last night—you said if you didn't have to do this, you wouldn't do it. You *don't* have to do it. You don't have to go down to Haven. I can take you away, past there, we'll find a place for us—"

"Madoc," she said, and now her lips trembled, but only a little. In her springtime eyes I saw a sheen of tears. "Don't you understand me yet? Don't you know that I have a . . . destiny." She blushed to use the poetic word. "I've made promises." She looked over her shoulder, to the river running, the cold swift grave of three elves who'd not found their way to freedom. "If my grandfather's work goes unfinished, how many more will that river claim, people so desperate for freedom they'll risk their lives—the lives of their precious babies—to have? I can save lives, Madoc. I can do that."

I went and sat beside her, shivering in the morning chill. I took her in my arms, some wild thought in me to lift her up and carry her away, or to lay her down and love her again, in desperation to bind her to me. She leaned against me, trusting, and I did nothing more than kiss her gently.

Homely, I'd said of her, and cataloged her every defect the first moment I'd seen her. Homely, how could I have thought so? She was the loveliest woman I'd ever known, her generous spirit shining in her eyes, the boldness of her heart seen in her every glance, even in the sad and sorry smile she gave me now.

"Please," she said, "help me finish what I've started. Please, Madoc, take me to Haven."

To Haven, to an old man waiting to wed her and coffers that would soon open and pour out the money needed to support secret efforts to free the Dragon Realms, to spirit refugees to freedom. Ah, Lady Usha Majere's lost causes.

My heart rebelled, rising angry in me. I would not lose this love I'd found, I would not turn her over to Lir Wrackham. I would not give her up!

But that rebellion of the heart was as hopeless as any lost cause you've ever heard of, I knew it when Aline lifted the locket from her breast, slipped the golden chain over her head. She pressed it into my hand, soft, she said, "I don't need it now, Madoc." Her eyes bright with tears, she whispered, "You showed me the truth of myself, the . . ."

Ah, she was Aline, my Aline. She blushed over the word, and would not say it.

"The loveliness," I said, my throat closing tight.

"Yes," she said, smiling a little. "Loveliness."

I loved the girl. Right to the bones of me, I loved her. Coward, elven Tarya had named me, the first moment she knew me she called me that, and she'd said so again on the day we left Solace. Well, she was pretty, Tarya of Qualinesti, and no doubt she was brave, but she'd been no good judge of character. I looked at the locket, that platinum square like a piece of forged starlight, and slipped the chain over my head. Warm from my lover's hand, it sat light as a sigh over my heart.

* * * * *

Lir Wrackham made me festive for his feast. He professed his gratitude for my good and generous care of his bride by dressing me in silk and satin. He gave me gold rings to wear, and he gave me boots of softest leather to put on my feet. He was a rich man, and so into my hand he put a bulging pouch filled with steel coins. "To thank you," he said, "to let you know how much I appreciate the care you took of my Aline."

My Aline . . .

He said that, a man who had never seen what the locket round my neck held, a man who knew how to look into a person's eyes and find the truth. A weedy old man with rheumy eyes and balding pate, his hands trembling with age, he said the name of my beloved as though he were speaking a prayer. In that way did he speak his marriage vows, looking long into the spring-time eyes of his bride. And she, head high, made her own vow to cherish and honor the old man.

I watched from the back of the great hall, the pouch of steel coins heavy on my belt, and if I'd worn fine clothes in the days before the wedding, I did not on the day the vows were spoken. I wore instead stout boots and tough woolen trews, a shirt of sueded leather.

"Traveling gear," said one of the guests, the only elf at the feast. "You don't look like a man who's going to stay long at the celebration."

"No," I said, my eyes on the bride, "I have an appointment in Solace."

He shrugged. "More's the pity. It looks like there's to be fine feasting here tonight."

I agreed that it did look that way. "But there's a lady waiting for me, and I don't like to keep her waiting."

The elf laughed, he said she must be a demanding lover, this lady of mine.

"Not a lover," I said, my eyes on the bride, Aline shining in gems and candlelight.

No, not a lover, but certainly a friend, one who'd sent me out on a long road to Haven, one who liked to redeem lost causes. She had, I realized standing there in Haven, considered me one of those, a man who couldn't see where true beauty lies, who didn't know what courage required.

Come back, Lady Usha had said when she sent me away, come back and tell me what Madoc Diviner divined from his trip.

A cheer rang through the hall, Lir Wrackham leaned close to kiss his bride. Aline, turning to accept his kiss, saw me. The old man's lips touched hers, her eyes met mine, and I gave the elf my excuses, saying there was still some light remaining to the day and it was time for me to go.

Blood Ties
John Grubber

"Come on, Oleth! Get your slow ass movin'!"

"Where are we going?" Oleth gasped.

"The cave!" Eliamm shouted as he jumped from the cart.

The cave was less than thirty feet away, but it might as well have been thirty miles as far as the terrified Eliamm was concerned. They could hear the footfalls of the gigantic beast splashing through the water behind them, moving closer, sounding like the thunder of a coming storm. The tylor—a creature that was part dragon, part something else horrible—wasn't clear of the swamp yet, but when it reached clear flat ground the gap between them and it would be closed in an instant.

The cave wasn't guaranteed safety, but it was their best hope. The brothers scrambled up a ledge, leaving the cart and moose carcass behind. The tylor gave a screeching roar that echoed through the trees as it emerged from the swamp. The reptilian monster smashed the cart to kindling with its huge clawed foot, dumping the half-skinned moose carcass onto the ground. The tylor reached the bottom of the rock face in the space of a heartbeat, its great splayed feet clawing the tallus-covered slope. Sniffing them, the tylor tilted its horned head and bellowed again.

Oleth, at age fifteen, was the younger of the two brothers and the larger, his size a result of spoiled indulgence and an avoidance of work. He had been first up the stone face, panic driving his heavy form ahead of his more athletic older brother. Eliamm had not panicked at the sight of the monster. He'd even had the presence of mind to grab their bow and arrows when they'd first heard the tylor crashing through the New Swamp.

They reached the cave, only to find it much smaller than when they'd played in it as children.

"I won't fit!" Oleth gasped.

"Sure you will! Suck in your gut!"

Oleth drew in a breath. Fear worked wonders and Oleth managed to squeeze his bulk into the cave that had been a safe haven in their youth, a place where two farmboys took refuge from pa's strap or two teasing younger sisters.

They were barely inside when the tylor slammed its head into the rock face, trying to force its fanged maw through the opening. The two young men scrambled to the back wall of the cave, pressing themselves against it, waiting, praying. Eliamm loosed an arrow at the tylor's horned head. Oleth cheered when the arrow hit, but it did no damage, bouncing off the thick brown scales and clattering to the cave floor.

Tylors are not known for their intellect and, after banging its head against the cliff face a few more times, the beast gave up and wandered away. Eliamm crawled to the cave opening and peered out into the growing darkness. The tylor had returned to the cart. The monster lifted the body of the moose, seized the head in its jaws and tore the head from the body. The boys sat silently in the opening, watching as two days worth of tracking went down the tylor's gullet in only a few bites.

Angrily, Eliamm launched another arrow. It bounced

off the thick scales. The monster didn't even blink. Its meal finished, its belly full, the tylor's head began to droop. With a snorting sigh, the tylor rolled over and was soon asleep, its bloated flanks rising and falling in a steady rhythm.

"Now!" said Eliamm.

The two slipped to the cave opening, hoping to sneak out while the beast slept. Eliamm stepped out, slipped on some loose gravel. Small rocks went bounding down the rockface.

The tylor muttered and stirred, half-opened one eye.

The brothers scrambled back into the shelter. Elaimm paced, frustrated, tired of being cooped up, eager to escape. Oleth holed up in the back of the cave and soon was snoring loudly, content to wait for the tylor to leave.

Near dawn, Eliamm woke with a start. The eerie sound that had wakened him was not a dream. The sound started as low, pulsating hum, grew to a high pitched whine, then dropped to the low hum again. The sound was repeated several times. He stared into the half-light, trying to find the source, but he couldn't see anything. He wasn't the only thing disturbed by the sound. The tylor woke up, clambored clumsily to its feet and set out, ambling off into the swamp the way it had come.

"Hey," Eliamm said, kicking his slumbering brother. "We can go now."

They stood staring gloomily at what was left of their cart. There was nothing left of the moose. No help for it but to go back home empty-handed.

Their father would hold them responsible for the loss of the cart, the supplies and the kill. Liam MacKeown wasn't a patient man. He wasn't unfair or harsh, but he brooked no excuses from his two sons. He would hear their story, scoff in disbelief, and then order them to clean the barn or muck the hogs as punishment. Their mother, Isabelle, would believe her sons. Rather, she would believe Oleth, her darling, who could do no wrong in her eyes.

The brothers trudged down the road, kicking rocks and laying blame. If Oleth hadn't panicked . . . if Eliamm had been a better shot . . . so on and so forth. The bickering continued as they rounded the last bend in the road that led to their parent's farm. Neither were paying any attention to where they put their feet and it took them both by surprise when Oleth fell into a large ditch and pitched forward, face-first, into the thick mud.

Cursing, he pushed himself up, used his shirtsleeve to wipe mud from his round face. Laughing, Eliamm extended a hand to help him stand.

"Who dug a pit there in the first place," Oleth grumbled.

Eliamm looked more closely at the pit. Not liking what he saw, he lifted his head, stared on down the road.

"It's not a pit, Oleth," he said quietly. "Not unless a pit's got toes."

It was a footprint. A footprint almost four feet long, with three broad toes. Beyond that was another foot print and still another. Vegetation was mashed and trampled.

The boys broke into a panicked run. The tracks led home.

"Ma!" Eliamm shouted breathlessly, charging into the yard. "Pa!"

"Kira!" Oleth hollered, calling their little sisters. "Selah!"

No reply. Not even the dog barked. Eliamm saw why. The dog's carcass, mangled and bloody, lay near the house it had died defending. Carcasses of other animals—cows, horses—lay scattered around the yard.

Flies buzzed and carrion-hungry birds flapped away in disgust, their feast interrupted by the arrival of the boys.

The house was wrecked. The walls were caved in, the roof had partly collapsed. The barn had been next to the house, but all that remained of it was a pile of splintered wood and stone.

They lifted the broken door that had been knocked off its hinges, entered the house. Their feet crunched on broken window glass and crockery. They crawled among the wreckage, searching for signs of life, calling until they were both hoarse.

Oleth began to whimper. "They're all dead! The tylor killed them all!"

"No, they're not dead, Oleth!" Eliamm said sternly. "Look around! There are bodies of the dogs and the cows, but no human bodies. They're alive!"

"Then where'd they go, Eliamm?" Oleth demanded.

"They probably went to the neighbors, to the Van Grutens," Eliamm said.

"You're taking this awful calm, Eliamm," Oleth said accusingly. "I don't believe you care what happened to them."

"I care what happened," Eliamm shot back. "But since nothing did, I'm not worried." He paused, looked around the wrecked house. "Did you notice something strange, Oleth? Every single thing of value we have is gone. Ma's jewelry, pa's money stash. Not smashed. Not broken. Just gone."

* * * * *

The boys ran across the fields, hope and fear lending them strength. But the moment the boys saw the Van Gruten's smashed fence, they knew what lay ahead and their footsteps slowed as hope died. Here were the same horrible footprints, the same death and destruction. Only this time, human bodies lay among the carcasses of cows and hogs. The bodies had been torn apart, some so savaged that the horrified boys could not recognize neighbors they'd known all their lives. By the signs, the Van Grutens, veterans of the Chaos War, had tried to fight the tylor. Spent arrows lay in the yard and Eliamm found a severed hand still holding fast to an axe handle.

Wagons were overturned and smashed like kindling, massive clawmarks digging deep into the weathered wood. The barns had been destroyed, but strangely, the house was relatively still in one piece, although windows were broken and the doors had been smashed in. The tylor's gigantic footprints covered the yard.

At the sight of the mutilated bodies, Oleth collapsed to his knees, heaved up his guts. Eliamm half-carried his brother away from the scene of the destruction, made him sit down beside the well in the back and drink some water. It was Eliamm who had to finish examining the bodies, search through the wreckage.

He came back to find his brother somewhat recovered, though Oleth sat in a huddled heap, tears streaking his face.

"They're not here," said Eliamm. "They're not among the dead. I found both the Van Grutens and their oldest son, Haim, but that's it. No sign of anyone else."

"Then where are they, Eliamm?" Oleth asked plaintively. "Where's our family?"

"How should I know?" Eliamm snapped, his nerves raw and exposed. The sight of those bodies and the realization of the cruel deaths they had died had shaken him to the very core of his being. He wanted very much to sit down and weep like Oleth, but Eliamm wouldn't let himself. One of them had to be strong. "I looked inside the house. Nothing's been taken. The gold candlesticks are on the table, along with the silver goblets that Mistress Van Gruten was so proud of."

"Well, of course," said Oleth. "What would the tylor want with silver goblets?"

"What would the tylor want with Ma's jewelry," Eliamm asked. "Yet it's gone."

Oleth looked at him and blinked.

"Listen!" Eliamm said. "Wagon wheels. Someone's coming."

The boys looked to see a brightly painted wagon rolling to a stop in front of the house. A small figure wearing a black cloak and carrying a large sack leapt from the seat to the ground.

"Fessik!" Eliamm breathed

He would have known that bright-painted gypsy wagon anywhere, as would most residents of the area. Fessik was a traveling merchant who always had something to sell, cure or curse. He journeyed from farm to farm, town to town. No one else dared travel at night, but darkness and the fear of the swamp's inhabitants did not stop the merchant.

Oleth jumped up, was about to call out. Eliamm clamped a hand over his brother's mouth.

"Keep quiet!" Eliamm whispered. "Let's see what he's up to!"

Fessik did not appear astonished at the sight of the carnage. He barely glanced at the bodies. He loped toward the house and walked straight inside. Eliamm's patience was rewarded a few minutes later when Fessik emerged from the house with the sack that was now bulging. He opened a door at the rear of his wagon, tossed the bag inside, withdrew a second empty sack and headed back for the house.

Eliamm broke into a run. Fessik's hearing was keen. He heard Eliamm before he saw him, turned and raced for the wagon. The trader was faster than he looked, and he was in his seat, reaching for the reins when Eliamm leapt onto him. Eliamm picked up the trader, hurled him off the wagon and into the mud. Eliamm jumped down after him, pinning his arms to the ground. One of the sacks tumbled out of the wagon, spilled it contents onto the ground.

Oleth grabbed a silver goblet and held it up for Eliamm to see. Reaching down, he picked up a glittering amethyst necklace and held it up, too.

"Thief, murderer!" Eliamm shouted. Grabbing the merchant's collar in both hands, he lifted the trader off the ground. "Where are they? Where are they?"

"I didn't steal it! I found it!" Fessik cried, half-choked.

Eliamm cuffed the trader on the side of the head. "What did you do to them?"

Eliamm pulled his hunting knife from his belt with one hand, keeping hold of the merchant's collar with the other. He stood up, dragging Fessik with him. Eliamm hauled the small man to the hitching post and bent him backwards over it.

Eliamm pressed the knife blade against Fessik's throat. "I'll ask you one more time," he said grimly. "Where are they?"

Oleth stared, shocked. "Eliamm . . ." he said hesitantly.

Eliamm flashed his brother a furious glance, and Oleth fell silent.

"I only steal from the empty homes!" Fessik wailed. "I didn't do anything to your family. They were gone when I got there—just like here!"

"So, you robbed our house, but had nothing to do with our family's disappearance?" Eliamm said, pricking the trader's skin with the tip of the blade, just to let him feel the pain. "How did you know when to come? You know where they are! Tell us!"

Blood trickled down the trader's neck.

"Eliamm, stop!" Oleth pleaded. "That's enough!"

"All right! I'll tell! The slavers take them. That's all I know, I swear!" Fessik pleaded. "I was at your farm two days ago, and they were all there, but when I came back yesterday—"

"When you came to rob it!" Eliamm interjected, shaking the trader until his teeth rattled.

"They were gone, the slavers had been there already!" Fessik whined. "They use the tylor. They send it in first, then they come in after."

Eliamm's mind filled with terrible visions. He saw his sisters put to work in a brothel. He saw his parents in chains. Liam would die before he was enslaved, though. Perhaps he was dead already.

"Where?" Eliamm asked, poking the knife in deeper.

Fessik shrieked in pain that was probably more imagined than real.

"No more! Please! Stop!" Fessik begged. "Three days east of here. There's a camp. I used to meet them near it."

"How do we get there!" Eliamm demanded.

Fessik stared at him. "You're mad! You don't know what you're dealing with!"

"Answer me!" Eliamm prodded the trader with the knife and this time the pain was not imaginary.

"They'll kill me!" Fessik gasped. "They'll know I betrayed them!"

"If you don't tell me," said Eliamm calmly, "I'll kill you myself. You have a choice."

The trader looked into Eliamm's eyes, saw his death there.

Fessik provided directions and even gave them his own crude map. Eliamm snatched it from him, turned and climbed onto the wagon.

"Get in, Oleth," he ordered.

When the trader started to clambor up onto the seat, Eliamm kicked him with his foot, sent the trader sprawling.

"Not you. Giddup," said Eliamm to the horse.

"You can't leave me here!" Fessik pleaded, chasing after the rolling wagon. "They'll send the tylor after me!"

"Good," said Eliamm.

"You won't find 'em, you know!" Fessik bawled. "Or if you do, you'll wish you hadn't!"

* * * * *

The red panels and yellow trim of the wagon were worn and faded, but the colors were still a bright contrast to the swamp's gloom. The cabin attached to the wagon was Fessik's home and it was filthy. Garbage littered the floor of the cabin. Dirty blankets lay crumpled on the hinged cot. Sacks of loot covered the floor. Eliamm told Oleth to lighten the load. Oleth shoved garbage, sacks, crates and barrels out the wagon's rear door. The horse gained speed.

"What do you think, Eliamm?" Oleth asked. "Are we going to rescue them?"

"Yes," Eliamm answered matter-of-factly. "They've got maybe a day's head start on us at most."

The ground flew past, the wagon bouncing behind the fast-moving horse. They took turns at the reins until Eliamm finally called a halt. It would take even longer, he told his brother, if the horse dropped dead on the trail and they had to continue on foot.

Oleth had cried himself to sleep inside the wagon, keeping his sobs quiet so that his brother wouldn't hear him. After a fitful few hours sleep, Oleth awoke to take the watch. Eliamm refused to sleep in the wagon. "I like to sleep under the stars," he said. He spread out his blanket on the ground.

Oleth absently poked the remains of the fire with a stick. Terrifying images of what might be happening to his family filled his mind. He did his best to forget his waking nightmares about what might be happening to his family, trying instead to focus on the task at hand, that of rescuing them.

Dawn came, a time of eerie silence in the swamp. The night creatures had ceased their nocturnal wanderings, but the animals of the day had not yet awaken. Suddenly, a low humming echoed across the swamp, rising, then lowering in pitch, and rising again. Oleth shook Eliamm awake.

"What's that noise?" Oleth asked fearfully.

Eliamm sat up. "That's the same sound I heard yesterday. When we were in the cave."

"What is it?" Oleth repeated. "I've lived in the swamp all my life, and I've never heard anything like that, Eliamm!"

"I don't know." Eliamm said, adding, "but it sure made that giant lizard run."

They ate a cold breakfast as they traveled. The speed of their horse and the lightness of their load was their advantage. They weren't being slowed down by prisoners. The tracks of the slaver wagon were easy to follow, made deep ruts in the damp mud.

* * * * *

The brothers followed the tracks for hours, until they were far away from their home. This was the farthest they had ever traveled into the swamp. This section, east of their home, was strange and unfamiliar. As the sun began to dip toward the horizon, the shadows that filled the swamp began to lengthen. With the rise of the pale moon came the mist, a thick fog that chilled them as they traveled. The swamp around them grew loud with odd sounds as the creatures of the night left their burrows and went hunting. The wind howled high in the treetops, insects sang to each other.

The fatigue of constant travel began to affect the brothers. Oleth staved it off by napping in the wagon, while Eliamm drove. Eliamm couldn't bring himself to leave his post, fearful that Oleth might miss some sign or take a wrong turning. Eliamm stayed awake, sitting next to Oleth when it was Oleth's turn to drive. Here and there, they saw tracks made by the tylor. The monster appeared to be trailing the slave wagons. Their fear increasing, the brothers continued their nightmare journey.

Every sound made them jump. Every creak of a branch, every rustle of leaves was something stalking them in the underbrush. Their progress slowed, and eventually stopped as exhaustion overtook them. They found a dry spot—a rarity in the swamp—and laid out their bedrolls.

When morning came, the humming sound of the previous two mornings came again, louder and closer than it had been the previous two times.

* * * * *

Shortly after midday, Eliamm stopped the wagon suddenly and leapt from the seat. He began running down the road, traveling about a hundred yards before turning aside to start climbing a tree. Oleth tied up the horse, grabbed a rusty iron axe out of the back of wagon and took off after his brother.

"I can see a wagon up ahead," Eliamm called down

from the branch. "It's in a clearing up beyond the bend."

"Are they in it?" Oleth asked. He started to climb into the tree.

"Keep down! You're too heavy!" Eliamm ordered. "I can't see inside—there's just a barred window on the back end. I don't see anyone on the wagon. The driver must have unhitched the horses to lead them to water. Now's our chance! Come on!"

Eliamm tumbled down out of the tree and ran down the road, Oleth following.

Nearing the clearing, the pair hid amid the ferns and vines, sneaking ever closer to the wood-sided wagon. It was huge, easily tall enough inside for Eliamm to stand up in. The wagon could carry twenty-five or thirty people and it must take a team of four horses to haul it. They could see green-gray smoke drifting out through gaps in the boards. Soft moans came from inside. Here and there a hand poked through the gaps in the wood panels.

"Keep watch!" Eliamm told his brother.

Oleth scanned the swamp around them for signs of the driver or crew. Eliamm began working at the lock on the back door of the wagon, trying to force the lock with his knife blade. All he succeeded in doing was breaking the blade on his knife.

Eliamm seized the axe and began to hack at the lock. The brittle iron axe-head cracked apart at the first hit. The steel lock remained intact. With a curse Eliamm hurled the axe-handle aside. Oleth picked it up again, thinking it might come in handy.

As he worked, Eliamm called out to those inside, but the captives made no intelligible response. They moaned and hummed, or babbled. Eliamm was digging at the wood around the lock with the remnants of the broken knife blade, when a thrashing sound in the undergrowth silenced him. The sound came from across the clearing.

Oleth saw movement in the plants and quickly pulled his older brother back into the tall ferns. Together the pair watched as the driver emerged from the bushes. He was alone, wearing a helmet topped with fanciful horns on his head. He wore a long dark cloak pulled tightly around him. As he shuffled past them, they saw that the cloak covered a huge hump on his back, a long black scarf covered his face. The driver appeared to be unarmed, and from what they could see, he was alone.

No sign of any horses.

Slowly working their way into deeper cover, the brothers prayed that the driver wouldn't look at the back-end of the wagon, where the dig-marks from the knife could be plainly seen.

The driver stood in front of the wagon. He reached into his cloak with heavy, gloved hands and drew forth an elongated disk attached to a long string. He began to twirl the disk around in the air. Faintly at first, but growing louder as it picked up speed, came the humming sound that had echoed through the swamp on previous mornings.

They could hear a crashing sound and suddenly the brothers knew what pulled the wagon. The tylor came thundering out of the swamp.

"Did you have good hunting this night?" the hunchback asked the tylor, as he hooked thick iron chains to the wagon, and then attached the chain to a leather harness around the lizard.

Within minutes, the tylor was hitched up. The hunchback snapped a whip and the wagon lurched forward, heading east, away from the lands the boys called home.

They hurried back to their own wagon.

* * * * *

"I don't understand," Eliamm said. "Why didn't any of them say anything to us? They all sounded . . . crazy."

"Forget about that. What do we do about the lizard?" Oleth asked, his voice quavering. "We could handle the driver, but not that thing."

"There's got to be a way," Eliamm said. "We just haven't thought of it yet."

They followed the slave wagon at a distance, easily keeping up with its slow pace. The road ran straight, so they stayed far back, keeping to its edges where they couldn't be seen. Being as close to the river camp as they suspected they were, neither of the boys wanted to take any chances. Time was running out. If they didn't rescue them soon, they would have to deal with more than a lone hunch-backed guard.

The slaver stopped frequently to toss large hunks of meat down to the tylor. As the sun hung low in the sky, the wagon stopped again, this time for the night, apparently. The driver laid a pack and a bedroll out on the wagon roof. Climbing down, he looped the chains of the tylor around a massive willow tree, securing them on a massive rusted spike driven into the trunk.

The boys found a small rock overhang, and proceeded to unpack their bedrolls. Oleth volunteered for first watch when he saw the fatigue on his brother's face, and, within minutes, Eliamm was asleep.

The next few hours passed slowly. Oleth distracted himself by looking up at the stars through the few gaps in the dense foliage. The swamp was strangely silent. Perhaps the animals feared the tylor. Oleth certainly did.

He watched the bright red star in the north sky wink down at the planet, and the silvery disk of the lone moon rise high into the sky.

* * * * *

"Oleth! Oleth! Wake up!" Eliamm shook his brother's sleeping form again.

Oleth opened bleary eyes. The moon was still high overhead, morning was still hours away.

"What—" he asked fearfully.

"I know how to save them, but we have to leave now! Come on!" Eliamm urged.

"What do you want to do?" Oleth asked. He was still half asleep, only barely registering the words.

"I'll explain while we travel," Eliamm said.

* * * * *

The sun was high in the sky. Sitting on the wagon seat, Oleth could hear the slaver wagon before he saw it. Wheels rumbled, chains jingled, the tylor's huge feet slapped the mud. Sweat trickled down his forehead under the black hood, and ran down his back. He stole a glance at his brother, hidden in the underbrush, who promptly pointed to the road with an angry glare.

"There's no way this will work," Oleth whispered to himself for the hundredth time. "I'm too big, Eliamm. He'll know right off."

They had backtracked down the road during the night. Finding a parallel trail, they followed it, driving hard all night, hoping against hope that it would lead them where they wanted to go and not into a bog. They were in luck. The narrow side trail rejoined the main road ahead of the slave wagon and less than a mile from where Fessik had told them he regularly met the slavers. The brothers then waited a little over two hours before they heard the wagon coming.

The slave wagon appeared rolling around the bend, the massive horned head of the tylor bobbing as it walked. Oleth's mouth went dry and his palms began to sweat. They had parked Fessik's wagon alongside the road where the driver would be sure to see it. They'd tied their horse to a tree a few dozen yards away. From its compliant behavior, they guessed that the horse had probably been to this spot many times. Even when the giant lizard was only a yards down the road, the horse barely reacted. Clearly, Fessik had been running his side business for a long time.

The huge wagon lurched to a stop. The hunchbacked figure rose from his seat and began climbing awkwardly down the side ladder. Oleth jumped down from the seat of Fessik's wagon at the same time. A wicked looking halberd was mounted beside the driver's seat. Oleth's heart was in his throat, fearing the hunchback would bring the weapon with him.

The hunchback left it in place, however. Unsuspicious, he advanced toward what he thought was his business partner.

Oleth kept the cloak wrapped around him, hoping that his bulk would be taken for that of the cloak. He and Fessik were about the same height, but Oleth was almost twice as big in the shoulders. Fessik's beard was duplicated with smeared axle grease. Eliamm had cut Oleth's curly hair until it resembled the merchant's grizzled locks. It wasn't a very good disguise, but it only had to work long enough to lure the slaver off the wagon and away from the tylor.

"We meet again, Fessik," the hunchback said, his low voice muffled by the scarf around his face. "And which of your customers are you selling out today? There better be more than two families this time! I'm barely half full!"

The hunchback extended a gloved hand. Oleth hesitated, but he couldn't do much except accept it. He clasped the hand in his own. He couldn't see the hunchback's eyes through the horned helmet, but when the handshake weakened, Oleth knew something was wrong. He tightened his hold of the hand. Shifting his weight and pulling, he flung the hunchback behind him, slamming him against the side of Fessik's wagon.

Eliamm burst out from the underbrush, axe handle in hand, as his brother tripped the hunchback, sent him sprawling on the ground. Face down on the road, the hunchback tried to get up, but a blow across the back from Eliamm sent him down again.

While his older brother kept the man pinned, Oleth ran to the slave wagon. He kept a fearful eye on the tylor, but the beast apparently knew Fessik, as well. The tylor shook its head and appeared to be searching for the meat it normally received when they stopped.

Oleth yanked the halberd from its mount beside the seat.

As Oleth ran back with the halberd, he saw that Eliamm had apparently gone mad.

His brother's face was fiery red. Fury blazed in his eyes. He swung the axe handle again and again, sent it crashing down on the helpless hunchback who writhed at his feet.

"Eliamm! Stop! You're killing him!" Oleth shouted, horrified.

Eliamm paid no attention. He kept raining blows, kept raving that this was for his father and this for his mother and this for his sisters.

Reaching his brother, Oleth grabbed Eliamm and halted the beating.

Eliamm rounded on him, fury contorting his face until it was as ugly as Fessik's.

"You can't kill him, Eliamm!" Oleth said. "No matter what he's done. That's makes us as bad as him."

Oleth held the halberd over the hunchback, blocking

any further blows from Eliamm. Eliamm's chest heaved with exertion and anger. After a moment, he grew calm and threw his club to the ground.

"Sorry, Oleth," he mumbled. "You're right."

Oleth was pleased. He could not remember Eliamm ever telling him he was right about anything.

The scarf that covered the hunchback's face was bloody, but he could still move. He started to get up, but found the endspike of the halberd pressed against his chest.

"Give us the keys to the wagon," Eliamm said.

The hunchback tossed the keys at them. Eliamm bent to pick them up.

Oleth was watching his brother and not the hunchback.

The hunchback rolled to the side, lashed out with a kick at the halberd, knocked it aside. Moving fast despite the beating, the hunchback was up and running. Before Eliamm could catch him, the hunchback had vanished, his dark form disappearing into the shadows of the swamp.

They didn't bother to chase after him. Figuring the hunchback had run to the slaver's camp for help, they had to get away from there as soon as possible.

* * * * *

The inside of the slave wagon was filthy. Human waste and blood covered the floor. The prisoners huddled together silently, eyes wide and glassy, barely reacting when the massive door swung opened. As Eliamm climbed into the wagon, he noticed the same greenish-gray smoke that they had seen the day before, drifting out of a metal-caged lantern on the ceiling. The smoke filled the wagon interior with a noxious fog, forcing him to retreat outside. Now he knew what had made the prisoners complacent.

The open door soon dissipated the smoke, but not its effects on the prisoners. Some of them were able to walk out on their own after some coaxing, but most had to be helped or carried. There was only thirteen people in the wagon. Eliamm noticed that their father wasn't among them. His fears had been realized. He could only assume his father was dead.

Oleth carried their mother in his arms, his eyes filled with tears. Eliamm sought out their two sisters, ragged and filthy and half-sick with the smoke. He cradled them in his arms, carrying them quickly out of the slaver's wagon and over to their own. They worked as fast as they could and soon had everyone tucked inside Fessik's wagon.

A horn call split the silence of the swamp.

"Whatever it means," Eliamm said, "it probably isn't good."

They doused the slaver's wagon with oil from the lamp, setting it ablaze as they fled. The tylor chained to the wagon came alive at last, bellowing in terror at the sight of the fire. It took off, running east on the trail, and vanished into the swamp, dragging the blazing wagon with it.

* * * * *

The brightly painted wagon trundled down the muddy road, its progress slowed by the extra weight of the people inside. Eliamm was at the reins, driving the wagon west, heading for the nearest shelter they could find. Oleth was in back with the prisoners, doing what he could to help them. The prisoners were in a sorry state. They were bruised and dehydrated; welts covered their bodies, as did festering scratches and insect bites.

They traveled westward for hours, the sun dipping lower and lower in the sky before them. Eliamm stopped only briefly to water the horse and let it rest. Periodically, the horn would again split the air, but it sounded farther and farther away. The prisoners fell asleep.

* * * * *

Oleth was half-asleep in the wagon when a tremendous jolt rocked the wagon. Oleth heard the aged roof above him creak under the force of some heavy weight. The wagon shock violently as footsteps stomped across the roof.

"Eliamm!" Olaf shouted.

A scream split the air. "Help! Oleth! Help!"

Oleth crawled over the bodies of the slumbering prisoners, finally reached the wagon door, only to discover that it had been barred on the outside. No matter how hard he shoved, the door wouldn't open.

* * * * *

A nightmare stood over Eliamm, wielding the axe handle Eliamm had used on him before. Eliamm pulled the horse to a halt, fearful that it would panic and run, wrecking the wagon and hurting the prisoners. He did not have time to defend himself and the hunchback had a clear shot. The creature struck Eliamm hard on the arm shattering the bone and driving it through the skin. Blood gushed from the wound

Eliamm dropped the reins, climbed up on the roof, thinking to hurl the creature from the roof. He froze in fear as he saw the huge black wings.

Moonlight illuminated dagger-like ebony tusks and a yellow-fanged maw. Spittle flew from its mouth as it swung the axe handle. What they had taken for a horned helm was actually horns thrusting up from the creature's head.

Eliamm gaped, horrified at this apparition, fear paralyzing him. He could do nothing but try to ward off the blows that rained down on him and cry out for his brother to help him.

"Do you know what I am, human?" the creature shrieked, laughing as it struck at him. "I am spawn! We serve Onysablet, ruler of the New Swamp! One day," the creature shrieked above the howling wind, "one day there will be enough spawn to drive you all from the swamp!"

The spawn brought the club down on Eliamm's back.

"Soon we won't need to hide under cloaks! Soon Onysablet the great dragon will allow us to reveal ourselves! We will rule here because we are united! We do not turn on each other like you humans!"

Again and again the club fell.

"You were going to kill me, weren't you? We do not kill each other. We do not betray our own kind."

The pain was too terrible to bear. Eliamm lost his balance, fell backward onto the wagon's seat. The spawn leapt down to land beside him, continuing to rain blows on the now unresisting form.

"Soon, Onysablet will rule supreme! All will fear her. All!"

The spawn continued to beat its victim until, with a grunt, it placed a clawed foot on the limp body and shoved it over the side of the wagon.

* * * * *

Oleth turned around and pulled out the halberd, hoping to get out and onto the roof. He could hear a low voice, muffled by the wood, and his brother scream again and again. Then Eliamm's screams fell silent and the wagon lurched forward suddenly. Oleth began kicking frantically at the rear door. The aged wood held firmly.

Oleth charged at the door with his shoulder. The door gave way with a splintering crack, flying wide open. Oleth fell headlong out the back of the moving wagon. He grabbed at the swinging door as he fell, his hand clutching at the handle. As his full weight yanked on the rain-slicked handle, he felt the door shift. His feet dragged though the muddy ground, one hand keeping desperate hold on the handle, the other on the halberd.

"Eliamm! Stop this thing!" Oleth roared.

But there was no answer, only a strange hissing sound.

Nails in the hinge were working their way out of the wet wood. The wagon bounced over a rut, the force jarred the nails out farther. The wagon was beginning to speed up, traveling downhill. The slope curved to the right abruptly, sending the wagon up onto its left wheels. It settled down again with a rocking shudder.

The door swung shut, sending Oleth forwards, giving him just enough time to loop one foot on the step before the door started to swing open again. Jabbing the halberd downwards, he buried the spike into one of the wagon's fenders, giving him a few seconds to search for a better handhold. He grasped hold of a lantern hook above the door.

Arms aching, he pulled his stout body up onto the roof, reached down to grab the halberd. He searched for Eliamm, but saw only a hideous winged monster in the driver's seat. Eliamm was nowhere in sight. Oleth crept forward, feet spread wide, holding the halberd horizontal, to balance himself on the roof of the careening wagon.

The roof was slick—slick with blood.

The spoked wheels rattled, as the wagon crossed on to a rickety wooden trestle. Grief and fear tore Oleth's heart, gave him courage. With a howl of rage, he swung the halberd. He tried to hit the creature in the back, between the wings. He missed, struck the shoulder.

The spawn whirled around, roaring in pain and fury. Green-black blood pumped out onto the wagon roof, smoking and sputtering in the moonlight. The spawn leapt up onto the roof, staggering slightly as it moved.

Oleth swung the halberd in a wide arc, to ward it off, the tip of the endspike grazing the monster's chest. Before it could continue its advance, Oleth had recovered from the swing, and pointing the halberd forward like a spear, he thrust forward.

The foot long iron spike slid past the creatures warding arm, driving deep into its belly and out its back. Oleth kept pushing, driving the screaming spawn toward the side of the wagon.

Blood poured from the creature's mouth. The dying spawn grabbed the handle of the halberd, tried wrench it from Oleth's grip. He held firm, and continued to push. The wagon rocked wildly as the maddened horse thundered down the road. With a final shove, Oleth pushed the spawn off the roof and over the edge of the bridge. Hanging onto the lurching wagon, he peered down among the rocks. All that remained was a tangle of broken bone and torn flesh.

Oleth ran to the front of the wagon, jumping into the seat and grabbed the reins. The horse slowed and the wagon came to a halt.

Leaping down from the wagon, Oleth raced back along the road until he found Eliamm.

Oleth cradled the broken body in his arms, carrying it back to the wagon, wrapping it in a blanket and gently laying it on the seat beside him.

Eliamm always liked to sleep in the open, under the stars.

Shard's Memory
Chris Pierson

Silence had once been a rare thing in Hybardin. The
Life-Tree, the giant stalactite-city that stood at the heart
of the dwarven realm of Thorbardin, had always been
filled with noise: hammers ringing at forges, haggling in
marketplaces, voices raised in song in ale-halls. The
commotion had been constant, and Hylar dwarves
learned from a young age to sleep amid the clamor. In a
city always abustle with life, silence spoke of emptiness
and loss. It was the sound of the crypt.

But quiet dwelt now in the city's cavernous halls.
Five years ago, the hordes of Chaos had attacked, and
the Life-Tree had cracked. Fissures riddled its rocky surface, and pieces had broken loose to fall into the black
Urkhan Sea. The lowest levels, in the stalactite's tip,
were nothing but rubble littering the wharf below. The
dwarves had been busy repairing the damage ever since,
but the scars of Chaos's onslaught remained. And worst
of all were the silences that ran through the city, like
veins of poisonous ore.

Morvik Narrowshaft followed such a vein, the scuff
of his bootheels the only sound. He strode down a broad
avenue on one of the city's uppermost levels, where the
manors of noble families stood. In times past, the street
had been a hive of activity. Children had laughed, adults

had called out to one another, pack lizards had pulled creaking wagons hither and yon. Now, though, the manors stood quiet as skulls, their windows dark. The iron gates lining the avenue silently rusted. Once-vibrant gardens were barren, once-bubbling fountains still. Rubble lay all about, mantled with dust.

Five years ago, Chaos had come to Silverspear Way. The shadow wights, beings of inky nothingness, had boiled into the city, laying waste to all in their path. Those they killed ceased to exist, as though they had never been. Within the manor grounds, heaps of armor marked where warriors had stood. Mounds of moldering clothes were all that remained of men, women and children. Not even the memory of the slain lingered, even in the minds of those who had known and loved them.

The shadow wights had swept from house to house, and while elsewhere the dwarves had fought or fled, the folk of Silverspear Way had never had a chance. One estate after another stood empty, the names of the clans who had dwelt within known only by the runes carved into the lintels above their gates. Hybardin was full of such places now, as were the other cities in the dwarf-realm: all of Thorbardin might have been so, had the High Thane of the kingdom not invoked ancient magic to thwart the invasion in the end.

Morvik held aloft a gleaming lantern, its light a sliver in the darkness. His other hand rested on the hilt of the sword that hung at his hip. Monsters had come to dwell in some of the derelict parts of the Life-Tree, as had bands of ruffians and scavengers who wouldn't think twice about slitting the throat of a lone, unarmed traveler. He rattled his scabbard now and again, making it clear to anyone who listened that he was capable of fighting back. If monsters or bandits lurked on Silverspear Way, they stayed hidden.

He stopped, gazing up at the runes above a gate that stood before a broad, slate-roofed manor. *House Ore-digger*, they declared. He frowned, trying to remember the Oredigger clan, but it was useless. Somewhere in the city's lore-halls, some roster would list the names of the dwarves who'd lived here, but there were no longer any faces or deeds to put with those names. The denizens of House Oredigger were lost, and by dwarven law the house would stand empty for a century unless an heir came forward with proof of his heritage. No heir would come, though—not for this manor, nor for any of the others that lined the avenue. Morvik bowed his head, his black beard bristling against his blue leather jerkin, then turned and walked on.

He stopped again four houses down, shining his lantern ahead. Its light fell upon a lone figure, standing outside another estate—a woman, whose tresses and cheek-whiskers glittered like polished copper. A glimmering lamp sat at her feet, bathing her in its ruddy glow. She was unarmored, and might have been prey for vagabonds, but for the sturdy warhammer slung across her back. She stood with her back to the street, staring in through the gates. Her fists were clenched about the bars, as though she could bend them apart with sheer will.

Morvik opened his mouth to speak, but his voice caught, and he cleared his throat twice before any sound would come.

"Lass," he called, "it's two bells past midnight. What are you doing here?"

She didn't move, except for a stiffening of her shoulders. "It's mine, Morvik," she replied firmly. "It will be mine again."

Sighing, Morvik started toward her. He glanced up at the rune-inscribed lintel: *House Ironsmelt*, it read. His hand moved away from his sword as he drew near, and he rested it on the dwarfmaid's arm. She didn't turn, keeping her gleaming eyes on the tall, domed manor beyond the gates. Morvik regarded her silently, then leaned in to kiss her cheek.

"Come away, Shard," he said. "It's late."

Her face grew stony, and her knuckles whitened as she gripped the bars tighter. "No," she growled. "This is my *home*, Morvik!"

He shook his head. "You don't know—"

"Yes, I do." She turned toward him at last. "I don't have proof yet, but I'll find it. I *am* an Ironsmelt."

Morvik looked away, unable to meet her fiery gaze. After a moment, though, he turned back. "Shard, come on. We'll talk about this tomorrow." He bent forward and pressed his lips against the corner of her mouth. "Please, love."

For several heartbeats she glared at him, then her gaze softened. She let go of the gate and slid her arms about him, and buried her face against his chest. They stayed that way a while, neither moving. When she pulled away, she said nothing; only nodded, favoring him with a faltering smile.

They tarried long enough to retrieve Shard's lamp, then walked away down the avenue, through the terrible silence.

* * * * *

Shard was not her birth name, but it was the only one she had. That was the trouble.

Not all the fighting during the Chaos War had happened in Hybardin. The shadow wights and fire dragons had attacked everywhere, from distant Northgate to the cities of Daebardin and Klarbardin, and even beneath the kingdom, where the dwarves' mineshafts snaked through the earth's bones.

Hroldeg's Delve had been such a place. It had been a fortress on the rim of a deep chasm, a safe place for the dwarves to store ore and rough gemstones before shipping them to the cities above. Morvik had been among the dwarves garrisoned there, guarding the riches within. He had no idea how many dwarves had been posted there, though he suspected there'd been more than two hundred. Of those, fewer than thirty had survived.

The word "battle" couldn't accurately describe what had happened at the Delve. In Morvik's memory, it was a slaughter. The shadow wights had been all but unstoppable: mortal weapons passed through them without effect, and only fire held them at bay. They could kill with a touch and tear through stone like wet parchment. Morvik's last clear memory before the killing started was of rushing up onto the curtain wall, summoned by the stone war drums atop the watchtowers, and standing shoulder to shoulder with his fellow dwarves as the darkness within the chasm came alive. Sometimes, in his nightmares, he could still see the shadows boiling toward him, misshapen, night-black claws groping for living flesh.

After that, memory became tricky. He could only remember flashes—the glint of steel, the sound of stone collapsing, the taste of blood in his mouth—and even in those, there were holes. Those voids had been his fellows: living dwarves who'd fallen to the shadowy horde, their names and faces now forever lost. Some, he was sure, had been friends and family; others he'd hardly known. They were all gone now.

In the end, the shadow wights had retreated, leaving the ramparts—what little of them remained—littered with the leavings of the slain, and a handful of confused, terrified dwarves. Morvik had lost both sword and shield, and had been one of the last of those who'd stood upon the northernmost stretch of the west wall. Elsewhere, the damage had been worse: the north wall, and the tower at its east end, had been utterly destroyed, with no one left alive.

So the survivors had thought.

When the fighting had ended and the wounded had been seen to, the dwarves had begun sifting through the ruins, seeking signs of the slain. They'd found nothing but axes and hammers, mail and helms—with one exception. Morvik had been digging through the rubble that once had been the north wall, pulling twisted breastplates and shields from the ruins, when he'd heard a soft moan—a woman's voice, beneath the debris.

He'd dug more furiously, desperation giving him strength to lift stones no dwarf should have been able to shift. He'd clawed his fingers bloody, but he'd reached her: a battered, bruised, and bloodied dwarfmaid clad in plate armor. Only luck had saved her life: the apex of an arch had come down over her, shielding her from the other rocks rather than crushing her. She hadn't been unhurt—her left leg had been broken and she'd suffered a concussion—but that she'd survived at all had seemed a miracle.

Worse than any physical injury, though, was that Morvik hadn't had any idea who she was. That realization had horrified him: he'd known the other survivors' names—even those he'd seldom spoken to—but hers was a mystery. He couldn't recall ever having seen her before. And when she stirred at last, jarred awake by pain as he splinted her leg, there came an even worse shock: *she* didn't know who she was, either. Her memory was completely, utterly gone.

It hadn't taken him long to realize what had happened: whatever magic the shadow wights worked to destroy those they killed had affected her as well. In recent years, Morvik had discovered that her case, while rare, was far from unique: a few hundred dwarves, scattered throughout Thorbardin, had suffered a similar fate. With no memories of before that time, those dwarves, whom their fellows called the Twice-Born, had had to begin their lives anew in the wake of the war.

Morvik had started calling the dwarfmaid Shard, after the broken stones that had buried her. She'd liked the name, and it had stuck. He'd tended her wounds, bringing her food and water while her leg mended. The dwarves had stayed at the Delve for a week after the battle, building cairns for the dead and sending search parties into the mines to dig out survivors. After that, they'd left the fortress, bearing riches and the wounded alike back to the cities above. Morvik had pushed Shard in a handcart on that long journey, and had stayed with her on the chain-pulled boat that brought them back to the sundered Life-Tree.

Many dwarves had lost their clans during the battle, and in the following weeks it became the norm for households to give succor to these unfortunate souls. When Morvik returned to House Narrowshaft—which had escaped most of the carnage—Shard came with him. Morvik's family had helped him care for her as she recovered from her wounds and tried in vain to regain her memory.

It was hard to say when his ministrations turned into love. It hadn't been sudden, but in hindsight it had been inevitable. By the time Shard could walk again unaided, she and Morvik had become smitten with each other. Most of the dwarves whom the war had orphaned— the Twice-Born included—left Hybardin after they recovered, settling in the ruins of the dark dwarf city of Daerforge and calling themselves the Lokhar, or the Unclanned. Shard, however, had remained after she became well again, for first weeks, then months. Morvik's family had welcomed her, for they were masons, and she'd proven able at the craft: somehow, her hands knew exactly what to do around cut stone and mortar. That was good for the Narrowshafts, for there was no shortage of masonry work in the broken city.

Love and work, however, didn't content her. Not knowing who she'd been, or what clan she'd belonged to, had been a hole in her heart. She'd hungered to find out something—anything—about her heritage. Morvik had been skeptical, but reluctantly he'd agreed to help her in her search. Together they'd pored over the lore-books of the Hylar, questioned other survivors of the Delve, even consulted fortune-tellers in the hopes of gaining some clue.

After months of searching, they'd had a break-through. The key had been Ernguth Ghaeril, a dwarf who'd been duty sergeant at the Delve. The dwarves on the eastern end of the north wall, where Morvik had found Shard—had all been of the same house, Ernguth's records had shown. Those dwarves had been from the Ironsmelt clan.

From that day on, though she had no memory of it, Shard had been certain she was of House Ironsmelt. Unfortunately, no other Ironsmelt had survived the Chaos War—those not slain at Hroldeg's Delve had died as the shadow wights ravaged the manors on Silver-spear Way. Not a single man, woman, or child of the clan remained, and the estate had been sealed, awaiting a new heir to claim it. Awaiting Shard.

Their troubles had started there. Shard had staked a claim on House Ironsmelt, but the reeve who judged such things sought proof of her lineage. All the evidence she had of her heritage was circumstantial, though, and in the end, the reeve had denied her claim.

This defeat had only strengthened Shard's resolve. She'd sworn House Ironsmelt would be hers, and nothing would sway her. This quest consumed all her time: she even stopped working to devote more effort to her research. Morvik's family tolerated this for a time, but with Shard's quest draining their coffers, they could only stand it for so long. Finally, as her search entered its third year, Morvik's father had asked her to leave. Grudgingly she'd complied, and Morvik had gone with her, moving into a smaller home in the Life-Tree's deepest levels.

That had been nearly three years ago; she'd made little progress since. She'd met one failure after another, but each only drove her harder. In her mind, it was not a matter of *if* she would reclaim House Ironsmelt, but *when*.

Morvik, on the other hand, remained doubtful. He loved Shard and wished to marry her—but no reeve would grant a nuptial writ to a member of the Unclanned. And his own family steadfastly opposed their union. Shard herself was more obsessed with her unknown past than with the issue of marriage.

Then, only half a year ago, Shard had had another unexpected breakthrough. She'd taken to making forays to Lobardin, the city of the Unclanned. On one such voyage, she'd found the Lokhar abuzz with excitement. Word had come from beyond Thorbardin that a Twice-Born human from Solamnia had found a way to regain his past. He'd caught a shadow wight, and had compelled it to reveal what he wanted to know. What was more, it hadn't even been the *same* shadow wight that had stolen his identity: all the Chaos-spawned fiends, it seemed, knew the names of the murdered, and would reveal them if forced by a Twice-Born.

The thought that she might be able to regain her identity had galvanized her, lifting her spirits higher than they'd been in years. Her obsession had taken on a new tenor, shifting from the search for knowledge to preparation for facing a shadow wight. She'd learned as much as possible about the foul creatures: they were indeed afraid of fire, their voices could paralyze a victim with despair, and they could only be harmed by consecrated weapons—which, with the gods gone from Krynn, grew rarer every day. Even so, she'd acquired two such sacred arms—a hammer and a sword—so when the time came, she would be ready.

Now, all that remained was to find a shadow wight. The fiends were scarce after the war, most having vanished when Chaos was defeated. But a few were rumored to remain. Shard went to Lobardin every week now, hoping to learn that one had been sighted somewhere in Thorbardin. So far, she'd been disappointed.

Secretly, Morvik hoped the disappointment would continue. The thought of Shard facing the fiends again worried him greatly. Yet he didn't tell her this—how could he, when only her quest gave her such purpose these days? So he sat by, waiting, and prayed her wish would never come true.

* * * * *

Upper Lobardin's main street was packed with dwarves of all descriptions. Unlike most of Thorbardin's folk, who prided themselves on the purity of their heritage, the Unclanned included folk from all the major peoples—Hylar, Daewar, Klar, Theiwar and Daergar. The city was divided into two parts, split by a deep rift a fire dragon had blasted into the stone. The Lower City, stretching along the shore of the Urkhan, was a maze of slums, lawless and dangerous. Going there unarmed and alone was to tempt getting one's purse—or throat—cut. Across the rift, however, the city was a different place. The Upper City was still poor, but for the most part it was safe. A community, of sorts, had risen out of the Lokhar's shared plight: adversity let dwarves who would have killed each other five years ago live in harmony.

Shard shouldered her way down the street, making her way through the bustling crowds. It was hard going, but in time she reached the intersection she sought: a narrow side street branching off the main boulevard. She pushed through the mob, toward a sign emblazoned with a coiled white dragon. The door beneath the sign was open, and song and laughter rang within. The smell of roasting cave-cricket meat wafted out into the street. Smiling, Shard strode toward Ice Wyrm Hall.

A disciple of Severus Stonehand was proselytizing by the door. Stonehand had been around for years, seeking followers to march forth and reclaim the ancient realm of Thoradin. His following was stronger nowhere than in Lobardin: the Unclanned, more than any others, were eager to seek a new home, there to start new lives.

Shard elbowed past the ranting preacher, throwing an icy glare when he tried to clasp her hand, then walked into the dark, smoky tavern.

The Twice-Born, who were a minority amongst the thousands of Unclanned, had staked out a few gathering places in Lobardin, and the Ice Wyrm was one of the most popular. Its proprietor, a grey-bearded Klar named Scree, was Twice-Born himself, and helped spread news among his kind. He had been the one who'd told Shard about the Solamnian who had

regained his name. She never came to Lobardin without visiting the Wyrm.

Scree was behind the bar when she came in, and
waved to her as she threaded her way among the tables.
She tossed a few coppers down, and Scree set a mug of
foaming black beer before her. She took a deep drink
and wiped her mouth.

"Bloody Stonehanders are back, I see," she said.

Scree made a sour face. "Can't make 'em stay away,"
he grumbled, waving toward the door. "I went after that
bugger with a table leg just the other night, but it weren't
no good." He hawked and spat eloquently in a spittoon
behind the bar. "So I've got good news, lass."

Shard drained her tankard, shoved it aside, and
leaned forward. "You've got something to say, say it."

The barkeep turned away, taking Shard's tankard,
and poured her another beer. She glared at him pointedly as he handed her the mug again.

"Oh, all right," he said at last, chuckling. "You've
suffered enough. I've found you your shadow wight."

She opened her mouth, then closed it again. "What?"
she asked. "Where?"

"Oh, that's the best part," he replied, folding his
arms. "It's at the Delve."

"The Delve?" Shard repeated. "*Hroldeg's* Delve?"

"Ayuh," Scree replied, nodding. "A Daergar patrol
ran into it, this past Agorin-day. It killed 'em all . . .
except one, who got away. Poor bugger was half out of
his wits when he got back. Last I heard, the Daergar
were talking about sending troops to get rid of the
accursed thing. I figured you'd want a shot at it first."

"Bloody right I do." Shard shook her head in amazement. "Who else knows about this?"

"No one *I've* told," Scree answered. "After all you've
gone through, lass, I figured you should be first to know."

"Thanks."

"Best be quick, though," Scree warned. "This won't stay secret long. You're not the only Twice-Born who's looking to catch a shadow wight."

Shard had been thinking the same thing. She rose, leaving her beer untouched. "You sure you don't want to come along?"

"No, lass," he replied, shaking his head, "but thanks. Some of us are glad not to know who we used to be."

Shard nodded, understanding. Just as her hands had known their way around stone, Scree had found he knew other things—how to pick pockets, how to slip a knife between a dwarf's ribs, and even less pleasant skills. To him, forgetting who he used to be had been a blessing, not a curse.

"All right, then," she said. "I'd stay to talk a while longer, but—"

"Go," Scree interrupted, waving her off. "Get out of here."

Turning, Shard hurried out the door. She knocked the Stonehander aside as she plunged into the crowd, bound for the docks of the Lower City.

* * * * *

Morvik had been at his family's manor all morning, working on plans for repairs to the bottom levels of the Life-Tree. He expected no one to be at the small dwelling he and Shard shared when he returned: Shard seldom returned from her sojourns to Lobardin before nighttime. When he got back, though, the door was unlocked. He reached for his sword—burglars weren't unknown in the part of Hybardin where he and Shard lived. Carefully, he eased the door open.

The entry hall was dark. At the far end, however,

golden lamplight glimmered beneath the door to the common room he and Shard shared. Morvik paused, swallowing: he could hear someone moving within. There was also another sound: metal rattling, as if the prowler were wearing a full suit of armor—

Morvik's heart sank. At once, he knew it was no burglar in his home. Feeling almost ill, he hurried down the hall and pushed open the door to the common room.

Shard looked up from where she sat as he came in. She was strapping her plate greaves on over her chain mail leggings. The rest of her was encased in armor as well, save for a few pieces—vambraces, gauntlets, her winged, visored helm—that she had yet to don. On the floor before her were a large, round shield, two leather packs, and a war hammer. It wasn't the same steel weapon she usually carried, Morvik saw: its head was silvery, with gold filigree. He recognized it right away as the blessed weapon she'd acquired to use against the shadow wight.

"Reorx's beard," Morvik swore. "You've found one?"

Shard nodded curtly, grabbing up her gauntlets and pulling them on. "It's at the Delve. I'm going. I'll be damned if another Twice-Born is going to beat me there."

Morvik walked to a stool and slumped down. He watched while she strapped on the last of her armor, then took a deep breath and let it out. "Shard, forget the shadow wight. Forget the past. Let's you and me leave Thorbardin."

"What?" She looked up, astonished.

"You heard me." He gazed at her, beseeching. "We'll go out into the world—names don't matter there. We can marry, live among the hill dwarves . . . or see the rest of Ansalon, if that's what you want. Maybe, if Stonehand ever takes back Thoradin, we can find a new home there. . . ."

Disappointment flashed in her eyes, and he fell silent.

"I thought you understood," she said. "I can't just leave, not when I'm so close to finding out who I am."

"You know who you are!" Morvik snapped. "You're Shard. The rest of it, that isn't you. It's someone you used to be."

"No, Morvik," she said. "I *am* an Ironsmelt. I'll have that back—the name, the manor—"

"To the Abyss with the manor!" he shouted. "Think about what you're risking, Shard. You could die. Who you were, who you are now . . . none of it will exist any more!" He walked across the room, and knelt before her. "Shard, you have my love. Isn't that enough?"

She stared at him for a long moment, then slowly shook her head. "I don't know. I don't think so."

He sat back, his face ashen, as she lifted her helm and slid it over her head. She left the visor open as she gathered her packs.

"I'm sorry, Morvik," she said, slinging her hammer and shield across her back. "I'll see you when I get back."

"No. I'm going with you."

Shard looked at him sharply. "I'm not asking—"

"You don't have to." He sighed. "I may not like you going back to the Delve, but if I can't stop you, there's no way I'm letting you do it alone."

With that, he turned and walked past her, into their bedroom to fetch his own armor. Behind him, though he couldn't see her, he knew Shard smiled.

* * * * *

Four hours later, a chain-pulled boat rattled across the black Urkhan sea, away from the Life-Tree. It pulled up to a broad stone jetty at the edge of the vast cavern, the lamp at its prow a feeble mote in the vast darkness.

Its pilot glanced about nervously as the craft bumped against the dock, then turned to his two armored passengers.

"This is it," he growled, gesturing down the shadowy jetty. At its far end, a tunnel opened in the cavern wall, like a throat of stone. "That's the old mine road. The rest of the journey's your own trouble."

Morvik stepped onto the dock, a hand on his sword. He wore the blessed blade Shard had acquired, in place of his usual weapon. He offered her his arm: she didn't need his help getting out of the boat, but she took it anyway. Her armor jingled as she stepped up beside him.

"You'll be back in three days, like we arranged?" Morvik asked.

"Aye," the pilot replied, his lips pursing to show how unhappy he was with the idea. His purse was full, though, and Morvik had promised to fatten it further when they returned to Hybardin. "I'll wait for an hour at midday—not a minute more. If you're not here by then, it'll be a long swim home."

"Fair enough," Shard said.

The boatman pushed off, his craft clattering away from the jetty. As his lamp faded in the distance, Shard lit a lantern of her own and closed the shutter. She shone its narrow beam about, warily searching the darkness.

They'd come here directly—they hadn't even gone to House Narrowshaft, to tell Morvik's family where they were bound. Now they were alone, darkness all about them. The dwarves didn't use this road much any more: quakes during and after the Chaos War had collapsed most of the promising mineshafts beneath this part of the kingdom, and had left the rest dangerously unstable. Standing here, surrounded by shadows, the only sound the lapping of water against the dock, the dwarves were certain that simple fear also had a lot to do with why their people had abandoned these tunnels.

They looked at the passage together, jaws clenched. "How long a walk is it?" Shard asked. "The only time I remember making this trip was you pushing me in that handcart after the battle, and even that's hazy."

Morvik furrowed his brow. "Eight hours, at a good march. Half a day if we're careful."

"Half a day, then."

He offered no argument. Shard leaned toward him and, on an impulse, kissed his lips. Then, holding her lantern ready, she started down the passage, into the earth's dark depths. Morvik paused, sliding his sword from his scabbard, then quickly followed.

* * * * *

The darkness grew smothering, sucking hungrily at the lantern's glow. Morvik had to sheathe his sword and light a second lamp, which helped matters somewhat, but even so the shadows hung over them like storm-tossed waves, ready to crash down as soon as either light faltered.

To make matters worse, the tunnel was far from quiet. The ravages of Chaos had weakened the passage's once-solid walls. Not a minute passed without the unpleasant crackle of shifting stone. Sometimes, the noise was faint, echoing up out of the gloom; other times, it was thunderclap-loud, bringing showers of dust and gravel pattering down.

Twice they heard even louder sounds, booming crashes that shook the stone beneath their feet. Later they found what had caused those ominous crashes: sheets of rock had broken loose from the ceiling and walls, littering the road with chunks of jagged debris.

They made their way around these obstacles carefully, eyeing the cracked stone overhead.

Time was difficult in such surroundings, marked only when one of their lanterns began to gutter, its fuel spent. Then they would stop, taking quick swigs of ale from their skins and replenishing their oil. They took turns at this, one always watching the darkness. If the shadow wight had ranged up the road from the Delve, it could swoop down upon them almost before they knew it. More than once, they jumped and reached for their weapons, their hearts triphammering in their breasts when the swaying lamplight made a shadow move unexpectedly.

They went on, hour upon hour, and finally they reached runestone markers proclaiming that Hroldeg's Delve lay ahead. Another hundred paces on, the tunnel widened into a vast cavern, whose full size was lost in darkness, beyond the reach of their lanterns.

Shard froze, stiffening as they stood at the cavern's edge.

Morvik reached across and took her hand. Their gauntlets scraped together. "Are you all right?"

"Yeah," she said. "It just all hit me—this is where I was born, in a way. It's where my first memories are."

They walked on. The ground was smooth and even, disturbed only by the stumps of stalagmites the dwarves had cleared away when they settled there. The ceiling was hard to make out, but the shadowy shapes of stalactites dangled down from the gloom. As they went, they passed heaps of rubble that had fallen from above, some of which would easily have filled the road behind them.

The worst thing, though, was the darkness: the cavern's size gave the gloom even greater weight. It was a strange feeling for Morvik: he'd lived here, as part of the garrison, for over a year before the Chaos War, and he'd never felt the heaviness of the shadows before. But then, in those days this had been a living place, where dwarves shouted and laughed and sang. Now it was empty, and something lurked in the darkness. Something that hungered.

"I can feel it," he murmured. "Can't you? Like something's watching us. . . ."

"Be still," Shard snapped, a little too quickly. She glanced about, throwing the light to their sides and behind them with her lamp. There was nothing to see— but that didn't mean there was nothing there.

They crept across the cavern, until at last a huge shape loomed out of the darkness: they had reached the Delve. The light of their lanterns fell upon an edifice of close-fitted granite blocks, a wall thirty feet tall and topped with crenelations. They shone their lamps to the left, where the wall ended in a stout, square tower, then swung to the right . . . and stopped, staring.

The keep had burst apart.

No one in all of Krynn worked stone as capably as the dwarves of Thorbardin. Dwarf-hewn fortresses had withstood wars, the breath of dragons, and even two Cataclysms. But here, the Delve's battlements had been torn asunder, blocks the size of houses strewn about like children's toys. Some had melted, then hardened again. It was just like Hybardin and the other cities had been, after Chaos's onslaught. The dwarves had been repairing those places for five years now, though; here, the damage was still fresh, an open wound.

Morvik licked his lips. "Think twice," he told her. "I'm not sure you want to remember what happened here."

She shook her head. "I'm not turning back." She swallowed, glancing around. "Come on. We have to get into the courtyard, away from these walls. If the shadow wight pulls one of them down on top of us . . ." She stopped, shuddering.

Morvik didn't respond for a moment, feeling sick as he stared at the rubble. Finally he nodded, waving the beam of his lantern. "Lead on."

Carefully, they started clambering over the ruined wall.

* * * * *

Little of the Delve still stood. The eastern wall and the towers at both its corners remained, as did parts of the north and south walls, though most of those had crumbled. The western wall was completely gone, its towers nothing but glassy, melted stubs. Within the courtyard, the donjon, barracks, and other buildings were piles of broken stone and splintered wood: some had caved in, while others had exploded, scattering debris all around. Amongst the ruins stood the cairns Morvik and the other survivors had built for those who had died in battle. Looking upon the makeshift graveyard, Morvik felt a tightness in his chest. He should mourn these dwarves, he knew. He'd fought beside them, had probably known them well. But how could he mourn when he couldn't even picture their faces, or speak their names?

Beyond the fortress, a deeper darkness beckoned. Hroldeg's Chasm, broad and all but bottomless, slashed through the ground. It cut across the southwest corner of the Delve, where the stone had given way and the wall had fallen into the abyss. The screams of the dwarves who'd ridden the battlements down into the pit echoed in Morvik's memory. Past the shattered wall, the bridges that had once spanned the gap had collapsed, leaving the far side, where some of the kingdom's richest mines had been, beyond reach.

They walked to the chasm's edge and peered down.
There was nothing to see, of course—there never had
been, even when the Delve stood strong and whole—
yet there was still *something* there. A presence . . . or an
absence . . . lurked down within the crevice.

"You feel it too?" Morvik breathed, glancing at Shard.
Ashen-faced, she chewed her lip as she gazed into the
depths.

She didn't answer at first. Then, blinking, she
nodded in reply. "It's cold," she said. "Like the mountain winds at midwinter." She blew out a shaky breath:
it fogged in the air.

"I remember this," Morvik agreed, stepping back
from the chasm. "When they came for us, it felt like a
blizzard was blowing up from the depths." He shivered. "How do we get to it?"

"We don't," Shard answered, glancing along the pit's
edge. She spotted an expanse that was relatively unclut-
tered by rubble, and started toward it. "If we can feel it,
sure as Reorx it can sense us, too. They can smell life, you
know—it draws them. If we give it time, it'll come to us."

Morvik chewed his moustache, his hand drifting to
the hilt of his blessed sword. He glanced away from the
chasm, then sucked in a quick breath. Shard stopped,
reaching for her hammer as she turned toward him. He
answered her worried look by pointing.

"Like it found them, you mean," he said.

Shard followed his gesture. There, some twenty paces
from where they stood—almost beyond her lantern's
glow—were several heaps of black armor. Even from a
distance, she could see they were tooled with the shapes
of talons, dragon wings, and leering skulls. Shields and
wicked axes and maces lay nearby. No dust shrouded
them: they glinted as Shard shone her lantern at them.
Daergar armor.

Neither of them spoke. They stared at all that remained of the dark dwarf patrol the shadow wight had destroyed. It was hard to conjure sympathy for the Daergar, who were the most cruel and vicious of Thorbardin's dwarves, but Morvik and Shard felt it anyway. No one, no matter how evil, deserved such a fate.

Shard drew her hammer and held it tight, squinting at the darkness that surrounded them. "Morvik," she murmured. "I want you to promise me something."

He glanced at her, his blade scraping as he slid it from its scabbard. Their eyes met, and he couldn't help flinching at the dread in her gaze. "Go on," he said.

"If this goes badly . . . if the shadow wight looks like it's going to defeat me . . ."

"Shard," Morvik hissed, "don't—"

"No. Listen to me," Shard insisted. "I've already lost one life to its kind. I don't want it to take yours, too. If it's going badly . . . if you think I'm going to die . . . then, if at all possible, I want you to get away. Leave me."

His mouth turned suddenly dry. He stared at her silently. "No," he said, more harshly than he intended. He took a breath and his voice softened. "I'm here with you now, to the last."

She smiled at him, but quickly turned away, staring into the shadows.

"Come on," she muttered at length, shouldering her hammer. "We'd best start clearing these stones away. The sooner we set the trap, the better."

* * * * *

They spent the better part of an hour toiling by shifting lamplight, lifting chunks of rubble and moving them aside. Several times they stopped, dropping their burdens to reach for their weapons, but nothing came for them, and nervously they resumed their labor. Finally they fell still, tired and aching, having cleared a circle twenty feet across of all debris larger than a pebble. They sat down to rest, breathing hard, and passed a flask of ale back and forth. Shard chewed on a strip of dried mutton as she pushed herself back to her feet, and walked to where she'd shrugged off her pack. With callused fingers she unlaced it, reached inside, and pulled out a small oaken cask.

"Here," she said, tossing the cask to Morvik.

He caught it, then got up off the stony floor. While he was rising, Shard produced a second cask, then tossed the pack aside.

They'd made a special trip to an herbalist's shop to buy the casks, before they left Hybardin. They were filled with *kharfa*, a runny oil made from mushrooms, which Thorbardin's dwarves used in warfare. Lit aflame, *kharfa* burned longer and hotter than pitch. Now Shard took a mallet and chisel from her pack and broke open her cask's lid. She handed the tools to Morvik, who did the same. An earthy stench wafted from the little barrels, stinging their noses.

Exchanging nods, they walked to opposite edges of the cleared area, then—with one last furtive glance into the gloom—upended their casks. Brown *kharfa* spilled out, splashing onto the ground. Slowly they backed around the clearing, pouring as they went. They traced a broad circle, each closing the gap where the other had started to pour. The casks were still half-full when they finished, so they covered each other's tracks, pouring more *kharfa* on top of what was already there. Finally, they flung the empty casks away.

"That'll do it," Shard said, eyeing the circle. "No

gaps anywhere, and it's thick enough to burn a good while. Get the tapers out, will you?"

Morvik, who stood next to Shard's discarded pack, bent down and rooted in it, producing a handful of crude, tallow candles. He set all but one of them down, then looked to Shard. "Now?"

She nodded wordlessly.

He went to his lantern, lifted its shutter, and touched the taper's wick to the exposed flame. The candle flickered as he walked back to where the other tapers lay. He let it burn a moment, then tipped it sideways, dripping wax onto the ground. When a small puddle had gathered he stuck the candle in it and left it there to burn.

Shard had told him of her plan back in Thorbardin. Knowing the shadow wight would be afraid of fire, she meant to use the *kharfa* to trap it. They would wait within the ring until the fiend appeared, lured in by the scent of their living flesh. Once it was within the circle, one of them would light the *kharfa* with a taper, penning it in within the flames.

"What about us?" Morvik had asked her, worried. "We'll be inside the circle with it."

Shard had nodded. "That's why we need the weapons. We'll fight the weakened wretch, and when it's beaten, I'll force it to tell me who I really am."

Morvik had his doubts about that part of the plan, even now. How could Shard be sure the shadow wight would even know what she wanted to learn?

"When it comes," Shard said, "it will talk to us. They killed wantonly here five years ago, but from all the tales I've heard they're usually much more subtle. It'll try to tell us we're worthless, that we're nothing. Don't listen to it, Morvik—if you do, you'll believe what it says, and you'll lose hope. You won't care about anything, even defending yourself, and it'll destroy you. So when it speaks, don't pay any attention. Talk to yourself, shout, sing . . . just whatever you do, don't listen."

Morvik nodded. A moment later he yawned. They'd been walking or working for nearly a day now, and though they'd drowsed in the chain-boat as it traveled from the Life-Tree to the old road, it hadn't been very restful. Shard yawned too, right after he did. Her face was haggard, her shoulders stooped, her eyes smudged and heavy-lidded. He was tired, but she was spent, worn out. Pity creased his face as he crossed the ring to join her.

"You need rest," he said, laying a hand on her arm.

"I'm fine," she muttered, and yawned again.

He shook his head. "No, you're not. You can't fight if you're exhausted, Shard. Get some sleep—I'll watch over you. When you're rested, we can switch places."

She hesitated, glowering, then shrugged. "All right. But watch yourself, Morvik. If you see or hear anything strange—*anything*—wake me right away. Understand?"

"Sure, lass," he replied, and kissed her cheek. "Now lie down before you fall down, will you?"

Smiling wearily, Shard eased herself down onto the stony ground. She rested her head on her pack and shut her eyes. In only a few moments, her breathing grew slow and even, and she began to snore softly.

Morvik bent over her, brushing her coppery curls with his fingers and watching the taper's light play on her face. Then he straightened, stretching. Blessed sword in hand, he sat beside her and turned his gaze toward the darkness, waiting for one of the shadows to move the wrong way.

* * * * *

The war drums thundered like a rockslide, filling the cavern with their din. Below, the dwarves of Hroldeg's Delve hurried this way and that, grabbing spears and shields, axes and crossbows. They pounded up the stairs to the battlements, armor clattering. Their troubled faces were hidden, obscured by the visors of their war helms. Officers barked at them, forming them into lines along the tops of the walls. The dwarves were well-versed at preparing for battle, having drilled at it often, and they moved swiftly and surely, weapons raised to face the foe.

At first, Shard thought it was just another drill, but there was something different in the air today: a strange energy, as though lightning had struck nearby. And cold—a frigid wind blew up from the chasm, fluttering banners on the towers and the tassels on the dwarves' helmets. Whatever was happening, it was no exercise.

Shard took her accustomed post, near the keep's northeast corner. To either side, warriors with the sigil of House Ironsmelt on their shields waited, weapons in hand. Shard glanced to her right, exchanging grim, faceless nods with her neighbor. She'd stood beside him many times, and they knew each other well. His name was . . . his name —

What *was* his name?

She stiffened, sudden realization striking her like a slap across the face. She didn't know who the dwarf to her right was. She twisted, craning to the left, but she couldn't think of the name of the warrior who stood there, either . . . or the one on the other side of him . . . or the next.

What's *my* name, for that matter? she thought suddenly, jolting herself a second time. Not Shard, not here. It's something else. . . .

Then she knew: it was the dream again.

She'd been having it, off and on, for the past five years. She knew immediately how it would play out, just as she knew it would fade to a featureless blur the moment she woke. It never changed: she found herself carried along, unable to change what she did, or what would happen. It was a terrifying, helpless feeling.

"Stand ready!" roared a voice. An armored figure strode down the line, a spiked mace in his hand. His horned helmet distorted his words, making them ring eerily. "Eyes forward, all of you! There's trouble coming!"

She stared at the officer, her brow furrowing. She should know him too. She could almost hear his name in her mind, but it remained just beyond her memory's reach.

The officer stopped before her. "I said eyes forward!" he bellowed, waving his mace.

But she didn't turn away. Instead she raised her chin. "Who am I?" she asked.

"*Now*, Reorx blast you!" the officer shouted, shoving her. She fell against a merlon, her armor clattering. "Eyes forward, or I'll gouge 'em out!"

"Just tell me my name!" she cried, but it was too late: still shouting, the officer had moved on down the line. Shard turned to the warrior beside her, who held a crossbow cocked and ready. "Please—" she began.

Before the crossbowman could reply, however, an icy gale broke over the Delve, striking it like a frost-rimed fist. The dwarves cried out in alarm, and all eyes turned toward the chasm. Shard looked too, though she already knew what she would see. A heart-beat later, a mass of darkness boiled out of the abyss, smashing against the keep's south wall. Several dwarves loosed bolts from their crossbows, or threw axes at the attacking shadows, but it accomplished nothing. The others raised their shields, locking them together into a wall, and stood firm, waiting, weapons ready.

"No!" Shard shrieked, horrified. "Get out of here! Run before—"

Suddenly, the black wave crested over the battlements. Dwarves shrieked, then the shadows fell upon them, obscuring them from view. When the darkness receded again, all that remained was a jumble of armor and weapons. Shard gagged, sickened, as she looked upon the leavings of the shadow wights' victims.

Then, with a loud, abrupt crack, the wall where the dwarves had stood split apart. Stone and mortar crumbled as the battlements collapsed, opening a wide breach and exposing the courtyard. Darkness flowed in, washing over everything, filling the inside of the Delve even as it flowed around the curtain wall, surrounding the outside as well.

Trapped, the dwarves braced themselves as the shadow wights slid up the stone edifices on either side, striking from front and rear at once. All around the Delve, screams of fear and pain rose, then suddenly stopped, replaced by the clatter of empty armor on the battlements. The dwarves vanished by the dozen, as if they'd never been. Stone roared again and again as parts of the wall, and the buildings within, fell to pieces. At the keep's northwest corner, the sturdy watchtower softened and wilted, melting like a candle.

Amid the carnage, a few dwarves held their ground, waving torches and lanterns to keep the shadow wights at bay. "Fire!" a woman's voice yelled from across the courtyard. "Fire stops them! Quick, find something to burn—"

A tremendous crash drowned out the rest as another segment of the south wall came apart. The shouter did not resume her cries.

Shard cast about, looking for a flame. A torch guttered nearby, and she lunged, pulling it from its sconce. A wall of shadows flowed toward her, down the battlements. Some of the dwarves before them—the ones with the Ironsmelt symbols on their shields—stood their ground; others broke and tried to run, their nerve gone. It made little difference; they all disappeared, their empty suits of armor coming apart, sending pieces skittering across the stones.

Shard raised her torch, waving it before her. "Hear me, Reorx," she prayed. "Deliver me from this darkness. . . ."

The shadows stopped, shying back from the brand's flame. Then they receded again like an ebb tide, making no sound as they went. Shard breathed a thankful sigh, but already she knew her relief would be short-lived. She'd used the flame before, countless restless nights. She'd driven off the darkness, but only for a time. And then—

A bone-shaking crack shook the battlements beneath her, then a second and a third, in quick succession. She shut her eyes and bowed her head with a resigned sigh.

With a sound like the death of the world, the wall collapsed. The ground dropped away beneath her, and she was falling among the crushing stones . . . falling—

* * * * *

Shard woke with a snort and sat up, a yawning pit in her stomach. The world spun around her as the dream frayed into wisps, then faded beyond recall. She didn't try to hold on to it; she'd learned, long ago, that it was impossible.

She sat on the stony ground, surrounded by what remained of Hroldeg's Delve. Beside her, a half-melted taper flickered; the stubs of three others stood close by. She blinked, startled—each taper could burn for more than an hour. Had she really been sleeping that long?

"You had a good rest," said a voice.

She jumped, gasping, and reached for her hammer before she realized it was Morvik. She glanced back to see him crouched behind her, his sword across his lap. He was pale, and his eyes were red-rimmed with fatigue. He wiped a hand down his face, blinking blearily.

"You were mumbling in your sleep," he said. "You had the dream again, didn't you?"

Shard nodded, sighing. "I think so." She pushed herself up, her armor clanking, then regarded him gravely. "You look awful."

He laughed roughly. "Thanks. I feel pretty grand, too. I was going to wake you soon anyway, lass—I don't think I can stay awake much longer. Can you keep watch for a few hours?"

"Of course," she replied with a smile. Her joints were stiff and her mind was still fuzzy, but Morvik looked far worse. She stood and paced around the circle, her eyes fixed on the darkness beyond its edge . . .

All at once she froze where she stood. She sucked in a breath, her nostrils flaring as she looked toward the chasm.

"Shard?" Morvik hissed sharply. "What's—"

She held up a hand and he fell silent. She squinted harder, searching the darkness. For a moment she'd seen something, out of the corner of her eye: movement where there should be none. She held her breath, waiting.

Then, without warning, it was back—a shadow that lurched to the left when the lanterns' flickering light made the others shift to the right. Her skin rose in bumps as she raised her blessed hammer.

"It's here," she whispered.

Morvik was beside her now, holding her shield. She took it and strapped it to her arm. "I see it," he told her.

Her eyes flicked toward him, and she frowned. He was peering well to the left of where she'd been staring. "You're not looking in the right place," she said, pointing with her hammer. "Over there."

"No," he said, nodding the way he was looking. "It's there. Don't you see it?"

And then she did—a swelling in the darkness, which stayed still while the shadows around it danced. She frowned for a long moment, wondering, then drew herself up. "Reorx's tangled beard," she swore. "That's not the same one I saw."

"Two of them?" Morvik gasped.

She nodded, spitting on the ground. "Kharas smite me—Scree said there was only one!"

Morvik was quiet for a long time. The tip of his sword quivered before him. "One for each of us," he murmured. "What do we do now?"

"Pray there aren't any more out there," Shard breathed. She glanced over her shoulder, making sure the darkness wasn't moving there too. "And make them come to us."

Slowly, they backed away from the shadow wights, toward the far side of the *kharfa* ring. Morvik stooped and pried the half-melted taper from the ground as they went. They both stopped just inside the circle's edge. Before them, the shadows wavered in the lantern's meager glow. All was still.

"Can we handle two of them?" Morvik whispered.

"Do we have a choice?" Shard replied.

Slowly, she reached up and lowered the visor of her helm. Morvik did the same, and she felt her stomach clench unpleasantly. She prayed to the vanished gods that she would live to see his face again.

Then, with unsettling silence, two patches of blackness broke away from the gloom and glided forward. Each had a vaguely mannish shape, though they had no features to speak of. They moved slowly, tentatively, to the edge of the ring . . . and stopped there, just outside the circle. Looking at them, Shard felt her mouth turn dry as old bones. Morvik, already weak with fatigue, was trembling openly.

"Remember—" she whispered.

Before she could finish the thought, the shadows surged forward, into the circle. As they did, Morvik turned and dropped the taper onto the *kharfa*. Flames, blue at their base and red higher up, sprang from the floor, then quickly spread, running in twin arcs around the ring.

The shadow wights froze in place, shrinking back from the blaze. They saw what was happening, but the flames were faster than they were: before they could flee, the ring closed behind them. They recoiled, then moved quickly into the circle's center. For the first time they made a sound: a vicious hissing, like twin geysers about to erupt.

"Now!" Shard yelled, striding forward with her hammer raised. "Quickly, before—"

"*Stop.*"

At once, Shard's body turned leaden. She came to an abrupt halt, halfway to the midst of the circle. The voice—cold, emotionless, yet still vastly compelling— had come from the shadow wights. She stared at them, terror swelling within her. These creatures, and their kin, had destroyed the Delve. They'd slaughtered hundreds of dwarves here—and thousands in the cities above. They'd stolen her past. Now here she was, face to face with them again.

And then she wasn't. She was looking at herself.

It was eerie, unlike anything she'd ever experienced. She'd seen her reflection before, in pools and mirrors, but this was different. The image moved of its own accord, rather than matching her. Its visor was open, revealing its face. It was *her* face, but it was a corpse: the skin was grey and waxen, the lips pulled back in a terrible rictus. The eyes had rolled back, showing dead white.

"What in the Abyss—" she breathed. None of the tales she'd heard over the years had said anything about this.

"That's because none who see this survive," the dead Shard replied. It spoke with her voice, but it was halting and toneless, each word an effort. Its toothsome grin broadened even more, the lips splitting as they stretched. "You pitiful child. Did you truly think you could defeat us with this paltry trap? Are you really such a fool?"

Shard shook her head angrily. "I want back what's mine."

"What's yours?" Dead Shard returned in a mocking, singsong voice. "You have nothing! Not even a proper name. You *are* nothing—you shouldn't even exist." Its face twisted into a derisive sneer.

Speaking was difficult. She couldn't look away from the apparition's glassy eyes. "You have to tell me. . . ."

Dead Shard only laughed—a mirthless, hateful sound. "I don't have to do anything," she snarled. "No. Coming here, you've only found the fate you cheated, five years ago. All you've done since you became Twice-Born—wasted. And you've doomed your lover also."

"Morvik?" Shard breathed. Behind her, Morvik took a step forward, but he, too, could not speak, could only stare.

"Dear Morvik," Dead Shard replied. "But then, what he felt for you was never truly love, was it? Pity, perhaps—the same as one feels for a starving dog. How *could* he love you? You were nothing, an empty shell, when he found you, and you're *still* nothing. When you're gone, what difference will it make? No one will even know you existed . . . not even dear, sweet Morvik, in the last, fleeting moments before he meets the end you chose for him!"

The world began to swim before Shard's eyes. She could feel herself fading—a strange sensation, but one she dimly remembered feeling before, five years ago, in this very place. Despair washed over her, blocking out everything else. Everything but the shadow wight's soft, seductive voice.

"Let yourself go," Dead Shard murmured. "Let it all go. There's so little to hold on to anyway, isn't there? It's so easy . . . it will all be better . . . when it's over. . . ."

Without warning, something struck her—hard—on the side of her head. White light roared within her skull, blinding her as she staggered sideways. She would have fallen, but something grabbed her arm and hauled her back, away from the shadow wight and toward the edge of the ring. She retched and tried to slump to the floor.

"Shard!" a voice shouted in her ear. Painfully loud, it roused her from her stupor. Her vision cleared, though her ears continued to ring. Morvik stood before her, gripping her shoulder with his right hand. In his left he held one of their lanterns, unshuttered and burning brightly. His voice boomed inside his helm. "Can you hear me?"

She tried to nod, but blood pounded in her ears and she nearly blacked out. "You . . . you *hit* me. . . ."

"I had to," Morvik replied. "It almost had you, lass. It would have destroyed you if I hadn't done something fast."

He was right—the shadow wight's words had lulled her, brought her to the edge of oblivion. And, for the second time, he'd saved her.

She smiled ruefully. "I'm glad *someone* was paying attention when I said not to listen to those things."

Turning, she glanced back across the circle. The shadow wights still lurked in the center of the ring, shying from the beacon in Morvik's hand. They were made of darkness again—Dead Shard was gone.

"What do we do now?" Morvik asked, raising the lantern. "We could try to run. Go through the flames and head back toward the surface. . . ."

Shard shook her head, her eyes fast on the shadow wights. but the flames surrounding them offered no escape. "We'd never make it. The fire wouldn't last long enough," she stated. "They're faster than we are—sooner or later, they'd chase us down." She hefted her hammer and brought up her shield. "No, we have no choice. We have to fight them."

Morvik bowed his head and blew a long, tired breath out through his lips. He'd sheathed his sword to pull Shard away from the shadow wights' grasp; now he slid it free once more, its silvery blade winking in the lamplight. He raised it and touched its blade to his forehead. Then he set the lantern down on the ground and shifted his shield back onto his arm.

"All right," he declared. "Let's finish this."

Side by side, they started forward. The shadow wights were only five paces away. Before Shard and Morvik had taken two steps, the dark shapes separated, gliding apart in opposite directions. The dwarves hesitated, then exchanged a quick nod and parted as well. Morvik moved toward the shade on their left, brandishing his sword. Shard veered right, raising her hammer in challenge at the shadow wight who'd taken her form, whose voice had nearly overwhelmed her with despair.

"Nothing, am I?" Shard snapped, shaking the heavy weapon. Sensing the blessing upon the hammer, the fiend shrank back. Shard grinned, quickening her pace. "We'll see who's nothing when this is over!"

She lunged, swinging with all her might. The hammer flashed in a deadly silver arc, its head parting the air with a low whistle. The shadow wight darted sideways and back, flowing away from the blow like water. Shard fought to arrest the stroke, then reversed it, lashing back with equal fury. Though it tried to slip out of the way again, the shadow wight wasn't quick enough. The hammer's broad head caught it where its ribs would have been, had it been human.

Until the blow landed, Shard had feared the weapon would pass uselessly through. Instead, though, the hammer struck home. The shadow wight's form didn't feel like flesh and bone—it was softer, with more yield, like a dummy stuffed with straw—but the impact still sent it reeling, jarring Shard's arm all the way to her shoulder. The shadow wight spun away, sliding toward the ring of flames, then halted, turning to face her again. It made a terrible hissing sound, like fat dripping into a cooking fire, and circled around her warily.

She turned with it, keeping the hateful creature in front of her. At the edge of her vision, she glimpsed Morvik stalking the other fiend, his sword flicking back and forth before him like a serpent's head. He was moving slowly, though: exhaustion had left him weak and clumsy. Shard almost watched him for too long: her shadow wight darted forward, arrow-quick, its dark talons groping for her. With a shout she leapt back, bringing her shield across to block the attack. Shadowy claws struck it, slashing through iron like it

Chris Pierson

was cloth. With a terrible screech, strips of metal tore away as she jerked the shield back. She countered with her hammer, landing a second blow. As with the first, however, it had little effect, save to make the monster glide back again, snarling.

They traded attacks several times more, the shadow wight ripping at her shield as her hammer pounded at it uselessly. Finally, a vicious swipe of its talons tore her shield in two, wrenching her arm as the metal gave way. She staggered, hammer flailing to drive the fiend back, and tossed the shield's shredded ruins aside. If the shadow wight hoped she would falter, it was disappointed: without pause she shifted her stance and her grip on the hammer, holding its long haft with both hands and glowering at the black abomination.

She snuck a sidelong glance at Morvik. He was still holding his own, though only barely. His shield was almost as badly tattered as hers had been, and his sword moved sluggishly as he lashed out at his foe. Still, it seemed he'd had better luck than her: his shadow wight was moving unsteadily as well. Even as she watched, one of his awkward thrusts struck home, driving through its leg halfway to the quillions.

Shard's opponent came on again, drawing her attention away from Morvik once more. The shadow wight swiped at her viciously. She ducked beneath its raking claws, which sheared one of the wings off her helm, then lashed out at its knees with her hammer. The blow would have crippled a man or dwarf, but it only pushed the shadow wight back again while she righted herself.

She groaned a curse at the dark, shifting form. It wasn't working—try as she might, she couldn't even wound it. She cast about, but there was nothing else to use against it: the lanterns were out of reach, and the only weapons that had a hope of harming the shadow wight were Morvik's sword and her hammer.

Her hammer . . .

Suddenly, she had an idea. On the back of the hammer's head was a thick, slightly curved spike, stout enough to punch through the sturdiest armor. She frowned at it, then shrugged and reversed her grip on the weapon, facing the spike outward.

The shadow wight crouched, poised to come in low this time. Shard shifted her weight onto the balls of her feet, waiting for it to move. She bit her lip, her hands twisting around the hammer's haft. Wait, wait—

The black shape surged forward. She nimbly twisted away from its attack—even so, one claw nearly tore through her left greave—then brought the hammer's spike down, hard, on the shadow wight's back.

A terrible shriek, like fingernails on slate, filled the air, jangling her spine. There were wisps of shadow-stuff everywhere, erupting from the creature's back; it fell, flattened by the blow, and more darkness boiled forth as she jerked the spike free. She leapt back as the shadow wight's clutching fingers tried to grab her ankle, then watched it thrash on the ground. Darkness continued to bleed from its wound as it turned itself over to lie on its back. It tried to rise, then collapsed and, with a soft, wheezing sound, came apart like an unspooling skein. Solid shadow dissolved into insubstantial fog, then vanished.

It wasn't dead—that was impossible, for the shadow wight had never truly been alive. It had simply gone back to the Abyss, whence it had come. One day, it might return. But, for now, it was gone.

Shard stared at where it had been, her heart thundering in her chest. She hadn't meant to destroy it—the wound had been more grievous than she'd intended. For a moment, grief clutched her heart. With the shadow wight gone, she couldn't make it tell her who she was. She'd lost her chance—

The sound of tearing metal roused her from her trance. She looked up, toward the other side of the burning circle. There, Morvik was losing his fight with the second fiend. The shadow wight had his shield in his talons, and was twisting it this way and that with brutal strength. The metal rended and ripped, and would have shredded Morvik's arm, were it not for his armor. He shrugged convulsively, trying to pull himself free, but he was caught. He stabbed with his sword, pricking the shadow wight once, twice, three times. Darkness seeped from the wounds, but they were shallow, and the fiend didn't seem to notice. It pulled even harder, and the shield gave way, breaking apart. Morvik stumbled back, then tripped and crashed to the ground. His sword skittered from his hand.

"No!" Shard shouted. She started to run.

The shadow wight was quicker. As Morvik struggled feebly to rise, it pounced. It swiped at him once with its talons before Shard hit it, first knocking it back with the flat of her hammer, then turning the weapon in her hands and slamming the spike into what would have been its gut, had it been human.

But the shadow wight wasn't human. It lurched back, tearing the weapon from her hands. She grabbed for the hammer's haft, but the fiend's black claws drove her back, then it reached down and seized the weapon for itself. Taking it in both its shadowy hands, it broke it in half like it was a twig, then hurled the pieces away. It wavered unsteadily for a moment, then began to surge forward, bleeding shadowstuff as it came.

Shard hadn't been still, however. Having lost the

hammer, she turned and dove for Morvik's sword instead. She came up with it, lashing out wildly, and the blade hacked deep into the shadow wight's side. The fiend stopped, drawing black from the glittering blade, then shuddered and collapsed in a dark heap, blackness seeping from its many wounds.

She started toward it, sword extended, fearing some trick. But it didn't try to grab her—it didn't seem to have the strength any more. It was fading ebbing away. She didn't have much time.

"Who am I?" she demanded, poising the tip of her sword above the shadow wight's throat. "Tell me!"

For a moment, the fiend was silent, then it barked a cruel laugh. "Very well," it said. "I know your name, Shard. I know every moment of the life we stole from you. I will tell you . . . but first, look to your lover."

Her skin turned suddenly cold and clammy. She turned, keeping one eye on the shadow wight . . . and let out a strangled cry.

Four jagged slashes marred Morvik's breastplate where the shadow wight's claws had struck him. The metal gleamed red with blood.

"He's still alive," Shard breathed. She turned back toward the shadow wight. "You could have killed him, I know. Why are you keeping him alive?"

"Because it pains you more this way," the darkness replied, its voice rasping with malicious delight. "I hold his existence in my hands. He will disappear, but slowly—and you will watch."

Her mind flashing white with fear, Shard ran to Morvik and knelt down by his side. The wounds in his chest were shallow, no more than deep scratches. They would have been of no concern, had they come from any other foe, but any wound from a shadow wight was lethal. Tears burned in her eyes. With fumbling

Chris Pierson

hands she reached up and lifted his helm's visor. Then she stared at his face, trying not to scream.

It was like looking at a specter: his flesh had turned white, ghostly. His eyes were pinched shut, his lips pulled back in an anguished grimace. He was not breathing.

And she could see through him.

"Morvik," she moaned. She reached out to touch his cheek, then recoiled when she felt her fingers pass through his flesh. "Oh, sweet Reorx . . ."

"Watch him vanish," the shadow wight hissed with sadistic glee. "He will die before me—I will see to that. And when he is gone, I shall tell you your name."

With a furious snarl, Shard thrust herself to her feet and whirled to face the dark form on the ground. She raised her sword. "And if I put this blade through you first?"

"Then he might yet live," the shadow wight replied. "But I will disappear, and you will learn nothing from me. The choice is yours."

Shard hesitated. The need to know who she was had driven her for the past five years—her whole Twice-Born life. It was before her now. Her chance had come.

But Morvik . . .

She could let him die. There would be no guilt—how could she regret the death of someone she wouldn't remember, afterwards? It was remarkably easy: she didn't even have to do anything. Only wait.

"You can do it," the shadow wight purred. "The passing of another minute, and you will regain a *lifetime*! And what will you truly lose, if he never existed in the first place?"

Shard looked at Morvik. She looked at the shadow wight. Then she stabbed the thing of darkness

272

through where its heart would have been, had it had one. She stepped back, leaving the sword embedded in its form.

"I'd lose my soul," she said. "How could I trade that for a name?"

The shadow wight unraveled and faded, like mist burnt away by the sun. The sword clattered to the ground.

Even before the blade came to rest, Shard was on her knees beside Morvik. She lifted his head and cradled it in her lap. It was horribly light, as though the helm contained only vapors. She bowed her head over his. Her breath came in hitching sobs, and hot tears streamed down her face.

The shadow wight tricked me, she thought. I'm going to lose him anyway.

"Morvik," she wept. "Morvik, please. I need you—more than I ever needed to know who I am. I see that now. Come back to me—we'll leave Thorbardin, like you offered to. We'll make our own way in the world; I don't need anything more. Just please, Morvik . . . love, don't leave me. . . ."

Then she heard the sweetest sounds she'd ever heard—in this life or her previous one, she was certain. Softly, Morvik took a breath.

She cried out, reaching for his face. Her fingers touched solid flesh—flesh she could no longer see through. Weeping tears of joy, she bent down and kissed his lips.

His eyes fluttered open, his mouth curling into a smile. "And hello to you, too," he murmured.

She began to laugh; it was a while before she could stop. When she did, she sat with her forehead touching his, and held him quietly.

"Lass?" Morvik asked after a time.

She looked down at him, unable to keep from smiling. "Yes, love?"

"Do you know who you are now?"

She was silent a moment. "Yes, I do," she said finally. "I'm Shard . . . just Shard."

Tactics

Richard A. Knaak

"No! No! No!" Tempion roared. "That's all wrong again! Do it like this! Adrian! Put the men in position so that we can show this lot what we want!"

In the shady spot where he was seated, Lord Cornwell sipped some water from his flask and watched Tempion, his second, try again to get the locals to follow through on a simple military exercise. The senior Knight of the Rose commanded a Solamnic contingent of but ten men, not an official unit of combat, but rather "observers" in this land where an unofficial war had grown worse over the past few months. The Knights of Takhisis, a vast brotherhood who had taken the rules of chivalry and honor from the Solamnics and turned those rules to the cause of darkness, had invaded the ogre lands. They had done so without fanfare, marching legions of ebony-armored warriors into the mountainous lands and destroying or enslaving every village in their path. The ogres, in turn, had fought back and now had begun to slow them a bit. But each day marked further inroads by the invaders and more and more corpses among the native inhabitants.

The aging commander squinted as he watched Tempion, a broad knight with a wide, crimson face, attempt to show one of the ogre warriors how he should stand when facing an attacker. It should not have mattered to the

Solamnics what happened here, for the ogres had always been a threat to humans, but the sudden rise of the Knights of Takhisis had stunned them, and each day the strength of the foe grew greater and greater. Eventually, there would have to be a war between the two knighthoods, but not yet, not now. Yet the Solamnics could not simply sit and wait. They had to discover what they could about the dark knights' tactics and weaknesses, which was why Lord Cornwell had been sent to this godsforsaken place. Which was why they were now attempting to teach ogres basic knighthood battle strategies.

Lord Cornwell wiped a bit of moisture from his thinning mustache. The gray-haired commander did not approve of this policy, believing that the ogres were best left on their own, to win or perish as seemed fit. He had fought ogres in the past, watched their monstrous fury pummel men to bloody gobbets. Truth be told, he hated the entire breed, but he had been given his orders. His superiors had deemed it a necessity to try to even the war out a little. Oh, the ogres would probably lose in the end, but by that time not only would they have weakened the Knights of Takhisis some, but Solamnia would have had ample time to plan the next move.

Of course, none of that mattered if the foul creatures never learned enough to make the effort worthwhile.

Rising with a sigh, the veteran warrior put away his flask. He watched with disgust as the ogres again misstepped through the drill. Amazing that they had had any success of their own before the Solamnics arrrived. But in one area, Lord Cornwell knew from reports, the dark knights had suffered such great losses, that they had temporarily turned their campaign to the rich lands to the northeast. That had given Cornwell and his band time to slip in and locate an ogre tribe open to a temporary alliance.

"You're well this day, human?"

The voice did not grate like an ogre's, sounding somewhat smoother, more cultured even. Cornwell still recalled the first time he had heard the unusual ogre voice, several weeks before, when out of the rocks and hills surrounding the small party had emerged more than sixty fierce warriors of that brutish race. Despite the difference in numbers, the knights had been prepared to fight, yet before the first blow could be struck, the leader of the ogres had materialized, stopping any attack. Weaponless, the figure, slight for an ogre but still taller than a human, had walked calmly up to the senior Knight of the Rose and extended his hands in ritual greeting.

"I am Guyvir, chieftain of the village."

Guyvir's face was not pure ogre, either. Oh, the bone structure gave hints of ogre lineage, as did the toothy smile, but the features and smooth words hinted at another ancestry, one not human but near enough. The chieftain might be called crudely handsome with his small amount of facial hair and great silver-black tresses falling past his shoulders. Emerald eyes, slanted, spoke of the other race which helped create this half-breed.

"My mother was an elf," Guyvir had explained immediately after meeting them. She had been a captive, of course, no elf or human maiden would willingly go to the arms of a brutish ogre. Yet Guyvir's father had come to worship his captive and if he did not permit her escape, neither did he mistreat. She had lived, resigned to her fate, finding solace in the child she had discovered she carried.

Despite the hardships, his mother had endured until Guyvir had lived for ten summers. From her he had learned various elfin skills, from diplomacy to use of the longbow. Those traits, plus the ones handed down by his father, had elevated him over others in the tribe and raised him up to chieftain. Lord Cornwell thought Guyvir the most likely reason the ogres here had enjoyed some success against the Knights of Takhisis.

"I'm well," Lord Cornwell finally replied to the patiently waiting Guyvir. It annoyed him that he had to look up at the face the half-ogre, but even with his mixed lineage the chieftain stood a head taller. "But, dammit, your warriors are taking too long to learn these maneuvers!"

"We try our best, but ogres, like other races, have grown accustomed to doing things their own way!"

Cornwell frowned. "Not acceptable! If you want to fight the Knights of Takhisis properly, you'll need to convince your warriors that primitive tactics won't hold back the tide of darkness forever!"

The chieftain shifted the bow slung over his shoulder. Of elfin design, it enabled him to strike a target as large as a mouse at twice the distance any of Solamnic weapon. Had all of Guyvir's subjects handled bows nearly as well, Lord Cornwell would have been very pleased. However, only a few ogres had shown any archery skills approaching competence, most preferring massive clubs or lengthy spears.

A clatter of metal, followed almost immediately by Tempion's frustrated shout, reminded Lord Cornwell that swords, too, were beyond the scope of most ogres. Some could wield them, of course, but not with the dexterity sufficient to prove more than a nuisance to a hardened Knight of Takhisis.

"I shall see what can be done," Guyvir returned, giving the commander a smile. "We're most grateful for your aid, after all, human."

"And we're glad to give it, of course! You know that!"

The half-ogre nodded. "The friendship of the

Solamnics means much to this village . . . but will any more of your knighthood be coming to help?"

Lord Cornwell fought to keep his ire down. This had been a point of contention with Guyvir since their first meeting. The half-ogre had wasted no time in asking when the rest of the Solamnic fighting forces would arrive.

The answer had left a sullen expression on his features. "No more will be coming?" he had said, incredulous. "They send only you to fight?"

"I am afraid that's not quite accurate. We won't be doing the fighting, but we will help you . . . organize yourselves for defense. Our mission is to only observe so that we can prepare for the future. It is your fight, not ours. I have my orders."

Guyvir's expression had darkened and he had bared his teeth, which Cornwell realized there and then had not been inherited from his mother's side. "And when is that future? After we're long dead or enslaved? I've heard that the Knights of Solamnia are champions of the oppressed . . . but that wouldn't include ogres, would it?"

Lord Cornwell had felt his face flush slightly. "My small band wouldn't be much aid to you in that respect, anyway, Chieftain Guyvir. We're less than a dozen men . . . but I bring with me men who can teach you what you need to know to harry and perhaps defeat the Knights of Takhisis."

He prepared to repeat his words now, but to his surprise, this time the obstinate chieftain backed down without further argument. Instead, the half-ogre glanced at his warriors and, in a softer tone, said, "They know that, without help, they will die, human."

"They don't have to, chieftain—"

"They will die. A matter of time, no more. We're few, the dark ones many. Luck has been with us, but we're ogres and your tactics are human."

"You agreed to this arrangement. We did not force it upon you."

Guyvir's smile held no humor. "I would agree to anything that gives us a chance to smash in the skulls of our enemies."

Cornwell forced down a shiver. "Now, now! We've had some luck so far, haven't we?"

"I would have more heads on the poles than those of just a few scouts. . . ."

The heads were a practice that the knights did not condone, but that Lord Cornwell had been unable to stop. Nearly a dozen rotting skulls, some still helmed, sat atop stakes at one end of the village, all trapped thanks to Solamnic tactics . . . then all brutally slaughtered by ogre rage. There would have been many more heads, but the knights had persuaded Guyvir to limit the practice to one "symbolic" trophy for each victory. Not exactly what his superiors would have preferred, but at least Cornwell could report results. Besides, no one had expected him to alter generations of bestiality in just the space of a few short months. Ogres were ogres. . . .

Still, Guyvir was right about one thing. His people were doomed to fail, to die, eventually. By that time, Cornwell and his band would be long gone, training others in skills and tactics. No matter what skills were taught to the savage ogres, however, they would be overrun in the end.

"I would ask that you send another message to your superiors, human."

"A message?" The graying commander pretended ignorance, but he knew too well what Guyvir intended to ask him.

"Tell them that this ogre chieftain bares his neck to them. Tell them that I will cast my weapon down at their feet, if they'll come and parley."

The half-ogre had offered the ultimate humiliation; he would surrender his authority and his life to the Knights of Solamnia if they would come in full force to oppose their dark counterparts. Guyvir meant every word of it, too. Despite his mixed heritage, the chieftain had proven himself honorable, willing to do whatever was necessary for the survival of his people. He had been in the front at past skirmishes, had put himself in harm's way again and again. During training, Guyvir had been the first to learn each step-through. In addition, the half-ogre had taken it upon himself to update the old, incomplete maps the knights had carried with them into these lands, providing extensive information that would have taken Cornwell and his men a year to compile. Tempion, ever suspicious, had even checked out as much as possible of Guyvir's geographical detail, finding no fault whatsoever. Guyvir was true and brave, for an ogre.

A shame such valor had to be wasted now. "As I have indicated, their answer will remain the same."

Emerald eyes lost some of their spark. "That is too bad."

The commander prepared to launch into another lengthy explanation about Solamnic beliefs and concerns, but just then an ogre warrior came trotting into the village. It was one of Guyvir's scouts. Lord Cornwell had to admit that the ogres made excellent scouts. Some of that credit no doubt went to the chieftain, who seemed to have not only inherited the elfin knack for understanding and memorizing the landscape, but had managed to impart some of that ability to his villagers.

The warrior fell to one knee before Guyvir. Massive, a foot taller than the chieftain, the newcomer had the typically grotesque, squashed face. Compared to him, Guyvir looked positively handsome, more elven.

The ogre pushed back an unruly mane of dark hair and growled something to his lord in the native tongue. Cornwell's eyes darted to Tempion, who understood the language far better thar him. His brawny second had already called a pause to the exercises and was starting toward them.

Guyvir barked something back, then glanced over at the Knight of the Rose. "Forgive me, Lord Cornwell . . ."

Without another word, both chieftain and warrior hurried off in the direction of Guyvir's dwelling, a simple stone and wood structure rounded at the top that was identical to other buildings in the village. Instead of doors, the hide of a bear covered the entrance, with smaller skins covering a pair of crude windows. The chieftain's home lay at the foremost side of the great meeting area in the very center of the village, where the inhabitants gathered each day to eat and drink. Even now, several ogre females, even uglier than their mates, were preparing the evening meal, some combination of local plants, lizards, and rabbit. Cornwell hoped it would taste better than last night's goat or else he would have to start sending his men out to hunt more, taking precious time away from their task.

There were some hundred or so inhabitants in Guyvir's village, making it bigger than some settlements, smaller than others. That meant between thirty and forty dwellings, all forming a circle around the common area. Surrounding the perimeter was a man-sized wall built from loose rock from the hillsides. Not enough to stop the Knights of Takhisis, but at least it would make an attack more costly. A previous village that the Solamnics had scouted as a possible training camp had been eradicated when the dark knight invaders rode straight into the village unhindered, without having so much as to leap a fence, or dodge sentries behind a wall.

"What was that, my lord?"

The aging knight stirred, looking at his second in command. Also a Knight of the Rose, the sandy-haired Tempion would succeed Cornwell upon his retirement. Tempion missed little and had extensively studied the rules of warfare as set down by the founders of the knighthood. Beside Common tongue and ogre, he could speak the languages of the elves, dwarves, the barbarians of the plains. True, his mustaches were thin and short, but the other knight was still young and Cornwell overlooked his slight deficiencies. He would value Tempion's sword arm, any day.

"I don't know, lad. The creature came running up to Guyvir, growled in that mongrel tongue of theirs, and then both ogres went hurrying toward the chieftain's hut!"

"Did you catch anything, my lord? A word? A phrase?"

"Nothing of importance." Truth to tell, he had not understood anything, but he did not intend to let Tempion know how poor was his knowledge of the local dialect. "But I think it would behoove us to know what so interested Guyvir."

The larger knight nodded. His hand slipped to the hilt of blade. "Shall I go see?"

"Let us both go . . . but first, how goes your tutoring?"

"As best as can be expect, my lord. They are not incompetent, but they resist any change. Add to that their thievery—"

"More thievery? Not another horse?" Just the other day, one of the Solamnic mounts had vanished, only to be discovered in the possession of one of the chieftain's scouts. The ogre claimed he had found the beast out on the plains, but none of the knights truly believed him.

"No, not since we got the other one back . . . and I still swear that warrior planned to eat him!" The animal in question had been Tempion's, so he took the incident personally. "This time, we're missing two daggers. I only noticed it now, although it must have happened some time ago. That makes three in the past five weeks. A sword, too, if you remember, right after we arrived."

"But Guyvir turned in that culprit, Tempion. Offered the ogre's own life, if we wanted punishment. I'll talk to the chieftain about it; tell him that such acts won't better relations with us. In fact, that gives us the perfect excuse to interrupt now. Come!"

The pair marched toward the chieftain's home. However, before they could reach the entrance, the grinning half-breed suddenly burst out, greeting both with open arms. Cornwell barely kept Tempion from unsheathing his weapon, so strangely exuberant did the chieftain appear.

"Friends! Humans! Lord Cornwell! News! News!"

Taken aback, the senior knight finally asked, "Good news?"

"The best! My scout reports a party of four dark ones riding into our vicinity! We can take their heads without any trouble!"

"Where are these scouts?" Tempion had still not removed his hand from the hilt.

"To the north. West of the twisting valley."

Cornwell vaguely recalled the winding landmark from the maps that Guyvir had given them. The eastern end of the valley disappeared off of the chart, though, for Guyvir said he had been there only once and that many years before. He could tell the humans little about the western part, save that the valley eventually opened up into level area, then an open plain. Cornwell had discussed exploring the valley with the possibility of reaching some of the eastern villages, but had delayed any final decision.

"How far west?" the younger Knight of the Rose persisted. Tempion always demanded specifics.

"A day, perhaps two. They ride south, directly toward this area."

Both armored figures glanced at one another. Scouts meant possible new incursions.

"We should investigate, my lord."

"Yes . . ." Cornwell rubbed his chin. "But I don't want them to know we're here. If they don't notice anything amiss, we let them go this time."

"Let them go?" Guyvir looked positively crestfallen. "They are the enemy! Their heads should decorate poles!"

"We'll let them go so that we can follow them back, find out how great a force they belong to. Then we can decide what tactics would make sense in the long-term, yes, Chieftain Guyvir?"

It took a moment for the half-ogre to reply and when he did, it was with his emerald eyes cast down. "As you say, human."

Cornwell clasped his hands together. "That's settled, then. Good! Now, Guyvir, if you'll be so kind as to come with Sir Tempion and myself . . ."

* * * * *

There were four of them, all right. An officer with a red cloak, followed in single file by three ordinary Knights of Takhisis. All wore sinister black helms and the skull and lily emblem on their breastplates. The small party moved slowly and cautiously, clearly aware that they were in enemy territory.

Cornwell watched from a rocky hill overlooking the

dark knights' route. The commander had taken with him only his small band of knights, the chieftain, and eight of Guyvir's best warriors. More than enough to handled the foursome if that proved necessary, which Cornwell hoped it would not. He wanted this patrol to return in peace, the better so that he could check on the strength of the force to which they belonged without raising suspicions. Originally he had intended on taking only the chieftain with him, but the half-ogre had insisted on bringing some of his own men, vowing to keep them under control.

The journey to the mouth of the valley had taken them more than a day, longer than the aging knight had wanted. He considered the job which had been done by the ogre scout, an arduous journey back and forth, and admitted to himself that the race was a hardy one, if nothing else.

Cornwell looked at the best map they had of the region. "Where are your warriors again, Guyvir?" he asked.

"There and there," the chieftain responded, pointing at a ridge and a hill just ahead of the patrol.

Tempion eyed the half-ogre. "They have been warned not to attack under any circumstances, right? This is reconnaissance, not one of their raids." The younger knight had not wanted to bring any ogres along. Tempion had felt that this operation demanded the expertise of the Solamnics, not the wild abandon of the locals. "We only want to observe these men."

"I have tried to convey to them what they are supposed to do."

Tempion did not look at all pleased at this ambiguous comment and started to say something, but Cornwell waved him to silence, for the patrol had come within possible hearing range. The Knights of Takhisis continued on at a steady pace. Finally, just yards from where the knights watched from overhead, the officer in charge raised his hand and called a halt.

The watchers could see why. The path ahead looked narrow and precarious, with many ledges and ravines, and the scouts would be better off walking their animals through it at a slower pace.

The four invaders had nearly reached the end of this treacherous part of their journey when several large, furious forms rose from the rocks above. Cornwell gasped and Tempion cursed. Both knights started to rise, but a body behind them collided with the pair, sending them sprawling. The senior knight looked up to see Guyvir pulling himself to his feet, calling out something angrily in the ogre tongue.

"Blasted beasts!" Tempion pulled his commander up. The pair reached for the chieftain.

"Stop them!" Cornwell roared.

The half-breed bared his teeth. "Too late, human! Too late!"

They gazed down to see the ogres already assaulting the four knights. One man lay dead, his head and helm a battered pulp. A second was trying to fend off an ogre with a club, but did not see another warrior with sword in hand coming up behind him. A moment later, the great blade pierced the back of his neck.

The remaining pair tried desperately to mount their animals. An ogre caught the officer's cape, but somehow lost his grip. Guyvir shouted, and the rider briefly looked up before urging his steed forward. His sole remaining comrade tried to follow suit, but two warriors dragged him off the saddle. He screamed, the cry cut off as one of his attackers broke his neck.

Lord Cornwell's eyes widened. The activities of the Knights of Solamnia had remained secret up until now.

If the escaped knight had seen any of them, if word went back that Cornwell's brotherhood had been training ogres. . . . "Stop him! He can't tell his superiors about our presence!"

Guyvir freed himself from Tempion's grip, then readied his bow with astonishing speed. He focused on the dwindling figure of the officer, but did not fire.

Tempion leaned into him. "Shoot!"

The chieftain released his shaft. It made a beautiful arc. The shaft bit into the man's shoulder, where the joints of the armor left unprotected flesh. Had Guyvir attempted such a shot, it would have seemed impossible. However, instead of downing the rider, it only made him flinch and wobble.

"He's getting away!" the commander roared.

"A difficult enough shot without this one roaring in my ear."

"Should we give chase?" Tempion asked.

"Give it a try . . ." Cornwell doubted his men's chances, though. Despite his wound, the officer rode like a demon, already disappearing in the distance.

Tempion already had two Knights of the Sword, Adrian and Bartik, in the saddle. Adrian muttered a word to Tempion, then the pair rode off.

Cornwell's second whirled on Guyvir, blade drawn. The furious knight held the tip of his sword to the chieftain's throat. "Give the command, my lord, and I will deal with this miscreant!"

"Sir Tempion! Remember yourself! Put down that blade!"

"We told him that his warriors had to let the patrol live!"

"He's correct," the half-ogre agreed, eyes steady. "You wanted the dark ones to live. I've failed you. Kill me."

"There'll be no more killing!" Cornwell snapped.

"Dammit, though, Guyvir, now he'll be able to report about us to his superiors!"

Tempion, his blade still at the ready, understood his commander. "We should not be here when they come back, my lord."

"No. . . it threatens everything we were sent in to do." They had intended on leaving Guyvir's village before long anyway. They had hoped to stay long enough to teach the ogres here how better to stand up to the Knights of Takhisis. Still, what other choice did they have now?

"Lord Cornwell . . . human . . . there may still be a chance."

The knights stared at the chieftain, Cornwell finally responding, "How's that?"

Emerald eyes widened in hope. "There's another path, one I'd forgotten until now . . . it could take us around to where the dark one must pass before he can rejoin his troops."

Tempion shook his head. "Impossible!"

"No, the dark one will have to ride through rough terrain! Our path will be a short cut!"

This interested the senior knight. "Where does this trail run?"

"Just east! We go up through the mouth of the valley, then around to the northwest again!"

"I do not recall such a route on the map," Tempion interjected with a frown.

"I haven't gone this way much in the past few years, human, but it exists! We waste time with arguing! My warriors can take the other path and hunt him down—"

"Your warriors have done enough already," Cornwell's fellow Knight of the Rose snarled. "My lord! This is for us and us alone to do! Without the ogres, we stand a chance of capturing the officer for questioning! Bring those blood-thirsty warriors along and we'll end up with nothing!"

"Let me redeem myself then! You and your men can go alone, but only I can lead the way!"

As the commander saw it, they had no other choice. Guyvir's warriors they could do without, but they needed the chieftain to show them the way. "All right, but let's be quick about it! He already has too much of a head start!"

Guyvir gave his warriors quick orders in ogre. As his people left, he rejoined the knights, who had already mounted. The half-ogre mounted his own pale brown charger, a steed, Lord Cornwell had reflected more than once, that would have made any Solamnic commander proud.

Like some barbarians and nomads, Guyvir rode nearly bareback, only a small, thin blanket underneath him. A few pouches hung from his belt. For weapons, the half-ogre carried a dagger and the bow that had failed him moments earlier despite his elfin reflexes.

With Guyvir taking point, the party rode off. Glancing at Tempion, Lord Cornwell noted how the other Knight of the Rose marked each detail of the landscape as they rode by, consigning the terrain to his nearly perfect memory, searching for any fault in Guyvir's map work. The commander knew that if his second found any suspicious fault with the direction they took, Guyvir would be challenged and might not live out the day.

On and on they rode, the half-ogre's massive mount proving every bit the equal of the Solamnic steeds. Guyvir's shortcut seemed genuine, for the band covered distance with little effort. The mouth of the valley opened high and wide for them, although it narrowed deep within. Fortunately, after a few minutes Guyvir turned north, leading the knights through a narrow but serviceable pass.

This at last led them to a ridge, where Cornwell caught sign of their quarry.

Half slumped over the saddle, the black knight still somehow rode on. He could not be more than a half a mile directly west. Cornwell glanced back, spied two dots—undoubtedly Adrian and Bartik—far behind them. The pair would have never caught up with the knight, but thanks to Guyvir's shortcut, the commander's small band would, and soon.

Guyvir led them around a dizzying trail that brought them nearer and nearer to the hunted. Lord Cornwell's hopes rose.

Then they had him. Tempion urged his steed ahead of Guyvir's, coming alongside the black figure. The officer pushed himself up and tried to draw his blade, but the Solamnic batted his hand away, then raised his own sword to the officer's breast.

"Yield!"

The Knight of Takhisis brought his mount to a halt. After a moment's hesitation, he laughed, a ragged sound. "I . . . yield . . . what few moments of life I have . . . left."

Only now did they see his terrible wound. It bled hard, torn open by the wild ride. The shaft remained fixed in his shoulder, the barbed end impossible to remove without agony.

Still, Cornwell knew that they had to try. Chivalry demanded it. "Reynard!" A somewhat stout Knight of the Crown straightened. Reynard had early on shown his gift for caring for wounds and had become, despite his youth, the unofficial healer of the commander's unit. "See if you can do something about his wound!"

Before the younger knight could obey, the officer

shook his head. He had not removed his helm, but they could hear his contempt in his tone. "Why bother when . . . when you'll only cut my throat afterward? Let me die honorably . . . if you can . . . still recall how . . ."

Tempion waved the tip of his sword near the man's visor. "Watch your slurs, dark one!"

"No slur . . . not after . . . not after what you did to Sir Hector, and his guard . . . filthy Solamnics . . ."

The man's words made no sense to Cornwell. "What the devil do you mean?"

The prisoner indicated that he wanted to remove his helm. After gaining Cornwell's permission, the man did so, revealing a bearded, brown-haired man with cultured features. His captors could see that pain wracked him, the officer's face was very pale. "From behind . . . yet! They never drew their . . . their weapons! You're no better than this beast . . . this beast over here . . ."

Guyvir smiled. "Your head will look good on a pole, human."

"Enough of that!" Cornwell demanded. To the captured officer, he returned, "We have done nothing like you suggested! We would never—"

"My lord!" interrupted Tempion. "Will you even listen to this one? The Knights of Takhisis might once have claimed some shadow of honor, but those days passed with the Chaos War! To even suggest that we could sink as low as them . . ."

"You're here helping the ogres, aren't you?" the prisoner pointed out with grim satisfaction. He looked away, then quickly stared once more at his captors. "You . . . you noble knights of Paladine . . . not really helping, *making* the ogres do your fighting f-for you! You ambushed my . . . my party with the same butchery as you did Sir Hector's! I saw the proof!"

"What proof, man?"

"The dagger . . . the tracks . . . more than enough proof of your foul presence!" Again the officer looked away briefly.

"Dagger?" An unsettling thought took root in Lord Cornwell's mind. "How long ago did this . . . incident . . . happen?"

"You . . . know! His blood is still fresh . . . fresh on your hands."

Not long ago. Cornwell glanced at Guyvir. "Chieftain—"

At that precise moment, Adrian and Bartik at last caught up to the rest of the party. However, with nary a word of greeting, Adrian stood up in the saddle and shouted, "My lord! We've been seen!"

The wounded Knight of Takhisis used the distraction to pull free his blade, but Guyvir saw him and acted swiftly. A dagger sank into the bearded knight's throat, sending him reeling back over his saddle.

"Guyvir!" the graying veteran shouted. "What do you think you're doing?"

"Never mind him, my lord!" Tempion pointed. "We were too late!"

At the top of a hill overlooking their present position, three figures on horseback watched the small party. All wore black armor.

"There were two more up there," Adrian said.

"At least five. Another patrol! We'll have to try to take them, too!"

Tempion frowned. "I do not think that a wise choice, my lord."

Cornwell might have argued, but he, too, then heard the blast of a horn. Another responded, then another.

"Paladine's sword!" the veteran commander murmured. "Their camp must be just over the hill! But . . . but what are they doing this far to the south? Guyvir!

Your scouts! They watch this region, don't they?"

The half-ogre wore a peculiar expression. Lord Cornwell waited in vain for Guyvir to answer, then another horn sounded, this one nearer and louder.

"They're coming over the hill!" Tempion roared.

True enough, more than a score of riders in black armor rose over the top of the hill, joining the others. Behind that score came at least that number again, and more and more, with no end in sight.

"How could they come so fast?" Bartik asked, as stunned as the rest.

"I think . . . " Cornwell began, unable to believe what had happened. "I think that they were already looking for us."

Tempion eyed him, slowly understanding. Guyvir, meanwhile, looked hard at the humans. "Well? They come! Do we fight or flee?"

Cornwell's second glared at the half-breed. "We cannot fight all those!"

"Then we must run! Come! I recall a way, a pass within the valley that also leads to the south!" With that, the chieftain turned his powerful steed around and headed east, not even waiting to see if the humans followed.

Lord Cornwell had every inclination of following. "You heard him! Ride and ride swift!"

"My lord?" Adrian had his sword half out.

"This is not the time to die in a one-sided battle! Come!"

By this time, at least a hundred of the black devils were surging down toward the Solamnics. Cornwell's charger moved swiftly, but still there remained a gap between him and Guyvir. Cornwell had to wonder how long their speed would hold. They had spent too long a time in the hot day futilely chasing the fleeing officer and now they had to ride faster than fresh riders who had been pacing themselves . . . tracking, no doubt, the trail of Solamnic horses.

Now he knew what had happened to at least one of the daggers and the misplaced horse. Some of Guyvir's warriors had made a foray against the invading knights without telling their Solamnic allies. They had made use of the humans' tools, but left traces behind that an experienced knight could read. For all his dislike of ogres, he had credited the half-breed at least with more sense. What disturbed him more had to do with the fact that Guyvir had then kept the matter a secret . . . but for what reason? Tempion pulled up alongside him. The broad knight signaled for his attention. "He seems to be leading us true!"

Cornwell agreed. They entered the valley. Instantly, shadows covered them, almost as if the sun had been eclipsed. Cornwell gazed up at the ominous walls of stone. Guyvir's mount had slowed, enabling the knights to catch up to him. Cornwell said nothing, choosing to save his energy for flight. A pass came up on their right. Cornwell felt certain that this was the route the chieftain intended to use for their escape. Guyvir crouched lower on his steed, urging it faster. The half-ogre stared at the opening—

—and rode deeper into the twisting valley.

The knights followed before they even realized. Tempion looked to his superior, but Cornwell shook his head. Forcing his mount to greater lengths, he came within shouting range of the chieftain.

"The pass! Turn back!"

"No!" called Guyvir. "Too late! They are too close! You must come this way!"

Cornwell looked back and saw that Guyvir spoke apparent truth. Their pursuers had picked up ground, incredibly. He guessed, to his dismay, that they did, indeed, numbered more than a hundred.

They had no choice now but to follow the half-ogre. The passage grew narrower and narrower and at one point the Solamnic party had to form a single file and keep riding as swiftly as possible. Fortunately, the Knights of Takhisis had to do the same and that bought Cornwell and his men precious minutes as the much larger force tried to maneuver its way.

Guyvir rode through this valley with more familiarity than he had claimed. Twice he avoided side passages that Lord Cornwell would have been tempted to try. Unfortunately, their pursuers stayed close on their heels.

"I will be glad when this valley opens up again!" called Tempion. The commander also felt the claustrophia, but tried not to show his fears. Then, to their surprise and horror, the narrow route ended abruptly. They pulled up at a rock wall, without so much as a crevice large enough for a rider and horse to pass through. Dead end!

"Where's the way out?" Lord Cornwell demanded of the chieftain.

Tempion realized the truth first and drew his blade.

"A trap! The ogre has led us into a trap!"

Cornwell glared at Guyvir. "Is this true?"

The half-ogre's face was set a mask, but his words affirmed the accusation. "I knew that the way ended here, yes."

"The stolen daggers! The horse too! You knew about them! You planned all this, didn't you?"

Tempion cursed. "By the shield of Paladine! Our enemies will make us all pay!" His anger grew. "But not before this one pays first!"

"Leave him, Tempion! That's an order!" Even

though he could hear the thundering hooves approaching them, Lord Cornwell needed answers to other troubling questions. "Your scout! He did not come back to report their appearance! He came to tell you that they had swallowed the bait, didn't he? You knew they'd come for us, thinking us base murderers! You have deliberately instigated trouble between our two forces, haven't you?"

"Only because it was needed."

"You've kept this secret for some time, waiting for the right opportunity, haven't you?"

"You're clever, human, and so correct." The half-ogre cocked his head. "But will you not ask the most curious question?"

"Which is?"

"Why I've trapped myself here with you humans?"

"Because you are a fool!" Tempion snarled. On horseback, he lunged at Guyvir. The half-ogre slipped to the side, and Tempion's sword only grazed his garments.

"No . . ." muttered Cornwell, suddenly looking up again and thinking of his earlier observations when they had first entered the tall valley. "No, we're the fools, lad."

Then the first of their pursuers rode into sight, a row of vengeful black warriors growing ominously larger by the moment. Cornwell ordered his men to form a row of their own and prepare to meet the foe.

"One hundred, if not more," Tempion rasped. "Give the order to charge, my lord. We will die with honor. We will show the black devils the difference between their goddess and Paladine."

The graying commander slowly raised his weapon. He hoped he would not have to let it drop, but prepared himself if it came to that.

The valley suddenly began to collapse from above.

That, at least, was Cornwell's first impression, but then he realized that from the very mountaintops tons of loose rock were being unleashed by figures . . . figures waiting . . . figures with a decidedly ogre cast to their features.

Caught unaware, the Knights of Takhisis fell easy victims. The first stones struck ahead of the front line, causing the men and horses to pull up while creating havoc in the ranks behind. When the avalanche grew and spread, havoc turned to panic as men trained for war found the very stones and earth attacking them. Rider crashed into rider as some sought to flee. While many were crushed, a few hardy souls attempted to continue forward.

"Paladine preserve us . . . " Bartik muttered.

How long the ogres had prepared for this, Cornwell could not say. Probably since they first had encountered the dark knights. Guyvir might have had the area prepared simply because he knew some day invaders would come in force. However long, his people had done their work well. Judging by the massive blocks that fell upon the dark knights, the ogres had chiseled loose much of the upper walls. They must have ridden out after the knights' departure, no doubt joining the eight warriors Guyvir had "sent away" after the initial attack on the patrol, and then simply waited for their master to lead the humans into the trap.

Everything else had been in place.

The enemy knights were hemmed in from the rear, too, their back lines slaughtered by an avalanche as great as the one burying the front.

A few riders managed to make it over the high rubble. Seeing them, Cornwell gave Tempion permission to meet them in battle. The other Knight of the Rose pointed his weapon, and with a cry led the men forward.

Swords flashed, but the few dark knight survivors had had their wills crushed and they swiftly gave way to the Knights of Solamnia. Tempion put his blade through a cloaked officer. Bartik did the same to a young warrior about his own age. Adrian suffered a shallow wound near his neck, but one of his comrades finished the attacker. It was all shamefully easy, considering how the dark knights had been beaten.

Lord Cornwell maintained his position, watching the ogres attack and keeping an eye on the chieftain, who had dismounted beside him. To the graying commander's surprise, a few bows appeared among the ogres above, the native archers proving far more adept at the art than he would have believed possible based from his observations during the past few weeks. He could see Guyvir's hand in that, too. The rain of missiles further decimated the ranks of the Knights of Takhisis, for the ogre bows were designed for ogre strength and sent thick bolts through armor.

The fighting began to die down. With but a few dozen or so warriors, the half-ogre had quashed a force several times greater. Few of the Knights of Takhisis still lived. Many of those breathed their last even as he watched, the victims unable to hide to escape the onslaught and butchery. Another smaller avalanche wiped out to a man a last group of some twelve or so desperate riders, a red-caped officer of high rank among them.

And then . . . it was over. The ogres were monstrously thorough and Cornwell suddenly realized that not only had none of the Knights of Takhisis escaped, none was permitted to survive. He turned to protest to Guyvir, but the half-breed's eyes warned him to remain silent.

The one matter for which Cornwell gave thanks concerned his own men: none had been killed. Adrian, Bartik, and two others sported wounds, but nothing life-threatening. Tempion remained untouched, but his expression indicated that the ghosts of this encounter would long abide with him. With the exception of Lord Cornwell, the dazed Solamnic knights had all dismounted, the better to let their exhausted mounts rest a little.

Cornwell's eyes burned. "You used us as bait," the commander finally uttered. "Bait!"

Guyvir looked surprised by his vehemence. "You've preached the importance of tactics, human! You should be pleased! Look what has happened! Look what a great victory has been won!"

Cornwell did look . . . and saw the carnage. He also saw the ogres moving through the dead, taking what weapons and items might be of use. He even saw one pull up the body of what appeared to be the enemy's Knight Commander and, with barely a thought, cut the head free.

Another trophy for the poles . . .

"This was not done with Solamnic honor! This would never have been done using Solamnic tactics!"

The chieftain nodded sagely. "True . . . which was why I used ogre tactics." Guyvir smiled coldly, showing his ogre teeth. "Your swords are welcome ever on our side, human, but I think the fighting ways of your kind do not work as well."

Suddenly, the aging commander noticed that several of the ogres had begun to accumulate around his party. Tempion and the rest noticed as well, Cornwell's second-in-command scanning the warriors with distrust.

The senior Knight of the Rose kept his his demeanor calm. "You are rejecting our aid?"

"Not rejecting, human friend! We've learned what we could. We've no more need of your teaching. We thank you for everything."

He realized that the ogres had learned far *too* well in some ways. They had played both knighthoods for fools. "What of us now?"

The smile grew colder, the teeth more dominant. Cornwell had never noticed how sharp ogre teeth could be. "We have no more need of you."

With a cry, Tempion swung his blade at the chieftain. However, with a speed that was inherited from his elfin mother, the half-breed moved aside easily, letting the trained knight stumble. The warrior nearest Tempion raised his club, striking the knight in the shoulder. The burly knight crumpled to his knees, his shoulder, his arm broken.

Guyvir shouted something in the native tongue to the warrior who had badly wounded Tempion. To Cornwell's astonishment, the ogres retreated a few steps.

The chieftain returned his attention to the humans. "My people are . . . very protective of me. You've my apologies, Lord Cornwell. If your healer can help your man, let him do so."

Cornwell gave such orders, but he had to ask, "What is the point? You plan to slay us all, don't you?"

"No . . . I plan for you to go."

The human's brow arched. "Go?"

"Back to your home. Back to the civilized walls of Solamnia. Now would be best."

His tone disturbed the knight more than even the cold smile. Understanding that argument could only lead to disaster, Lord Cornwell signaled his men to mount, watching closely as Reynard helped Tempion up onto the saddle. Tempion gritted his teeth, but he

Richard A. Knaak

nodded to his superior, indicating that he would be able
to ride with them.

The ogres had somehow cleared a path along the carnage and rubble, a rough road, but one that the knights'
horses would be able to traverse. Without another word,
Cornwell turned his mount from the chieftain and
started to lead his battered troops out of the valley. He
wanted nothing more than to be far from this place, far
from his humiliation.

"Human . . . Lord Cornwell!"

He looked back at Guyvir.

"Don't feel so bad. You taught well. You taught us
much that we needed."

"I fail to see what, sir!"

The teeth in his smile seemed endless. "There're
many similarities between your warriors and the dark
ones. Your actions, your tactics . . . your perceptions. I
promise you; we'll remember those similarities and
what we learned from your teachings and we'll spread
it among our kind. You'll be very proud of how well
we've learned to fight against the invaders . . ."

And anyone else after that, Cornwell realized. Perhaps . . . perhaps his superiors had not thought far
enough into the future, when they launched their program of training ogres to deal with the dark knights.
Perhaps the Knights of Solamnia had contributed to the
making of a more fearsome foe . . .

He turned away, disturbed by his thoughts. The
ogres did not stand in their way as they departed the
area, the horses picking their way over stones and
corpses. Lord Cornwell could feel Guyvir watching
them. The Knight of the Rose could not suppress a
shiver. Asking forgiveness from whatever powers still
watched over the mortals of Ansalon, he found himself
hoping that this war would be a bloody one for both

sides . . . and that a certain half-breed chieftain would be counted among the dead.

If not, then in a few years the Knights of Takhisis might prove the least of Solamnia's problems . . .

The Raid on the Academy of Sorcery

Margaret Weis

He would not give up. He would try the spell again.

"Though I have no idea why," Ulin muttered beneath his breath, "for it won't work."

In truth, the "why" was his father. Ulin had watched Palin Majere cast the same spell over and over until the words to the spell thickened on his tongue. Sometimes the magic worked, but more often, these days, the spell did not.

When that happened, Ulin watched his father grow old.

Palin had never before now seemed old to his son, not until this last year, when the wild magic his father had, in essence, "discovered" began to slip through his fingers like quicksilver. At first Palin had blamed his ineptitude on the infirmities of age, although that seemed implausible. His father, Caramon Majere, was still hale and hearty into his eighties. Palin had lost nothing else to age. Although he was of slender build, like his uncle Raistlin Majere, Palin was not cursed with ill-health, as had been his uncle. Palin was active and in good physical condition. His mind was keen. He enjoyed being out-of-doors, enjoyed walking and riding. He still liked a game of goblin ball and often outplayed the young scholars who did nothing all day but keep indoors with their noses pressed between the covers of a book.

Ulin realized now that his father had never truly thought the dwindling of the magic had anything to do with a dwindling of his mental or physical capacity. Palin had wished it to be so. Wished it desperately. He would have made that sacrifice gladly rather than come to understand the truth.

The spell Ulin was attempting to cast was a simple one—he was trying to put a wizard lock on a door. He drew in a deep and cleansing breath, endeavored to clear his mind of all nagging worries and cares—a difficult task, these days—and closed his eyes, concentrating on the magic that he could feel in the stone floor beneath his feet, feel in the cool stone walls at his side, feel in the wood of the door itself. That was the frustrating part. He could feel the magic. He knew it was there as he knew that blood ran red and warm in his veins. He could feel the magic flowing into him, but when he attempted to make the magic work for him, it was as if some other mouth than his was gulping it all down before he could get a draught. When he tried to cast the spell, he was left with nothing inside. He was drained, empty, the magic dissipated.

Ulin sighed, brushed irritably at some annoying insect that he could feel crawling on his skin. Gnats, he thought. Or fruit flies. He would have to remember to see if the servants had left open the cellar door again. As for this particular door, he glared balefully at the inoffensive object as if it were personally responsible for thwarting him and even gave it a swift kick in his frustration.

Sighing and muttering imprecations, he took out an ordinary iron padlock from the pocket of his robes, affixed it to the door, and locked it with an iron key.

"A sad pass we've come to, isn't it, Ulin?" said a voice behind him.

"What do you mean, Lucy?" he asked with forced cheerfulness.

"You tried to cast a wizard-lock and it failed," she said.

Ulin smiled ruefully and shrugged. "You know me. Ham-fisted. Butter-fingers. I should be a cook. I wouldn't be a bad cook, you know. The alchemy, that's much like cooking. One reason I enjoy it. A pinch of this. A cup of that."

"It's not just you, Ulin," she said. "It's—"

Ulin put a finger to his lips, glanced around swiftly to see if anyone else was in earshot.

"We're alone," she said, exasperated. "Look, Ulin, it's no use going on this way. Pretending everything's right when it's not. You and I both know the truth. Some of our pupils know the truth. That's why they're leaving. The masters know the truth. That's why your father disbanded the Conclave. The magic is failing. It's not just failing you. It's not just failing your father. It's failing all of us!"

Ulin didn't answer. Turning away from those green eyes that had the disconcerting habit of seeing inside his head, he gave the padlock a vicious tug. The lock held. Satisfied, he dropped the heavy key into a pocket. —"Time was when we didn't need locks on the doors here at the Academy. But these days, with the madness for god-crafted artifacts and their value so high, my father felt it was unwise to leave the mage-ware room free for all to enter. I suppose he's right, though I do detest these iron padlocks. They tell everyone who passes by, "Hey! We have something valuable in here! And we figure you'll steal it!" Wizard-locks at least have the advantage of being subtle and invisible."

He glanced back at his companion hopefully. "I don't suppose that you, Lucy—"

She shook her head. "My spells have been working about half the time. And if I put a wizard-lock on, odds are I might not be able to take it off. I'd rather not try. The fact is, Ulin . . ." She hesitated, as if unwilling to impart bad news.

They had been friends for years, ever since his arrival to take up his post as Assistant Master at the Academy. He understood her silences now as well as he understood her spoken words. The bond was that close between them.

"No, not you, too, Lucy," he said quietly, taking hold of her hand. "You can't leave. What we would do without you?"

Those were the words he said with his mouth. The words he said in his heart were: What will *I* do without you?

Plump Lucy she was called or Plain Lucy, to distinguish her from another Lucy who had been a student at the Academy. Although that other Lucy had left, the appellation had stuck, much to Ulin's indignation. Lucy wasn't beautiful, by any means, not like Ulin's mother Usha Majere, not like Mistress Jenna, not like Ulin's late wife Karynn. But Lucy's smile, which brought a dimple into each freckled cheek, could warm Ulin like spiced wine. Her rolling laughter could tease him to laughter, even in his darkest moods. Her green eyes sparkled in his dreams.

The green eyes were not sparkling now. They were shadowed, distressed. Lucy was his closest friend, his dearest friend. He had not thought he could ever love anyone again after his young wife had died untimely, stricken by a plague for which the healers had no cure, a plague most believed had been inflicted on them by the monstrous green dragon Beryl. Ulin had been away from home searching for magical artifacts. He had arrived back just in time to hold his dying wife in his arms. His heart had died then, too, or at least he wished it so. But he was young himself, only in his late twenties, and his heart had a perverse way of continuing to beat. Now it seemed to have found a perverse way of allowing him to love again, to find pleasure in life again. He had begun to think that Lucy might become more than a friend to him and he had hoped, on occasion, that perhaps she was thinking the same way.

"Ulin, I don't want to leave," she said, holding his hand fast. "But, let's face it. I'm not earning my keep. I have only two pupils. Another left last week. I tried to talk him into staying but his parents said that they weren't paying good money for no results. They're making him a carpenter's apprentice and I can't say that I blame them. At least he'll be taught a skill that will gain him a living. As for the other pupils, they can join the class with Master Dowlin. He's lost several of his, as well."

"Stay here and do research, then," Ulin said. "Alchemy is a fascinating study, Lucy." His golden eyes gleamed like the precious metal they resembled as he thought of it. "It's much more satisfying than magic. I'm relying on myself, my own creativity and intelligence, to create something—not on some force that comes from the gods or from the air or the ground or wherever. Magic maybe works with you and maybe it doesn't. Magic is completely unreliable. I control my experiments, Lucy! I do." He thumped himself on the chest. "And, if my measurements are correct and accurate, the chemicals *always* react in the *very* same way *every single time*. No guess work involved. No wondering if this time the magic will work for me, or if this time it will fail. I must show you, I've just come up with the most amazing concoction—"

He paused, then said contritely, "I'm sorry. I know you're not interested. And you don't have to work with my smelly old chemicals. There's a lot of work to be done cataloging artifacts and old spellbooks and scrolls—"

"Cataloging them to sell them," said Lucy gently, folding her other hand over Ulin's. She smiled as he shook his head stubbornly. "I saw Mistress Jenna here last week. I know what your father is doing."

"They're old friends," Ulin said.

"That may be, but she's also the largest dealer in magical artifacts in all of Ansalon and although I don't know this for a fact, my guess is that she left with several choice ones tucked away safely in her robes. Your father's selling off his own collection to keep the Academy going, isn't he, Ulin?"

He wanted very much to say no, but he knew he could not lie to the dimples and the freckles and the green eyes.

"I've seen the change in him," Lucy continued. "Everyone has. We're all worried about him. He's thin and gaunt. He avoids all of us. He won't speak to anyone. He spends all his time locked in his study."

"He's studying new spells," Ulin said, and the excuse sounded lame, even to him.

Lucy just shook her head. "I'm proud, Ulin. I've made my own way in life since I was little. I've supported myself and my family. None of us ever took a copper we didn't earn and I won't start now." She squeezed his hand. "Cheer up, dear friend. The moment the magic returns, I'll be back. You won't be able to keep me away, not with a hundred wizard-locked doors!"

Her laughter made Ulin smile, but the smile didn't

last long. He was tempted to ask her to stay because of him, because he loved her, but this wasn't the right time for those words. A declaration of love now would be mistaken for charity. He'd had countless opportunities before this. For one reason or another, he'd never taken them. And now, when he desperately wanted to tell her, the time had passed.

"Where will you go?" he asked. "What will you do?"

"I'm a good teacher. If I can't teach children to read the language of magic, then maybe I can teach them to read Solamnic or Common. Your grandmother Tika's come up with the idea of a school for the refugee children. Better than having them run wild in the streets, she says. She's offered me the job. The pay isn't much, but I'll have room and board at the Inn—" She halted, chuckling. "Ulin, you look just like a landed fish."

"You're not leaving!" he said, gaping and staring. "You're not leaving Solace!" He caught her in his arms and hugged her close.

He held her for a long time, reveling in the warmth of her body, the smell of her chestnut hair. She clasped him just as firmly, nestled her head into his chest. In that moment, everything was settled between the two of them, though neither of them spoke of it aloud.

"I was looking for your father," she said, emerging reluctantly from his embrace. She glanced toward the door across the hallway, where Palin had his study. "I wanted to tell him myself. That is, if he'll even see me—"

"He's not here," Ulin replied. "No, that's the truth this time." Palin had made it a practice lately to tell his son to say that he was away, when in fact he was locked up in his study, searching for some reason that the magic was failing. "He's meeting with the commander of the Solamnic garrison here. They sent for him.

There've been reports of troop movements in the east. Dark Knights massing on the Qualinesti border. They think the dragon may be gathering her forces to attack Haven."

Lucy's forehead crinkled in a frown. "But what about the pact of the dragons? Beryl—the old green bitch—should know that if she attacks Haven, her cousin Malys will have something to say about it."

"Pact!" Ulin snorted. "As if any of us really thought the treacherous beasts would honor a pact. The key word is "honor" and we know that none of them can probably even spell it!"

"What does your father think?"

Ulin sighed, shook his head. "I have no idea. He's not talking to anyone these days, Lucy. Not even my mother. But then, she's gone so much of the time. Her portraits are in such demand . . ." Recalling vividly the last violent clash between his parents at home, he let that subject lapse.

"I'd like to see this new concoction of yours," Lucy said, hoping to cheer him.

"Would you?" Ulin brightened.

He always considered himself homely. He was rail-thin and gangly with his grandfather's big bones but no meat to cover them. The mirror showed him only his inadequacies. It never showed him what other people saw in him, for only the mirror of the soul can do that. His face was transformed in his eagerness.

"You'll find this really interesting," he said, walking with rapid strides down the hall, tugging her along after him. "I guarantee it."

At the end of the corridor stood a laboratory that had been established for the use of students and masters. Only a few years ago, the laboratory had been crowded with mages practicing their spellcasting, studying the nature of ancient artifacts, creating their own magical devices. The laboratory was almost completely empty now. Ulin and his father were the only two who used it and Palin was here rarely. The twenty or so masters and students still in residence at the Academy were busy researching ancient texts, hoping to find clues as to why the wild magic had suddenly ceased to work for them or, if it did work, why it was unpredictable and unreliable.

Ulin entered the laboratory, hustling Lucy along with him.

She coughed and wrinkled her nose. "It smells dreadful. What have you done? Invented gully dwarves?"

"That's the brimstone. Or maybe the saltpeter." Ulin led her to a large stone table covered with numerous black splotches, as if someone had been mashing blackberries. The room reeked with a peculiar acrid odor that made Lucy sneeze violently. Several large crocks holding various substances were lined up on the table.

Lucy glanced at the black splotches. "If you're searching for gold, you've missed the mark."

"Bah! Gold!" said Ulin. He sat down at the table. "What I've created is much more interesting than gold."

"What *have* you created?" Lucy looked around. "I don't see anything?"

Ulin grinned shamefacedly. "Well, maybe "creation" isn't the right word. Watch this."

"I have here a small sampling of saltpeter. Did you know," he added, mixing the strange concoction together, "that my great uncle Raistlin used saltpeter to fool his enemies into thinking he was working magic when he was really too exhausted to cast a spell? Watch this."

He struck a spark from flint. The spark landed on

the white, crystalline substance and it flashed brightly, so brightly that Lucy blinked. The flash vanished almost immediately.

"Impressive," she said dryly. "He must have scared a lot of goblins in his time."

"He did, so my grandfather told me." Ulin dipped a scoop into one of the crocks, drew out six measures of a black powdery substance. "Charcoal," he said. "Add to that one measure of brimstone." He dumped in a bright yellow powder and continued to talk while he mixed his concoction assiduously. "Well, that started me to thinking. What if I could make the flash do something. Something more than just flash. Like lightning. Lightning gave me the idea of using brimstone. I began trying various substances—

Ulin halted in his mixing to look up at her. "I was never a very good mage, Lucy. I was born into a world the gods had forsaken. A world where godly magic was lost. True, my father found the wild magic, and that helped sustain him and the other mages. Somehow, I never took to it. Or it never took to me. Father says I lack discipline and perseverance. I used to think he was right, but now I'm not so sure. I seem to have all the discipline and perseverance I need when I'm pursuing my alchemic studies. I spend hours here and never notice the time pass at all. But trying to cast magic leaves me frustrated and with a pain in my belly. And that was in the days when the magic was working! I'm much happier here in the laboratory than I am in the mage-ware room."

"I think your mother was scared by a gnome when you were in her womb," Lucy said, teasing.

"Maybe so." Ulin laughed. "I'll have to ask her." Having mixed together the substances, he packed the resultant powder into a small salt cellar. "Now watch this. You better stand back."

Lucy retreated backward, holding her nose. She had been involved in some of Ulin's experiments before and knew that, if nothing else, they tended to be odiferous. Flint and tinderbox in hand, he held his arms outstretched over the salt cellar. He struck a spark over the salt cellar and jumped back.

Again a flash, but this was accompanied by a loud bang. The salt cellar blew apart, bits of it flying all over the laboratory. The force of the blast shook the stone table and the floor on which they were standing.

The noise was alarming, deafening. Lucy hastily covered her ears, but by that time, the boom was over, like thunder after a lightning strike. She blinked, staring at what was left of the salt cellar, which wasn't much. Ulin's face was blackened with powdery residue and had a bloody gash on his forehead from where he'd been struck by a portion of the salt cellar. He never noticed. He gazed at his achievement with pride.

"I'd say that would definitely put the scare in more than a few goblins, wouldn't you, Lucy? I call it 'thunder powder.' Come closer. It's safe now."

"What did you say? I can't hear you." Still keeping her hands near her ears, just in case the thunder powder was not yet finished thundering, Lucy advanced cautiously, staring warily at the black splotch on the table, as if fearing it might go off again. "That was very nice, Ulin. Very . . . entertaining."

"Yes, I know," he said gleefully. "It can blow up great huge piles of stones. One day last week I took it out into the woods and I did just that. Then I blew a boulder out of the ground. After that, I blew up a tree stump. You could hear the explosion for miles." He smiled impishly, looking very much like a mischievous small boy. "When I came back into town, people were out looking at the sky for storm clouds. That's what gave me the idea for the name."

He began to pour out more powder. "If you had enough of this stuff, you could knock down a stone wall. Like one of these walls here." He waved a hand vaguely.

"I think your father might notice one of his walls missing," Lucy said.

"Don't worry," Ulin said, looking at her with the same impish grin. "It's just a theory. One I won't be testing. Would you like to see it again?"

"Uh, no," she said, adding hastily, at his look of disappointment. "It was quite impressive, Ulin, but my ears are still ringing! Maybe some time we'll . . . uh, blow up stumps together. We'll take a picnic lunch . . ." She couldn't help it. She began to giggle.

"Laugh at me, will you?" he said, pretending to be hurt. "I don't mind. You unbelievers may scoff now, but when the time comes, when you absolutely *have* to have a stump removed, you won't be laughing then, will you, Mistress Lucy?"

She pursed her lips, eyed him critically. "You look a fright. You've got black stuff all over your face and hands. And you've got a cut on your forehead. Come along and wash up like a good boy and make yourself useful. Help me pack my things and carry them to the Inn."

"Yes, ma'am," he said, playfully meek. Sliding off his tall stool, he finished the destruction of his person by wiping his powder-stained hands on his robes.

Lucy herded him from the room, looking very much like a short, plump sheepdog harrying a tall, thin sheep. Once they were outside the laboratory, though, he halted.

"You should have seen how high that stump flew up into the air!"

"You," said Lucy, giving him a shove in the direction of the washroom, "are incorrigible!"

* * * * *

Lucy's possessions were few. Ulin carried the iron-banded box that held the few magical artifacts she'd managed to acquire over the years. Lucy carried a wicker basket filled with her clothes. The two crunched companionably through the dried, dead leaves of autumn, admiring the beauty of the flaming reds and yellows of the leaves that still clung to the branches. The two enjoyed each other's company, as always, but Ulin was glad when the Inn came in sight. The handles of the box were digging into his palms. Lucy was huffing and puffing with the weight of the basket and they had just mutually agreed to set down their loads and rest a spell, when the town bell began to clang, sounding the alarm that would call all citizens of Solace to the central square.

The bell was rung by the sheriff and then only in dire emergency. The clanging could mean anything from a child lost in the woods to a barn catching fire to the approach of a flight of dragons. The smith in his leather apron came running, leaving his apprentices to mind the forge fire. Women came clattering down the stairs that led to the tree-top houses, wiping away flour from the day's baking, carrying babes in arms who were too little to be left at home alone. Old folk, who had been basking blissfully in the sun, perked up on hearing the bell and reached for their canes. Dogs began to bark wildly and small boys, like squirrels, slithered and slid down out of the trees.

"We'll drop off this stuff and go see what's happening," Lucy said and Ulin agreed.

Picking up their burdens hastily, they hurried toward the Inn. Halfway there, they saw Palin Majere. He was walking with rapid steps against the flow of the crowd, heading for the Academy. His head was down, his hands folded in the sleeves of his robes.

"Father!" Ulin called.

Palin either didn't hear his son over the commotion or he was deliberately ignoring him. He kept walking.

"Father!" Ulin called more loudly and made a move to intercept his father.

Only then, when Palin had practically walked into his son, did he lift his head. His face was grim. His eyes shadowed.

"I don't have time to talk now, son," he said brusquely, starting to pass by. "I am in a hurry."

"What is it, Father?" Ulin demanded, detaining him. "What's going on?"

"Beryl is preparing to attack Solace," Palin said.

Ulin stood gaping at him. "But . . . that's ridiculous, Father. Is she insane?"

"I don't know whatever gave you the impression the dragon was sane to begin with," Palin retorted. "Ridiculous or not, the knights have received reports that a force they have been watching, led by Dark Knights, is not marching to Haven, as was thought. They have turned toward Solace, coming up from the south. The knights are planning to march as swiftly as possible to meet their advance long before they can reach our city. We're calling out the town militia. I was on my way back to the Academy to collect some of the artifacts that have to do with battle-magic."

"I'll come with you," Ulin offered.

"And I will, too," Lucy added stoutly.

Palin was shaking his head. "No, I need you both to remain in the Academy. The pupils should not be abandoned, nor the masters. I want you to go back to the Academy, son. Make sure everyone remains calm."

"You don't think the Academy will be attacked, do you, father?" Ulin asked.

Palin shrugged his shoulders. "Lord Warren is confident that the knights will halt the enemy's advance. Our scouts report that the force is a small one. The Dark Knights are getting cocky, he thinks, to attack with so few men. I'm more worried that a few of Solace's own ne'er-do-wells might decide to take advantage of the turmoil to do a little thieving. And now I *must* be going. May luck be with you and with us all this day."

He left them abruptly, without waiting to hear their answer, taking it for granted they would do as he bid them.

"Well, that's that," said Ulin, grunting as he hefted the box. They started once more for the Inn. From the square, they could hear the loud and authoritative voice of Lord Warren formally calling the Solace militia to arms. "No glory in battle for us. Only stanching Master Thomas's nosebleed that he always gets when he's over stimulated."

"But your father's right, you know," said Lucy, lugging the clothes basket. "The pupils can't be left alone. Goodness knows what the little dears would do. Half of them in hysterics and the others ready to rush out to fight. And the masters no better, some of them. To tell you the truth, I don't really think I'd be much good in a battle." She glanced down cheerfully at her plump body.

"Whether we are or whether we're not, it looks like we're not going to get the chance to find out," Ulin said and he sounded glum.

* * * * *

Wary of the dragon lurking so near their borders, the knights and the Solace town militia had long been preparing for just such an eventuality. The muster of troops was swift, for they had practiced monthly, and within six hours after the first reports came in, the knights were riding southward, followed by a regiment of doughty, arms-bearing citizens. A small force had been left behind under the command of Caramon Majere, who ordered everyone to fill whatever containers they could find with water in case the dragons launched a fiery assault against their city.

Riding at the head of his column of knights, Lord Warren turned on his horse to motion to an aide. "Where is Master Majere?"

"Riding by himself at the back of the column, sir," the aide reported. "At least that's where I last saw him."

Lord Warren nodded. "Tell Master Majere I want to speak with him."

The aide raised an eyebrow, looked shocked.

Lord Warren said gruffly, "Very well, damn it, ask Master Majere politely if it would be convenient for him to speak with me. Civilians," he muttered after the aide had departed.

Palin rode forward along the long line of men-at-arms and knights to confer with the knight commander, Lord Warren. The two were not exactly friends, but they held a mutual respect for each other. Lord Warren was completely opposed to the use of magic in battlefield situations, believing firmly that the men required to guard a spell-casting mage could be of better use elsewhere on the field. But he was forced to concede that on occasion, magic had its place, particularly pyrotechnics, and so he had asked the mage to ride along. Lord Warren trusted immeasurably in Palin's good sense and his courage, if he did not trust completely in his magic.

"Master Majere," Lord Warren said. "Thank you for taking the time to speak with me."

Palin bowed from the saddle, wordless. He wore a hooded traveling cloak, kept the hood pulled low over his face. Removing the hood, he found, merely encouraged people to talk to him.

Lord Warren cleared his throat. He found speaking to the shadowed face extremely disconcerting. "I know you mages have your secrets and all that, but I need to know . . . in order to plan the attack, mind you, I need to know . . ."

"What magic spells I intend to use?" Palin finished, as a way of bringing the conversation to a swift conclusion. "Certainly, my lord." Palin reached into a pouch, produced a rosewood box, banded with silver. He opened the box to show twenty silver balls nestled in red velvet. Each ball was decorated with runes engraved upon the sides.

Lord Warren eyed the silver balls warily. "What do they do?"

"Toss one of these on the ground in the midst of enemy cavalry, and it will burst apart, sending out a swarm of magical insects. Their bite is like that of the horsefly, only a hundred times more painful. They will drive even the best-trained war-horse mad within seconds, send him plunging out of control, thus completely disrupting a cavalry unit, rendering them not only useless in the field, but making them a danger to their own troops."

"Amazing," said Lord Warren, impressed. He could well gauge the value of such a weapon. "How does it distinguish friend from foe?"

"It does not, my lord," Palin replied, not bothering to hide his scorn.

Lord Warren frowned. "Then what good is it, if it drives the mounts of my own knights crazy?"

Palin endeavored to curb his impatience with those

who were magic-ignorant. "My lord, you need only attach one of these silver balls to an arrow and have your best archer send it flying deep into the enemies' ranks. Your knights will remain unaffected so long as they keep out of the spell's radius for fifteen minutes. After that, the spell will dissipate, the insects disappear."

"I see." Lord Warren was pleased. "I'll have our best archer assigned to you, Majere. But you won't fire until you have my signal?"

"Of course not, my lord," Palin said coldly. "I have had some experience in battle myself, my lord."

"That's good," said Lord Warren, relieved. "That's very good."

Palin started to ride away, then paused. "My lord, don't you find this all rather odd? I know something of military matters from both my own past experience and that of my father. This seems a very small force to send out against a city as well-prepared for attack as Solace."

"Bah! These Dark Knights have a new leader now. A man named Targonne. He's an accountant, an office-flunky. Not a general. He knows little of military matters, so our spies tell us. His own officers have no respect for him, though they're all terrified of him. He gained his post through assassination, you know. This is probably some hare-brained scheme of his thinking to catch us napping." Lord Warren grunted. "He'll find that we're awake. Wide awake."

Palin remained unconvinced. Turning his horse's head, he rode back to the rear, well behind the knights, behind even the footsoldiers. Palin was troubled, but unable to explain his anxiety. As he had said, the actions of the Dark Knights made no sense to him and he could not, as could Lord Warren, so easily pass off their actions as being those of an obtuse commander. Whatever else the Dark Knights may be, they were not stupid and they did not allow stupid people to remain in positions of command.

Palin could not explain it, but he had the strangest feeling that he was riding away from battle, not toward it.

*   *   *   *   *

"So you see, there is nothing to worry about," Ulin told the assembly of students and masters. "The knights have everything well in hand. According to my grandfather, they face only a small enemy force and will likely rout it without any problem. My father has asked that we continue with our daily routine—" He paused, checked a sigh. "Yes, Mistress Abigail?"

The small red-haired, sharp-eyed, sharp-tongued little girl was the bane of the masters' existence. She was one of those extremely intelligent children who are brighter than most of the adults around them and who make no secret that they hold the adult world in contempt. When the other students had departed the school, saying they had nothing left to learn since the magic was failing, Palin had hoped that the one good which might come out of this evil was the departure of Mistress Abigail. Sadly, she stayed on. Word was that she terrified her parents and that they were quite content to let others deal with her.

"What if the knights don't hold them?" she asked petulantly. "What if we're attacked?"

"That's a very unlikely possibility," said Ulin, striving to remain patient. Lucy had just stanched Master Thomas's nosebleed and now Ulin could see the boy's eyes starting to widen in terror. "Very unlikely," he said emphatically. "We are in a secure fortress. The walls of this building are made of stone and very thick. The gate is guarded by a powerful magic spell. Nothing can possibly harm us."

"A dragon could," said the little girl.

"Dragon!" Master Thomas's chin quivered. His hand flew to his nose.

"Tilt your head back," Ulin snapped. "We are not going to be attacked by dragons. Return to the classroom, all of you."

"Blue dragons with lightning breath," hissed Mistress Abigail, leaning near Master Thomas and contorting her face grotesquely. "They'll breath fire on you and your flesh will snap and crackle and turn black. And after they cook you they eat you! They start by biting off your head—"

"Oohhhh," Master Thomas moaned. Blood dribbled down his nose and into his mouth.

Ulin, with a grim face, marched Mistress Abigail to the library, figuring that an afternoon of dusting books would settle her much too vivid imagination.

The day passed in relative quiet at the Academy of Sorcery. Master's Thomas nosebleed finally stopped. Mistress Abigail was sent to bed early as a reminder that it wasn't nice to frighten little boys.

Or big boys either, for that matter.

"I think you should stay here," Ulin said to Lucy. "Not go back to the Inn. Not tonight."

"Is that a proposition?" she asked, her dimple flashing.

"No." Ulin flushed. "I didn't mean it like that. It's just— Well, I don't want you in Solace in case anything should happen. Not that I think it will, mind you, but . . ."

"I'll stay," she said. "I was planning on it in any case.

Master Thomas was in such a state I had to cast a sleep spell over him. A sleep spell, mind you!" she reiterated proudly. "The first spell I've cast in days. And I cast a wizard-lock spell on the mage-ware room. I think it's the state of crisis. Brings out the best in me. It won't stop a dragon, but—"

"Dragons!" Ulin grimaced. "You've been listening to Mistress Abigail. You know, I think I'd rather face a dragon than ever again spend five hours alone with that little imp. She asked, by my count, seven hundred and eighty-five questions, of which seven hundred and eighty-four could not possibly be answered by the great Astinus himself. And the seven hundredth and eighty-fifth was 'How do babies get inside a mommy's tummy?'" He sighed deeply, then cheered up. "I don't feel much like sleeping. What about a game of fox and hounds after you cast the spell? Will you be fox or hounds?"

"Hounds," said Lucy promptly, heading off for the mage-ware room. "Two coppers a point?"

"It's a deal." Ulin went to find a deck of cards.

* * * * *

"That's it!" Lucy said wearily, tossing in her hand. "I give up. You win."

"You owe me"—Ulin peered down at the slash marks he'd made on a chalk board—"eight steel and ten coppers."

"You cheat," Lucy accused. "I know there were six huntsmen in that last hand, when there's only supposed to be four in the deck. I would have called you on it, but I was too tired."

"I do not cheat," Ulin returned indignantly. "If you'd just learn to count the cards when they fall—"

The town bell rang out, wildly, frantically. At almost the same moment, someone was heard bellowing from down below.

"Ulin!" a voice shouted. "Open the gate!"

"Grandfather!" Ulin said, jumping to his feet.

"You don't suppose—" Lucy couldn't finish the thought. It was too terrible to speak. "Ulin, we have all these children!"

He was up and gone, dashing down the stairs, taking them recklessly two or three at a time in his haste to reach the door. Lucy caught up the skirts of her robes and followed as fast as she dared.

Ulin threw open the main door. He ran across the courtyard that was rimed with frost, spent several moments wrestling with the enormous wooden bar that held the gates closed. He was thankful that he didn't have to contend with removing a wizard lock. He pulled open the gates.

The Academy was located several miles outside of Solace. Built on a hilltop, the tall towers and high walls made of it a small fortress. The night air was chill and crisp. The full moon shone brightly and the grass beyond sparkled with frost. Caramon Majere was big and brawny still, though he was in his eighties. His hair was iron gray, but his eyes were clear and keen, his body unstooped and unbowed. He loomed large against the starlit darkness. Behind his grandfather stood two big draught horses, hitched to a hay cart. Caramon had driven here in a hurry, apparently, for the horses were puffing and blowing, sending up clouds of breath that smoked in the chill air.

"Grandfather! What—"

"We were duped, Ulin," Caramon said bluntly. "The knights have gone off on a wild kender chase. I sent some of the lads out on patrol to the west, just in case.

The lads have come hot-footing it back with word that a small force of draconians is headed this way."

"They're going to attack Solace!" Ulin gasped.

"Not Solace, grandson," said Caramon, placing his hand on Ulin's shoulder. "The Academy of Sorcery."

"No! That can't be! How do you know, Grandfather?"

"I had lads posted in the lookout towers high up in the vallenwoods," Caramon answered. "A force of about seventy-five draconians passed right underneath them. They could hear them talking. The draconians were all excited about the loot they were going take from the Academy and how Beryl is going to reward them for every magical artifact they bring to her. And double that reward for any mage they capture alive."

"The knights," said Ulin thickly, his brain stumbling around like a drunkard. "The army—"

"I've sent word," Caramon said. "Mistress."

He doffed his cap and nodded his head to Lucy, who had come to join Ulin and now stood calm and mute at his side, offering her silent support.

"But they can't possibly return in time," Caramon continued, replacing his cap. "If they force-marched all night, as they planned, they will have covered some thirty miles by now. The men and horses will be exhausted. They couldn't possibly turn around and march back to Solace without rest. The quickest they could come would be tomorrow night. And that's many long hours away."

"Still, we could hold out until then," Ulin said hopefully, fumbling his way through the fog of fear and dismay to see clearly at last. "The Academy walls are stone, thick enough to withstand even a draconian assault, especially from a small force. We have a store of artifacts, some of them meant for battle-magic, to say nothing of our spell-casting— What is it, Grandfather?"

Ulin asked sharply, noting Caramon's grave expression. "You're not telling me something."

"The draconians spoke of dragons, Grandson. We don't know . . . the lads didn't see any, but . . ."

"Dragons! Then perhaps we will be safe and Solace is their target!"

"Ulin," Lucy chided him. "What are you saying?"

Realizing what he had been wishing, if not exactly saying, Ulin felt his face flush. "I'm sorry, Grandfather. Of course, I don't want Solace to be attacked. It's just . . ." He looked behind him, at the stone walls standing tall against the stars, gleaming a soft pearl gray in the moonlight. "My father loves this place, Grandfather. He will be devastated."

"Buildings can be rebuilt," said Caramon briskly. "The Inn's been burned down and built back twice in my lifetime and better each time. But lives once lost cannot be recovered."

"You're right, of course," Ulin agreed. He was calm now and in control. "We have the children to consider, as well as the masters." He looked out to the courtyard. "That's why you brought the cart."

"I'll take them to the Inn," said Caramon. "Make haste! We don't have much time!"

Lucy was already racing back across the courtyard. Ulin followed her, thankful that they didn't have their full complement of students. He woke the masters and explained the situation. Fortunately, they kept their heads. They woke the children, soothed their first startled fears and, wrapping them in blankets, hustled them out of the Academy to the waiting cart. They were told was that they were going to Solace to stay in the Inn of the Last Home for a little while. All the children knew Caramon, who was a favorite. The sight of his jovial face, calm and reassuring, set them at ease, and the idea of a ride in a hay cart at this time of night, when they should be in bed, more than allayed any terrors.

Mistress Abigail guessed the truth right away, of course, but kept her mouth shut and was actually seen to be daubing Master's Thomas bleeding nose with a handkerchief in a motherly fashion and admonishing him, once they were settled in the cart, to tilt his head back. When all were packed in, Caramon looked down from his place on the seat of the hay cart to Ulin, who was standing in the gate, with Lucy staunchly at his side.

"Ulin—" Caramon began.

Ulin shook his head. "I'm staying here, Grandfather. I can't let all our artifacts come into Beryl's possession. I have to make some provision for them. But Mistress Lucy will go with you."

"Mistress Lucy will not, thank you, Master Ulin," Lucy returned placidly. "You better be on your way, sir," she said to Caramon. "Don't worry! We can manage."

Perched on the driver's seat, the whip in his hand, Caramon seemed about to argue. Realizing that time was running short and realizing, too, that what Ulin said was right, that they could not allow such powerful artifacts as Palin had collected to fall into Beryl's claws, Caramon urged them not to take any unnecessary chances and then snapped the whip over the horse's ears. The big animals lunged forward, pulling their heavy load with ease. The cart's wheels went spinning up the road, heading into the thick woods.

The night was eerily quiet once they were gone. Ulin peered intently into the trees, but he saw no movement. Draconian raiders would be silent and circumspect. He had no doubt but that they'd never see them until they were upon them. As for the dragons, the first they would know of them would be the terrible debilitating dragonfear, which robbed a man of his wits, his courage and, most horribly, even his will to live. Whatever Ulin did, he must do now, before the fear rendered him helpless as a child, lost and forsaken.

"What *are* we going to do, Ulin," Lucy asked, as if she'd heard his thoughts. "They could be on us at any moment." She helped him swing shut the heavy gate. "They could be out there right now, for all we know."

"Yes," he said. He slid the huge bar into the gate. He paused to consider it. "When the Academy was first built, my father and the other mages cast a powerful spell on this gate, a spell that is supposed to activate if anyone attempts a forced entry."

"Do you think it still works?" Lucy asked.

Ulin shrugged. "Who knows? I guess we're about to find out." He glanced at her sharply as they hurried back across the courtyard. "Are you all right?"

"No," she returned cheerfully. "To be honest, I'm so scared I could run away down that road this moment and probably beat the horses back to Solace. But I'm not leaving you behind. Especially since you have a plan. You do have plan, don't you?"

He smiled ruefully, took hold of her hand and squeezed it tight. "Yes, I have a plan. But it's dangerous and I'm not sure you should be here, Lucy. It might fail."

"Can you use my help?"

"Yes," he admitted.

"Then let's get to it. What are you going to do? We can't hide the artifacts. The draconians will almost certainly find them and if they don't, the dragons will. Reds have a nose for magic, or so I've heard."

"I'm not going to hide them," Ulin said. "I'm going to bury them."

* * * * *

The captain of the draconian raiding party was a large aurak named Izztmel. He was already a favorite of Beryl's and this night's raid would go a long way toward increasing his influence with the dragon. The raid was Izztmel's idea, based on a "conversation" he'd had with a young human magic-user, a friend of Palin Majere's.

A month ago, Izztmel had come across the unfortunate young mage, capturing him as he was attempting to return to the Academy from a journey to the Tower of High Sorcery at Waywreth, a Tower Beryl longed to acquire but which the wizards managed to continue to successfully conceal from her.

The young mage had not provided any useful information regarding the Tower, but he had revealed, before he died, the fact that Palin Majere, fearing Beryl might stumble across the Tower, had a great many valuable magical artifacts secretly stored in the Academy.

When Izztmel suggested to the dragon that they raid the Academy, Beryl embraced the idea. She had never breathed a word to anyone, but she had felt a decrease of her own magical powers in the past few months. In her heart, she feared that her cousin Malys was responsible, but Beryl also had to consider that the culprit might be these troublesome human mages at the Academy. Beryl gave orders for the Dark Knights to feint an attack coming from the south, drawing out the garrison of Solamnics and the Solace town militia, leaving the Academy isolated and undefended.

Izztmel had pointed out that this would leave the rich city of Solace undefended, as well, but Beryl had refused to even consider attacking Solace. Her cousin Malys would almost certainly view this as a breaking of the pact and Beryl was not strong enough yet to win a battle against the immense and powerful red. But Malys would not mind a little midnight raid against an Academy whose mages had on more than one occasion thwarted the great red's ambition to rule all of Ansalon.

Solace's time would come, but it was not now.

Izztmel and his small force of raiders marched from Beryl's lair, heading toward Solace, keeping under cover. In the meantime, the Dark Knights marched from another direction, making their movements as open and blatant as possible.

A few hours past midnight, the main body of the draconian raiding party joined up with their advance scouts, who had been hiding in the woods ever since sundown, keeping watch. Izztmel noted with disappointment that lights shown in some of the windows of the immense stone structure. He'd been hoping to catch them all asleep.

"Your report?" Izztmel asked one of the scouts.

"Sir." The scout saluted. "They were tipped off. Your force was seen by some humans hiding in the trees."

Izztmel muttered curses. "I thought I smelled human flesh in the forest. I couldn't spare the time to check it out. Have they all fled then? Taken their goods with them?"

"They loaded some of their young into a wagon," said the scout. "Your orders were not to do anything that might alert them and so we let the wagon leave. That was about an hour ago. But there are still at least two mages inside. We heard them talking. They said they were going to stay to protect the artifacts. We haven't seen them come out."

"Excellent," said Izztmel, rubbing his clawed hands. "Two prisoners and all the artifacts. And no one defending the place. We have only to wait for the reds—"

"Sir," one of his draconians called, "you can see the red dragons just coming over the horizon."

Izztmel, looking to the west, saw the shadows of dragon wings blotting out the starlight.

"Launch the attack," he ordered.

The word passed quietly down the line from one draconian to another. They drew their curved bladed swords and ran over the frost-rimed ground toward the main gate. They ran in silence, no cheering or yelling. Reaching the gate, they halted.

"Bring up the battering ram," Izztmel ordered.

Draconians carrying an enormous iron-shod ram ran at full speed toward the gate. The ram struck the gate and instantly disintegrated as if it had been made of ice, not wood. But the draconians who had been holding onto the ram flew backward, struck by an unseen force.

"Some sort of spell on it, sir," reported one of the draconians.

"You don't say." Izztmel sneered. "Stand back, the lot of you."

Approaching the gate, he held out his clawed hands, brought his spell to mind. He could feel the power of the spell on the gate working against him. He could feel, too, those little annoying stinging gnats or whatever insects seemed to flock around him when he was spellcasting. His spell wavered and for a moment he thought he'd lost it, and then suddenly the spell on the gate snapped. Izztmel's magic flowed inside him, warm and exhilarating. The magic flared from his hands, forming a wall of fire that struck the gate and set it ablaze.

Now yelling wildly, the draconians battered down the flaming gate and dashed through.

* * * * *

At the sound of the shattering boom of the battering ram, Lucy flinched, spilling some of the charcoal she was scooping into a barrel.

"Careful," Ulin said coolly. "We don't have all that much of this stuff that we can throw it around."

"I'm not throwing it around," Lucy snapped. "I'm shaking like a leaf. You did hear that, didn't you? They're out there!" She lifted her head fearfully. "And something else is out there, too! Something awful!"

"Dragons," he said grimly. "That's the first taste of the dragonfear. Fight against it, Lucy. The dragons aren't close yet. And hopefully it will take them some time for the draconians to break the gate down." He carefully scooped up the small amount Lucy had spilled and poured it into the barrel. "Now we put the lid on these two."

"Why a lid?" Lucy asked nervously.

"Because I've discovered in my experiments that the thunder powder is more effective when it's contained than when it's loose."

Ulin hefted the barrel filled with the black powder and, carrying it carefully, hauled it down the hallway to the room where the artifacts were stored. Lucy brought the other barrel. They had only managed, in the short time they had, to produce an amount of the thundering black powder sufficient to fill three barrels, two large and one small. Ulin placed each of the large barrels at the foot of two load-bearing columns that stood near the door to the mage-ware room.

"Now, if I'm right," he said, eyeing the barrels and the columns and glancing up at the massive stone ceiling above, "when these two go off, the force of the blast will knock down the columns and that will cause the roof to collapse on top of the artifacts. Not even the dragon will be able to get to them then."

The dragons were drawing ever nearer. He could feel his stomach start to clench. He took in a deep breath to calm himself.

"*If* you're right," Lucy said. She looked skeptical. "Ulin, you blew up a *salt cellar!*"

Ulin shrugged. "Whether I am or not, there's not much to be done about it now."

Upending the third small barrel, he poured lightning powder on the floor all around the other two barrels. Then, continuing to pour out the powder, he started backing down the hallway.

"What's that for?" Lucy asked.

"This is how I'll set it off," Ulin said. "Let me know when I reach the end of the corridor. I can't see where I'm going."

"We're here," Lucy announced after a moment.

"Good thing," Ulin grunted. He had nearly emptied the barrel. He straightened, grimacing from cramped back muscles.

"Grab one of those." He indicated the torches set in sconces on the walls. "We'll need it."

"You want to light a torch!" Lucy stared at him. She held up her blackened hands. "We're covered in this stuff!"

"It won't hurt you," he said patiently. "It needs to be contained, remember? Just be sure not to set off that trail of powder. Not yet."

There came the sound of yelling, triumphant, terrible.

"They're through the gate," said Lucy, her face livid. "Hurry, Ulin!"

He reached up to grasp hold of one of the iron sconces made in the shape of a gargoyle that lined the walls. Removing the flaming torch from the sconce, Ulin heard the small click of a hidden mechanism. He grasped hold of the sconce and turned it to the right until he heard another click. He then turned the sconce back to its original position and there came a third click. After a pause, during which Ulin nervously chewed on his lip, certain his invention had failed, there came a grinding sound. He sighed in relief and, grasping Lucy's hand, darted into the opening created by a sliding panel in the wall.

"That's remarkable!" she said, impressed. "I didn't know this wall did that!"

"Only my father and I know about it," Ulin returned. "It was designed for just such an occurrence. It was my idea," he added with a touch of pride that not even his fear could obviate. "Hand me the torch. Now get out of here, Lucy. Start running." He pointed down the long narrow corridor that disappeared into the darkness. "The tunnel comes out in the woods near my father's house."

"I'm waiting for you."

"Lucy, damn it!" Ulin glared at her, but she simply glared right back. He didn't have time to argue.

There came a shattering crash, as of wood splintering and breaking. Fearful shrieks of glee split the air. The draconians had entered the Academy.

Ulin touched the end of the torch to the trail of lightning powder. It sparked and caught fire. The flame began to eat up the powder, moving relentlessly across the stone floor to the barrels. Ulin watched a moment to see the flame racing along the trail of powder. Then he grasped hold of a length of rope that hung from the ceiling and gave it a sharp tug. The sliding panel reversed its movement, closed off the opening.

"Run!" he shouted. "Don't worry about being modest, girl! Gather up your skirts and run like dragons were after you."

"Very funny!" Lucy grunted, and did as she was told, hiking up the skirts of her robes practically to her waist and haring off down the long tunnel with Ulin pounding along at her side.

They ran and ran and listened with stretched ears, waiting for the explosion. Time passed and there was nothing. Nothing except the echoes of their own footfalls.

"Shouldn't . . . something . . . have . . . happened . . . by now?" Lucy gasped with what breath she had left.

"Yes," said Ulin, his own voice tight with despair. "It should have. We've failed."

* * * * *

After a night spent lying wrapped in his blanket on the cold, damp ground, broad awake, staring at the stars, trying to put a name to his fears, Palin had just managed to fall asleep when a hand shook him.

"Sorry to wake you, Master Mage," said a voice. The face was lost in the darkness. "Lord Warren would like to speak to you. He says it's urgent."

Palin tossed off his blanket, followed the lord's aide back to the Knights' command tent. The camp was an uproar, officers shouting, waking the men, calling for their horses or their squires. Palin wondered that he'd been able to sleep through it.

"Here's something damn odd, Majere," said Lord Warren, his face grim. "My scouts have just come to tell me that the enemy's gone."

"Gone, my lord?" Palin repeated, still stupid with sleepiness.

"Gone. Vanished. The whole lot of them. Melted into the night. Do you know what this means?" Lord Warren didn't give him time to answer. "It means that this was a feint. We've been hoodwinked! It means that while we're lolly-gagging like a bunch of idiots down here, they're attacking Solace!"

Fear twisted inside Palin and now his fear had a name. Lord Warren was wrong. Beryl didn't want Solace. She wanted something much more valuable to her than Solace.

Drawing a ring from out a pouch, Palin slipped it onto his finger and vanished.

"We're turning back," Lord Warren began, but he found himself talking to empty air. He blinked, stared. "Majere?"

No response.

"Mages," Lord Warren muttered and left his tent that was already, by his command, being taken down around him. "Strange chaps. Even the best of 'em."

* * * * *

"This is the mage-ware room," said Izztmel, staring intently at the closed door and comparing it to a crude map he'd drawn from the description of the Academy that he'd wrung out of the tormented mage. The four draconians who had accompanied him bunched up behind him to get a look. He glanced around. Yes, this fit with the description. On the lowest level in a narrow corridor down from the laboratory. Several large columns lined the corridor. The only thing that was out of place was a wooden barrel standing beneath one of the columns near the door. The barrel was covered with a black powdery substance that had been spilled all over the floor

"What is this filthy stuff?" Izztmel demanded, suspicious. "Second! Come forward."

"Yes, sir." The bozak approached warily.

"Go examine that stuff more closely," Izztmel ordered. "Tell me what it is."

The bozak crept forward, his eyes fixed on the

powder, ready to bolt the moment it seemed inclined to do something alarming. The powder appeared innocent enough. He bent down, stared hard at the substance, taking care not to step in it.

"There's a track of the stuff that leads off down the corridor, sir," he reported.

"Well, go investigate it!" Izztmel ordered, seething at the loss of time. He was so near the magic. The feel of it made his scales click in anticipation.

The bozak tramped down the hall. "It looks like someone tried to use this to start a fire, sir," he reported. "Part of it's burned at this end."

"Humans! Just like their tomfoolery," Izztmel muttered. He reached down a claw, dipped it in the black substance and brought it to his nose. "Charcoal." He sniffed again. "Rotten eggs and horse piss. Some sort of magic, perhaps. Whatever is was meant to do, it obviously fizzled."

"Now there's magic," he said, pointing toward the iron padlock. "I can smell it!" His tongue slid out between his teeth in his eagerness. "Their precious artifacts! Wizard lock, iron padlock. A child could break through these."

Izztmel wove a spell with his hands. The wizard lock shivered, but held. He strengthened the spell and at last felt the magical barrier give way. Now there remained only the iron padlock. He called the words to a lightning spell to mind, pointed his finger at the door lock.

The magic flashed from his clawed finger, sizzled near the barrel . . .

*　*　*　*　*

Ulin and Lucy stood at the edge of the woods, their hands clasped together, watching fearfully the two enormous red dragons flying in lazy circles above the Academy of Sorcery. Outside the smoldering gate, a draconian patrol walked, keeping a look-out for anyone who might disturb their looting and ransacking. They obviously did not expect to be interrupted, for they grumbled and swore in their uncouth language, complaining about being left out here while their comrades were scooping up all the treasure.

From inside the Academy, Ulin could hear raucous laughter, the sounds of furniture being smashed, desks hacked to pieces, glass shattering. Every blow seemed to strike him personally. The fiends were wrecking the place. Anything valuable they found they tossed out the broken windows to be retrieved later and carried off.

"You did all that you could have done, Ulin," Lucy said softly, her voice shaking.

"It wasn't good enough," he returned bitterly. "That's the story of my life. Nothing I did was ever good enough! Not for the magic. Not for my wife . . . "

Lucy gasped, dug her nails into his flesh. "Who's that?"

A figure had suddenly materialized in the courtyard; a figure that for a moment seemed to Ulin's startled vision to have been spun out of starlight and moonglow. And then, in the next horrified instance, he recognized it.

"Father!" he shouted.

But the draconian patrol had also seen the figure and they were much closer.

"Father!" Ulin shouted again. "Behind you!"

Palin turned. Seeing the draconians, he raised his hand, prepared to cast his spell . . .

A tongue of flame shot up from the Academy. The flame flared higher than the tallest Tower. The light of the flame was so bright that it blinded all who looked at it. And then came the thunder—a concussive blast that rolled out of the Tower, rumbled over the ground that shivered and shook with the shock wave. The blast knocked Palin flat and sent the draconians reeling backward. The dragons flying above the Academy flailed about, enormous wings beating frantically to carry them out of harm's way. The blast tore the heart out of the Academy of Sorcery.

Rubble and debris flew high into the air, and then crashed down to the ground in a deadly hail storm that snapped off tree limbs and sent huge chunks of stone bounding over the ground like pebbles.

Oblivious to the danger, Palin jumped to his feet. He screamed something, words Ulin could not hear for the awful rumbling of the Academy walls collapsing. The great Tower teetered and then it fell with a deafening crash. Flames leapt up, lighting the darkness, changing night to terrible day in an instant. Smoke roiled into the air.

The draconians, stunned, stared in baffled amazement at the flaming building. One of them pointed up at the red dragons and shook his fist.

"Blundering idiots! What'd you have to go and blow it up for?" he screamed. "Some of our boys were still in there!"

"Not to mention the loot!" another shrieked.

The reds ignored them. Their night's work was finished, albeit in an unexpected manner. Singed and battered from the blast, they took flight, heading for home. In their report to Beryl, they would place the blame for the explosion on the aurak Izztmel.

"We won't go back empty-handed," said a draconian, eyeing Palin. "We'll take this human scum with us at least. One of their filthy wizards is better than nothing."

"Father! Look out!" Ulin shouted.

Palin stood staring at the end of his dream. He neither saw nor heard anything else.

Ulin started to race toward him. Lucy flung her arms around him, held him fast.

"You can't help him, Ulin!" she said. "They'll only capture you, too. We'll tell your Grandfather! He'll send out a rescue party. The draconians' trail will be easy to follow. Ulin, don't do this! Don't!"

The draconians seized hold of Palin. Still dazed from the blast and, perhaps more, from the sight of his beloved Academy going up in flames, his dream going up in smoke, he didn't fight or struggle. He did not look at them, as they chained his arms behind him. He did not speak. He watched the fire until the draconians hustled him off, and even then he twisted in their grasp to stare behind him.

"You can let go now," Ulin said, his voice ragged from the smoke.

Slowly, Lucy released her grip.

He looked weary to the point of dropping. Tears streaked his charcoal-blackened face. The gleam of madness had died out of his eyes, leaving them dark and empty. Lucy's own tears slid unchecked down her cheeks. In the distance, they could hear the bells in Solace ringing again, calling out those left in the town to come fight the fire.

"Much good it will do them," Ulin said bitterly.

Reaching into his pocket, he took out a sheaf of notes. He ripped them in half, ripped the halves in half, ripped those into fourths and continued ripping until the ground was covered with small bits of paper no larger than the ashes and cinders falling down on top of them.

"My notes on the thunder powder," said Ulin. "And the formula." The notes shredded, he put his hands to his head. "I wish I could tear them out of my brain the same way!"

"Magic could have blown up the building," Lucy said, thinking to comfort him. "You might have cast a spell . . ."

"Magic is a skill, a discipline, an art. The use of magic requires study, sacrifice, concentration. The thunder powder"—Ulin glanced back at the blazing building and shuddered—"any thug with half a brain could use it, Lucy. What have I done? What dreadful power have I brought into the world? I wish I had never conceived of it."

"At least no one will know," she said, soothing him and calming him. "They will think it was the dragons that destroyed the Academy."

Ulin crushed the shreds of paper with the heel of his boot. "No one will know," he repeated. "No one will *ever* know!"

THE SOULFORGE
MARGARET WEIS

The long-awaited prequel to the bestselling
Chronicles Trilogy by the author who brought
Raistlin to life!

Raistlin Majere is six years old when he is introduced
to the archmage who enrolls him in a school for the
study of magic. There the gifted and talented but
tormented boy comes to see magic as his salvation.
Mages in the magical Tower of High Sorcery watch
him in secret, for they see shadows darkening over
Raistlin even as the same shadows lengthen over all
Ansalon.

Finally, Raistlin draws near his goal of becoming a
wizard. But first he must take the Test in the Tower
of High Sorcery—or die trying.

THE CHRONICLES TRILOGY
MARGARET WEIS AND
TRACY HICKMAN

Fifteen years after publication and with more than
three million copies in print, the story of the world-
wide best-selling trilogy is as compelling as ever.
Dragons have returned to Krynn with a vengeance.
An unlikely band of heroes embarks on a perilous
quest for the legendary DRAGONLANCE!

THE LEGENDS TRILOGY
MARGARET WEIS AND
TRACY HICKMAN

In the sequel to the ground-breaking Chronicles trilogy, the powerful archmage Raistlin follows the path of dark magic and even darker ambition as he travels back through time to the days before the Cataclysm. Joining him, willingly and unwillingly, are Crysania, a beautiful cleric of good, Caramon, Raistlin's brother, and the irrepressible kender Tasslehoff.

Volume One: *Time of the Twins*
$6.99 US; $8.99 CAN
8307
ISBN: 0-88038-265-1

Volume Two: *War of the Twins*
$6.99 US; $8.99 CAN
8308
ISBN: 0-88038-266-X

Volume Three: *Test of the Twins*
$6.99 US; $8.99 CAN
8309
ISBN: 0-88038-267-8